1851

Charlotte Treleaven Comes of Age

To Ann,
with kind regards,
Patricia R. Olds.

Patricia R. Olds

Strategic Book Group

Strategic Book Group
P.O. Box 333
Durham CT 06422
www.StrategicBookClub.com

ISBN: 978-1-60976-381-7

This book is dedicated to everyone who has helped me in its process; particularly my husband, for his patience; and my two sons, who set me in the right direction when this 'awkward computer thing' wouldn't do what I wanted it to do.

Chapter One

✦

Robert Hattenbury, at the prompting of several letters from his mother, finally came home to the family seat in East Cornwall in early summer of 1830.

He arrived one pearl fresh morning and Mrs Hattenbury was naturally enchanted to see him. But during the first few days at home, he was scarcely in the house at all, quickly falling into the way of catching up with old friends and acquaintances.

One evening however, Sophie finally secured his company to herself and how very happy she was to do so. Apart from the pleasure of seeing him, there was a matter of some importance she wished to discuss with him, to whit: his marriage. Robert, it should be said, had not mentioned marriage; the plan was his mother's.

Sitting in the drawing room with her son after dinner, and drinking an excellent glass of port with him, she broached the subject. "Robert, darling, is it not time you were thinking of settling to the married state?" she asked.

Stretching out long legs comfortably and running the stem of the port glass between his fingers, Robert said lazily: "I am in no hurry, Mama."

His mama's reply dispelled his lazy air completely. "Well, now you are done with Mrs Lerpiniere, it might be a good time to think of acquiring a wife," Sophie mooted. "You are certainly of an age."

"Barbara Ler . . . how did you . . ." Robert's blue eyes had widened with a surprise bordering on shock.

"Darling, gossip rides a very swift horse," Sophie responded. *Her* eyes held a decided twinkle. "We hear most things eventually, even down here in our Cornish depths."

Subsiding into his chair, Robert's gaze remained upon Sophie's face, thoughtfully digesting what she had said. Eventually he said: "Setting aside the indelicacy of your remarks, why, Mama, should my marriage suddenly occupy your mind?"

"Because I have a candidate for you," Sophie told him with a charming smile.

"Indeed?" Robert cast his mind around the local belles, knowing it must be a local girl or Mama would not have required his presence at home. "Who might the lady be?" he enquired complacently, knowing of none he could recall.

Mrs Hattenbury then delivered her second astonishing surprise of the evening.

"Charlotte," she said; and Robert nearly fell off his chair in shock.

"Do you mean Charlotte Treleaven?" he asked incredulously, "little Charlotte?"

"The very same," agreed Sophie, nodding and smiling.

Recovering his savoir faire Robert said: "You are funning, of course, Mama." He spoke with studied irony and a certain amount of amusement. When it became apparent that she was not, he laughed aloud. "No! It is a suggestion too ridiculous for words. Charlotte is a child."

"Not at all, dearest," Sophie assured him. "Charlotte too is of an age."

"Mama!" Robert's brows rose aloft. "Miss Treleaven cannot yet be sixteen while I, let me remind you, am nine and twenty. You are *seriously* asking me to propose marriage to a schoolgirl? I think not," he ended dismissively.

"Miss Treleaven?" Sophie queried gently. "You always called her Charlotte as a child. Think how well you dealt together then. She adored you. You loved her too; did you not?"

Robert protested: "Yes, of course I did but she was a mere babe and the timbre was familial. Marriage is entirely different; it would be akin to marrying a sister," he averred and added: "at all events, I am perfectly satisfied as I am."

"You may be satisfied in the particular, Robert, but your situation is not perfect. Mistresses, to which you allude I take it, do not increase your land holding by as much as a tittle," Sophie pointed out reasonably, speaking of the 'light skirt brigade' for the second time that evening, as though accustomed to discussing her son's mistresses every day of her life. "Nor do they provide acceptable heirs generally speaking. Only think how embarrassing to our dear Prime Minister that his brother, Marquess Wellesley, has so many illegitimate offspring to be stumbled over in town." She might have given examples much closer to home, the Carrs for example. "Marriage to Charlotte would satisfy in all particulars, and I was not thinking of an immediate nuptial. Take time to become reacquainted. Then you could make a declaration of intent and marry, say, after her birthday next year."

Robert gave his mother a level glance as she adjusted an elegant shawl about her shoulders. Sophie was now forty seven but he thought how little time had changed her: gracious and cool, her skin sweetly scented, fair hair tucked neatly into a cap, she seemed curiously untouched by life.

"I could make a declaration but shall *not*," he replied pointedly. "Such a marriage could only make me a laughing stock. Besides," he added dismissively, "say what you will she is a mere schoolgirl and would bore me to death in a week."

"If you allow, Robert, I must disagree. Charlotte is everything a girl should be: sweet-tempered, delightfully amusing, and on the way to being a beauty, not at all boring I assure you. Indeed, she will make you an admirable wife.

"As to young brides, they are not so unusual. You see them everywhere. I was only sixteen when I married, as was Alethea when she did. Now I think of it, I remember my mother speaking of a lady she met when taking the waters at Spa one year. The girl, a Madame de Golifet, had been married two years and was not fifteen even then!" she brought out triumphantly.

"Mama," Robert raised his eyes to the ceiling in exasperation, "that must have been at *least* fifty years ago and it alters *nothing*. Miss Treleaven is still not suitable for me." He was losing patience in earnest now.

"I hesitate to contradict you again, Robert," Sophie said, apologetically, "but I truly believe you are wrong in thinking thus. Charlotte is not your usual run of girls. She is very mature, from the circumstances of her life, and from having been raised and educated with a much older sister; nor is she still in the schoolroom. Truly, dear heart, if youth is your only objection to Charlotte time will provide the remedy."

"This I do not dispute," Robert observed dryly. "Ask me again later, if you must. I do not object to a sensible marriage in principle, just not this one at this time. What would I do with so immature a bride in town?" he ended disdainfully. There was a great deal more to Robert's last remark than was apparent, from the circumstances of *his* life.

Sophie did not take Robert up on his final comment. Instead, after the smallest pause, while she raised an eyebrow every bit as mobile as her son's, she said gently: "Alas, Robert, I do not like to remind you but time is only on Charlotte's side. In a few years she might consider you too . . . well . . . *too* mature. The boot might then be on the other foot, with Charlotte finding *you* a bore, an old fuddy-duddy even."

These measured, softly spoken words sent temperatures in the drawing room plummeting. Clearly, Robert could not credit the evidence of his own ears. There was a moment of incredulous silence as Sophie, not without effort, held her son's coldly furious gaze.

"Indeed," he said with icy emphasis, replacing his glass on the table carefully. "Let me tell you, Mama, no woman has yet complained of boredom in my company."

"No dear, of course not, but . . ." Mrs Hattenbury hesitated, with an air of genteel dilemma, then said apologetically: "I believe we are speaking of mistresses again. They cannot be expected to complain because of the . . . well . . . the nature of their situation. Wives are a rather different matter. *Their* regard has to be merited."

Sophie's emphasis was masterful and Robert hard put to contain his wrath. Face tight with effort, jaw rigid, he drew a deep breath and rose from his chair, holding his tall, well-made figure very straight.

"You are impossible, Mama," he ground out finally. Not trusting himself to say anything else, he turned in his heel and stormed out.

Mrs Hattenbury's lips curved in the tiniest of smiles as she watched him go, but the satisfaction of jolting his complacency, done simply to make him think, was very short-lived. The worries remained: Alethea's problems; and what to do about her darling boy.

She sighed, reflecting on the physical likeness between Robert and his late father: the shapely blond head and fine blue eyes, his face and lips handsomely moulded, the tall and upright stature. Her son was as temptingly beautiful as ever his father had been.

But where Francis had entered early into the matrimonial lists, Robert showed not the least sign of discontinuing his present lifestyle, to whit: sporting a succession of lovely (one assumed they must be lovely or they would not be seen on *Robert's* arm) paramours and, from his usual detached viewpoint, apparently looking upon marriage with an unfavourable eye.

To say that Robert was detached, however, was not to say he was cold. He had a formidable temper when roused and was then . . . how shall it be put . . . best not crossed? Nor was he emotionally shallow. He was simply a man who held himself well in check, never given to easy exposure of private feelings. Sophie often thought that he was a sophisticated and rather cynical version of his papa; a far more complicated man, hard even at times.

Still, if gossip were true Robert was quite unlike his parent in one particular. It was said of him that he was very casual towards his paramours and quick to lose interest after the initial conquest. Sophie's husband, dead now more than four years, had been a man of very warm impulse towards the fair sex, his mistresses enjoying lavish and undivided attention from him. He adored them even more if they became enceinte, fecundity bringing out his most endearing and protective qualities.

Sophie had basked in the full glow of Francis's love the first year of their marriage and when she told him she was pregnant he was delighted. Alas, tragedy came in the wake of Robert's difficult and protracted birth: the young couple listened in horror as Dr Henders warned them that there must be no more children or Sophie would die.

Stark news!

Francis and Sophie stared at each other over the yawning chasm which had opened between them; and no bridge over it!

After an extremely difficult period of adjustment Francis, with pain, apology and relief in his eyes, kissed Sophie's hand and removed to a separate establishment in town. She remained with her infant son in Cornwall, leading a life that was now, it has to be said, rather empty: even darling Robert, adorable though he was, could not wholly compensate for the loss of an adored husband.

Sophie did love Robert but initially, it must be admitted, she resented the havoc his innocent coming wrought. She often wondered in later years if her early reserve towards him was the cause of Robert's detachment; but then, more comfortingly, she postulated that being without a father's guiding hand for much of his life must have been partly responsible. Francis came home to Cornwall only rarely, usually in the summer months.

Indubitably, Robert had always been self-contained and, as an only child, self-willed too. He disliked being thwarted and could be overbearing if he were. Growing up in a female household, and of dominant disposition, he usually went his own way. Like the proverbial horse he might be taken to water but could not be made to drink. Indeed, he was more likely to dig in his heels. Sophie knew this only too well which was why, seeing Robert's resistance to the match with Charlotte, she now intended to change tactics.

It was a marriage she desired ardently for a variety of reasons, not least a wish to see her son happy. She could not have said he was *unhappy* precisely; yet she sensed a lack in his life; purpose perhaps? If this were so, could not union with a loving wife better fulfil him? Of *course* it could.

This was where Charlotte entered the picture. She was exactly the kind of girl Sophie envisioned; warm-hearted and generous but with that spicing of ginger needed to thaw Robert's starchy reserve. His wife would also need courage to stand against him in overbearing mood. Charlotte, by nature and training, had more than enough of that sturdy quality.

See how well she had looked after her gentle, disorganised mother, with a maturity far beyond her eleven years, after her sister, Jacinta, married and went away to Scotland. Yes, Charlotte was a truly supportive daughter who would make an equally supportive wife. For Robert and Charlotte it could be a match of mutual benefit and satisfaction, a match made in heaven.

The proposed marriage also had other advantages; for Alethea and herself, for example, providing them with enduring companionship for their declining years.

Friends since childhood, she and Alethea had made their come-out together. At a ball one evening, they met Francis Hattenbury, newly arrived from Cornwall that season. Together they fell in love with him but it was to a love-dazzled Sophie he later proposed. Alethea stoically suppressed her own sharp disappointment and was the first to congratulate them.

Then Alethea received a proposal from Jake Treleaven. He was a dark and attractive Cornishman, a close neighbour and friend of Francis. She did not love him; indeed, she never ceased to love Francis; but it was thought to be a good match at the time and she accepted Jake at her parents' urging. For Alethea there was also the added incentive of continuing her friendship with Sophie at their new homes in Cornwall.

It was as well her affections were not engaged with Jake for he was an indifferent husband. He was neither demonstrative nor understanding; worse, he drank heavily. Thus, when he died from a feverish liver, some ten years ago, his death brought only relief. It left Alethea free to lavish affection on her two daughters, Jacinta, who was then twelve, and Charlotte aged five. Poor Alethea lost four other babies to an early grave, one before Jacinta, and three after; hence the age gap between the two girls.

Life had not been kind, neither to Alethea nor her friend; but where Sophie was financially secure Alethea had the added difficulty of penury with which to contend. Jake, alas, had also been a gambler, who left his family without reserves, fortune dissipated in paying off his debts.

Now the Treleaven affairs were alarmingly close to ruin, with the threat of having to let go of the estate and move to Scotland as pensioners of Jacinta's husband. If this happened Sophie would not only lose a loved friend but also dear Charlotte, who was the darling of her heart next to Robert. Such a thought was not to be endured and the obvious solution to the difficulties was, without doubt, an advantageous marriage.

Enter . . . Robert!

Why *not* Robert? It seemed delightfully obvious to Sophie: Robert happy; Charlotte secure; ruin averted; friendships comfortingly continued. Was all this good fortune to be set aside because her son turned obstinate? No! Sophie would not see the perfect solution lost for a whim, not if she could help it.

***

It was still light when he left the house, so Robert fetched the dogs from the stables. He took them down to the lake, where the simple act of throwing sticks for Brutus and Caesar to retrieve helped dispel the fury his mother's remarks had roused.

How dare she imply he was a bore? She knew parental respect forbade that he retaliate to the insulting thrusts. The remarks themselves had been bad enough, but further to say that Charlotte Treleaven, whom he remembered from Jacinta's wedding as a skinny little girl with red pigtails, might find *him,* a cosmopolitan man-about-town, boring was absolutely infuriating! It was also patently ridiculous.

What was Mama up to? Was she trying to goad him into an offer? Did she think him so complete a slowtop as not to see the goad? Well, if he had anything to do with it, and make no mistake about it he *had*, Mama was about to eat her words.

Over tea he spoke coolly to Sophie thus: "Mama, I was extremely angry with you tonight. Indeed, so much so, I was obliged to leave you or say things I would regret."

"Robert, darling, I know. Please forgive me. Truly, in trying to pursue your happiness," she stretched out a conciliatory hand, "I forgot the respect which is your due. I do apologise."

Such a handsome apology must ameliorate wounded feelings and it certainly worked upon Robert. However, he was not deflected from his purpose.

"Nevertheless, you must be made to see for yourself the ridiculosity of the proposed match. Invite Mrs and Miss Treleaven to dinner before I leave for Brighton. Observe us together and see how very unsuitable your scheme is."

Robert was conscious of the concessionary nature of his offer, rather than simply giving his mother an outright refusal. In fact, generous was not too strong a word to describe it he believed. Imagine his chagrin, therefore, when Sophie laughed and responded dismissively.

"My dear, it is not necessary. You go off to your pleasures at Brighton with my blessing. I shall try to find another solution." In this there was no hint of reproach, she knew, just the smallest, barely detectable suggestion of a little selfishness on Robert's part.

"Another solution?" Robert frowned. "To what may I ask? I understood we were discussing matrimony. And, Mama, are you trying to make me feel guilty?"

"Yes, we *were* discussing matrimony but as you do not care for the match there is nothing more to say," Sophie responded. She rose and hugged him warmly. "This business need not concern you; and of course I am not trying to lay guilt upon you. There is no reason to reproach yourself."

Robert defended his cravat. "I am perfectly aware of that, Mama and I do not. Why should I, indeed?" He then asked suspiciously: "Are you concealing something from me? No," he said, changing his mind rapidly before she could respond, realising it would only prolong a conversation of which he was already tired, "pray, don't answer that. Simply do as I say. I *will* have this awkward situation disposed of as I wish. Issue the invitation." He shrugged broad shoulders irritably, the question settled as far as he was concerned.

Sophie smiled as she observed the familiar mannerism. "How like your father you are, Robert; and how well that blue jacket becomes you," she said lovingly.

"Do not try to cozen me, Mama," he advised dryly, giving her a level glance. "Papa may have fallen before you every step of the way, no doubt he had his reasons, but I am not he."

For a startled moment Sophie wondered if Robert alluded to her husband's unconventional lifestyle. If so it was for the first time. However, the clock striking the hour of ten saved her the necessity of a reply. All that was further said came from Robert as she retired to bed.

"Mama, if by 'another solution' you mean to suggest a different match, please do not. When I choose to marry it will be to suit me not you."

***

Next day Mrs Hattenbury, looking her usual neat self, visited Alethea at Crane Lodge. She was met by her equally neat friend but where Sophie's figure was trim Alethea inclined to plumpness. Both ladies had greying fair hair and pink complexions. As frequently happens with close friends, they had grown to look alike over the years, slim and plump versions of each other. They kissed in greeting and passed into the house, meeting Charlotte in the hall.

Charlotte did not look like her mama. Both in looks and intellect she took after her late father. Fortunately, she had inherited her mother's gentler disposition but with a much firmer edge to it. Physically, her father's black hair and Alethea's fair locks had combined in their daughter to produce an abundance of glossy chestnut hair. As yet she spurned tight curls bunched at the temples, or the equally fashionable straight bands. Charlotte had neither time nor money for fashion. She wore her hair tied back, to reveal a fine brow, wide-set grey eyes, dainty nose and a mouth which smiled easily. Her complexion was too brown to be de rigueur, from spending a good deal of time in the garden, but golden skin did not detract from a face which was already pretty and promised greater loveliness to come. Her slim figure, though, was well disguised by clothes which had seen many years of stalwart service, let down and out several times since new.

"Charlotte," Sophie greeted with warm affection, holding out her arms.

Her greeting was returned with a hug before Charlotte led a way to the drawing room. With the two mamas seated, stools at their feet and fans to hand, she asked if they would like a glass of wine.

"Should we, so early in the day?" her mother asked, looking guilty. Both Sophie and Charlotte laughed at her predictability. When she and Sophie took wine together Alethea quite often opened with this remark, or something similar.

"Of course," Charlotte encouraged robustly, "there is no sin in this. Now what shall it be . . . Pansy or Primrose?" Wine poured, Charlotte left them to their own company and went about her tasks.

Sophie opened immediately, her tone clearly suggesting more than she actually said. "Robert invites both you and Charlotte to dine with us tomorrow."

Alethea drew a quick breath. "How kind of dear Robert. You spoke to him?" she asked eagerly.

"Yes, but Robert says Charlotte is not mature enough for him."

Alethea's face showed how keenly she felt this disappointment to their hopes. Sophie went on swiftly to reassure her. "It is all nonsense, of course. He has not seen her since Jacinta's wedding and has no idea how she has grown. *And* he rather changed his mind, if only from irritation, when I said she probably would not take him because she might find him boring."

Alethea gave a horrified gasp, which was quickly hidden behind plump fingers. "Yes, wasn't I naughty?" Sophie laughed, agreeing with the unspoken comment, "but it put Robert absolutely on his mettle and he has now agreed to see her. I am perfectly sure that is all it will take. Darling Charlotte will do the rest and Robert will be enchanted. Wasn't I clever?"

Alethea was not so sure. "Ought we to persist in the face of Robert's reluctance?" she asked worriedly.

"Why ever not? It would be foolish to give up so admirable a scheme for want of a little spirit," Sophie said firmly. "If Robert and Charlotte fall in love it will make everything so beautifully simple."

"That is true, dear, but only if they *do* fall in love." Alethea was still not entirely convinced. She knew well the trials of a loveless marriage and did not wish that for her darling Charlotte, no matter how convenient.

"Naturally. All *we* shall do is give them the opportunity. Now, Alethea, say nothing of this to Charlotte."

The only information relayed to Charlotte was Robert's invitation, to which she replied: "Oh, splendid. I shall like to see Mr Hattenbury again."

***

Social nicety being what it is there was nothing in Robert's demeanour to suggest he was 'looking Charlotte over' when he greeted her on arrival at Hattenbury next day.

She could not have known, therefore, that Robert's immediate reaction to her was one of incredulity that his mother, even for one *moment*, could have proposed for him so unsuitable a bride. She must have taken leave of her senses!

Although Robert's gaze no longer rested on Charlotte as they progressed into the drawing room, his inward eye still saw, with astonished exactitude, the unfortunate picture she presented.

Never had he seen such a sartorial disaster as Charlotte's dress . . . without a hint of fashion and with clear lines of demarcation where it had been let down at the hem. Had he been asked, he would swear it was the very same dress she had worn to her sister's wedding four years ago, a schoolroom gown, clothing a body unremarked by any apparent womanly curves. And though her glossy hair was beautiful it was not dressed but simply held back with a ribbon.

Alas, even had he been thinking seriously of Charlotte, which he was not, she would not do, having neither address nor style, no presence nor maturity. She simply was not his counterpart in any way. And this girl was presented to him as a wife? It was ludicrous. Whatever was Mama thinking?

Oh, true, Charlotte's lovely grey eyes were as wide and candid as ever, her smile as warm, as he freely acknowledged, looking at her with a brotherly eye, but this could not make up for her manifest shortcomings as a bride. No, indeed, it was impossible.

Robert had no malicious wish to disappoint his parent, no matter her apparent disregard for the respect which was his due, or his feelings for that matter, but there was a definite limit to filial duty, very definite, and this was it.

Charlotte on the other hand, although she greeted Robert in her usual friendly fashion, was very favourably impressed with him. In the period since their last meeting she had matured emotionally if not, as appeared, physically, and now for the first time Charlotte saw Robert as a man, a perfectly splendid one at that!

Splendid! There was no other word to describe that elegant, manly physique, those lovely blond curls and sparkling blue eyes. He was a veritable Adonis! So why had no one snapped him up yet? What was wrong with him? There must be *something*. No man this heavenly could remain unattached without just cause. Thinking about it, as the evening progressed, she remembered that Jacinta had frequently said he was arrogant and could be crushing. She, herself, vaguely recalled from childhood how pointedly he ignored one when he chose. That must be it. He was high in the instep.

But it seemed not. Over dinner he listened when addressed, laughed when amused, and had none of the usual taciturnity associated with a Cornishman, speaking eloquently on various interesting topics. Furthermore, he declined to sit alone with the decanter after dinner but joined the ladies immediately, to drink his port companionably while the two mamas tatted and Charlotte entertained them with a piano recital.

Music was the love of Charlotte's life and she a gifted performer, soon lost in the joy of her art. Robert was agreeably surprised, not having heard her playing since the dreaded scales period.

"You play well," he commended.

"Now, darling, you see why I wished *you* to persevere with the pianoforte. You and Charlotte could have given us a duet," Sophie mooted mischievously. Robert cast her an irritated frown, her alter meaning not lost on him.

"What, Mr Hattenbury! Too idle to practice?" Charlotte ribbed.

Mr Hattenbury was not amused. He raised a lordly brow, looking down his high-bridged nose, and when he spoke Charlotte immediately recognised his cool tone. "You are too kind, Miss Treleaven," he said. What he actually implied was that she was an impertinent chit.

Charlotte blushed but her glance remained steady on his face. "I merely joked, Sir. I would never presume to patronise *you.*" As she spoke Charlotte was aware that she had called him 'sir' for the very first time.

Robert's haughty look was modified as he picked up the unconscious flattery of her emphasis. "Is this to say that you are perfectly prepared to patronise others than I?" he queried, a slight smile quirking his shapely mouth.

Seeing him relent his inimical attitude Charlotte's sparkle returned. "Certainly not, Mr Hattenbury! How could you think me so ill-bred?" she protested demurely. "In fact, to prove how *well*-bred I am, I propose a chess match, wherein you may beat me soundly because I am an indifferent player. You play excellently well, or so Aunt Sophie says. What do you think? I promise not to make too much fuss if I lose."

"If, Miss Treleaven?" Robert said confidently, rising to his feet. Blue eyes glinting with pleasurable anticipation for the first time that evening, pique forgotten, he extended an inviting hand to Charlotte. "Come, let us engage."

Now there was a phrase with which to conjure, thought Sophie.

Three short games later a thoroughly trounced Charlotte was still at the chessboard. "Uhm . . . how mortifying to be so soundly beaten," she observed.

"May I suggest . . . a little more practice, Miss Treleaven," Robert said, cool and provocative. Charlotte laughed, unoffended.

"Touché," she conceded, "but, Sir, I have no opponent as skilled as you to practice upon. Give me a game on a regular basis and see how I improve."

"Are we done now?" Robert asked.

"Not unless that is your wish. For myself, I am not so feeble as to give up at the first hurdle. I may beat you yet."

"I very much doubt that," Robert said, amused, and he was right.

Charlotte's efforts were not crowned with success that night, not on any front, although some light-hearted arguing between the chess players did re-establish their old friendly rapport; as was noted by the watching mamas.

The tea tray was rung for and Charlotte presided over it. This, Robert assumed, was part of her presentation. In this assumption he was wrong since Charlotte was unaware that she *was* being presented. No, she performed with ease from long habit, handing out the cups with never a drop spilled. Busy as she was, she did not notice how closely Robert observed her.

This young man was somewhat in the process of revising his first estimate of Charlotte. An evening spent in her company had reminded him of how engaging she was. In this she had not changed and for so young a lady she possessed both natural sang froid and grace. Her manners were pleasant and open; she was as his mother had said, accomplished of both intelligence and talent.

Unfortunately, none of these mitigating factors could overcome the predominant difficulties, vis-à-vis marriage, making it all the more of a pity that Charlotte was without address or any kind of town polish.

This was not an insurmountable barrier of course, but it would take time before a good modiste and hairdresser could sort out all Miss Treleaven's problems; she also needed to grow a little, here and there.

However, what *was* insurmountable was the lady's unquestionable immaturity. She was not his equal in elegance, in experience, or social accomplishment. They were a world apart, a complete mismatch. Charlotte was undeniably charming and would make an excellent wife one day, of that he had no doubt; but not for him. Such a thought was plainly ridiculous. Of this, Mama must now be aware.

***

At evening's close Robert politely handed Mrs Treleaven and Charlotte into the carriage. He bowed to them, the door was closed, and the carriage started down the gravelled drive.

In the carriage, Mrs Treleaven drew a contented sigh. "Was that not a *most* enjoyable evening, dearest?" she asked.

"Very much so, Mama," Charlotte replied enthusiastically. "It is very pleasant to have Mr Hattenbury home again after so long an absence. Let us hope he makes a more protracted stay this time." She laughed. "Did you notice, Mama, that he treated me rather more as a grown-up tonight, exhibiting the veriest nicety of town manners? However, I have no doubt that on less formal occasions he will soon fall back into his old way of ignoring me."

With her own hopes uppermost in mind, Mrs Treleaven ventured daringly: "Perhaps not, dearest. Perhaps he will fall in love with you."

Charlotte fell into an instant fit of the giggles, and said: "Mr Hattenbury? Oh, no I think not. He is far too elevated for me, as was plain this evening, in spite of all his politenesses."

"How can you tell, Charlotte? Mr Hattenbury was most attentive to you, admiring your pianoforte recital, for instance," Alethea pointed out.

"He was only being polite Mama. Do you think if Sophia Bond had also been a dinner guest he would have distinguished me with his attention? No, I assure you, he would not," Charlotte averred cheerfully, knowing she spoke the exact truth.

Alethea sighed, feeling disappointed, because she suspected Charlotte was right. "What a pity," she mourned.

***

Since Charlotte had been unaware of Robert's examination of her it was as well she was not cognisant of his inner feelings towards her either, nor his perfectly plain expression of them when he returned to the drawing room.

Where he had been anticipating rueful acknowledgement of his mother's, perhaps understandable, mistake (his was not a grudging nature after all) he found no such thing. Far from it! He was brought up short by Sophie's look of eager expectation.

"Mama!" he exclaimed, frowning in perplexity.

"Well, my darling boy, was I not right about Charlotte? Is she not the most delightful companion one could wish for?" Sophie asked, smiling joyfully. "She is so right for you. Oh, this was the happiest of evenings, was it not? And see how well you two dealt together."

Robert looked at his mother dumbfounded for a moment. "Do my ears deceive me?" he asked eventually. "Surely . . . surely, Mama, you cannot have missed seeing that the match you propose is impossible! Miss Treleaven and I are *totally* unsuited! Never would I have chosen one such as she for a life partner. What, am I worth so little?" he asked, clearly offended.

As he spoke, the look of joyful anticipation on Mrs Hattenbury's face gradually died. At first she found it difficult to comprehend Robert's feeling of ill usage and felt shocked by his contemptuous dismissal of Charlotte, when she had thought . . . had so hoped for his happiness. How was it possible that he could speak so slightingly of dearest Charlotte?

Silent for a long moment, giving back Robert's stare as she adjusted to her son's antipathy, Sophie said eventually: "No, Robert, I must confess I saw no such thing. To me you appear eminently well-suited, even happy together."

"Mama! Happy together? Well-suited?" Robert was incredulous. "How can you *possibly* say such?" He shook his shapely head in sharp disbelief. "*I* am a man of the world and Miss Treleaven scarce more than a schoolroom miss! Have your senses gone begging that you cannot see the disparity between us?"

Robert swung away from Sophie, running a hand through his hair as he began to pace the Turkey carpet, talking all the while. "It can only be that you are blinded to the reality of Miss Treleaven, and her inadequacies, by your obvious affection for her but . . ." he turned back to Sophie, "have you looked at her . . . *really* looked at her?" he demanded. "You cannot have done, for if you did you would have seen what I saw ~ a girl without 'ton' or address, wearing the most appalling gown, her hair a disaster which, I swear, never had benefit of a hairdresser's scissors." He drew breath.

"And *this* is what you would have me take to wife? Am I of so little worth in your eyes? Am I to be made a laughing stock simply for your wish? Oh . . ." Robert's voice, which had risen with indignation, now dropped to a lower register. His hand resumed the destruction of a once-neat hairstyle. "How infinitesimal your regard for me that you would even *think* to propose so inadequate a bride."

At this point in Robert's peroration, Sophie rose to her feet. She gathered herself together and spoke quietly, no longer joyful but looking sad and diminished. "You are being inordinately intemperate, Sir, far more than the situation warrants and you have denigrated Charlotte more than enough. I will hear no further insults against her." She bent upon her son a glance compounded of anger and sorrow, and added: "I will only say that if your prideful conceit is such that you cannot see beyond it to the beauty of Charlotte's character, I must pity you." Sophie drew breath. "However, since you have made your feelings abundantly clear we will speak no more of this. It is finished. Goodnight." She turned to the door.

"Pray, do not walk away from me, Mama. This discussion is not ended," Robert said angrily, frustrated at his mother's abrupt termination of the conversation. He still had much to say and did not care to be unjustly accused of conceit without an opportunity to defend himself from the charge.

Sophie paused politely and said: "Excuse me, Sir, I am very tired. I really cannot talk any more."

***

Robert did not sleep well. Next morning he did not ride before breakfast, but retired to the library with the Morning News when he had eaten. There he awaited Mrs Hattenbury's rising.

After breakfast Sophie found a smiling Robert in the hall. Mother and son observed each other silently for a moment. Robert saw how tired and dispirited his mother looked. He held out a hand to her.

"We did not finish our conversation last night, Mama, and we must. It will not do to have unpleasant feelings hanging over us," he opened.

Sophie knew he was right. An unhappy night's reflection had shown her that in view of how things had transpired, she must cease meddling in Robert's affairs, and be completely open with him in regard to her reasons for wanting him to marry Charlotte. Indeed, it would have been better to do so at the outset, she conceded, except that her dream of happiness for Robert and Charlotte had seemed eminently achievable. It could have happened naturally had life's cards fallen more favourably.

"Of course, Robert, come into my sitting room. We can be cosy there."

Once they were settled Robert spoke. "Before all else, Mama, allow me to apologise for my intemperate speech last night. It is true that I was incensed, in the matter of conceit, of which you accused me, (conceit? It still wounded) but that is no reason to give myself licence to castigate you as I did.

"On reflection, I realise that you acted in good faith in presenting Miss Treleaven; for love of her, I doubt not. I did not see this at the time," he conceded, "and, I must tell you, I had forgotten what a delight Charlotte can be; in this you were also right. I was quite disarmed, I have to confess." Robert had been leaning towards his mother while he spoke. He now sat back and steepled his fingers before beginning again.

"The thing is, Mama, I don't believe you have looked clearly at this situation from my point of view. True, I must marry eventually because the house needs an heir. Believe me sincere when I say I would oblige you if it were possible. However, in the circumstances . . ."

Seeing where Robert was heading, knowing it would be profitless and not in chime with what she must reveal, Sophie interrupted him politely with these words: "Forgive me, Robert, but this is not necessary. You made your decision last night and I have accepted it. No further justification is required."

Initially, Robert was a little piqued to be cut off so abruptly but when his mother continued his attention was fairly caught.

"Also, I have not been quite open with you," Sophie confessed. She was twisting the fringe of her silk shawl unconsciously. "I owe you an explanation. But where to begin?" Sophie hesitated, the problem seeming too large to explain in a few words. Silence obtained for some moments.

Robert, catching the hint of tristesse in his mother's face, and thinking it may have been as a result of last night's quarrel, said gently: "Am I such an ogre you cannot talk to me, Mama? Come. I promise not to shout at you again."

Sophie returned his encouraging smile. "Of course you are not an ogre, my Robert. No, I hesitate from not knowing where to begin, as I said."

"You could start with 'not quite open'," he suggested, his look faintly quizzical. "In what respect?"

"Charlotte," Sophie said simply.

At this succinct reply, Robert laughed. "Now why am I not surprised?" he asked with a touch of irony. He leaned to take Sophie's hand. "What have you not told me, dearest Mama?"

Twice Sophie's lips opened and twice closed before the right words came to her. Eventually, she said: "In proposing marriage between you and Charlotte I truly thought you could be happy together. This was my *chiefest* purpose but not my only one. I did not disclose all my reasons for wanting the match." Sophie drew a quick breath, her fingers tightening under Robert's. "There is another vital consideration. Charlotte *must* marry advantageously or the Treleavens are ruined."

Robert frowned. "Ruined? How so?"

Sophie's gaze, full of her anxiety, centred on his face and she said: "There is no money left, Robert. They stand at the edge of ruin. Indeed, their unfortunate situation began with Mr Treleaven's death; his heavy gambling and drinking debts had then to be paid, you see; but nothing became particularly apparent until after Jacinta's marriage. After then their financial problems seem greatly to have accelerated. Now, in spite of darling Charlotte's valiant efforts ~ she's the one who keeps the house going you know, because Alethea has little skill in that direction ~ now, they must make a choice: Charlotte to marry well, or leave here to become dependants of Jacinta's husband."

Anxious glance still fixed on Robert's face, Sophie appealed: "Now, don't you see, dearest, why I thought, for all the reasons I put forward, that if Charlotte were your wife it would answer every purpose; would it not? And I *know* she would make you very happy."

Before Robert could respond to his mother's appeal, Sophie broke out with obvious, heartfelt distress: "Oh, Robert, darling boy, I cannot bear to lose the society of these dear souls so close to my heart. What *am* I to do without their company? Who will be here to share in the dark or happy hours of my day?" Sophie, it was, who now grasped Robert's hands in her own. "Dearest, won't you reconsider?" she urged. "Every difficulty would then dissolve in the mist; all will be righted; made well. Don't you see?"

"Yes, I do see, Mama," Robert agreed when she had finished speaking, his look becoming grave at the serious nature of her disclosures. "But I still think your proposal will not serve here, much as I would like to oblige you. I cannot marry Charlotte because . . ." he hesitated briefly, not wanting to offend his mother again, but knowing it must be said, "Mama, in elegance, in experience and social accomplishment, Charlotte is not my equal."

"But," Sophie pointed out with sharp perception, "those persons who *do* have these accomplishments seem not to have satisfied you to date, Robert."

He could only acknowledge this thrust without conceding it and move on. "Nonetheless, whatever you say, Mama, I must and will, return to my stated belief, which is that Charlotte is not yet suited to marriage. In a few years more maybe. No," he averred, "what we must do is to find another solution."

"What, Robert?" Sophie cried in some desperation. "I have wracked my brain repeatedly and come up with nothing."

The 'what' was a question Robert would need time to consider, since his mother's revelations were a bolt from the blue. So thinking, he said: "Give me time to come up with something, Mama, and, pray, do not distress yourself further." He patted her hand consolingly and disengaged her hold. "Leave this with me." He looked her straight in the eye, lowering his head to do so. "A solution *will* be found, I give you my word. This need trouble you no longer."

"Oh, darling, thank you." As Robert rose Sophie rose with him. She embraced him in a grateful hug. "You cannot know how relieved I am to hear you say this," she said with heartfelt relief.

"You know, Mama, you *should* have told me of this sooner."

"When are you ever here to be the recipient of confidences, Robert? Four years, it is, since you were last at home." Sophie's tone was wistful and unconsciously accusing.

It struck Robert as deeply as had her earlier cry of 'who will be here to share in the dark and happy hours of my day?' and came as an unintended reproach. He felt culpable because he knew he had been remiss in duty to his mother. Indeed, he had always bitterly blamed his father for neglecting Sophie and now he had been guilty of the same omission. But, for one reason or another, returning home had been too painful since his father's death; and in truth he had not suspected that his mother would miss him. He now saw that in this he had been wrong.

"I *am* here now, Mama," he comforted gently, "and shall bear you company."

On which note Robert departed!

***

When he was gone Sophie called up the carriage and was driven to Crane Lodge. Once there she wasted no time in imparting the bad news, not wishing Alethea to be held in suspense.

"Alas, Robert will not be offering for Charlotte." A disappointed 'oh' escaped Alethea's lips. "I know," Sophie said, "I am as upset as you but Robert says he is not a suitable match."

Kindly, Sophie reversed Robert's actual summation. It was enough that Charlotte had been rejected. No-one else need know she had also been found wanting; unjustly so in Sophie's opinion.

"Oh, Sophie, dear, how very disappointing." Alethea's disappointment was palpable. She was close to tears, voice quivering. She reached for her handkerchief and found none. "We had such high hopes; did we not? But there," she drew a steadying breath, "if it is not to be I must try not to mind." Although she said nothing of it Scotland loomed large in her mind.

Sophie passed Alethea her own handkerchief. "Pray, do not be distressed, Alethea, because all is not yet lost. Now, are you composed?" Receiving a slightly woeful agreement Sophie went on to disclose the budget of her conversation with Robert. "A solution *is* to be found. Robert will deal with it all and Scotland, he assured me, need never figure in our thoughts again," she ended comfortingly.

Mrs Treleaven's worries were considerably eased by Sophie's reassurances, and while neither lady could think of what Robert might do, both were confident he would do something because he was a man of his word. Each lady therefore was more cheerful than either had earlier expected to be, notwithstanding the blighting of their hopes for darling Charlotte.

***

On leaving his mother Robert went riding with Brutus and Caesar running at his heels. His thoughts were still centred on the problems of the Treleaven ladies. He realised he would need to know a good deal more of their financial affairs before coming to any helpful conclusions regarding their unfortunate situation.

He did wonder briefly why more help was not forthcoming from Jacinta. Only the smallest consideration brought him to see that it was unlikely the Reverend Macgregor's stipend could furnish the Crane estate's needs, in addition to his own family. In this he was correct; it could not. Jacinta did send her mother a little something each quarter but Robert, of course, knew nothing of this.

As for Charlotte, it was a pity she was so young because much of what his mother, irritatingly, pointed out in regard to his own lifestyle was correct. It was high time he was married. He had been aware of this for some time. The difficulty lay in finding a reasonable candidate, again as his mother had noted, equally irritatingly. Robert wanted someone of excellent character; reputation above reproach; intelligent (vapid girls, alas, seemed on the increase) and, if possible, a girl who was attractive in person and disposition. So far no such figurehead had appeared on Robert's horizon, though not for want of looking.

Mama was also right about the paramours. Barbara, the present incumbent, was still exciting but had become proprietorial and too open in expressing it. This was quite unacceptable, particularly in another man's wife, since it left Robert open to gossip. This was anathema to him, for *he* would not willingly add to the gossip already surrounding the family name.

Mistress Lerpiniere's behaviour was one reason he had come home this summer, Mama's summons providing the perfect excuse. It would do no harm to show Barbara he was a free agent. A few weeks in Brighton without him would serve to remind her that it did not pay to be possessive towards a lover. He still meant to go to the seaside, because he had promised to join Charles there, but only after Barbara had had time to reflect.

Robert rode across field towards Berriowbridge and thereafter the river Lynher, making for the woods at Nodman's Bowda. Presently, his thoughts were interrupted by a cheerful hail.

"Hallo there, my boy." The grey-haired man who accosted him was on foot. Robert drew hard rein and returned the greeting.

"Mr Hearl Rodd. How are you, Sir?"

"Still able to walk my boundaries, as you see, young Robert."

Smiling, Robert dismounted to shake hands. "And what of the family? They are all well?" he asked.

"Yes, but come and see for yourself. They will be pleased to renew acquaintance, such a stranger as you have become these last years. Is your harvest in yet?" Mr Hearl Rodd enquired. "No? Well, visit after harvest. Catch up the news then," he suggested sensibly, from a farmer's viewpoint.

"That would be most enjoyable," Robert agreed.

"Fine. Bring that pretty mama of yours and the Treleaven ladies." With a friendly nod the older man turned away.

Robert remounted and very shortly turned back along the river, cutting through the trees at Bathpool. He went down into the valley, recrossed the river, and spurred up the hill on the far side. Briefly he reined in, looking back down the valley before continuing on into the hollow where Crane Lodge nestled. Also briefly, he considered calling in to apprise the 'Treleaven ladies' of their invitation to Trebartha but he was hungry and home was only six furlongs distant.

Robert was busy for the next few days discussing farm strategy with his agent, Jethro Bligh. They mooted an increase in the herd of steers, debating a purchase from Launceston in July, or Tavistock Goosey Fair in September. Crop rotations were planned and the problems accumulated since Robert's last visit sorted out.

Then hay harvest was upon them. The Hattenbury tenants and neighbours rallied to help, praising heaven for fine weather. Mrs Hattenbury was kept busy organising comestibles, knowing that prodigious mugs of cider and large numbers of pasties were going to be tucked away before all was safely gathered in.

Hay harvest was drawn to a pleasurable close with an evening of song and dance, which everyone declared capital entertainment. Later, all went home satisfied if a trifle tired and, in some cases it must be admitted, somewhat disguised. Happily, the persons involved were few and of maudlin rather than quarrelsome temper, so it could be truthfully claimed that the harvest had gone off very well.

At evening's end Robert placed a hand upon Charlotte's arm. "Come and see me tomorrow. I have some several things to impart to you, Charlotte."

Charlotte thought Robert rather peremptory in his mode of request but since he had called her by name in a pleasant, friendly fashion, rather than addressing her as Miss Treleaven, she decided to overlook his failing this time.

Chapter Two

The following day both Sophie and Alethea felt enervated. When Charlotte said Robert wished to see her Alethea urged her daughter to go alone to Hattenbury.

Mr Hattenbury was out when Charlotte arrived, while his mother was enjoying a cup of hot chocolate. Sophie invited Charlotte to join her and she accepted with alacrity, chocolate being a rare treat in her own home. Later, they repaired to the garden to take the air and admire Sophie's beloved rhododendrons.

Francis had given her the first bush as a hothouse plant many years ago and was frankly sceptical when his wife suggested planting it out. Contrary to every expectation, the shrub flourished like a native in Cornwall's acid soil and many more rhododendrons, of differing size and glorious colour, had since joined the forerunner, creating a dazzling display when in bloom.

"Don't these look lovely, Aunt Sophie," Charlotte remarked, smiling.

"Absolutely. I asked Robert to order me some more and mean to plant them there," Sophie indicated the space she meant, "between here and the Laburnum by the lily pond. It will close that gap, which is quite draughty when the wind comes off the north coast, I find."

Head to one side, Charlotte considered this plan, her glance taking in the formal garden where they sat. Beneath their feet was a terrace of blue Delabole slates, with plants set amongst them in artfully arranged spaces. There were also large marble urns filled with flowers and herbaceous plants. To the right of the terrace, behind massed clumps of evergreens, myrtle and arbutus, the parkland rolled away in a long slope down to the lake. To the left was the rose garden. Fronting the terrace, down a wide, shallow flight of steps, was the lily pond of which Sophie spoke.

There was a gap which, Charlotte agreed, might be decoratively filled with rhododendron, so giving the garden complete seclusion, making of it an oasis of calm and beauty, like a jewel set in the austere grandeur of surrounding moorland, where granite tors rose in ragged peaks to the sky. The rock was blue-grey at this time of day but was often a luminous pink in the glow of evening.

"I must remind Robert again," Sophie said.

"Of what, Mama?" Robert asked, appearing behind them.

"Oh, hello, darling." Sophie glanced up at her son, but though he spoke to her it was upon Charlotte that his gaze rested. She recalled his attention. "To order me another Rhododendron."

"I haven't forgotten," Robert responded and gave his mama a kiss of greeting. His eyes returned to Charlotte. "Walk with me down to the lake, Charlotte," he said and offered her a hand.

Unaccustomed to the practiced chivalries she took it awkwardly, but once having done so wriggled her fingers in his palm to take a firmer grip, to Robert's secret amusement. After a polite farewell to Mrs Hattenbury, who showed every indication of settling for some time, they strolled off hand in hand.

"Did you enjoy your ride?" Charlotte enquired of Robert.

"Tolerably," he replied.

"Does that mean yes or no?" she asked forthrightly with a small frown. Charlotte liked clarity.

Again Robert was amused. "It means a little of both but mostly yes," he explained, humouring her. "I have been to Trebartha at Mr Hearl Rodd's invitation."

"So that, presumably, was the mostly yes part."

"It was. The no part consisted in riding out early. After yesterday I would have been happy to join Mama in doing nothing."

"Spend the rest of the day easefully," Charlotte advised, her kindly tone making Robert feel all of his twenty-nine years. She felt no diminution of energy after her labours of yesterday, *and* early this morning, and looked positively blooming.

"Perhaps," he agreed. "However, we are not here to discuss the state of my health but to arrange a reward for your harvest help. I thought you might enjoy a pleasure trip."

Charlotte looked up, her eyes sparkling with sudden excitement. "A pleasure trip? Oh, yes, lovely! But," she added, mindful of Christian duty, "it is not necessary to reward me, Mr Hattenbury."

"I am happy to hear you say so," Robert commended her virtue, as he properly ought, "but you shall still have a treat; the mamas, too, if they wish."

Hearing this gladly confirmation Charlotte experienced a leap of anticipation which found physical expression. She squeezed Robert's hand excitedly and began to skip along at his side. This necessitated a quickening of his pace to keep up and he protested jokingly.

"Charlotte, not so fast; remember my enervated state for which you earlier professed concern, if you recall."

She moderated her step but was not noticeably abashed at his stricture. "Of course, Sir. I would not occasion distress to your poor old bones, not for the world," she teased. Then seeing his startled look, and overcome with mirth, she promptly collapsed against the arm she was supporting so solicitously. Her laughter was quite infectious; Robert, too, was obliged to laugh.

"My dear, Charlotte, have you no respect for your betters?" he admonished with a raised finger. "Let me tell you that if you dare laugh at me again, which I see from a quivering lip you *are* in danger of doing, you will find yourself making a swift trip into the lake courtesy of these old bones."

Try as she might Charlotte could not stop laughing." "What a whisker, Sir. You mean no such thing," she spluttered."

"Do not put me to the test if you value your skin," he warned; at which Charlotte experienced a surge of unholy glee and rose to the dare.

"I do not believe you, Mr Hattenbury," she chanted provocatively, giving him a glance of unmistakeable daring. Just in case however, she prepared to take flight.

Alas, before the words left her lips Robert's hand tightened on hers and he dragged her, will she, nill she, down to the lake's edge. There, with his other arm at her waist, he held her teetering over the water. She cried out in laughing alarm.

"No, no, Sir! I do believe, I do! No!" Her voice rose on a shriek, half laughing, half fearful as he swung her out a little further. "Oh, pray, don't be so horrid. You know I did not mean it."

Eyes alight with devilment, Robert lowered his arm even further. Charlotte saw the lake water rising to meet her and clung yet harder to he who was sole barrier between her and a wetting.

He asked conversationally: "Do you remember falling into this lake when you were small, Charlotte? I fished you out then but now I am thinking it is time to throw you back in," he suggested wickedly.

"At this late date, Sir? Oh, no, don't. Please accept my apologies instead, I implore," she entreated breathlessly; at which, Robert relented. He returned her to terra firma, his arm tightening around her waist in support as he did so, swinging her to face him, breast to breast.

Charlotte clung to Robert as she regained her footing and, clinging to him, suddenly and disconcertingly, became aware of the strength of his body, his hard muscles and male scent. She felt strangely disoriented for a moment and to cover her confusion said quickly: "I did not think you would take me at my word. I thought you much too sophisticated to indulge in silly games, Sir."

Indeed, had any one of Robert's social circle seen him now they would have been perfectly astonished. The suave Mr Hattenbury larking? Impossible!

"Life is full of surprises, Charlotte, as you will find. By the bye, do stop strangling your tongue with my title every time you address me. Call me Robert, as you were used to do."

"Was I? I don't recall that, Sir."

Charlotte was pleasantly surprised, as well she might be, at Robert's licence to use his given name. It was an honour.

"It came about because of your difficulty in getting an infant tongue around the name Hattenbury but since you were an adorably sunny little girl, and much petted by all, no-one minded."

"No-one being you, do you mean?" Charlotte asked, smiling in delight at Robert's description of her smaller self. She had quite recovered her lost equilibrium.

Robert glanced down at her, standing beside him. He was smiling too. "Meaning me, Charlotte," he agreed.

"Dear Sir, how perfectly lovely." She pressed against his arm in an excess of warm feeling towards him and in so doing experienced again that heightened awareness of him. "How could I have forgotten how kind you are?"

Robert laughed. "How, indeed? But come, down to business; we have things to settle." Their walk around the lake was resumed and he asked: "Now, in the matter of your reward, what would you like?"

Charlotte thought for a moment. "You said the two mamas could also enjoy the pleasure trip, so should we wait and hear their views, Robert?" There it was. She had used his name for the first time.

"No, it is your treat, although we may discuss it with them later if you choose. I thought you might enjoy a day at Looe."

Before Charlotte could respond to this suggestion Robert went off on a train of thought sparked by mention of the seaside village.

"I had a treat of my own there when I was a child." He did not reveal that for him the treat had mostly consisted in a day of rare companionship with his father. "Papa and I got a lobster, I seem to remember." He was contemplative, his eyes distant. "How long ago that seems now."

"You still miss him, of course." Charlotte was sympathetic, hearing in Robert's voice something he was unaware of betraying.

For a moment Robert was inclined to resent Charlotte's remark as impertinence, but the expression in her lovely eyes was so patently sincere the resentment died. Instead he found himself agreeing with her.

"Yes, I do," he said slowly. "He was so little at home when I was growing up. It was not until I went up to Oxford I began to know him better." He gave a resigned shrug. "Such are life's vagaries, I suppose."

Charlotte pressed his hand in warm sympathy. "You do have some good memories of him, though."

"Better half a loaf, you say?" Robert stopped to consider Charlotte's earnest, upturned face. "You are young to be acquainted with the virtue of consolation," he remarked thoughtfully.

"I was thinking of Jacinta. I missed her terribly when she went to Scotland; indeed, I still do, but it's no use upsetting Mama with talk of missing my sister."

Ostensibly, as she spoke, Robert was studying Charlotte's pretty face but inwardly he was contemplating the essential loneliness her words revealed, reinforcing what his mother had told him. It was no life for a lively young girl, he concluded, but equally it was not something to be discussed right now.

He took on a brisk air. "Well, Charlotte, we are getting away from the subject and *that* must be your fault. *I* do not meander all about a point and never come to it."

Charlotte laughed, cheerfully refraining from pointing out that it was he who had wandered and not given her time to answer his question.

"You mooted Looe, Sir," she said, "and that I would like. I am certain I would love the seaside; to walk on the sand, feel the wind blowing in from the ocean and tugging at the hair, singing in one's ears. How wild and beautiful that must be."

Full of enthusiasm for her topic, Charlotte glanced up and saw Robert regarding her with unconcealed amusement. She blushed and said defensively: "Of course you think this romantical nonsense, no doubt."

"No such thing, poppet," he contradicted, rather less than truthfully and gave her a quick, reassuring hug; which Charlotte enjoyed, close contact with Robert's person, she had discovered that morning, being an unexpected source of pleasure. "But if the mamas are to join us we should hope for more clement weather. It would be most unfortunate if we lost one, or both, over the harbour wall in a gale; wouldn't it?" he conjectured amusively, smiling blue eyes resting on her indulgently.

Seeing him thus, Charlotte thought that Robert, in this unexpectedly playful mood, was something of a revelation. Gratifyingly, the aloof and frosty 'town' Mr Hattenbury seemed to have been replaced by the gentler Robert of earlier days, to his great advantage and Charlotte's pleasure. To experience stimulating companionship, such as she was enjoying with Robert this morning, did not often come her way.

Further, but a little puzzlingly, she had also discovered that in his physical person Robert had the power to overset her usual equilibrium. To be near him, to feel his touch, had set up quite distinct and hitherto unknown sensations in her body. It was hard to describe exactly but was rather like a ripple of deliciously pleasant sparkles running through her from head to toe, 'knocking her all of a heap', as Morley might have said; which also made it disturbing since she was not used to such sensations.

She had noticed how handsome Robert was at the supper party, but not then experienced this acute awareness of him, and maybe never would if he had not let down his guard before her today. He would have remained the Robert of her childhood hero-worship days.

At this point her introspection was interrupted. Robert reclaimed her attention and went on to tell her of a second treat in store; the Trebartha breakfast. Charlotte thanked him prettily, although privately unsure this would be quite the pleasure he anticipated. For her, going into company always set up the thorny question: what was she going to wear?

***

Next morning, Mr Hattenbury went riding before breakfast. This time he did call in at Crane Lodge. He had been thinking of Charlotte as he rode and realised, with some astonishment, how much he enjoyed her company yesterday. She had behaved with such natural charm he had been disarmed, light hearted in fact. It reminded him of old times. In retrospect, he was startled at the speed with which the familial camaraderie of earlier years had been re-established.

Equally, he was surprised to find she sometimes appeared to know his mind as though it were her own. This, he realised, must be no more than happy accident because there were few points at which their minds could meet considering the disparity of taste, age and culture between them.

With Charlotte in mind it appeared entirely natural that he came upon her in the garden. She was working with Morley, their old retainer. He called a greeting; Charlotte waved but did not stop her labours.

"Hallo. What are you up to?" he asked, dismounting.

"Gathering peas for today's dinner. Would you care to help?"

This would not have been one of Robert's preferred activities but he agreed cordially enough, turning over horse and dogs to Morley before asking Charlotte what she wanted him to do. In the event, it must be said, he contributed more to conversation than physical labour as Charlotte quickly noted.

"You have an excellent kitchen garden, Charlotte," Robert observed, looking at rows of healthy fruits and vegetables filling a space bordered on three sided by low hedges and on the fourth by a hot house.

"A combined effort by Morley and me; he does the hard digging and I the planting. The rest we share equally."

"That is quite a project with beds of this size. You like gardening?"

"I used not to," Charlotte confessed candidly, "but needs must. It's lovely to have our own garden produce, I must confess, and Mama thinks my green fingers nothing short of miraculous."

"Who would not be overcome with admiration," Robert agreed absently, his mind inwardly noting that Charlotte's gardening activities must be a sign of the Treleaven's straightened circumstances.

"What a whisker!" she said bluntly. "You are simply putting on polite manners. I expect you really think it the greatest bore imaginable."

Robert's wandering thoughts were brought sharply into focus by this remark, and he was quick to take up the challenge. "I did not say I like toiling over weeds but I would not decline to partake of the comestibles," he countered.

Charlotte popped a pea pod and offered him its succulent contents.

"What? Eat them raw? I rather hoped you would serve them to me cooked and on a plate. However, if this is the extent of your hospitality I accept perforce," he said, tossing the peas into his mouth.

Presently they went up to the house, carrying the vegetable basket between them. Charlotte said: "Stay for breakfast, do. Mama will be delighted to see you."

"Should you not ask first?"

Charlotte said confidently: "No. Like Aunt Sophie, you are always welcome."

"I take it she is still a more than regular visitor," he observed dryly.

Charlotte chuckled. "Oh, yes. The mamas frequently enjoy what they call a 'cosy prosy' and if you were to ask me what they did at such a time, on a given day in their youth, I could tell you without hesitation or fear of contradiction. I could describe their gowns or their beaux with equal exactitude."

Robert mistakenly commiserated with her. "Poor poppet, how boring."

"No; I did not say as much," Charlotte denied, looking a little affronted.

Robert stopped walking. Because they held the basket between them, so did Charlotte perforce. "I see I have offended you. Forgive me. I only thought you would find younger companions more entertaining. You cannot have many interests in common with the mamas. Are there not other activities more appealing to your tastes?"

As he spoke wide grey eyes were searching Robert's face. Charlotte's mouth looked vulnerable but when she spoke her words were plain enough. "Youth and the middle years are not mutually exclusive; nor is it entirely impossible for *some* of us to do what is unappealing; such as you, Sir, gathering peas."

After delivering this broadside Charlotte gave the basket a sharp tug and marched off with dignity, leaving Robert torn between annoyance at the implied criticism and amusement at Charlotte's wit. Amusement won. He laughed.

Hearing Robert laugh at her, Charlotte was mortified. She picked up her skirts and ran, unaware that he called after her.

***

Mrs Treleaven was surprised to see Mr Hattenbury stroll into her hall but made him very welcome when he explained that Charlotte had invited him to breakfast.

"Oh, is she with you?" Alethea asked, looking around his shoulder.

Robert smiled charmingly and explained: "She went to deposit her garden spoils in the kitchen, and I am come to claim my reward for the help I gave. Shall we?" He offered Alethea an arm. "Charlotte is a keen gardener it seems."

Mrs Treleaven allowed herself to be led into the drawing room. "She *is* clever at growing things, Robert. Oh . . . may I call you so, dear? I always think of you in the familiar since your mama speaks of you by your given name and so, of course, I think of you by it also, even though we have not seen you for some time and you have become quite the stranger."

Mrs Treleaven's conversation became convoluted, (a not unusual occurrence), the outcome being that Robert agreed she might use his given name. It was simpler. He wondered at his mother's thinking her friend uncomplicated. He always found her confusingly vague. She appeared even more so today.

Robert did not realise that it was he who had thrown Alethea into confusion, and that his unexpected appearance had made her wonder, quite hopefully, if darling Charlotte had been the draw.

"Perhaps, I, too, should revert to childhood usage and call you Aunt Alethea," he suggested, settling her into a chair. His chivalrous effort was wasted. No sooner was Mrs Treleaven seated than she sprang up again.

"What am I thinking of? You would like a glass of wine, of course." She crossed to an oak cabinet and brought forth a small assortment of bottles. "Oh, but it is too early . . . before breakfast. What *am* I thinking of?"

"Later, possibly," Robert said, hard put to conceal a smile when he saw what was on offer. It was definitely a widow's wine list; pansy, blackcurrant and whortleberry.

"Your dear mama and I often take wine together," Alethea confided, "not that we drink great quantities you understand," she added guiltily, the perils of strong drink so indelibly imprinted on her mind that guilt came to her easily in this regard, "but it does stop the onset of a dry throat when one is talking. Charlotte teases us by saying that Sophie and I enjoy feeling guilty at our small indulgence but this I cannot allow. I do not believe it sinful to drink *home*-made wine. I am certain it would not be counted as strong drink. What do you think, Robert?"

Robert's thoughts were unrepeatable so he said nothing. But as he listened to his hostess with every appearance of civility, he wondered what he had let himself in for by accepting the breakfast invitation. A widow's wine and stultifying conversation? He was inclined to make his excuses but manfully resisted the temptation. He had offended Charlotte and could not leave without making amends. However, he was still annoyed at becoming embroiled in such a ridiculous situation. It was too parochial for words.

"Who gathers the fruits for your brewing? Charlotte?" he asked abruptly, frowning at his thoughts. He suspected that this was another result of their penury.

Alethea misinterpreted the frown as disapproval and launched nervously into speech. "With Morley's help, naturally. She grows some fruit in our garden . . . but you know she is a keen horticulturalist. You remarked on it yourself only a short time ago; did you not?"

"So I did," Robert agreed dryly.

At this moment Charlotte appeared and was greeted with relief by both occupants of the drawing room, Mrs Treleaven feeling that her daughter could now take up the burden of conversation with Robert because he had grown to be quite formidable in some ways.

Robert was also grateful for the interruption. Frown disappearing, he got to his feet to greet Charlotte. Her face was no longer stormy and he assumed their quarrel had been forgotten. He soon discovered how wrong he was.

"We are choosing an after breakfast wine, Charlotte. Shall you join us?"

"I? Certainly not! I am too young to partake of wine," she said pointedly. "I know nothing of your London ways of course," she spoke as though of a den of iniquity, "but here, in Cornwall, the Methodist persuasion strongly condemns the habit of drink." Almost she tossed her head at him and as he saw this, a slow smile lit Robert's now wickedly sparkling blue eyes. "However," Charlotte added, "that is nothing to the point. Breakfast is served. Shall we go, Mama?"

"Do you tell me Mr Sherwell has converted you to the Methodist belief?" Robert asked ingenuously as they walked into the dining room. "I thought you firm in the church of the realm. Do you no longer worship at North Hill?" He feigned surprise, his look grave.

"Naturally, we still attend St Torney's," Charlotte said, annoyed and a little confused. "There is no question of a conversion," she went on tartly, disdaining Robert's helping hand at the table. "What are you thinking, Sir?"

"I beg your pardon," Robert apologised, effectively taking the wind out of Charlotte's eye, "but knowing Sherwell's sentiments with regard to drink, when you spoke of the Methodist persuasion, I naturally thought . . ." He allowed the rest of his thought to remain unspoken but the budget of it hung in the air.

"I meant that in this part of Cornwall, which has been influenced by the Wesley brothers, drinking is frowned upon. That is all."

"Not at my harvest gathering, it wasn't," Robert replied as he raised his glass of small beer to Charlotte and then saluted her mother with equal deliberation. To Alethea he said, making it sound as though they were partners in sin: "It seems that Miss Treleaven dislikes the habit of drinking even this innocent brew, Aunt Alethea. Presumably she disapproves of us too."

Devilment was in his eyes as he gave Charlotte a sideways glance. She caught the brilliant blue flash and could not prevent an exclamation of chagrin, particularly when she saw her mother's distressed looks.

"Now, Mama, pray do not feel guilty." Charlotte spoke soothingly. "Mr Hattenbury is not referring to you." She returned her attention to him. "You are well aware, Sir, that I was not condemning the mamas' small indulgence."

Robert smiled winningly, his eyes wide and sparklingly blue. He addressed Charlotte with the same pointed formality she used to him. "I quite understand, Miss Treleaven. You are directing the finger of scorn at *my* dissolute ways but, I do assure you, I shall imbibe only the same wine you think suitable for our mamas. I feel sure that if it is of *your* culturing it cannot be the devil's instrument. Holding the views you do, could you otherwise bring yourself to make it?"

This masterly speech threw Charlotte into confusion. She scarcely knew how to answer without embroiling herself further.

"No, no, I did not mean . . . I did not say you were . . ." she stopped, feeling guilty when she saw his sorrowful look. But then she saw his shapely mouth quiver and knew he was ribbing her. She blushed and succumbed to laughter; against her will it is true. Robert also laughed.

Having listened to the young people's altercation with dismay, the bewildered widow now joined in the laughter headily, vastly relieved to feel the dissipation of stiffness in the atmosphere.

Breakfast was not dull after all. Mrs Treleaven said little but neither of the others felt a lack. Indeed, Robert was surprised how quickly time flew.

***

After breakfast, as the three loitered, replete, at table, Robert introduced the topic of Charlotte's reward.

Alethea was thrilled for her daughter and charmed by Robert's kindness in forwarding Charlotte's pleasure. But that was only until she heard of the proposed attraction: Looe. Then her happy smile died, the becoming pink blush in her cheeks faded and she was clearly unhappy.

"Oh . . . no . . . Robert, dear . . . if it please you . . . not Looe. Could we not go to . . . go to . . . to Launceston?" With this happy solution coming to mind Alethea's voice rose hopefully. "Yes. That would be quite delightful; would it not, Charlotte?"

Charlotte gave up Looe easily since her mother did not want to go there. "Of course, Mama. We can climb up to the castle. Now *that* I shall enjoy."

Robert was more curious. "What have you against Looe, Aunt Alethea?"

It was a reasonable question but he received no plain answer from a clearly uncomfortable Alethea, only a welter of disjointed phrases telling him nothing.

Seeing her mother's discomfort Charlotte stepped in. "Mama, Looe was no more than an idle thought. And now *that* point is settled, Robert has some further good news." Charlotte turned to Robert, giving him the floor for the new topic.

Intrigued, curious, but too polite to pursue the matter of Looe further, Robert took up smoothly where Charlotte left off.

"Yes, it is another treat. We are all invited to take breakfast with the Hearl Rodds next week. Their nephews are in residence so it should be a lively morning."

Mrs Treleaven was immediately diverted and her first thought on hearing the news, as with Charlotte, although in Alethea's case uttered aloud, was: "But what shall you wear, Charlotte?"

Having turned her mama's thoughts into happier channels, Charlotte had no wish to burden her with awkward questions of an inadequate wardrobe. She said cheerfully: "There is plenty of time to think of that. Now, Mama, why not go and write up your diary? Uhm?" Charlotte went to her mother and helped gather up her shawl and handkerchief.

Alethea said goodbye to Robert, who was now also standing, and tripped away upstairs. In truth she was relieved to go for the Looe business had brought back some very unhappy memories. To be private at this point was a blessing she welcomed.

***

"What was that all about?" Robert asked when Mrs Treleaven had gone.

"I'm afraid I don't know," Charlotte replied truthfully, "but if Mama doesn't want to visit Looe, no more do I. Honestly, Robert, I have long wished to explore Launceston castle but never had the opportunity. I shall enjoy it excessively." Charlotte's eyes were sparkling with anticipation, her enthusiasm boundless. "We could take a picnic. Won't it be delightful, Robert?"

"I'm sure it will," he agreed, smiling at her pleasure in so simple an expedition. "That being settled," he held out a hand, "walk me to the stables and tell me all about your pretty flower garden on the way."

Charlotte obliged happily, while Robert listened more with heart than ears, until he asked presently: "Have you forgiven me yet?"

"I believe I must," Charlotte responded, "for if I do not you will begin to tease me again and it is quite provoking to be full of smiles when what you *want* is to show disapproval." Her expression was a mixture of irritation and amusement.

Robert drew her to a halt. Hands light upon her shoulders, he turned her to face him. He was smiling but his voice held serious undertones when he asked: "Will you fly off the handle if I reintroduce the topic?"

"No, I won't, but what makes you critical?" Charlotte was genuinely puzzled.

"Not so, Charlotte," he denied. "I simply thought, naturally I believe, that you would prefer to spend time with people of your own age."

"Perhaps, but there are few living here. You are our closest neighbour and you are never at home." Interestingly, although she did not notice, Charlotte now bracketed herself together with Robert in terms of companionship, whereas, only last week, she had remarked to her mother that Robert was far above her touch.

"What happened to the Laskey brood who rented one of your cottages?"

"Gone to Plymouth. They were never accepted here; French connections and a different faith; hopeless."

"I see." Robert spoke absently, thoughts ranging over the immediate country. "You are right, poppet. There are no suitable companions to hand. Poor sweet."

She bridled, colour rising. "Waste no sympathy on me, Sir. I am not poor, nor shall I be sweet if you continue in this vein."

Robert drew back, laughing. He put up his hands as though for protection. "Pray do not eat me, Miss Treleaven," he protested through his laughter. "indeed, I mean you no harm."

Charlotte's ruffled feathers subsided. "I am not lonely, if that is what you think. I am too busy to be lonely."

"Busy at what?" Robert asked as they began to walk on. He suspected he already knew the answer to that question, as Charlotte confirmed.

"Organising Mama, mostly," she replied, after several moments of thought. "She is a little mazed at times . . ."

Robert started to laugh and Charlotte gave him a challenging look but he shook his head, disclaiming any malice. "What else do you do, apart from organising your mama?"

Charlotte deftly deadheaded some straggling flowers. "Well, I have my piano of course. And then there is the house and garden work. This time of year we are particularly busy with preserving, jam making and wine culture." She looked conscious but her voice defied him to comment.

"Of course," Robert agreed gravely but Charlotte saw his mouth quirking the tiniest bit. She moved on to the next bed. He followed. "What are these?" he asked.

"Night-scented Stocks," she replied briefly and went on: "In winter Mama and I do the needlework. In spring we set the house to rights . . . and so on through the year. There is no time for boredom, I assure you."

Robert took her hand again and they resumed walking in silence. Ostensibly he was observing the flowers but his thoughts were entirely with Charlotte, reflecting that the life she described was far from normal for a girl of her class and age. She might easily be speaking as the matronly wife of a farmer not the daughter of a gentleman. Clearly, her activities reflected their reduced circumstances. She would hardly be expected to stock their cupboard, or do serious gardening, in the normal course of events. Gardening might serve as a whim of the late queen but not for Charlotte.

She would of course be expected to know household management but her present life was neither suitable nor desirable in one so young, no matter how capable. The seriousness of his mother's misgivings had been brought home to him quite forcibly this morning.

He cast a glance at Charlotte and the picture he saw was of a pretty girl in a shabby frock, her face gently moulded. In repose her mouth sometimes had a tiny droop, giving her a vulnerable look, until one noticed the determined lift to her chin. It would be at one's peril to miss that.

His gaze travelled to the tender curve of Charlotte's neck and shoulders, where luxuriant dark chestnut hair (not red as he had recalled) tumbled down over a breast only very lightly formed in womanly mould, scarcely at all in fact. He saw slender brown arms and the hand in his was not the usual smooth, pale member he was used to caressing in moments of dalliance. The thought made him laugh aloud.

Charlotte gave him a glance of enquiry. He released her hand and slipped an arm over her shoulders. "Come along, dear heart. I am for home since I am obviously holding up your many labours. But first I must thank you for a most delightful day."

Looking up at him, with a mischievous glint in her eye, Charlotte asked: "What made it so delightful? That I persuaded you to engage in labour not to your taste, or that I twice quarrelled with you, Sir?"

Amused, Robert responded: "No the delight was in your entertaining person, not your sharp tongue."

To this, looking even more mischievous, Charlotte replied: "I believe I can recall a time when you named me 'pesky' so delight is a decided improvement on that; don't you agree, Robert?"

Robert laughed heartily but refused to be drawn. He ruffled Charlotte's hair. Then he put a hand under her chin and turned up her face, dropping a light kiss on her cheek. Her skin was smooth and warm and she smelled just as delectable as the fruits in her conservatory.

He made his excuses to Mrs Treleaven via Charlotte, who responded very quietly, bemused by her first kiss and, again, sharply aware of Robert's person. During their altercations this morning, yesterday's attraction had been subdued under irritation but with his kiss it sprang back into life, leaving her wanting more of him and his company.

Off he went, giving her a cheerful wave as he gave his horse the spring, entirely unaware that the salute he had given her so casually was a momentous event in Charlotte's life.

When he was gone Charlotte stood rooted for a few moments with a hand to the kissed cheek wondering if, perhaps, Robert was beginning to think of her with admiration. Or, commonsense coming to the fore, did he think of her as a child to be amused. This, on balance, seemed more probable.

That same commonsense told Charlotte to keep her fancies in check. Nevertheless, it was pleasant to remember the touch of Robert's mouth and the warmth of his chest under her hand.

Had he been privy to her thoughts, Robert might have been given pause for thought, reminded, as his mother had said, that Charlotte was no longer a schoolroom miss. Since he was not Robert rode away blithely, reflecting on a very pleasant day.

***

When Robert reached home it was almost dinnertime. His mama kissed him in greeting. "You were gone a long time, darling. Have you been to Bicton?"

"No." Robert laughed. "I was less than a mile away at Crane Lodge. Aunt Alethea invited me to breakfast and I stayed on. You were not alarmed by my absence?" He was perfectly collected.

"Naturally not, dearest," she replied, as cool as he. That part of their conversation ended here; so short, so interesting to Sophie. Robert had spoken without apparent reserve but still given her several things to mull over.

For instance: Aunt Althea? Since when had he reverted to titling her thus? He had been known to refer to her as 'your odd friend' when the mood was on him. Also, leaving home that morning, he made no mention of visiting Crane. What had drawn him there? Charlotte, perhaps? Mrs Hattenbury smiled inwardly at the heartening possibilities raised by such an idea.

"Mama." Robert recalled her wandering attention. "Tell me; why is Looe village anathema to Aunt Alethea?" he asked. "I suggested a pleasure trip there for Charlotte but she would not hear of it."

"Ah." Sophie's mind flew back down the years and she remembered instantly the time that had given Alethea so strong a distaste of Looe. "I know precisely why, Robert. It is because our two families made a visit there one day, when darling Charlotte was two or three years old. You were away at school.

"Everything went splendidly; we lunched well at the inn . . . and the day is so indelibly imprinted on my mind that I still recall what we ate. We had *the* most delicious pasties, followed by strawberries and cream.

"Then, being overstuffed, we walked to the end of the quay, where stood a large granite slab conveniently placed to do duty as a seat. Alethea and I accepted the stone's mute invitation gladly, whilst your papa and Mr Treleaven took Jacinta and Charlotte to the beach to trawl for gemstones. Apparently, Lord Falmouth said he found some there and . . ."

"Yes, yes, get to the point, Mama," Robert interrupted impatiently. "I've visited Falmouth, at Tregothnan and found him rather too ready to show off his collection, be it never so valuable."

"Valuable, indeed, Robert. It is said to be worth over £15,000," Sophia said in awe.

"Mama!"

"Of course, dearest. Well, coming to the crux of it, when we later crossed over the river and began climbing the hill to Hannafore Point, Charlotte was eager to run on ahead, to look at those cottages clinging to the hillside among the trees there. Mr Treleaven called her back, for her own safety no doubt, but the darling baby did not hear him and continued on her course. He ran after her and then, Robert . . ." Sophie took a breath, grimacing and shaking her head in disbelief, even at this late date, "then, Robert, he beat her with his cane, stroke upon stroke upon stroke, while she, poor darling, sobbed that she had not heard him call and was very sorry.

"He seemed not to hear a word she said, merely repeating with each stroke, that he would not have her disobey him. Of course," Sophie paused, giving Robert a look that said much, "he *had* been drinking. Poor Alethea was near to fainting with horror; Jacinta was in tears; and I was stunned that he could treat his own sweet child in that way. And it wasn't the first time he'd done such, you know.

"Anyway, your father prevailed upon him to return to reason with soothing words and a restraining hand; and then we came home, in very sombre mood." Sophie paused before ending: "And that, Robert, is why Alethea so disliked your suggestion. She has never forgotten that day. In her mind the village is forever associated with Charlotte's beating. That man drew blood from her, you know."

Robert frowned in disgust throughout the telling of Sophie's tale, and then said: "I never realised he was such a monster, Mama."

Sophie shrugged. "You were only a boy, darling, and away at school during the latter years, so never saw the worst of it when he was drinking very heavily; and, I must say, I liked him when he was younger. He was intelligent and could be perfectly charming when not in drink," she said.

"Humph," observed Robert, "that is not much of a recommendation *and*, I suppose, also explains Aunt Alethea's preoccupation with the evils of what she calls 'strong drink'," he added thoughtfully. "I would not have teased her had I known."

"How teased, Robert?"

"No, Mama," Robert stated firmly, getting to his feet. "I have no intention of regaling you with that story. The two of you can pick the bones out of it to your hearts' content when next you meet.

"However, there is on other thing. This Trebartha breakfast seems to be problematic for Charlotte. She has nothing to wear, I understand. Has she a dress in her wardrobe that could be updated pro tem, do you think? I have already had some provisional thoughts about their financial situation but this is more immediate."

He kissed her and was off, leaving Sophie to think pleasurably over her son's obvious interest in Charlotte's concerns and thinking that maybe, just maybe, she had been right after all.

Luckily for Robert's peace of mind, he knew nothing of that which exercised his mother's so pleasurably and that night, after a day of unimpeachable rectitude, he retired to take the untroubled sleep of the just; which came to him as anticipated but much earlier than when he was in town.

***

Discussing various projected activities over breakfast next morning, Sophie tentatively brought up the subject of Brighton, vis-à-vis: if Robert still intended to go.

To her relief he replied that he was too busy to leave home at this time. "I've been invited to shoot at Rose Craddock and Bicton, among other things."

"Also, darling, you should think of making an appearance in church. Mr Trelowary will be offended if you do not."

Robert agreed, without marked enthusiasm. "Incidentally, can you arrange Charlotte's trip to Launceston with Aunt Alethea?"

"I'll pop over to Crane this very day."

"Now why am I not surprised at that revelation," Robert observed dryly. Sophie merely laughed.

***

She sent no message to Crane, both houses exchanging informally, but set out in late morning. On arrival Alethea came to greet her. Arm in arm they walked into the house, and Alethea said excitedly: "Robert was here yesterday. Did you know?"

"I did, Alethea, and was so surprised to learn he had spent the day with you. Was he with Charlotte the whole time?"

"Yes, oh yes," Alethea nodded vigorously, "but, Sophie, you have no idea of my duplicity. I ought to be ashamed but somehow I am not. Perhaps I should pray extra hard when I am next in church."

"Possibly, dear, but do tell me . . . what did you do?"

"I watched them walk in the garden when Charlotte thought I had gone to write up my diary," she confessed simply.

Sophie's scruples were not so finely tuned. "And? What did you see?" she prompted, without the least hesitation.

"Well . . . first they walked; then they stood by the flower beds while Charlotte tidied away the dead petals; next they spoke, and then . . . oh Sophie . . . Robert kissed her! Can you imagine? He kissed her." Mrs Treleaven's sigh was of pure happiness.

"What! Kissed her?" Sophie was astonished. "Alethea, are you sure?"

"Would I relate such a thing if it were not so?" Alethea asked indignantly.

"Goodness! I cannot believe it! You are sure you did not make a mistake?"

"Sophie, no!" Alethea protested. "I saw Robert place his lips to Charlotte's cheek. Come to the window and I can point to the very spot where he embraced her." Mrs Hattenbury, in the act of rising, was so surprised she sank back into her seat.

"Embraced her?" she echoed. It seemed improbable that her cool and self-contained Robert was seen to be kissing, *and* embracing, the very girl he had dismissed as absolutely unsuitable marriage material only a few days ago! She began to laugh, feeling giddy with mirth. "Alethea, do you tell me that my son embraced your daughter, in your garden, in full view for all to see?"

"Indeed, only I saw, I hope, but, yes he *did,*" Mrs Treleaven brought out triumphantly. She took Sophie's arm and drew her to the window. Pointing to a clump of foxgloves, she said: "There. First he held her hand, then he put an arm about her and then he kissed her. I saw it all. Is it not wonderful? Or . . . oh dear, Sophie, do you condemn me for spying?"

"No. I only wish I had seen it all, too." Mrs Hattenbury sighed enviously. "Think what this could mean, Alethea," she said, allowing hope to rise. "I know Robert has said Charlotte is not right for him but he *did* come to see her, and if he kissed her . . ." She did not continue this tantalising line of thought. Instead she asked: "What had Charlotte to say?"

"I do not know for I was not supposed to have seen." Alethea looked faintly shocked and then doubtful. "Should I have asked her?"

"My dear friend, no. Excitement has addled my wits. We must not meddle and possibly raise Charlotte's hopes unwisely. We must leave it to Robert. It is therefore better to stay silent. But Alethea," Sophie added robustly, "that is not to say that we may not *hope*. If Robert and Charlotte marry she will not be lost to us as Jacinta was and it will solve every difficulty.

"Only think . . . what else is there for her in this part of Cornwall? One of the Buller boys from Looe would suit her but, let it be faced, for her to live there is no better than Scotland when winter is upon us because the roads are quite impassable. Were she a Mrs Buller we would rarely see her and what use is that?"

"Yes, and then Mr Tregodick's son is already betrothed," Alethea continued where Sophie had left off, "while the Wrayes would want a dowry. Mr Rodd's nephews are not yet up to scratch and of the Baring-Goulds only Charles is presently at home."

"Oh, no, he is a pleasant young man but I think him quite unsuited to Charlotte's temperament; too clerical," Sophie decided. "His brother, Edward, who looks divine in regimentals, is rather like Robert and would be equally suitable in certain respects but he is seriously courting Sophia Bond. There is no-one else suitable near at hand who comes to mind. No," was Sophie's final, firm dictum, "it has to be Robert."

Chapter Three

That evening, on his way to dine with Richard Tregodick, Robert surveyed the familiar country scenery, the fields and folds of the countryside, the unmistakeable, timeless face of the Cheeswring quarry, stark against the skyline. He was finding it extraordinarily pleasant to be home and meant to come more often; though possibly not in the tourist season since Cornwall had now become part of their lexicon.

Robert remembered his young self sneaking away from his tutor one time, to spend a day at the quarry. He had assuaged his hunger with the whortleberries growing there in abundance. He also remembered being dreadfully sick as a result. The caning earned for his truancy had not been pleasant either.

That had been the year of the Methodist revival in Cornwall, when the people of the near-by village of Coad's Green converted the old blacksmith's shop in Penhole Road to a Sunday school and Meeting House.

That was also the year Bonaparte was dethroned. Robert could still remember the excitement generated when the mail coach brought down the news, the rejoicings and celebratory firing of redundant warning beacons. He and Jacinta had been allowed to build their own bonfire, on which they daringly burned Napoleon's effigy. Later, they went to Plymouth on the ferry, to see his ship, the Bellerophon, brought to harbour. Robert smiled. Yes, it had been a long time ago and Charlotte not even thought of.

Following a new train of thought, Robert now speculated that Richard, with whom he was to dine, would have made an excellent husband for Charlotte had he not already been engaged to a pretty heiress, Miss Julia Langford, from Twowatersfoot, a small village on the other side of Liskeard. Her father had a pretty estate down in the valley there, with a trout stream running past his door and plenty of duck for the shooting. In addition Miss Langford was an attractive girl, not much in the way of conversation but a trim figure, so Richard was positively eager to submit to wedlock's bond. Alas for Charlotte, although on reflection, maybe not; unlike Miss Langford, Charlotte had plenty of conversation; too much for Richard's taste probably.

All thoughts of Charlotte fled from Robert's mind when he entered the Tregodick house and a smile of anticipation lit his face as he heard the gusting, masculine laughter issuing from behind closed doors. It promised to be a thoroughly entertaining evening.

***

That promise was fulfilled but the price paid was a thumping headache next day, which made *his* the kind of company best avoided. Charlotte, coming down the lane to Hattenbury and meeting Robert ahorseback, was unaware of this. She was extremely surprised therefore, when he demanded, frowningly, and without as much as a token good day: "Where the devil are you going?"

Her smile of greeting died. "On an errand to your mother, Sir," she replied, looking uncertain.

"Unattended?" His tone was arbitrary. It brought a mortified flush to Charlotte's cheeks.

"Why not?" She blinked as she looked up at him. "Are you suggesting Mr Pearse will set the dogs on me if I cross his fields? It is more likely Mrs Pearse will call me in for buttermilk and a piece of her Heavy cake. Excuse me for pointing it out, Mr Hattenbury, but you seem bad-tempered. Since I am not I bid you good morning, although I suspect such will *not* be the case for you."

With this tart rejoinder Charlotte made to pass on, all her pleasure in seeing Robert dissipated. He leaned down to retain her with a hand on her shoulder. His frown had disappeared and he seemed amused.

"Pray, Charlotte, do not be so waspish. I was only thinking of your good." She tried to brush away the detaining hand without success.

"I take leave to doubt that, Sir. You are merely venting your ill temper on me and I do not choose to be your butt. Unhand me please."

"No, Charlotte, truly." Robert's demeanour softened. "Had you read the Morning News you would know there are three escaped criminals abroad in this area. They are making for Liskeard, where one of them has family. This would be their route."

With this reasonable explanation Charlotte's anger died. "Why did you not *say* so?" She glanced over her shoulder as if expecting the miscreants to appear at any moment. Robert laughed and held out a hand.

"Oh . . . get up before me, do. I'll take you to Mama. Put your foot across mine. Ready? Heave."

Charlotte landed on the horse in a heap. She had been more vigorous in aiding her ascent than either Robert or his horse anticipated. It took a few minutes to quiet the animal and get his passenger in order, none of which did much for an aching head, as straightened lips and muttered imprecations testified. Charlotte leaned back on his arm, giving him a decidedly mischievous glance.

"You *are* bad-tempered," she observed. "I said you were." Her pleasure in him was quite restored somehow, even though he was not his usual charming self.

Robert's arm tightened around her, which she did not mind in the least despite the martial glint in his eye. "Incorrigible child, you will come by your just desserts if you provoke me, and so I warn you, but not because I am ill tempered. My patience is thin because I have the headache. No!" he said, with a force he had instant cause to regret when he saw Charlotte's mouth shaping a saucy retort, "don't you dare say it's my own fault."

"Nothing was further from my intention," Charlotte said demurely, "but since *you* said it first I think it's probably true. Imbibing last night, were you?" She gave Robert a look of singular sweetness, sympathetic and disarming.

Looking at her fresh face, its compassionate expression, Robert felt the curdled knot inside him unravel. He relaxed in the saddle, returning Charlotte's smile but honestly disclaiming any right to her sympathy.

"Yes, I was, having a very convivial evening with Richard Tregodick's family and I am not now feeling the thing. It *is* my own fault, of course," he said ruefully.

Charlotte twisted about and took Robert's face between her hands. "Then you obviously need to be kissed better," she said and did so, meaning to salute his cheek, but finding only his mouth free since her palms framed his face.

Her kiss was a fleeting touch of lip to lip, in no way ardent, but it silenced them both. Charlotte blushed, horribly aware of having committed a social solecism, of doing what she quite clearly ought not to have done. Robert, she saw, was looking decidedly odd.

"Mr Hattenbury . . . oh! Pray, *do* forgive me! I did not mean . . . oh, murder! What must you be thinking?" She pressed both hands to her own hot face, quite unable to look at him. "That was not at all what I meant to do. I only thought . . . oh, how dreadfully embarrassing."

Yet, was it not, perhaps, what she had meant to do? Had she not wished, when he kissed her cheek the day before yesterday, to feel Robert's mouth upon her own? Oh, no, surely, she could not be so forward?

Robert quickly regained countenance. "There is no need to be embarrassed. I accept your kiss in the soothing spirit intended, thank you." He raised her chin. "Look at me." She did so, still blushing. "I am not disconcerted and nor must you be. Understood?" When she nodded, although still looking conscious, he drew a breath and said: "Right. Now for goodness' sake, let's get *on*." He jerked the reins to turn his mount and headed back down the lane.

"How long are you staying with Mama?" he asked, setting Charlotte on her feet at the front door.

"Not long. I have things to do at home."

"Very well but await my return. I shall take you home."

"There is no need," she demurred.

"There is every need," Robert insisted firmly. "We cannot be certain the ex-inmates of Bodmin gaol are not in the neighbourhood. Now mind me in this, Charlotte." He emphasised the point with a firm grip on her shoulder.

"As you wish, Sir."

Charlotte did not care for his arbitrary manner but was in no mood to cross him, feeling subdued after her faux pas. Additionally, he was now in a happier frame than when they first met, and it would be a pity to send him off in a fresh state of irritation. There was one other consideration; it would be pleasant to enjoy his company again.

***

Robert returned home well before luncheon. Sophie was surprised to see so early a return. She was also relieved to note that the thundercloud her son wore earlier was entirely gone.

"I did not expect you yet, Robert. The fresh air seems to have done you good. You are looking better," Sophie greeted.

"I am home early to tell you that we are invited to visit the Langfords at Twowatersfoot ~ Richard Tregodick's new family," he added in an aside for Charlotte's benefit. "Miss Langford's parents are anxious for her to meet prospective neighbours before the wedding, so that all will not be strange to her." Turning directly to Charlotte, he told her: "The invitation includes you and Aunt Alethea."

"Us?" Charlotte said, in pleased surprise. "Oh, how splendid!"

"When is it to be?" Mrs Hattenbury asked.

"The family are fixed at Kelly Bray until Saturday week, the twenty sixth. Mr Langford proposes that we travel back with them."

"No, I meant the wedding," Sophie corrected. She began gathering her things, ready for a remove to the terrace where a light repast awaited them.

"Mama!" Robert's expression was pained. "Why ask a question and not wait for an answer?"

Sophie laughed. "Come into the garden and tell us *all*."

"So, then," Robert began, when plates had been passed around, "the wedding is in September, and . . ."

"What of your visit to Brighton, Robert?" Sophie interjected.

"Postponed, pro tem," Robert replied briefly. "However, since I am home early specifically to impart this news to Charlotte, may I be allowed to do so, Mama?" How studied his patient tone.

"Pray do," Mrs Hattenbury replied, perfectly collected.

"Thank you, Mama." Robert bowed to her from the waist, punctiliously, before turning to Charlotte, who was trying to stifle her laughter at the spiked exchange between mother and son.

"Sit with me, Charlotte." He extended a hand. "You, I feel sure, will be delighted to lend me an ear," he remarked laconically.

"Certainly," she said with alacrity. "How could I do otherwise after such a pointed remark? But why are *we* invited, Robert? Mama and I don't know Miss Langford."

"When I told her you were younger, prettier and a nearer neighbour than I, she was eager for your acquaintance," said Robert, in plain mode.

"How kind," Charlotte commended warmly, leaning forward to press his arm, her hand lingering upon his sleeve for a moment. "I have never been so far afield as Twowatersfoot and shall *so* look forward to it. Mama, also, and all due to your thoughtfulness, Robert. It is quite as Aunt Sophie often says, you really are a darling," responded Charlotte, in loquacious mode.

"For heaven's *sake*, Charlotte, you are infuriatingly like Mama at times. Am I never to get a word in edgewise? Altogether, it has been that sort of day." He put a hand to his temples.

"I beg your pardon, Robert. Please, do continue," she coaxed. He relented into the ghost of a smile.

"Very well. As I have already tried to tell you, several times," he emphasised pointedly, "we shall leave here on Saturday, two weeks from today, and plan to stop at Webb's Hotel in Liskeard for a meal before travelling on to the Langford home."

"For how long is the invitation?" Charlotte asked, mentally wondering how Crane would go on without them. Something would have to be arranged.

"No time limit was stipulated but I believe we may stay for several weeks if we wish. I think you will like Miss Langford, Charlotte. She has a sweet disposition though, alas, little conversation. If you become bored with her I can always teach you backgammon to pass the time."

"Such nobility," Sophie murmured.

Robert eyed her with suspicion. "What is that remark to the point, Mama?"

Mrs Hattenbury twinkled merrily. "Shall we see any gentlemen except at meal times? In my experience they are either out with guns or immured with the port."

Robert, in the matter of this visit at pains to be of service to Charlotte, and not feeling quite the thing even now, was not amused. "Why doubt my word?" he enquired irritably. "Let me tell you, Mama, I accepted this invitation for . . . your pleasure more than mine."

His pause was barely perceptible but the glance he bent in his mother's direction was plain and she understood immediately. The visit had been arranged for Charlotte. Again Robert surprised her.

Charlotte, no slowtop, also understood, realising from a full heart how much Robert was putting himself about for her. He was sacrificing his own plans in the interests of her pleasure. Equally she understood his frown, the hand to his brow.

"Have you still a headache, dear Sir?" she asked solicitously, with a glance of concerned enquiry. "I will bathe your forehead with lavender water if you wish."

Robert smiled. "Not necessary, thank you, but you could massage my temples if you chose. Should you do so, I want no accompanying strictures on the evils of drink such as I have already heard from you. Knowing one has brought about one's own indisposition is sufficient punishment."

"As if I would," Charlotte demurred, laughing softly at his aggrieved tone. She went to stand behind him and began to soothe his temples. After a few minutes Robert relaxed visibly, eyes closing as he murmured appreciation.

"Ah . . . better," he sighed, and lapsed into silence. She continued her comforting ministrations and presently, with another releasing sigh, Robert settled his head against Charlotte's breast.

Sophie Hattenbury was a very surprised spectator of the intimate scene being enacted before her eyes, thinking that both participants in it seemed peculiarly at ease with each other on such short reacquaintance, particularly within the social parameters Robert had previously set out. And how was it Charlotte had already known of Robert's indisposition? Why should he give her licence to abate it? Here was food for thought.

Opening reluctant eyes, for he was pleasantly comfortable, Robert became aware of his mother's interested gaze. He sat up, stilling Charlotte's hands, the faintest of flushes colouring his cheeks. "Thank you, Charlotte; that is better."

"I am glad to have helped, Sir." Charlotte did not add that it had been quite delightful to be at liberty to touch him so freely.

Fortunately for Robert's countenance, which, through Charlotte, had twice been set awry that day, a message was brought requiring Sophie's presence elsewhere. By the time she returned Robert and Charlotte were discussing the outing to Launceston.

"If you do not mind sharing the treat you could invite Miss Langford and Richard to join us. It would be a tangible expression of goodwill and you would be known to each other before going to Twowatersfoot."

"What a good idea, Robert," Charlotte agreed. "Did you mention it to them?"

"No; I thought it better coming from you."

"I shall write directly when I go home," Charlotte promised. "In fact I should go soon." She looked at Robert.

"I am quite at your disposal," he said and got to his feet, offering Charlotte a hand; and now, knowing her better, it was not a polite extension of the fingertips but a wholehearted offering of the palm.

Charlotte took his hand confidently and they went off down the garden, clasped hands swinging between them. Charlotte was obliged to skip now and then, to keep pace with Robert's longer stride, which he did not think to moderate in consideration of her shorter legs.

They did not go far. Taking a short cut through the orchard, Robert saw his old swing suspended from the leafy boughs of a tree. He looked at Charlotte speculatively.

"Are you too old to enjoy a swing?" he asked.

"Not if you mean to push me," she replied demurely.

He agreed with easy good humour. "I seem to recall having done so before. Let me try first. It may no longer be safe."

He tugged on the chains vigorously, using all his body weight. The swing held firm and in a few minutes Charlotte was high in the air, her chestnut hair flying.

Once she was well launched Robert came to the front of the swing, standing clear of Charlotte's out-thrust feet since, as in all else, her participation was enthusiastic. He watched tolerantly, taking a vicarious pleasure in her enjoyment.

Gradually, the swing's momentum lessened. At shoulder height, Charlotte called out: "Stand clear."

The swing started on its downward arc and Robert saw Charlotte release the chains. Realising she intended to jump, he moved forward hastily. "No, Charlotte," he cautioned, "don't be reckless."

Too late! Even as he spoke, she parted company with the seat and sailed through the air with arms outstretched.

She might have landed safely but for Robert's intervention. She was distracted and came down in an untidy heap. He caught her up swiftly.

"Fool!" he snarled furiously. "What in God's name were you thinking of? You could have broken your neck. Oh, Charlotte . . . idiotic child! Are you hurt? Let me see you . . . let me see. Oh, I could murder you for giving me such a fright."

Anxiety was the prime cause of Robert's fury. Charlotte did not see this. Every bit as furious as he, she responded angrily.

"I am not hurt but it is no thanks to *you*. It was your fault that I fell! Ouch!" She emitted several involuntary groans as various parts of her anatomy, separately and together, protested. "I would have been perfectly safe had you not jumped out like that. And you call *me* fool?" she ended in high dudgeon.

Robert was shocked to rigidity at her temerity in addressing him thus. He was silenced momentarily, unable to believe his ears. When he could speak, incensed, he ground out: "Insolent girl! Hold your tongue! How *dare* you take exception to a just rebuke? You might have broken every bone in your body. Did you think of that?" he demanded, his fury increasing when she made no answer. "What? Have you nothing to say now?"

Charlotte, with a fulminating heart, said: "Indeed, I do, Sir, but you commanded me to hold my tongue. Which shall it be . . . speak or not speak? I *wish* you would make up your mind what you want," she demanded in louder, angrier tones, struggling to regain her feet.

"How childish, Miss Treleaven. Have you no countenance?" Robert dismissed, his anger hardening to icy contempt. At the same time, he helped Charlotte rise with automatic chivalry. Restored to her feet, he began dusting her down.

"Leave me be." She fended him off without ceremony. "I never met so infuriating a man in all my life. Childish, you say, childish? If that is not pot calling kettle black, I do not know what is."

For a brief space they stood face to face, both glaring at and thinking vituperatively of the other, until, as eye bonded with eye, Charlotte saw the shadows beneath Robert's blue orbs. She remembered his indisposition. Of course, this was why he was short-tempered and she should not have ill-used him.

All her anger dissipated, she reached out to him impulsively. "Oh, dear Sir, I do apologise. Let us cry truce. You are perfectly right to upbraid me. I should not have flown up in the boughs because you did. Forgive me, please," she appealed.

Still angry, Robert did not relent immediately. "Don't speak of flying into the boughs, Charlotte. You have already done too much of that for *my* taste."

There was a moment of conscious silence as Robert realised the peculiar aptness of what he had said. Charlotte saw it at the same time and the absurdity of the situation in which they were embroiled struck home. First came a reluctant smile and then a small giggle from Charlotte, followed by a complete eruption of mirth from both which obliged them to support each other against the imminent possibility of collapse.

When they were more collected Robert dried Charlotte's eyes with his handkerchief. "Perhaps it was my fault a little," he conceded, "but you should not behave so. Young ladies swing decorously. They do not jump up and down like monkeys, frightening all and sundry. I had forgotten what an imp of mischief you can be."

Charlotte might have objected to such a description as applied to her but she did not. To be standing close to Robert, within the circle of his arm as she now was, felt most agreeable and the warm feelings engendered by his nearness gave her a strong inclination to do, and be, exactly what he wanted.

"As you say, Sir, I shall be more sedate in future," she promised.

"Very commendable," Robert commented dryly, "but in case you might, accidentally of course, fall into more mischief I think I should take you home right now." He started down the orchard without more ado.

At Crane Lodge Robert gave Mrs Treleaven all the news. When it had been assimilated, he saluted her cheek in farewell. After a brief hesitation he also kissed Charlotte's cheek and then walked back to Hattenbury in leisurely fashion, inspecting Home Farm crops as he went.

Later that day he joined his mother at dinner. With Charlotte in mind, it was of her he first spoke.

"Mama, you really must preach a gospel of caution to Aunt Alethea in regard to allowing Charlotte out unattended. She ought to have a chaperone. To be without one, as I found her today, is neither safe nor appropriate."

Sophie's own concern was evident in her reply. "Unfortunately, Robert, it is not as simple as that."

"How so?" It seemed straightforward to him.

"There is no-one to attend Charlotte. Crane only has Megan, their one servant, and she cannot be spared."

"Only one domestic?" Robert thought he had misheard. "You say Charlotte and her mother run that great house alone?" He was frankly astounded.

"They have no choice," Sophie answered with unassailable truth.

"Good God, what happened to their other servants?"

His mother shrugged expressively. "Without money to pay them they had to be turned off. Robert, I *did* tell you Alethea was in difficulties."

"Yes, but I did not realise to what extent!" Robert could still scarcely credit it. "Had I known I would have acted more swiftly on their behalf."

"Please do, darling. Their situation is grave and something *must* be done soon. Since you do not wish to marry Charlotte, another candidate must be sought; meantime . . ." she did not need to say more. Robert quite took the point.

"Yes, yes, Mama, I will look to it immediately. I shall send for Roddick Sampson and see what can be done," he assured her. He went on in a slightly dry tone: "Now I see why you were so willing to sacrifice me to the cause."

"Would it be such a sacrifice, darling?" Sophie appealed. "You and Charlotte deal so well together now she is grown, I thought . . ."

"No, Mama," Robert broke in firmly, to avert the raising of unrealistic hopes. "Charlotte and I deal well together because we are like family, as you saw earlier today, but nothing else is possible. Our lives are too disparate."

Robert had a sudden mental picture of his erstwhile mistress, her flagrant allure and the response it aroused in him. To dwell on Charlotte in the same context was unthinkable. "No," he said in sharp reflex. "No, Mama," he repeated more gently, seeing her disappointment, "but something will be done I promise you. Meanwhile, with regard to Charlotte's safety when she is abroad, she must be provided with a horse at least."

"Let her have Dulcima. I no longer ride her. There may be a problem though. Charlotte is very proud and pride matters a very great deal, as *you* are well aware, Robert, so she must be gifted carefully."

"Leave that to me," Robert responded, ignoring his mama's pointed reference and privately resolving that Charlotte would do exactly as she was told.

***

Before consulting with Sampson, the lawyer, Robert made it his business to ride over the Crane estate to see how things stood and found, as his mother had said, that it went ill with the Treleavens. The land was unhusbanded, the cottages untenanted and falling into disrepair in some cases. The field hedges had not been pleached for some time; they were wild and disorderly, and the meadows were thick with overgrowth. As for Crane, the house was sound but needed refurbishment, both inside and out. Clearly, it would take a deal of money to set things right, the question being: where was it to come from?

Selling up was not the solution since it would leave Charlotte and her mama homeless, and in its present state Crane would not fetch a good price; the money thus obtained would not last long. Therefore the plan was not viable; nor was Scotland.

This left the equally unsuitable solution of Charlotte's marriage. Yes, she would marry eventually but not as an expedient and certainly not yet. First she had to grow to full womanhood. She must also make her come-out if she were to find a husband. Unlike Jacinta's husband, matrimonial prospects did not usually come riding in uninvited. Duncan Macgregor had been a guest preacher at St Torney's and he fell in love with Jacinta on first sight, very shortly thereafter sweeping her off to Scotland as his wife.

The more he thought, the more Robert came to one obvious solution; that he should buy the estate and leave the Treleaven ladies in situ. There would then be money to put everything to rights. At a later date, when Charlotte *did* marry, and depending on her husband's circumstances, Crane could either be bought back or gifted as a dowry.

Knowing such an action would take time to put into effect, Robert did not immediately disclose the plan to buy Crane to Mrs Treleaven. Instead he enquired sensitively into her immediate finances.

Alethea felt no discomfort in disclosing this information to Robert. Sophie had said dear Robert would find a solution to her difficulties. Therefore she reposed perfect confidence in him and spoke unreservedly.

As a result of her disclosures Robert made some funds available immediately. These were in exchange for running his sheep on her land for fresh grazing, of which Crane had an abundance, and was something he'd already thought of as being of possible advantage to both parties. This put an immediate, and very welcome, sum of money into the Treleaven exchequer. It also gave Robert time to consult with his man of business as to ways of implementing the larger plan.

Alethea told Charlotte of the sheep-grazing arrangement and she welcomed it equally with her mama.

Of his other plans Robert said nothing pro tem, although he often stayed to keep Charlotte company during his visits to Crane but not, it must be revealed, when she worked in the kitchen garden. Once was penance enough for any man he felt.

For her part Charlotte thought how exciting life had become since Robert's advent. She hoped he would not go off to Brighton too soon. The prospect of a return to old routines was less than appealing. She little realised that when Robert's plans came to fruition old routines would no longer pertain.

***

Tuesday, the day of Charlotte's treasured excursion, dawned cool but clear, the sun promising warmth later. Miss Langford and Charlotte quickly became acquainted, and were on the way to becoming firm friends when they arrived in Launceston. This was mostly due to Charlotte's warm reception of the other girl's confidences. From what Julia said, it appeared her fiancé's virtues were many. Having no cause to believe otherwise, Charlotte was sincere in congratulating Miss Langford on securing a true matrimonial treasure in Mr Tregodick. The two mamas, it must be confessed, shared an amused smile at the girls' artless exchanges.

Strolling around the town when they arrived at their destination, Mr Hattenbury hugged Charlotte to his side. "Are you content, poppet?" He was an indulgent companion that day, ready to smile on her without need for reason.

"Ah," commented Mr Tregodick sagely. "I could not think why you should want to come here, Robert; not quite your style; but now I understand." He was looking at Charlotte as he spoke.

She laughed, saying with disarming candour: "Too tame for sophisticated Mr Hattenbury you think? Yes, it is my treat because he is also kind Mr Hattenbury."

"Idiot . . . kind Mr Hattenbury, indeed," Robert mocked, and ruffled her hair

Charlotte, of course, retaliated. "You can be . . . when you choose!" She skipped off, laughing playfully over her shoulder.

Miss Langford was amazed at Miss Treleaven's temerity. *She* was acutely in awe of Mr Hattenbury and would never dream of addressing him so cavalierly.

Looking up at the castle, Robert observed to the mamas: "It's quite a climb. Would you ladies prefer to drink coffee at the inn while we four make the ascent?"

The two mamas, following his gaze, quickly agreed. They thanked Robert for his thoughtfulness and waved the party off, watching them go down the hill to the castle entrance. Then they retraced their steps round the square to the inn (where Robert had earlier bespoken dinner for six) and the landlord's private parlour.

Comfortably settled, Sophie said: "Clearly, Richard knows Robert would not normally indulge in castle climbing."

"Oh, Sophie, you know dear Robert's coming here is only a politeness towards the young ladies," Alethea responded generously.

"Yes," Sophie agreed, "at least . . . one young lady." The two old friends exchanged speaking glances.

***

They were not alone in commenting upon Robert's indulgence towards Charlotte when, after dinner at the inn, they decided to take a look-in at the shops.

As usual, Charlotte was attached to Robert's hand as they walked, looking up to his superior height frequently as they argued lightly: of what Miss Langford and Mr Tregodick could not hear because they had fallen somewhat behind, Robert, also as usual, walking quite quickly.

Miss Langford, one hand resting decorously in the crook of Mr Tregodick's arm, as befitted an engaged couple, commented: "Miss Treleaven is not at all afraid of Mr Hattenbury, is she? I quite tremble to see how free she is of his person. She even addresses him by his given name! Can you imagine? I would not dare."

Richard glanced at her sweetly serious face. "They are like family together and one is never in awe of a brother," he explained, matter-of-factly. "If I am to tell the truth, Miss Langford, it would not displease me to hear my name on *your* lips."

She blushed and would not look at him. "I could not," she whispered, much confused. She had never heard her mother address her father by anything other than his title. Richard's free hand covered hers.

"No-one is close enough to hear. See, the two ladies have stopped at the boot maker's shop. I expect you could if you tried," he murmured coaxingly; and after a while it seemed she could, although it still felt very daring.

Presently they caught up with their party, who were now conjoined at the boot maker's. Charlotte was exclaiming at a handsome sign above the shop which, appropriately, took the form of a boot. This one was painted eye-catchingly gold and was well known in the area; as was the boot maker for the quality of his wares. Mrs Treleaven drew attention to a pair of pretty blue kid pumps in the window.

"They would go well with Charlotte's best dress," she said. Then, throwing caution to the winds in the light of her new found substance, decided that her daughter should have the shoes if they fitted her, or order some if they did not. Thus, it fell out. An ecstatic Charlotte came out of the shop, the proud possessor of a pair of beautiful blue kid pumps.

The rest of that golden day passed perfectly and it was with untold regret Charlotte heard Robert say they must take the homeward road. She did not want her lovely day to end but, as with all things, it had to. In a short time they were heading for their homes, first going to Kelly Bray to drop off Richard and his fiancée.

At Crane Lodge, Robert dismounted to see the Treleaven ladies safely into the house. A happy Charlotte thanked him for her wonderful day. Then, in a perfectly natural manner, she gave him a hug. Robert responded with a quick hug of his own and kissed her cheek before saluting Alethea similarly and saying goodbye.

***

Robert's man of business rode away from Hattenbury House leaving his client in thoughtful frame of mind, very thoughtful, indeed; but he also left him with a useful interim solution to the Treleaven ladies' financial problems.

On opening this same topic with Roddick Sampson, meaning to ask ways and means of implementing his plans to buy Crane, Robert had been astonished to hear the lawyer's response.

"If I may be permitted, Sir, would it not be a simple matter to reinstate the annual sum of three hundred and fifty pounds which your late father paid into the Treleaven estate from his private funds?" he suggested.

Since Robert knew nothing of any such sum he was naturally very surprised. Further enquiries elicited the information that the said pension began the year of Mr Treleaven's death and ceased the year Robert's father died, no contrary instructions having been received in this regard.

"Why was it paid?" Robert asked.

Sampson, not having been furnished with any reason for the said payment, could not tell him. However unsatisfactory this lack of explanation, Robert did not hesitate to accept so easy a solution of the problem in hand.

"Reinstate the pension immediately," he instructed.

Roddick Sampson, also acquainted with the Treleaven affairs, asked forthrightly: "Sir, would you require me to make any additional recompense for the four years unpaid?"

"Yes, of course," Robert agreed, picking up instantly on the significance of the four years. It had not been Jacinta's wedding but his own father's demise which precipitated the Treleaven decline! But what had been his father's obligation to Jake Treleaven's widow? Clearly, his mother had not known of the pension or she would have told him. The only person who must have known was Aunt Alethea. Here is where he must direct his questions.

This he did, having required Sophie to send the carriage for Mrs Treleaven. Alethea looked a little apprehensive on being ushered alone into Robert's study but he soon reassured her. Since she had received no explanation as yet, Sophie was rather affronted at being excluded.

"Dear Aunt Alethea," Robert began, "it has only lately come to my notice that you have inadvertently been wronged. Why have you never spoken to me of the unpaid income from the Hattenbury estate?" he asked gently, taking her hand.

"Why . . . Robert . . . dear . . . I . . . I did not realise it was still to be paid. I understood . . . when your dearest papa died . . . that the obligation was at an end," she responded in her usual, somewhat confused manner but with perfect openness.

"No, no, that is not the case. Its cessation was a mistake," Robert assured her. "The obligation is on the family not its individual members. It must continue to be disbursed and, naturally, you will also receive the four years of unpaid funds." There was a pause before Robert, with purpose aforethought, gently admonished her, saying: "Aunt Alethea, you should have *told* me. Had I known, the monies would, of course, have been paid to you. "

"Oh, Robert, dear kind boy . . ." Alethea pressed his hand feelingly, "had you been here, and had I known I should, naturally, I would have told you. But when your dear papa spoke of having an arrangement with my late husband I simply assumed it to be a personal matter between them. Francis . . . oh, excuse me, Robert . . . I mean, your father . . . well . . . that is . . . he said that it was the business of none but he and Jake and that I was not to think of it. Naturally, after that, I did not wish to offend him with impertinent questions. I never realised, therefore, that it was a family matter until you now have mentioned it."

Listening to her explanation, Robert came to the conclusion that Alethea's simplicity of mind might be irritating at times but in this instance it was his friend, making his part in the proceedings easy. How Charlotte would react, her mind being much sharper, was open to question but all in good time in that quarter.

"I only hope this business has not been too great an inconvenience to Crane," Robert said, knowing full well there had been a great deal more than inconvenience but wishing to leave Alethea's pride intact.

"Well . . . a little perhaps," she confessed, "but now all will be righted." On saying these words aloud the reality of them came home to Alethea; her face lit with a wide smile of relief and thankfulness.

Impulsively, revealing much more than her 'a little, perhaps' she burst out: "Oh . . . and now Charlotte can have a new gown for Trebartha! How delightful that will be."

"Indeed," Robert agreed, inwardly thinking that a good few other things must also change in Charlotte's regard.

Mrs Hattenbury's acceptance of the news was immediate and unquestioned in Alethea's presence. Only after her friend, still in a happy daze, had departed for home to give Charlotte the news, did Sophie question Robert more closely.

"I know no more than I have told you, Mama," he responded, shaking his shapely head. "The pension is not in dispute, only why it was never mentioned. Can you throw any light on it?"

"I can only think that Papa knew Mr Treleaven's financial affairs were in wild disarray and made this arrangement to secure Alethea's future," Sophie responded thoughtfully. "That would be very like him; would it not? Of course, he would have worded it kindly to spare Alethea's feelings, not wanting that she should be made to feel it was charity." Sophie's words carried a ring of truth as Robert recognised.

"As you say, Mama, and it makes the way forward much easier. Now we can concentrate on plans for Charlotte's future in more leisurely fashion. There is no immediate need for . . . wedlock, for example?" Robert teased, giving his mother an engaging smile.

Sophie responded in like manner. "It will certainly give her time to mature. You did say, did you not, darling, that you would consider Charlotte for a wife when she has grown a little?" Sophie mooted innocently.

Robert burst out laughing. "Mama, what a little opportunist you are."

Chapter Four

When Charlotte taxed Robert about the stipend, as he knew full well that she would, he was fully prepared.

"I knew nothing of it, Charlotte," he stated with perfect truth. "It came to light when I was speaking to Sampson on a different topic. It appears to be a matter of honour, or possibly business, between my father and yours." Seeing Charlotte open her mouth to question what matter of honour or business, Robert added hastily: "What *that* was we shall never know because no record was made. All I *can* say with certainty is that the stipend is honourable and *must* go forward. Indeed, it should never have ceased. That was an oversight which is now rectified.

"As to the time when it was not paid, if, having had the opportunity to think it over, you and Aunt Alethea feel that interest should be paid on the lost funds, I can only agree and will see that it is done."

Robert's last suggestion had Charlotte frowning in perplexity. As he'd intended, it fixed her mind forward of awkward questions to which he had no answers.

"Charge interest? Robert we could never do such a thing. What? Would we be so ungracious?" she protested.

"The Crane estate is entitled, Charlotte. It is within your legal rights," Robert pointed out punctiliously.

To speak of Crane estate and 'legal rights', in relation to the annual pension, was a master stroke. Presented to Charlotte thus, it made the whole arrangement less personal and more of a business matter.

"I am certain Mama would not wish to penalise you for an unintended oversight, Robert. The fault was not yours," she reasoned.

"Charlotte . . . thank you. That is very forgiving," Robert said warmly. "I cannot help feeling that I *should* have known of this sooner and still feel some discomfort, but since you exonerate me, as did Aunt Alethea, may we now drop this subject for my peace of mind and speak of other things?"

As Robert was smiling at her most winningly and had drawn her into his arms, Charlotte was perfectly agreeable, her senses immediately plunging into that delicious state of distraction which close proximity to Robert induced in her.

"Of course, dear Sir," she murmured, eyes dropping to his chest where her hands now rested, the comforting beat of Robert's heart beneath them.

"That is my good Charlotte," Robert said softly. He drew her closer in gratitude for her easy compliance, and also relief at having come through some decidedly choppy waters unscathed.

Was there something in his voice, although she knew not what, that made Charlotte look up at precisely the moment Robert's head came down to press a kiss of gratitude on her brow? Did he really mean to cover her mouth with his own?

Whether by accident or design he never afterwards knew. What *was* indisputable, was that the commendatory salute he intended, rapidly became an embrace of dancing senses and passionate involvement, one that raised the steady beat of Robert's heart to a pounding crescendo.

For Charlotte, Robert's kiss was a revelation, as satisfyingly dreamlike as any she had ever imagined receiving from him. It left her trembling, feeling warmed and cherished, her whole body tingling, vibrantly, wonderfully aware of every facet of Robert's physical person in all its masculine promise.

So it was that with this, her first real kiss, Charlotte left the world of childhood for ever and entered the adult sphere, from which she would never now re-emerge.

When their lips parted Robert looked distinctly shaken. Releasing her, he said quickly: "Good God, Charlotte, what am I thinking of? I do apologise. What a bully you must think me." Then he laughed off the incident as though it were nothing: which of course it was.

Charlotte, who had been enjoying only the most delightful sensations until he spoke, caught his discomfiture and blushed guiltily.

"Well I expect you are but I am becoming quite used to your bear hugs," she blurted in quick confusion. Realising what she had said, she blushed even more rosily and dashed away, leaving Robert acutely uncomfortable; but when they met again at church he was his usual collected self, entirely at ease; consequently, so was Charlotte.

After service they followed the Hearl Rodds out of church. Mr Hearl Rodd repeated his invitation to Trebartha and the following week was decided upon.

That day Charlotte was up early and waiting in the hall when Robert called for them. Mrs Treleaven not yet being down he used the intervening space to cast a discerning eye over Charlotte's attire.

There had not been time to procure Charlotte a new gown, so she was wearing her only good summer dress of white French lawn, on the sleeves of which she had sewn some sky-blue ribbons, to make them resemble the currently fashionable beret sleeve. She had also lengthened the skirt with a ribbon frill at the hem. The gown was far too snug a fit but she looked fresh and lovely and was, of course, proudly sporting her new blue pumps.

Aware of the sartorial deficiencies of her wardrobe, she asked, with a shade of anxiety: "Will I suit?"

"You look charming, poppet," Robert complimented her, at which she smiled instantly. His commendation was all she needed for perfect ease.

***

Charlotte had not been to Trebartha before and was entranced to see the lovely old house appearing through the trees as they travelled up the drive.

"It has probably stood there since Norman times," Robert told her. "Naturally, it has been modernised over the years," he added with a grin, as neat gardens and sweeping parkland testified.

On arrival, they saw groups of people walking near the house. A pair of gentlemen horse-riders was cantering through the trees to the stable block. Robert recognised the two young men.

One was Algernon, the Duke of Northumberland's brother. The duke owned Werrington estate, north of Launceston. The other was Charles Baring-Gould from Lew Trenchard (the very same Sophie had dismissed as unsuitable for Charlotte) a young man of twenty-four years, expecting to be instituted rector of Lew Trenchard in the near future. He was a friend of Mr Hearl Rodd's nephew, another Charles, who was also making his career in the church; at St Torney's eventually, which was in his uncle's gift.

Mr Hearl Rodd awaited them in the breakfast room. With him was his brother, the Reverend Edward Rodd; Edward's wife Harriet, and their sons Francis and Robert. Also present were the Rashleighs of Menabilly, relatives of Mrs Rodd on her father's side; Mr Coryton who was a connection on the side of Mrs Hearl Rodd, plus the Sanford ladies and two Misses Glyn. Other guests were still arriving.

Charlotte was initially apprehensive of so large a party, but she was naturally gregarious and soon overcame her shyness. Having been introduced to the assembly, she quickly became a general favourite, faces softening to smiles on all sides to see her artless vivacity and pretty behaviour. With such a reception, noted with swelling pride by her mother and Sophie, she was soon enjoying herself immensely.

The Misses Glyn talked needlework with Charlotte, after admiring her gown and learning she had adorned it with ribbons herself because, she told them: "Mr Hattenbury said it would make me look fashionable."

Francis and Robert Rodd treated her with a kind of brotherly camaraderie throughout the morning and Charles Baring-Gould, whom Charlotte thought very handsome, even forgot his priestly dignity long enough to play shuttlecock with her.

For Charlotte it was a brilliant occasion and she was quite reluctant when thoughts of leave-taking were voiced. However, she ran as bidden to tell Robert the mamas were ready to leave at his convenience.

He was at a distance across the park in conversation with their host. They were obviously discussing the house because the older man was pointing out various aspects of the front elevation, Robert nodding and looking interested.

Charlotte slowed as she drew near, not wanting to intrude, but Robert signalled her to approach them. She stood quietly, leaning against his arm, her two hands clasped over his, until Mr Hearl Rodd finished speaking. Incredibly, he was relating a plan to take down lovely old Trebartha Manor and erect a lofty, modern mansion in its place. *How criminal*, thought Charlotte, and almost said so aloud when politely asked her opinion. Luckily she restrained her tongue, saying it sounded an interesting proposal. Then she passed her message to Robert and ran back to the mamas, skirts flying buoyantly. Robert smiled as he watched her go.

"Taking little thing." Mr Hearl Rodd was also smiling. "Not yet out," he remarked, noting her schoolgirl dress.

"No, Sir, but she soon will be."

Later, after taking leave of the Hattenbury party, one Miss Glyn said to the other: "It looks as though Miss Treleaven has taken Robert Hattenbury in tow; don't you think? Pity. I rather fancied him myself. He is very handsome."

The second Miss Glyn responded: "But could you live with his pride, sister? He is something starchy and correct."

"Not with Miss Treleaven, I observe."

"Then perhaps they are well matched."

***

In the carriage going home, Charlotte sat beside Robert, leaning contentedly on his arm, bonnet discarded.

Mrs Treleaven said: "Such charming company; was it not? A most delightful morning altogether; don't you think, Charlotte dear?"

"It was, Mama," Charlotte replied with a happy sigh.

Robert looked at her indulgently. He had seen how gracefully she conducted herself in company this morning. After a few months finishing in Bath, or London, Robert did not doubt she would make a successful season. He had not missed the interest glinting in the eyes of several young men on being introduced to Charlotte, despite her youth. Plainly, she would have no difficulty attaching a worthy young man at the appropriate time.

"You were certainly a hit with the gentlemen I noticed," he observed.

Oddly, this thought gave Robert no pleasure although he recognised that as Charlotte grew and matured it would be inevitable. He looked at her, taking in the lustrous hair and glowing complexion, her sparkling eyes and artless animation. She was pretty, she was enchanting, and he did not relish the thought of losing her company too soon.

Unmoving against his most comfortable arm, Charlotte, in response to his comment, mused: "Only after the fashion of treating with a new puppy, I think."

The acuity of her remark surprised Robert and brought a smile to his lips. It was, he thought, a comforting observation. Feeling protective towards her, as he did, it was anathema to think of her belonging to some amiable young buck, particularly when he studied the smiling curve of her mouth and remembered how he had kissed that same sweet mouth only last week. Of course it had been a little reprehensible but no harm was done. After all, she was like his sister, he thought, remembering selectively. Anyway, there was a good deal to be sorted out at Crane before Charlotte could be launched on society.

In response to her comment, he said: "I am not so sure of that, poppet. I, for one, have never seen Charles Baring-Gould slough off his clerical dignity so readily. He was quite taken with you. How do you fancy being a clergyman's wife? Two in the family? Now that would be an accolade."

"As to that, Sir," said Charlotte, settling herself ever more comfortably against Robert with a happy sigh, "I cannot believe I would make a good helpmeet for a clergyman. Jacinta has the right character for it but I haven't enough gravity."

"Anyway, it is not time for you to be thinking of marriage," Robert responded.

'I would with you, Robert', Charlotte thought. Of this he naturally knew nothing, since what she actually said was: "Not with any of today's candidates."

'No,' Robert reflected silently, *'not for Charlotte the tribulations of marriage just yet.'* Aloud, apropos of nothing, and to her pleasure, he said: "You are a perfect treasure, poppet."

The watching mamas also thought so but their chiefest joy was in hearing Robert voice the sentiment.

However, Robert's thinking in relation to Charlotte's marriage was faulty in one respect. She would not regard it as a tribulation. She was energetic by nature and training. Through circumstance she had been brought up to a life of industry, not idle pleasure. The thought of taking on the management of her future husband's house would have left her undismayed, particularly if the house in question had been . . . Hattenbury?

***

Robert was away for two days, staying with the Baring-Goulds at Lew Trenchard, over the border in Devon. Charlotte did not see him again until Saturday when they set out for Twowatersfoot. When she did see him her heart swooped with happiness.

"You are looking most handsome today, Sir," she greeted, excitement sparkling in her lovely grey eyes.

"Handsome is as handsome does," he responded with a grin, gallantly handing her into the carriage after the two mamas. A groom rode behind with the horses, one for Robert and one for Charlotte's use at Twowatersfoot.

The journey to Liskeard was quickly accomplished. The chaise drew up before the columned portico of Webb's Hotel in good time to greet the Langford family, who were waiting in the vestibule.

Every politeness completed, and without more ado, the party was ushered into the dining room, where they partook of a generous three-course dinner which, at one shilling and nine pence per head, was excellent value.

No time was wasted in getting underway at meal's end and carriages were soon taking the long, upward hill to Dobwalls. It rose out of the open, rolling valley which housed Liskeard. Then they took the Bodmin road, thereafter descending steadily into the very different, narrow and wooded valley of Twowatersfoot, so called because at that point the rivers Fowey and St Neot meet. Riverside House, the Langford residence was aptly named, therefore.

***

Church and walking was the order next day, the first of the visit. Walking at Twowatersfoot was particularly delightful since the whole valley was scenically superb; heavily forested, an abundance of sparkling waters, and with the road to Bodmin winding through the trees beside the river for much of its way. It was richly rewarding to ramble the picturesque coolth of the pines and watch the sun-dappled waters. Charlotte loved it, so different an experience from her own native moorland. It was a satisfying expansion of horizons for her adventurous spirit.

Nothing further was planned for Sunday because energies must be reserved for a picnic visit to Restormel Castle the following day.

In preparation, Charlotte read Leland and Norden's guidebook, (thoughtfully provided by Mr Langford), which told that the castle, dating back before the fourteenth century, had belonged to the first Duke of Cornwall, known as the Black Prince. He was so called because he always wore a feather-plumed helm and black painted armour into battle, so that his valour could be easily distinguished. He was indeed a valorous man, as fearless and as handsome as his father, King Edward the Third, by all contemporary accounts, said the guide.

Thus primed, Charlotte was as ready as any to mourn the castle's sad decay. Hers was the first eager eye to catch a glimpse of Restormel, showing through the trees on a promontory above the town of Lostwithiel. When they reached the ancient pile, or what remained of it, little more than a ramparted high wall, enclosing a circular area some hundred feet in diameter, she could not wait to begin exploring.

She and Miss Langford, both historically minded, examined the ruins thoroughly; the tower, the chapel, and several other uncategorised apartments; but it was only Charlotte who earned Mr Hattenbury's disapprobation in doing so.

This occurred when she came right to the edge of the unrailed rampart and waved energetically to the company far below. Robert, talking to Richard, did not see her until Mrs Treleaven's quavering voice, uttering his name, caught his attention.

"Mr Hattenbury, dear . . . look!" His eyes followed her gesturing hand and he saw the intrepid Charlotte.

"Good God, you idiotic child, get *back* from the edge!" he bellowed, making frantic shooing movements with his hands. The urbane Mr Hattenbury bellowing? Indeed, he was!

Without so much as an excuse-me to the rest of the party he strode off, running swiftly up the steps to the ramparts. Seizing Charlotte, he dragged her away from the edge, will she, nill she, down to safer areas.

"Oh, you limb of Satan. What did you think you were doing?" he hissed between clenched teeth.

Charlotte took exception to his rough usage and said so. "I was perfectly safe, and I am *not* idiotic," she protested furiously. "Twice, now, you have given me that appellation and it is simply not true!"

Robert's anger equalled hers. "You could have slipped . . . *anything* might have happened. Oh, Charlotte, what is to be done with you? At least think of your mama before you get up to these pranks. She was terrified when she saw you."

Not only Mrs Treleaven, it seemed. Robert's face was pale, his eyes dark with imagined horrors. He was also trembling, Charlotte saw in disbelief, only then realising what a shock she had given him. Her fury died instantly and contrition took its place.

"Robert, dear Mr Hattenbury, I am so sorry." She put her arms around him for comfort. "I did not think. You're right, I am idiotic," she said gently and leaned her cheek against his jacket front. "Dear Robert, please forgive me. I won't do it again."

Over her head, Robert saw a tableau of suspended animation, every eye upon them, some looking distinctly amused. He broke from Charlotte's hold and faced her about. "Look," he said harshly, "see how you have frightened everyone. Go and make your apologies at once, especially to your mama."

Charlotte went without demur, leaving Robert to take a steadying breath and pull down sharply on waistcoat and cuffs before rejoining the others. Luckily, the unfortunate incident did not mar the occasion and Charlotte apologised so heartfeltedly, she could not but be instantly forgiven.

Not by *all* it is true, but even Robert had forgiven her at day's end, when she soothed his irritation with a recital of music by his favourite composer, Krieger; which music, it could be observed, was so soothing as to send several older members of the party into a doze. Charlotte pulled a droll face, which Robert properly ignored, but one corner of his shapely mouth lifted with a hint of amusement.

***

Several days passed in doing very little except walking the grounds, there being no parkland because of the nature of the terrain at Riverside. However, as the Langfords were excellent hosts their guests were soon off on another excursion; to Lanhydrock.

The Honourable Mr Agar and his wife were not then in residence but as Lanhydrock House was considered essential viewing (Charlotte's guide book said so) the visit was arranged under the auspices of Mr Glyn, a close neighbour of the Agars, and father of the Misses Glyn Charlotte had already met at Trebartha. Their party was to see the house and then partake of a cold collation.

As is usually the case, the ladies were more enthusiastic at the prospect than their escorts; they were dutiful at best. Nothing deterred, carriages were soon bowling over the handsome old bridge at Resprin and on up the sycamore avenue to Lanhydrock gatehouse. The mansion came into view, with the church beside it and a stand of tall beeches behind.

The house, beautiful but by no means fashionable, was a low granite structure, occupying three sides of a quadrangle. It had embattled parapets and stone-framed windows. The outer wings of the house were joined by an iron railing enclosing a gravelled courtyard. Gates, in the centre of the rail, opened onto a path which led directly to the two-storied porch. Here, the Agar steward waited to greet Mr Langford's party.

"I have never understood the female passion for poking around other people's lumber. What can be of interest here that you will not find at home?" Robert mooted innocently and was instantly disabused by a chorus of feminine dissent.

The tour began in the Great Hall, progressed via the Billiards Room, (where the gentlemen showed a lamentable tendency to linger but were firmly encouraged to go forward) and ended in the Upstairs Gallery. The gallery was a hundred foot in length to the inch.

"This is interesting," Charlotte said, pointing to the gallery ceiling. It was covered in a profusion of plaster figures set in panels, which in turn were surrounded by smaller panels, all highly ornate, the whole depicting Old Testament stories.

"Would you like it at Crane?" Robert asked in disbelief.

"As to that, no, but it suits here; don't you think, Robert?"

"No; and let me tell you this, the Agars don't like it either."

"Oh, do you know them?" Charlotte asked, diverted.

"Acquainted, rather, but I do know their son. Ah! Now here is a thought," Robert paused, his eyes dancing wickedly. "He is twenty or so, exactly the right age for you, darling Charlotte, and if I were to . . . let us say . . . fix you up with him, you could be mistress of this ancient pile and admire the ceiling every day."

"Mr Hattenbury, pray hush, someone may hear!" Charlotte exclaimed scandalised, looking around quickly. "And what do you mean by 'fixing up? I'm not Restormel, you know. You make it sound as if I were collapsing."

Robert cast an eye over her slender form. "Not that I can see," he observed. There was a quite different gleam in his eye now.

"In any case," she went on, ignoring his last remark, "I did not say I wanted to live here. I merely thought the ceiling attractive, but you are at liberty to disagree."

"I most certainly do. However, I have not the least objection to your thinking it pretty," he said with conscious graciousness. To that sally Charlotte only tutted.

The remaining tour of the house was quickly accomplished, after which they were led to the dining room where a cold collation of bread, meats and cheeses was laid out. To finish, there was a choice of fruits from the various estate gardens.

After lunch, and a suitable pause for the purposes of digestion, Julia expressed a wish to see the Well Garden. Here, there *was* a well, once used by St Petroc's monks when they were in residence at Lanhydrock before bad King Henry's Dissolution.

On reaching the well it looked none too safe. Remembering Restormel, Robert kept a close rein on Charlotte, making sure to stop a discreet distance from the well's crumbling stone surround. "Far enough, Charlotte," he cautioned, when she wanted to go for a closer inspection.

"It does not look safe," Sophie added.

Not one to give up easily, Charlotte looked up at Robert in enquiry and observed: "Mr Tregodick has taken Julia to see it." He gave her a clear and eloquent glance, saying nothing. Charlotte stayed where she was, at Robert's side, and was rewarded for her obedience with one of his lovely smiles; which did not go unremarked by the parents.

Later, when they were all walking the shrubbery, Richard and Julia fell behind. Glancing over her shoulder, Charlotte saw how absorbed they were in each other and felt a little . . . what? Envy, was it?

"Robert is that what it is like to be in love?" she asked. He followed the direction of her gaze.

"Are you asking for symptoms?" he responded, amused.

"Of course not," Charlotte disclaimed impatiently, "but thinking of Julia and Mr Tregodick, well . . . she speaks of him often when he is not by her and has a . . . a sort of glow when she *is* with him. Is that love?"

Robert looked sideways at Charlotte's earnest face. "I have never been in love so I cannot say, but you may be right." He laughed. "Shall I confess that I once thought myself in love with your sister?"

"Did you?" Charlotte found this highly diverting.

"Alas," he elaborated, "Jacinta did not reciprocate. She boxed my ear smartly and that was the end of my tendre. Was ever a man so deceived in his expectations?"

"Robert, no!" Charlotte was horrified but giggled at the same time, a hand to her mouth in a vain attempt to conceal her mirth.

"Heartless creature! You care not a jot for my injured feelings," Robert reproached her spuriously.

"Dear Sir, I do," she spluttered, "and really, I wonder at Jacinta's temerity. I would not dare to treat you so cavalierly."

"Shall I chance my luck, then?" Robert's eyes were dancing, the assumed reproach quite gone.

"What do you mean?" she asked, puzzled.

"I was trying to kiss her at the time," he explained, and laughed aloud to see Charlotte's eyes widen in startlement.

"Come along," he prompted, taking her hand and urging her onwards, because she had stopped walking in her surprise.

After a moment's thought Charlotte spoke again. "Robert?"

"What now, little inquisitor?"

"You once said Mr Tregodick was lucky to come by a quiet and biddable girl of Miss Langford's stamp. Do you admire her too?" Charlotte's tone was unconsciously wistful, thinking how unlike she and Julia were, although why this was a matter for concern she had yet to contemplate.

Robert grinned. "I certainly admire the charming property she brings with her. I could grow inordinately fond of that trout stream," he said wickedly.

"Robert! How venial," Charlotte condemned him cheerfully, swinging their clasped hands between them as they walked. "Anyway," she added, reverting to their previous topic, "Jacinta would never have suited. Her disposition is too serious for you but exactly right for the clergy."

"Very true," Robert agreed.

Presently, leave-takings were made and the Langford party arrived back at Twowatersfoot in time for a late supper; after which it was bedtime, and a well-earned rest from the labours of leisure.

***

Despite Charlotte's propensity for alarms and scares, it was Robert who fell victim to an accident. On Thursday morning the gentlemen decamped with guns or fishing tackle, according to taste, while the ladies walked to the weir. This was a well-known local sight.

Returning to the house they found Robert, alone, back from the pigeon shoot. He sported a large bump and an ugly bruise at his right temple, but made hasty reassurances as to the state of his health when it seemed the mamas might fuss.

On seeing his injury Charlotte felt sick with concern and could not speak. Not knowing its cause, Robert took this omission kindly and extended a hand in mute invitation, wanting her by him. Charlotte went to him and he rose to his feet.

"Come and be my good angel. Sit with me in the veranda's shade." He took her arm and led her out through the open glass doors of the drawing room. Mrs Hattenbury made to follow but Robert stopped her. "No, Mama, please do not fuss over me. Charlotte's company will suffice."

"What happened, Robert?" Charlotte asked when they were seated, suppressing her sick shaking.

"I walked into a tree bough, would you believe? Stupid, stupid thing to do. I was concentrating so hard on the game I simply did not see it." He was clearly angry with himself. "Not wanting to spoil sport for the others, I returned early."

Standing at the glass door, Sophie overheard Robert's explanation. "Poor darling, I hope it did not ruin your entire morning," she said. Beside her, Alethea murmured sympathetically.

Robert was in no mood for polite exchanges and said bluntly: "Of course it did, Mama, but there is nothing to be done about it now. Oh, damn!" He put a hand to his brow. "I left my gun in the stables. I must retrieve it."

"I'll go, Robert," Charlotte volunteered, rising. He detained her without haste.

"I am perfectly able to collect my own gun, thank you. The blow I took may have addled my wits a trifle but it did not render me physically incapable."

"I only thought to save you the exertion."

"For which I thank you, but the answer is still no. Guns can be dangerous. I would not have mine go off in your face."

"Was it left cocked?" That *would* be a surprising thing for Robert to do.

"Charlotte!" He was affronted at her assumption. It looked as though she too was about to incur his wrath.

"Then where is the danger to me?" she asked reasonably.

"There is none. Oh, Charlotte!" he exclaimed irritably. "What an idiotic conversation this is. Look . . . let us start again. I was merely thinking of volatile powder. Accidents do happen. Witness me."

Charlotte saw that mixed in with Robert's ill temper there was a glimmer of amusement. She played on this, seeing a way to lighten his mood of self-disgust.

"They do indeed, Sir. One hears stories of the most practised shots being downed by volatile powder." She used a consciously soothing voice.

"Precisely." Robert was mollified.

"In which case, are you not as likely to be injured as I?" she asked rationally, tilting her head towards him, a smile in her eyes.

Robert could not but agree. "Since this is so, by all means, let it be me who is the further injured party, if any," he said firmly.

Charlotte leaned forward and took his hand, saying warmly: "Dear Mr Hattenbury, how generous. Yet," she looked doubtful, shaking her head, "I do believe Aunt Sophie would be most unhappy in that event. After all, Sir, she is your mama, and would not at all like to see you shot . . . particularly when you already have a nasty bump on your head."

Robert was momentarily at a loss, until he saw where Charlotte was leading him. He began to laugh. "Do stop this nonsense, Charlotte," he pleaded, "and give me peace of your arguing."

"Dear Sir, it is not my intention to plague you. It is only that I, too, dislike the notion of your being shot. We all do," she said, gently pacifying, her sympathetic gaze centred on his face.

"I am not going to *be* shot," he reiterated forcefully, laughing in spite of himself, and holding his head. "Pray, do not make me laugh, Charlotte. It hurts. Stop trying to humour me, provoking girl."

Her purpose accomplished, Charlotte desisted. "As you wish,

Robert, except to say that if you are not in danger neither am I. Let's go together."

Robert threw in the sponge. "So be it. But, dear heart, you will pay for this caprice when I am feeling more the thing, believe me," he promised, pulling her to her feet. With Charlotte tucked up under his arm, they walked off, and Robert was heard to say, feelingly: "Women!"

Mrs Langford, who had overheard their conversation from the drawing room, smiled at the mamas and commented: "Pray forgive the naughty allusion but it seems Miss Treleaven will not have difficulty in bringing shot to bear on *this* bird."

"So we are hoping," Sophie confided candidly.

Miss Langford did not feel qualified to comment but later relayed the conversation to her fiancé. "I understood from you that they were as brother and sister, but it seems not from what was said."

"I know nothing more than I told you." Richard shrugged off the subject; but he remembered it at a later date.

Meanwhile, Robert and Charlotte completed the retrieval and were walking back to the house. Alone with her he could let down his guard.

"It hurts like the devil," he confessed ruefully, in response to her sympathetic enquiry. "To tell the truth, I wish we were at home in Mama's garden, with you soothing my brow as you did once before."

"Could I not do you the same service here, Robert?" she asked softly, grey eyes anxious upon him. "I dislike that you suffer."

"You and I, both, my angel," he said with feeling, "but one cannot be private here and I have no wish to expose my frailties to the concourse."

"What about the summerhouse? No-one would be there at this hour. If you went on ahead, I could run back to fetch some witch-hazel from Mama's medicine chest. It is the swelling on your head that causes the frightful throbbing, you know. If we reduce the bump, your pain will ease," she explained.

Such a prospect was infinitely appealing to one who was enduring a pounding headache. The plan was instantly endorsed and Charlotte sped off, stopping only to murmur to Mrs Hattenbury of their whereabouts, and the reason thereof, before returning to Robert. He was now lying his length on a sofa in the summerhouse. Within minutes his head was resting on a soft cushion in Charlotte's lap as she gently applied a cooling witch-hazel pad to his temple.

"There, dear Sir, is that not better?"

Of itself, her quiet voice was a blessing, her breath a sweet zephyr on his face. Patiently, she rewetted the pad when it dried, continuing to minister to Robert's need. Eventually he drifted into slumber.

He slept for perhaps half an hour, while Charlotte watched over him tenderly, fanning away darting summer insects which occasionally invaded the quiet garden room. She was so absorbed in him as to be quite unaware that her back was stiff from sitting still, or that one leg, from the weight of Robert's head, had gone to sleep.

Indeed, such was her joy in serving him, of having him so completely to herself, her breast ached with the pleasure of it. She longed for . . . she knew not what, except that it took all her resolution not to caress his beautiful sleeping face, or kiss his lips. That would have been wrong, she knew, and might have wakened him.

Presently, the mamas appeared. Charlotte placed a hushing finger to her lips. Both ladies sat down quietly, not to disturb Robert. But something in the altered air must have alerted him because he stirred and came awake. Somnolent blue eyes gazed at Charlotte; he smiled.

"My beautiful angel," he murmured, kissing her fingers. Eyes closing again, he turned his face into her lap, breathing in the fresh scent of her body, holding her hand to his cheek.

"Here are the mamas, Robert, come to see how you do," Charlotte told him softly. Gently, her free hand touched his head. "Are you feeling better?"

Stirring again, he stretched and sat up unhurriedly. "Thanks to you, Charlotte, my headache is almost gone. It feels as if the bump has gone down considerably," Robert said, touching his forehead. He turned his gaze to the mamas. "Is she not an angel?"

Alethea answered earnestly: "Oh, indeed, Robert, she always is."

Charlotte pooh-poohed this assertion laughingly. "I am not, Mama. Remember how fervently you agreed with Robert when he recently called me a limb of Satan?"

"Oh, but that was different, dearest. That was when . . . well it is true you were a little . . . but then it is so rare that . . ." Alethea became rather flustered.

"Stop, Mama," Charlotte advised, much amused. "You cannot advance down the road you are taking. It is a dead end I fear."

Charlotte attempted to rise but stumbled because the circulation had not been fully restored to her sleeping limb. Robert reached to support her until she could stand unaided. "A small exchange of service," he said, stroking the back of his hand down her cheek.

"Entirely apropos in the circumstances, since you have made use of Charlotte quite cavalierly, have you not?" Sophie commented, rather dryly.

This was the first time she had spoken since coming into the garden room, although her eyes had been very attentive. Not waiting for a response, she went on to advise Robert, thus: "It was wondered where you were and, as you are looking dishevelled, darling, it might be better if you took the back path into the house. The other sportsmen have returned and are taking coffee in the drawing room."

"As you say, Mama." One could see the habitually self-possessed Mr Hattenbury take over from the disarmed Robert of a moment ago. "Thank you, again," he said to Charlotte and was off.

***

So far only short walks had been taken. When Robert had recovered from his injury Mr Langford mooted a longer ramble; to Taphouse.

Mrs Treleaven, on hearing his description: "We shall follow the river for a mile or so, then cross the bridge and climb the long winding lane to Taphouse," felt her heart quail. Her ears were quite closed to his following comments, which explained: "The beautiful scenery is ample compensation for the necessary exertion." In truth, she was too busy sending out unmistakeable 'help' signals to Sophie to hear anything further at all.

Mrs Hattenbury did not fail her. "Shall you mind if Mrs Treleaven and I stay here, Mr Langford? I am certain the scenery is all you describe but I am afraid we shall spoil your pleasure, less robust walkers as we are." She smiled deprecatingly.

Robert raised a disbelieving brow at this gentle fiction. Sophie frowned him down. Charlotte, perfectly understanding the situation, giggled and her voice wobbled when she promised her mother a full description of the walk on their return.

Going by pairs, the walkers set off and found their host's summation to be exact. Each lady received the help of a male arm during the steeper parts of the toilsome lane, until emerging onto a narrow plain at the top.

"Aunt Alethea had more sense than we," Robert observed. There was no need to moderate his voice for the others were a little behind.

He lowered himself to the grass. Charlotte sat beside him and asked: "Are you very tired, Sir?"

"Hot more than tired."

"You *were* rather going at a gallop. No-one else is in sight."

"I wanted the climb over and done with. Think of the relief of going back down, Charlotte." Robert put an arm around her shoulders and pulled her near. How easily his arm seemed to settle on her when they were close.

"Poor old thing," Charlotte teased. "I shall need to support *you* over the worst parts on our return."

Looking at her vivacious face, so close to his, Robert could see tiny beads of perspiration beading her upper lip. Unthinkingly he bent towards that smiling, pink mouth, so temptingly near, and murmured her name. "Charlotte."

'Robert is going to kiss me," she thought, heart leaping with excitement, and could almost taste his lips on hers. But disappointingly he drew away. Following his gaze, she saw Mr Tregodick and Julia come into view. Robert got to his feet and gave Charlotte a hand up.

"What, only now here?" he ribbed Richard.

"Mama and I stopped to pick flowers," Miss Langford explained. "Aren't they pretty?" She showed them to Charlotte.

Mr and Mrs Langford hove into sight. Julia's mother carried a bunch of moon-daisies and poppies, the latter already drooping in the heat, but they lasted long enough for the girls to make chaplets for their hair.

"Very pretty," Mr Langford complimented them.

Taphouse was quickly explored and beakers of cool buttermilk purchased from a wayside house before the walkers started for home.

During the walk Richard spoke of the forthcoming annual wrestling match taking place in London. This year's Cornish contestants, Rodda and Moyle, were both particularly good and expected to win their bouts. Richard planned to see them and invited Robert to join him.

"I *was* thinking of going to Brighton but there won't be time if I go to London." Robert shook his head. "I don't know where the time has flown this summer. I meant to be off by now."

"Had you an inducement to stay?" Richard asked, dipping his chin in Charlotte's direction. Robert feigned surprise, eyebrows aloft. "I rather thought you interested," Richard added. He had not missed the near embrace.

"Good heavens, no. Charlotte is like a sister to me," Robert responded but his cool reply left the other man unconvinced. He merely grinned.

The conversation changed but Richard's observations were still on Robert's mind. He did help Charlotte on a particularly declivitous bend but walked apart from her after this, sharply aware of his friend's eyes upon them.

Charlotte questioned him with a glance that he affected not to notice. Instead, he talked of the next evening's entertainment, when carpets were to be rolled back for an evening of dance.

This was Mr Langford's plan. He was a doting parent and proud of his daughter's dancing prowess, Julia having been taught by the celebrated dancing master Mr Dawson of Truro.

Charlotte, not having enjoyed the benefit of a dancing master, celebrated or otherwise, was less keen; as she told Robert. "I can scarcely dance," she confided apprehensively. "Could I play for the dancers, instead?"

"No," Robert said decidedly. "How will you learn if you never practice?"

"But what if I make mistakes?"

"Better to do so in private than a public assembly. Practice now will put you in good trim for the London assemblies when you are out."

Charlotte sighed. "To speak of London later is no help now. It is tomorrow that looms large," she said gloomily.

Seeing her still anxious, Robert spoke more kindly. "Stop being such an . . ." he nearly said idiot but stopped himself in time, "such a gudgeon, Charlotte. No-one is going to eat you." Then, with the look of a sacrificial lamb, he added: "If you are *really* worried I will undertake to run through some steps with you in the morning." Now it was Robert's turn to sigh, while Charlotte's face lit with relief.

"Will you? Oh, thank you, dear Sir. I am so afraid of making a cake of myself. Oh, you are kind." Normally, she would have squeezed his hand in gratitude. This time she could not because she was not holding it.

"I shall not be kind if you tread on my toes and so I warn you. I am more likely to box your ears," he threatened. Charlotte was not deterred. She had seen the smile in his eyes, as he glanced at her under his lashes, and gurgled with happy laughter.

"Since you appear in benign mood today, I shall press my good luck and remind you that you promised to teach me Backgammon. When do you mean to retrieve your promise, Robert?"

"When I am ready," he replied. Again Charlotte was sanguine and rightly so. After dinner, when the gentlemen rejoined the ladies, Robert beckoned Charlotte to the backgammon board.

Later she went to bed happily, Robert's praises ringing in her ears. How lovely! He was pleased with her again; although, had it been imagination to think she somehow incurred his displeasure earlier?

Chapter Five

Robert was not so pleased with her next day. Pained, both literally and figuratively, would be a better description, because there were times when Charlotte landed heavily on his toes during the dancing lesson in spite of her small stature. When this happened he castigated her freely, somewhat to Mrs Treleaven's distress, (she was playing for them), but Charlotte was unaffected by his grumbles and even laughed.

At lesson's end Robert mopped a perspiring brow. Sinking to a sofa, he said: "Still heavy over the fences but better, I think. Don't you, Aunt Alethea?"

"Indeed, I do, not but what I thought Charlotte danced well before," Alethea answered equivocally, caught between her desire to agree with Robert without being disloyal to her daughter.

"Mama, I did not dance well and you need not scruple to say so. I believe I have improved with Robert's teaching, and now hope not to disgrace myself this evening." She turned to him confidently. "*You* have to dance with me first, Robert. If you do, others will think it safe to do so."

He groaned. There was no way to avoid this fate since he, it was, who had insisted on her dancing. "The things I find myself doing for you, Charlotte!"

"Why? What else have you done?" she enquired ingenuously.

Only when he opened his mouth to tell her, did Robert realised she had floored him. He closed his mouth again. "Uhm," he said, frowning repressively; but as she watched, Charlotte saw that his eyes were dancing. After a moment, an appreciative smile began to curve his lips and he burst into laughter. "What a minx you are, Charlotte!" he said at length. He extended a hand and pulled her down to the sofa. "You are the naughtiest creature imaginable," he said without heat.

"Untrue, Sir, or you would not be smiling," she responded with certainty.

"Nonsense."

Charlotte's answering smile died. Regarding him intently, she began to play with the buttons at his waistcoat front. "Why were you cross with me yesterday?"

"Was I? I don't recall it," he extemporised lazily, knowing exactly what she meant. He stroked a wisp of hair from her forehead.

"I thought I upset you," she persisted. It was Robert's turn to regard her.

How delightful, how pretty Charlotte was, epitomising the very best expectations of nubile youth: how impossible to explain anything of yesterday to her.

His hand covered hers. "Dear Charlotte, my upsets, real or imagined, are rarely prompted by you. As your mama is wont to say, you are a darling poppet." His words, he thought, were well chosen.

Charlotte was sharply aware of the warmth of his chest under her hand. She sighed happily, pleasure flooding her keenly at his touch, the message of which was far different from his words. "How kind, Robert," she said, wanting, abruptly and quite fiercely, to kiss him, to taste the sweetness of his mouth.

"After this morning I quite believe I am," he agreed complacently. Shortly, he thrust himself upright. "Let's walk upriver before coffee." He raised an enquiring brow at Alethea. "You will not join us, I believe," he said with lordly assumption, shrugging broad shoulders into his jacket.

Since she had already experienced a walk along the narrow and rugged upstream path, and not altogether to her enjoyment, Mrs Treleaven was happy to agree. They left her tidying music sheets on top of the piano and departed through the French windows.

"Phew!" Robert exclaimed as they came out in the sun. "It is really hot today. Would you prefer not to walk, Charlotte?"

"It will be cooler among the trees." She had no mind to give up the pleasure of his company simply because it was hot.

Along the first stretch the path was wide enough to allow of two walking abreast, and Charlotte slipped her hand into Robert's welcoming palm. Coming to a small, sun-lit clearing they both instinctively halted to look back downstream.

"I adore this walk, Robert, don't you? It is so peaceful and mysterious, and the river seems almost to speak to one. I wonder how many others have stood here in the past, listening to the water, and watching the wind-ruffled leaves of the trees."

Robert glanced at her dreaming face and unthinkingly drew her close. She turned and nestled into his arms, mmm-ing softly. He held her for a moment, resting his chin on the top of her head.

"Are you glad you came?" he asked, releasing his hold as they walked on.

"Oh, yes. How about you?"

"Of course . . . good food, good company, who could ask for more?"

"What about Brighton?"

"Ah, Brighton," he mused, adding teasingly: "But had I gone there I would not now be enjoying this delightful walk with you, would I?" Charlotte's heart swelled joyfully. Robert might only be funning but it was still a pleasant sentiment to hear.

They came to an obstruction on the path, an exposed tree root in the riverbank. The ground fell away sharply behind it. "Wait, Charlotte," Robert cautioned. He jumped down and held up his arms to swing her down beside him. "And watch out for my feet. They have already suffered much in your cause today."

Charlotte laughed. "They may be in for more shocks this evening," she riposted cheerfully and Robert groaned.

However, he bore up perfectly well, dancing not only with Charlotte but each lady present, and they were a large party because eight of the Langford neighbours had been invited. Robert still managed to look as if enjoying himself.

***

At a late breakfast next day, Sophie remarked to Alethea on the evident change in Robert. "I scarcely recognise him these days. His reserve is quite gone and he has lost the restlessness which usually typifies his behaviour at home. He seems happy with the tamest of domestic enjoyments nowadays. I cannot help but think this is due to Charlotte's influence. How else explain such a dramatic difference in him, Alethea? Nothing else has changed that I can see.

"As you know, he can be frightfully intolerant and aloof when he chooses," Sophie went on, unusually loquacious, "but he never is so with Charlotte. Last night, when they were dancing, I thought how contented he looked." She added meaningfully: "Another thing, Alethea, if you recall, Robert was never one to accept comfort, even as a small child, but twice recently he has let down his guard with Charlotte, and I confess to being astonished at the degree of intimacy exhibited between them after his accident."

"Yes, and Charlotte has changed too," Alethea observed when Sophie paused long enough for her to get a word in. "She has been so quiet since Jacinta left us but now she sparkles. Indeed, when Robert was teaching her to dance yesterday she was so pert with him I trembled to think how he would respond. But he was not at all put out, and though he called her a minx he was very caressing with her."

"Isn't it lovely to see?" Sophie beamed. "I really am beginning to think that our hope of a match is not as impractical as Robert led us to believe. I always thought that when he came to know Charlotte again he would fall in love with her."

Sophie's judgement was not quite in line with Robert's thinking. It is true that when they were en famille he was completely at ease in Charlotte's company, remembering what a heart-warming and delightful child she had been. He still found her delightful, but stimulating in addition, now that she had grown; she was also witty and totally without guile or affectation. He couldn't remember when he had last enjoyed being at home so much.

Furthermore, Charlotte's conversation was sensible, which was also a refreshing change. Most fashionable young women nowadays seemed to mouth nothing but inanities in Robert's experience. Oh, yes, he liked Charlotte very much; very much indeed at unguarded moments, and these seemed to arise with artless ease.

Perhaps this was because of their early life associations, and close family links. As a consequence, the formality usually pertaining between the young and unattached was not much in evidence in their case. This may also explain why he had fallen into the habit of petting Charlotte, as one did easily with family members, quite without intention but simply because it came so naturally.

Again, she had many exemplary qualities Robert found endearing, not least a devotion to her scatty mama, cheerfully shouldering the burden of their shared problems. This was a most admirable characteristic and it gave Robert a strong desire to be of service to Charlotte, to protect her and give her both his time and attention.

However, in company with Charlotte socially, the case was rather different. For example; to be shown their relationship through Richard's eyes yesterday had been a distinct shock, and brought him up short. What he had seen then made him decidedly uncomfortable as he remembered the familiarity with which he was apt to treat Charlotte. While she was lovably vivacious, and undeniably pretty, she was not, and did not look, entirely grown up. Her conversation might be adult: her person definitely was not. Alone with her, conversing or pursuing activities of mutual interest, he was unaware of discrepancies between his mental picture of Charlotte, the one created by bonds of affection and intellect, and Charlotte as she really was: a physically immature young girl. Under the gaze of society he was much more aware and, naturally enough, did not wish to be thought importunate, or be brought into ridicule by inappropriate feelings.

But of Robert's private thoughts the two mamas knew nothing, and so continued to speculate happily when they were on the way to Glyn House later that day, to visit Mr Langford's boyhood friend.

Glyn House, rebuilt on the site of an old mansion destroyed by a fire that also destroyed an antiquarian library acknowledged to be one of the finest in the country, was a handsome residence in modern style.

Although low in structure, to follow the lie of the land, it had many commodious rooms, particularly the library although, as one might expect, it was not yet fully furnished with books.

"Libraries cannot simply be thrown together," said Mr Glyn, shaking his head regretfully, as he told the visitors of his many fine books lost to the fire. "However, time must soften the blow," he added philosophically. He then changed both his subject and facial expression, beaming jovially as he said: "Now, ladies, I am reliably informed that it would please you to look over my house; is that right?"

The gentlemen of the party politely declined to view the mansion, preferring to escape to the gardens, and it was here that the female contingent joined them in due course.

Glyn House had been built at the bottom of a gentle slope in a small valley. It was, therefore, sheltered from the winds. On a sunny day, such as this, the air was pleasantly balmy, taking into account the estate's close proximity to the moors, as several of the guests observed.

Shortly, Charlotte set out on a tour of the gardens with Robert, Mr Percy (another guest), and one of the Misses Glyn. Charlotte remarked admiringly to Miss Glyn on the garden's great loveliness. "Thank you, Miss Treleaven. As you see, we are keen gardeners here," Miss Glyn replied.

"Are you also a lover of the landscape, Miss Treleaven?" enquired Mr Percy.

"Oh, yes," she responded enthusiastically, "my garden at home is well stocked with a wide variety of flowers and shrubs."

"May I ask your favourites?" Mr Percy cast Charlotte an admiring glance.

Finding another keen cultivator, she was happy to furnish him with this information. Thereafter, they proceeded to exchange all those things dedicated gardeners are apt to go over with each other, to their mutual enjoyment if not always to their listeners.

Charlotte was delighted with her new companion, pleased to find someone with a common interest. In the course of their long talk, she and Mr Percy fell behind, leaving Mr Hattenbury to do the honours by Miss Glyn.

Robert did this admirably, since he was a well-bred young man, but he did miss Charlotte's conversation. At one point he glanced back, to see Charlotte and her escort perfectly engrossed, heads together over an herbaceous clump.

Straightening up Charlotte said: "Is it not astonishing how many separate parts a flower has . . . so intricate yet so perfect?"

"Equally, this is the case no matter whether the tiniest moorland flower or the largest cultivated bloom," agreed Mr Percy. He gave Charlotte an enquiring glance. "If you are interested in wild flowers I can show you some quite beautiful ones growing not far from here."

"Oh, yes, please. That would be delightful," Charlotte said with great interest.

Charlotte's mother and Mrs Langford then approaching, Mr Percy lost no time in putting his good idea to them. Mrs Treleaven raised no objection but believed Robert should first be consulted.

This appeared perfectly reasonable to Charlotte and she flew after Robert, who was now well ahead with Miss Glyn. She seized his hand, breathlessly explaining all about Mr Percy's notion. "What do you think, Sir?"

He frowned slightly, disengaged her clinging hand, and said coolly that he would think about it.

"Could you do so *now* please, or it may be too late to arrange an expedition. Please, dear Sir, do say yes," she urged him eagerly.

"I see you are a true aficionado," observed Miss Glyn. Charlotte acknowledged this remark without taking her eyes from Robert's face.

"I have said I will think about it," he reiterated with finality. With that she had to be content but the disappointment she felt in Robert's cool response clouded her lovely grey eyes. Her radiant smile dimmed. She had been certain he would agree instantly.

Later the ladies were drinking lemonade on the terrace, while the gentlemen of the party elected to go riding across moor. Mr Percy looked for an opportunity to ride with Mr Hattenbury, wanting to find out his decision on the proposed expedition. It struck him as odd that Mr Hattenbury should have jurisdiction over Miss Treleaven's doings, because he knew from asking that they were not related. Possibly he was her guardian, although he seemed young for that role.

Mr Percy opened a conversation, to discover what he could. "Sir, I hope you will not think me impertinent if I comment on Miss Treleaven's charm of countenance."

"I am sure she would be happy to hear the sentiments you express," Robert responded politely but was not thereafter more forthcoming.

Mr Percy tried again. "Is she in your charge, Mr Hattenbury?"

Robert put up his brows. "Forgive me, but I do not see how that can be of concern to you," he said coldly. Mr Percy flushed at his tone and begged pardon.

"It was not my intention to be inquisitive, Sir. I simply thought that as she must apply to you for permission . . ." Mr Percy's voice trailed away when he caught sight of Mr Hattenbury's rigid expression. When Robert replied his accents were glacial.

"You do well not to continue, Mr Percy. Further, allow me to tell you that the wild flower expedition will not be possible."

He elucidated no further and Mr Percy did not care to persist. He retired, feeling decidedly hot under the collar, and thinking that any admirer of the enchanting Miss Treleaven would need to be intrepid, very intrepid indeed if the formidable Mr Hattenbury had first to be braved.

Mr Hattenbury, the formidable, did not enjoy his ride and was glad to leave Glyn House. No further mention was made of the proposed outing before they left.

Charlotte, waiting for something to be said, and disappointed that it was not, received no enlightenment until they reached Riverside House, Robert being silent on the return journey. When she began talking he told her plainly to be quiet, extremely annoyed with her, as Charlotte was fast becoming aware. Hurt by his shortness, she subsided into her own corner of the carriage, taking comfort in the surprised looks of the two mamas.

Robert's spirits recovered over dinner but he had little to say to Charlotte and she felt the omission deeply. This was her first experience of his cold front and she did not like it: she had grown accustomed to basking in the sunshine of his approval. She did not know what she had done to annoy him but had every intention of finding out as soon as possible. She wanted her own, kindly Robert back.

After dinner, the gentlemen were slow to join the ladies in a postprandial walk but the two parties eventually met up on the terrace. Charlotte sat close to the drawing room door, keeping an eye out for Robert. When he came he was with Richard and she spent several frustrating minutes trying to catch his eye. He seemed in no hurry to look her way but, when Richard was drawn to Julia's side, she seized her chance.

"May I speak with you, Mr Hattenbury?" she addressed him formally.

"Of what?" He stood tall and aloof.

Charlotte glanced around. "I would prefer to speak privately, if I may."

"As you wish." Robert led her to the small withdrawing room, where he took up a stance before the fireplace. Charlotte stood a few paces away and spoke without preamble, as direct as ever.

"You are distant with me, Sir, which makes me think I have caused offence. What did I do?" she asked candidly.

He gave her an unsmiling look, seeming to pursue an inner train of thought. When he answered it was indirectly. "Are you aware it is socially inappropriate for a lady to be exclusive with gentlemen for great lengths of time?" he asked coolly.

Charlotte looked perplexed. "What do you mean, Sir?"

Robert transferred his body weight from one foot to the other and clasped his hands behind his back. "I mean that you were much too private with Mr Percy today. Such behaviour must occasion talk."

Charlotte looked even more perplexed, eyes blinking in confusion, her lips moving as she absorbed what Robert was saying.

"But . . . we were only speaking of flowers. Are you inferring I ought not to have stayed with him so long? Was that wrong?"

"It was rather," he agreed, still very cool. "You were also somewhat *too* enthusiastic in putting forward Mr Percy's fine plan. Such enthusiasm might also be misconstrued." He ended on a much sharper note than intended.

"Well . . . but . . . I thought it was a good idea. I was certain you would too," she explained haltingly. Robert's expression did not change. "Robert? Sir? I do not understand." Her anxiety grew. "I am most sorry if I transgressed," she apologised and waited, looking fixedly at Robert.

There was another pause, longer this time, before he said harshly: "You spoke only of flowers you say, yet Mr Percy put several impertinent questions to me when we were riding. He appears to have developed a very swift tendre for you which made me wonder what you had said to encourage him. Would he otherwise have spoken to me so eagerly?"

With these words Robert had come to the seat of his anger, as was now quite clear to Charlotte. She might reasonably have enquired why Mr Percy should be obliged to ask anything of Robert in her regard, but no such thought occurred.

"Robert!" She started forward with outstretched hands, which came to rest upon his coat front. "Robert . . . oh, Robert, I said nothing, I promise you. I did not, truly. You must *know* I would not." Large, distressed grey eyes stared up at him. "Dear Sir, I would never willingly offend *you*. Please believe me."

So heartfelt and sincere a plea must strike deeply at any heart and Robert, no man of iron where Charlotte was concerned, began to relax visibly. Behind his back hands which had been tightly clasped, relaxed their hold and gravitated towards Charlotte, settling naturally upon her waist.

"You were not engaged in such intimate conversation as is commonly called flirting?" he asked, even as he did so knowing that it was no part of his duty towards Charlotte to ask her such questions. In this respect he had no duties at all.

"No, *indeed*, I was not," Charlotte exclaimed earnestly.

And was there something in Robert's voice, an expectation so subtle he was unaware of revealing it, which prompted her to rise and clasp her hands about his neck, to cling to him without reserve and be murmurous with him? No matter its prompt, the effect of Charlotte's loving attention was immediate. Falling to the temptation of her sweet, pink mouth Robert gathered her close and kissed her. What man could resist?

So heady was the pleasure of that kiss, it took long, absorbed moments for Robert to realise what he was doing, that he was being extremely indiscreet to hold Charlotte breast to breast, as he was, in full view of any who might come into the room or pass the window. He took a deep breath and gently eased her away.

"I am sorry, Charlotte, it is not for me to question your behaviour." Now she had been so adorably submissive and he was thinking more rationally, the two not unconnected, Robert realised he had been unreasonable. He also knew why but could not acknowledge it, even to himself.

"Indeed, Robert, you were not at fault. How can it be wrong that you wished to save me from censure?" Charlotte said.

Her approbation left Robert distinctly uncomfortable since he knew himself undeserving. "We are not in agreement on that point, Charlotte, so let us agree to differ and put the incident behind us," he suggested obliquely.

Charlotte accepted this suggestion willingly and went away to tidy her hair, which had become disarrayed in Robert's embrace, while he returned to the terrace.

Later, listening to Charlotte play the piano to accompany Julia's singing, he reflected on what had happened and vowed to be a great deal more circumspect in his dealings with her in future. He must not treat Charlotte with the familiarity he had used to her earlier, nor expect to have more of her than was socially acceptable.

Neither must he take exception to the normal exchanges she made with young men. She did not belong to him and he must not behave as if she did. One day Charlotte must marry. That had to be faced.

***

Mr Hattenbury's party stayed two days more at Riverside. During this time, Robert did his utmost to keep his relationship with Charlotte on a familial plane and she accepted this. Nevertheless, he was thankful that they were never alone together.

As for Charlotte, she was happy to be with Robert daily. He was her familiar, indulgent companion once more and though he did not kiss her again, she was always suspended in that delicious state of possibility. Lying in bed at night, drifting into sleep, it was thrilling to relive how it felt to be clasped to the length of Robert's warm, strong body and feel his mouth caressing hers, to imagine that it might happen again soon. He was *so* delicious.

Finally, the visitors took leave of their new friends and returned to Coads Green, happy in the promise of an exchange visit later in the year.

Chapter Six

Home again, Charlotte fell into her normal routine and was busy catching up on a backlog of work built up in her absence. Additionally, while they were away, there had been a new arrival at Crane. This was their new housemaid, Minna Drew. At Robert's request she had been found for them by lawyer Sampson.

As Robert had previously pointed out to Alethea, at just seven pounds per annum for a live-in maid, she could now afford more help in the house. Alethea, still overwhelmed by her changing fortunes, had not, at that point, come round to practicalities. When Robert added that another maid meant more freedom for Charlotte, Alethea agreed instantly.

However, it meant less freedom initially because Charlotte had to train the girl. Alethea, alas, was not best fitted for this task. As a result Charlotte's time was too much engaged for her to ride out with Robert, as she had become used to doing, and she missed him dreadfully. Often, at the end of her day, she felt an aching void of 'no Robert' centred somewhere around her midriff. Then, such is the malignity of fate it rained heavily for several days. Again she did not see him and wondered if he were missing her too.

During this time Robert became restive. He spoke of joining Charles in Brighton, privately aware he would not be averse to renewing another relationship although, he acknowledged, the attraction was no longer as it once had been.

Sophie did not relish the prospect of losing Robert so soon. Certain his discontent was because he was missing Charlotte, she sent a note to Alethea. She asked if Charlotte might come to her, because she was not feeling quite the thing and would welcome an enlivening presence.

Charlotte came as soon as she could, well wrapped against the still-falling rain, and found Sophie lying on a sofa. She confessed to a scrimmet of a headache, which cooling applications of rosewater soon dispersed. Later, she listened contentedly when Charlotte played the piano.

"Will you play that beautiful Kreiger minuet, my love?" Sophie asked.

This was the sound to greet Robert when he returned from church, wet and irritable, not much spiritually refreshed it must be said. He paused to listen, realising, with rising spirits that Charlotte was in the house. He lost no time in repairing to the drawing room, where his entrance went un-noticed by an absorbed pianist. He joined his mother quietly.

Robert listened to Charlotte play for half an hour, thinking ironically that it did more for his soul's good than Mr Trelowery's best sermon. Then, becoming impatient for her attention, he crossed the room to stand behind Charlotte. She became aware of him when his hands covered her eyes.

"Guess who?" Robert asked, leaning over her. Feeling his presence, Charlotte's heart leaped with joy. Then his hands fell to her shoulders, where they remained to exert a caressing pleasure agreeable to both.

"It could only be you, dear Sir." Charlotte tilted up her head to him, revealing a radiantly smiling face.

Robert's gaze slid down the smooth column of her throat. "Why so formal?" he asked simply to make conversation, while he refreshed himself with the essence of Charlotte, absorbing her perfume.

"Shall I call you Mr Hattenbury, Sir, instead?" Charlotte teased. She too was only making conversation as she tried to still the racing tumult in her blood.

"Not unless you wish to incur my displeasure," he told her with mock severity. Unceremoniously, he shuffled her across the piano stool and sat close to her, thigh to thigh, he facing one way and Charlotte the other. For a moment he was silent, looking at her and smiling. Then he said softly: "You have neglected me shamefully lately, poppet." His voice reproached her but his eyes were laughing, flashing brilliantly as always when he teased. One hand caressed her arm lightly. He raised her fingers to his lips and Charlotte shivered.

"Then, clearly, I must make amends; but how? I can think of nothing," she said shaking her head playfully, while perfectly sanguine of his response.

"Worry not, Charlotte. I shall think of something," he promised, "but for now come and play chess with me." Hands at her waist, he lifted her from the piano stool and led her to the chessboard. "I have only had Mama as opponent since I last saw you and she is hopeless. No challenge at all."

Sophie acknowledged his censure unoffended. It was worth it to see Robert's gloom drop from him like an old cloak. She was right. He *had* missed Charlotte.

***

Later, when Charlotte was ready to leave, the rain had stopped although leaden-grey skies still loured. Robert said he would take her home ahorse rather than call out the carriage for such a short journey.

When told of it, he had been annoyed to hear that Charlotte walked down, asking her where was Dulcima, to which she had replied: "I did not wish to soak the gentle beast for so little cause."

"Nonsense," he reproved brusquely, "her coat is waterproof. Remember that in future." This was Mr Hattenbury at his most autocratic.

"Yes, Robert." This was Charlotte, very demure.

Her cloak was sent for from the kitchen, where it had been drying, and Robert's horse brought to the door. Mounted, he waited impatiently for the groom to throw Charlotte up and then they were away, cantering easily.

After a few minutes he slowed the animal's pace, his need for haste gone once they were in motion and Charlotte was in his arms. Holding her, he felt wellbeing flow into him and recognised the impetus of his impatience to be away. He fitted Charlotte more closely to his body. He pressed his face to her hair, breathing in her scent, and said simply: "I missed you, poppet." How complex an admission that was for Robert; what happiness it brought Charlotte.

She turned up her face to his. "And I you," she confessed. "I so much enjoyed being with you at Riverside. Having no work to do was heavenly."

Robert's brow loured like the skies above at the mention of work and he straightened. "You should not have it to do here, Charlotte. Your life is nothing *but* work. Is not the new maid taking on some of your tasks?"

Robert's shortness put Charlotte's murmurous tone to flight. "When she is trained she will, of course, be helpful," she replied, a trifle tartly.

"Why cannot Aunt Alethea undertake the training?" Robert demanded.

"Robert Hattenbury! Have you seriously thought that question through?" Charlotte demanded in her turn, but now she was laughing up at him.

"Uhm." Robert took her point immediately and a reluctant grin tilted one corner of his mouth. "I see what you mean; and, no, I wasn't thinking clearly. My concern was to see you freed from the tyranny of constant labour. We must make more haste to right things at Crane. I have been remiss in this."

"The problem is not yours, Robert."

"No, Charlotte, don't argue with me." He frowned at her. "Your problems *are* mine. I caused them. I'll speak to your mama tomorrow. She will listen to me," he said with certainty. Subject dealt with, he eased Charlotte back into his arms and spurred on his horse.

Charlotte was both amused and irritated by his casual assumption of authority but knew he was right in what he said. Looking up at him, she asked: "Are you cross with me, Robert?"

His face relaxed into softer lines. "Of course not; it is your situation, rather. I am never angry with you, sweet heart," he said; which lordly declaration dispelled Charlotte's slight diffidence and made her laugh.

"A noble claim, Sir, but patently untrue. If I may make so bold, I can recall numerous occasions when you were extremely irritable with me.

For example: when I danced on your toes; if I go walking alone; argue with you or keep you waiting. Shall I go on?" She was careful to omit any mention of Mr Percy.

Robert turned in at the gate of Crane. "Oh, possibly irritable, at times, but never angry. You cannot accuse me of that."

Mr Hattenbury had a short memory when he chose. Charlotte could have done so with ease; that she did not was pure philanthropy.

He got down from Blackboy and reached for Charlotte. She slid into his arms but when her feet touched the ground Robert did not release her. He did not want her out of his hold and, knowing why, drew her closer. He gazed down at her, brows quirking into a quick frown, but not one of anger Charlotte recognised.

She looked back at him, waiting for him to tell her his thoughts, her face serene. But she was acutely aware of him on several levels; physically for the nerve-tingling pleasure of his nearness and emotionally for the reassurance she always felt when he held her. There were also other things she had not yet defined.

Robert was silent, seeming to struggle with something he wanted to say, his face a little strained.

"What is it, Robert?" Charlotte asked softly. But for Robert it was too soon.

"Nothing." He shook his head and gave her a one-sided smile. "However, Charlotte, I am holding you in a bear hug. You know what comes next I believe?"

Charlotte said nothing but her breast tingled with anticipation, and she made no attempt to avoid Robert's mouth as it claimed hers. Indeed she rose to meet it.

That kiss was different from any other he had given her, more deliberate in eliciting a response, more positive in showing his own pleasure, and Charlotte's lips parted naturally under his. Experiencing the sweetest sensations imaginable, she pressed closer and clasped her hands about his neck. When their mouths parted she sighed murmurously and rubbed her face against his, the smell and taste of him such heaven she was reluctant to release him, wanting more than he offered.

After a moment, he held her away and ran a gentle finger down her nose, to trace the outline of her lips, still sensitive from his kiss. The fleeting caress made Charlotte shiver. Robert laughed softly to see her involuntary reaction.

Then he spoke. "There are ways out of all difficulties, my love." He did not say what, or explain what he meant.

***

Sophie and Alethea had recently embarked on the ambitious task of making a set of wall hangings. They were being stitched in French Knot (similar to the much admired panels adorning the walls of nearby Cotehele House) and very time consuming that would be, so it was a gargantuan task to undertake. But as the wall hangings were to be a wedding gift for Robert and Charlotte, such was the two mamas' confidence in this happy outcome, nothing was too much trouble although, naturally, no mention was made to the intended recipients.

However, when looking for the patterns, Sophie found several lengths of long-forgotten dress fabric, bought and never used, which she thought Charlotte would like. There was an aquamarine Macclesfield silk; a short piece of sky blue satin, intended as a waistcoat for Robert, but alas never made; several pieces of cambric, and a large bale of lustrous, rose-coloured *Peau de Soie,* once meant for a ball gown.

Sophie called up the carriage and took these treasures to Crane without delay, thinking the time immediate to extend Charlotte's wardrobe now that her social life looked set to expand. Also, here was a thought, if Robert found Charlotte attractive in her old clothes how much more enchanted might not he be to see her more flatteringly adorned? Not, of course, that clothes really *did* 'maketh man', but it was certainly a considerable help.

Charlotte was ecstatic when she saw the fabrics and began instantly to think of what to make, heavenly vistas opening to her inner eye. She dreamed of being arrayed in fashionable rose pink, gliding across the ballroom floor; or charming Robert in the aquamarine silk, or . . . she came back down to earth and her usual sensible self; or having the cream cambric made into a day dress that actually fitted her.

At dinner the talk was still on fashion. Robert was now present, having ridden back from a sporting morning spent with the Wrayes at Rose Craddock.

"We are thinking of calling on the dear dressmaker in Callington," Mrs Treleaven informed Robert with a beaming smile.

"Do you call this lady dear because she is expensive, Aunt Alethea, or is she so well known to you as to merit the term as an endearment?" he asked, straight-faced but with a gleam in his eye Charlotte recognised instantly.

Robert's gentle satire put Alethea into a fluster. "Well . . . I do not think her expensive . . . no, of course not, or we should not then engage her services. Nor do I know her intimately . . . not but what I know her to be good with a needle, as your own dear mama can testify. But . . ." Alethea's rambling explanation ended when Charlotte giggled.

"Robert is teasing you, Mama. Do not rise to his bait. It only makes him more provocative," she warned laughingly.

"Is he, dearest? I expect I would have noticed in a minute or two," her mother responded equably.

This exchange set the tone for a light-hearted dinner hour and though there was no more talk of sewing, Charlotte's absentminded conversation told Robert she was still thinking needle and thread.

She was in no way absent when she strolled with him in the garden after dinner however. The atmosphere was redolent with the scent of sun-warmed flowers rising headily into the air, the recent heavy rain having produced an abundance of new growth everywhere. Charlotte's hand rested on Robert's arm as they walked and she was gratifyingly attentive to him later, making not the smallest objection when he slipped an arm about her waist and drew her close. Indeed, she was most helpful in this endeavour, leaning into him at such an angle as to make his kissing her very easy, if he chose. Which, gratifyingly, and delightfully shiver-inducing, he did.

Inside the house, as so often, the mamas were discussing their offspring.

Sophie opened. "Robert forgot all about Brighton, and being gloomy, when Charlotte appeared. It *is* she who alters him and, you notice, he is never repressive with her. He is indulgent, rather, and so warm towards her I scarcely recognise him at times. This cannot be happy chance I feel."

"You have said exactly what I was thinking although, naturally, I offer no criticism of dear Robert. He is always polite but, I must confess, there are times when he is so enigmatical I am nonplussed. However, Charlotte never seems to find his conversation confusing and that is what matters."

Alethea's observations amused Sophie and she laughed, but readily agreed. "Still, enough of that. Now what about the dressmaker? Shall we go the day after tomorrow?" Alethea seconded this suggestion enthusiastically.

Not much later, Robert reappeared with an arm around Charlotte. He wore an air of contentment, a glow that was reflected in Charlotte's face. *They look so right together,* Sophie thought joyfully, and prayed for a happy outcome to their hopes.

"We mean to visit the dressmaker on Wednesday, Robert. Will you ask Bligh to engage us for luncheon at the Bull, and also inform Mrs Buckingham of our intention to call? We'll need him to escort us into Callington too," Sophie said.

"I'll take you, "Robert offered.

"What, Sir? Do you mean to sit in while we discuss styles and patterns, or call upon your superior opinions as to skirts and sleeves and trimmings?" Charlotte enquired demurely, eyebrows quirking.

"Good grief, what a fate! No, thank you," Robert declared, with the air of a man having a narrow shave, "No," he added, "I am coming because it is market day and I want to look over some yearlings with Bligh." So much for Charlotte's hopes.

***

Wednesday came. They started out, with the female contingent in the carriage and Robert and Bligh ahorse, arriving at Callington in good time to sit down to luncheon at the Bull. Later, the two sexes parted to pursue their separate agendas.

Mrs Buckingham welcomed the ladies to her house in Laburnum Row; the fabrics were displayed; Charlotte's measure was taken and decisions were made.

She was to have an evening toilette in the *Peau de Soie*, although not quite the grand affair of which Charlotte had dreamed, an afternoon gown from the Macclesfield silk, and an everyday dress from the cream cambric, a piece of which Charlotte had previously reserved to make a shirt for Robert's birthday gift.

Before their escort arrived to take them home, Mrs Buckingham promised Charlotte the evening gown for the following Tuesday, which, as it happened, *was* Robert's birthday. The seamstress also said she could manage the day dress by then and the Macclesfield silk the following week. On this very cheering note they left for home.

***

On the return journey Charlotte was lost in happy dreams of Robert's reaction when she appeared in her new finery. He had yet to see her in a really grown up gown so he *must* be surprised. She was brought down to earth at Tregodick House in Kelly Bray, where they stopped for a brief visit. Dismayed, she heard Robert say that at the market he had met Sir William Call, son of Sir John Call, one time Member of Parliament for Callington. In concert with Willy Wraye, with whom he had been at the time, he was invited to Whiteford House for a few days fishing, this being the banker's preferred relaxation. His relaxation was easily indulged because there was a river running through his grounds.

Robert then revealed, with a touch of amusement, that the Bart was fond of fish to the point of sinking ornamental ponds in his lovely gardens. "These are purely for decoration, not sport," he said, tongue-in-cheek. He turned to Charlotte. "Now here is something to interest you, poppet. Whiteford House has seven entrances, fifty two doors, and three hundred and sixty five windows, an oddity, I think you will agree. I shall regale you with a full description when I return."

"When do you go, darling?" Mrs Hattenbury asked. She noticed Charlotte's disappointment at the news but it was soon dispelled by Robert's answer.

"Friday 'til Sunday," he said briefly, before turning his attention to Richard. "Incidentally, Richard, Wraye is off to the wrestling match in London week after next. I told him we were going and he suggests we meet up."

"No Brighton, then?" Richard asked.

"No, not this year," Robert said without a sign of regret. "My good friend, Charles Knox, spoke in his last letter of travelling to Italy in the autumn. I may take him up on that instead."

"Lucky dog," Richard said with cheerful envy. "No trips to Italy for me. I shall be leg-shackled by then."

"So you will," Robert said, and for no reason at all his eyes flew to Charlotte.

She was in conversation with Miss Hamly, Mrs Tregodick's companion, and did not see his glance. Richard did and wondered with secret amusement whether Robert might also have good reason not to go to Italy. It looked as though the wind lay in that direction for all his protestations to the contrary. There was a definite look of leading strings about him when he and Miss Treleaven were together. Still, as in his own case, it took a while for a man to realise he had been downed.

Richard thought it typical for Robert to fall victim to Charlotte's refreshing naiveté, after having had his pick of polished metropolitan beauties for several seasons past, but as she plainly adored him (a glowing face showed that when her eyes lit on him) it was not to be wondered at. It was exceedingly heart-warming to be loved with uncritical devotion, as he had discovered for himself.

Moreover, being Cornish, Miss Treleaven would understand Robert fundamentally, in a way the English could not. There was no denying that even those educated out of the county rarely lost their essential Celtic differentness and always hungered for home, no matter how long they were away. It looked as though Robert's homecoming call had sounded; and no bad thing, judging from his looks, for now he was much less the structured cosmopolitan of recent years and more his true self, as he had been before all that Society nonsense took hold of him.

Robert became aware of Richard's amused glance and turned it off with a joke. "There is always a remedy if your new life proves unpalatable. You could follow the example of that fellow from Lanivet."

"What fellow?"

"The one who sold his wife at Bodmin market," Robert replied.

"Sold his wife?" Richard echoed, laughing.

"Aye, that's so," his father confirmed. "I believe he got a sixpence for her. It was all writ up in the Morning Post. I remember your pa telling me of it, Robert. You were there at the time I believe."

"I was," Robert confirmed, enjoying the ladies' scandalised looks. "I remember it very well. As I recall the woman was knocked down to a soldier. Let me think . . . it was about November time and very wet that year, as I recall, and it cannot have been more than a dozen years ago."

"How looked the wife, Sir? Was she happy with the arrangement?" asked Miss Hamly, with compassion in her glance.

"That I do not recall, but the erstwhile husband looked relieved," Robert replied. This remark drew forth general laughter which increased when he added: "So it's off to market with Miss Langford if she proves too difficult, Richard."

"I shall give her a fair trial first," joked Richard, amid more laughter as the cups were passed around.

The visitors left shortly as the skies were beginning to lour.

***

Next day, the rain having amounted to little, Robert called to take Charlotte riding. "Look," he tempted, "I've brought a picnic to take to the Hurlers."

Needing no temptation, she agreed happily, the new maid now being able to separate milk and make cream, which were Charlotte's usual tasks at this hour. She flew upstairs to change.

Robert was not slow to appreciate the pair of delectable ankles she showed on her hurried ascent. Mrs Treleaven, following the line of his eye, felt obliged to explain, in some embarrassment, that darling Charlotte had grown so much these last months she really was in need of the new gowns ordered.

With a slow smile, Robert responded: "I see no need to complain," which he certainly would *not* have said had he been less aware of Charlotte and more aware of Alethea.

His comment threw Mrs Treleaven into deeper confusion. Hastily, she changed the subject. "Do you mean to celebrate the Summer Solstice this year, Robert, dear?"

This erstwhile pagan festival was celebrated in Cornwall by the lighting of a string of bonfires on all the high promontories from Kit Hill at Callington, westward to Penzance. Fires were lit at midnight, followed by singing and dancing, not to mention a copious consumption of spirituous drink, accompanied by the carrying of torches and the lighting of tar barrels.

"Do you consider it a suitable festival for Charlotte to observe?" Robert asked curiously. He knew from past experience that when wine started to flow, festival night was not always decorous.

"These last few years we have watched the Caradon bonfire from your dear mama's drawing room and light a small fire for the workers in the field where the well is . . . in case of emergencies, you know," Mrs Treleaven explained earnestly.

"Oh, I see." A much diluted event. "Let the practice continue, by all means," he said absently. His attention had been captured by Charlotte's swift reappearance.

He went to the staircase with outstretched hand. "You have a commendably unfeminine attitude to punctuality, infant. You were not gone above five minutes."

"Keep you waiting, Mr Hattenbury? I would not dare," Charlotte returned playfully. How many were the pet names he used to her, rather as to a dear child, but he did not always treat her as a child.

With Dulcima saddled Robert gave Charlotte a leg up and they were away, across field to Upton Cross and thence through Minions to the

Hurlers. Surprising to Charlotte, there were two or three parties of excursionists viewing the stone circle when they reached the spot. Robert was amused to see her astonishment.

"Did you not know it has become fashionable to gawp at our monuments, Charlotte?"

"Really?"

"Indeed; ancient Druidical remains and modern mansions alike come under scrutiny. Werrington Park is thick with them in summer. Why do you think I tactfully refused Northumberland's invitation to visit?"

"Fancy coming down here just to see these old stones! It passes belief."

"You were not averse to viewing a mansion or two when we stayed at Riverside," Robert mused.

"Yes . . . but that was different," Charlotte defended herself.

"Of course, dear heart," he agreed.

Chuckling, he spurred on his horse, skirting the stone circle and striking out for Craddock Moor, scaling its highest eminence before reigning in. Looking back, they saw tiny, doll-like figures moving among the stones. Tregarrick Tor lay to the south; at the base of Craddock's west slope was a tangle of bracken and rough grassland; but here, on the summit, was splendid isolation, a world separated from the bustle of life below, and silent, save for the gentle blowing of the horses and the occasional jangle of their harness.

Charlotte turned up her face to the sun and closed her eyes, sighing contentedly. "How I love the moors, Robert. Who could live anywhere else after knowing this desolate splendour?"

Surveying the countryside lazily, Robert answered without turning his head. "Who says you must?" He headed south to find a patch of ground smooth enough to set out the picnic. Charlotte followed.

After they had eaten Robert stretched out on his back. He closed his eyes but soon found the sun too hot on his face. Winningly, he asked Charlotte to make him a shade. Sportingly, she did so and he settled in comfort. In no time he was asleep.

The sun was equally hot for Charlotte but the pleasure of observing

Robert's beautiful face, unguarded in sleep, and gently touching his blond curls was more than ample compensation. Moreover, gazing down at him, she realised that the emotion she felt, growing ever stronger in her whenever they met, was love, deep and constant. She loved him with all her mind and body. She knew that now, knew she would always love him and, most miraculous of all, she was almost certain he loved her, that he would soon tell her so and show her his love. How she longed for that moment.

As once before, she guarded her lover patiently. Presently he awoke, and his brilliant blue gaze centred on Charlotte, the sight of her bringing a smile to his lips. Slowly he sat up. "Beautiful Charlotte," he murmured, his voice husky from slumber and rested his head in the curve of her shoulder. He rubbed a cheek against her velvety skin and then his lips. "Uhm . . . lovely."

For a long moment he stayed thus and then sat back, running a hand over his hair and yawning. He stretched hugely and turned on his stomach, idly plucking a grass stalk. Charlotte eased her limbs, cramped from their recent immobility. There was a companionable silence between them.

"Shall you mind my going to Whiteford?" he asked presently. Charlotte looked surprised. What rights had she in this matter?

"Why should I?" she countered. He turned, smiling, and tickled her nose with the stroil he'd been chewing.

"I have no reason to suppose you should. That was not what I asked. But since I seem to spend a large part of my time in your company, I thought you might miss me, just a scrimmet." His eyes flared attractively, courting her agreement.

"Oh, I see." She wrinkled her nose, now itching from its contact with the stroil. "Yes, but I have much to do. You will be home again before we have had time to miss you." In saying this Charlotte was less than candid, but only because she thought it no part of her prerogative to resent Robert's comings and goings; or, at least, not to say so.

Unaware of this, he felt piqued by her cool response. It did not please him. "You missed me when last we were apart, or so you said. Why not now?" he demanded. "Clearly, it is conceit on my part to imagine you enjoy my company."

Charlotte laughed at his injured tone and instantly repented her reticence. She stretched out beside him, saying: "I have no right to object to your going away. That is not to say I shall not look forward to your return with pleasure. There . . . does that restore your self-esteem?"

These sentiments held a charm which smoothed the frown from Robert's brow. Nevertheless, he was surprised Charlotte had so quickly grasped the reason for his pique. Further, that the sentiments she expressed had such power over him.

"Yes, it does, and for that you shall be rewarded," he promised.

"Oh, lovely," said Charlotte and raised her face for a kiss.

This wonderfully honest response was yet another surprise. It quickened Robert's heartbeat in stunned delight, sending his blood spiralling. Unfortunately, Charlotte saw only the surprise. She blushed and retreated in confusion, thinking she had transgressed social bounds.

"Forgive me, Sir, I did not mean to be forward but I thought . . . I mean . . . I quite see that I mistook the matter. I am so sorry," she apologised in a rush and made hurried movements away from him, her embarrassment acute.

"No, Charlotte, indeed, no. Don't retreat, my darling, no!" Robert enjoined urgently. He moved quickly, to grasp and hold Charlotte. "You made no mistake, truly you did not. No, Charlotte." She was still trying to rise. "Stay, do."

Charlotte ceased to struggle but a face resolutely turned away from him revealed that she still felt awkward. Robert shifted his grip, banding her arms less tightly, holding her more gently, more lover-like. His voice reflected these feelings when he spoke.

"Charlotte, you did not mistake me. My surprise was that you caught my intention so quickly. I had forgotten how swift-witted you are," he murmured into her ear. "Darling . . . look at me; won't you?"

Heartened by his tone more than the explanation, Charlotte drew a tremulous breath and slowly turned her head. The tender expression in Robert's eyes reassured her.

After a moment spent studying his face, she asked hesitantly: "Is that true, Robert?"

"Yes," he said simply. He was easy under her scrutiny.

"I thought . . ."

"No, you were wrong," he interrupted. Then, giving her a half smile, he remarked: "Indeed, you have often surprised me with your acuity, Charlotte. Why I should not have expected it this time is puzzling."

Charlotte relaxed still further, her face beginning to reflect the smile on his. "If I have made a fuss over nothing, Robert, I beg your pardon."

"As you should," he said with mock severity, "for in so doing, you have deprived me of the pleasure of your kiss these five minutes past. In which case, I believe we should speak of punishment rather than reward; do not you?"

She looked a trifle wary. "How punish, exactly?"

"Like this," he said, dropping a kiss on her nose tip. Then he kissed her cheek, his mouth rising by small degrees to an eyebrow, whose silky outline was slowly traced. Then his caressing lips found her ear and the most deliciously shiver-producing spot exactly beneath it.

Charlotte drew a shaken breath and instinctively raised her chin as Robert's kisses rained across her throat, searching out a resting place behind her other ear, his teeth gently nibbling its lobe.

"Is this not exquisite punishment, Charlotte?" he murmured.

"No, Sir, it is no punishment at all," she whispered, hands beginning to cling, her body shaping itself more closely to his, "except to you, perhaps, since you have said you care for no delay in kissing my lips."

He gave a muted laugh. "Little witch. Even now you would best me."

No answer was forthcoming because, as he spoke, his mouth covered Charlotte's, nudging her lips apart, encouraging her to respond to the overt invitation he gave. When she did answer, with a shy tip-touch of her tongue to his, Robert's heart leaped, the pleasure he felt so profound his body became indiscreet in its reaction. At this, caution urged him to break off the embrace. Reluctantly he did so, taking a deep breath and opening his eyes.

When she felt him withdraw, Charlotte gave an involuntary murmur of protest. There was an impetus in her, which Robert both felt and saw, to reclaim his mouth and hold him close. Again, he experienced a sharp pleasure surge in his body and would have surrendered without resistance had she persisted; but Charlotte too withdrew.

After a while he said: "We should track for home."

Charlotte looked up at the sky, as blue as Robert's eyes. "Yes," she agreed. "I cannot leave poor Minna to the cows again." She began to pack up their gear. Robert remained where he was and watched her, his expression hard to define.

Charlotte was beginning to recover from the deprivation of never having quite enough of Robert and now said, gently ironical: "I would not have the least objection to your helping me, Sir."

Robert grinned and rose. "If I must." He whistled up the grazing horses, which came to his call, and they set out for home, both silent on the return journey.

When they set down at Crane, Charlotte's ruminations prompted her to arrest Robert with a hand on his arm. "Robert, I have a question for you. Will you answer it with perfect truth, if you please?"

"Of course, cherub. What is it?"

It took a while for Charlotte to come to it but eventually, she said: "You spoke earlier of my surprising you by being quick-witted. Is that the whole explanation? Or is it that you suspected me of flirting with you, as you believed I did with Mr Percy? I hope not for I would not willingly do anything which lowered me in your esteem. I did not mean to be forward with you, if that *is* what you thought."

"My darling girl, of *course* not! Charlotte, listen to me . . . with regard to Mr Percy, the truth is that I was put out because you spent so much time with him, when *I* wanted you." Did Robert realise how revealing was that remark? "You did not behave badly and I should have told you so plainly at the time. But, I have to confess, I was rather ashamed of my ignoble behaviour and for this reason said nothing. I was a cur to put my own comfort before yours and you need not scruple to agree with me."

This drew a smile from Charlotte. "You would not be best pleased if I did, Sir," she observed from past experience. "But, Robert, I was only interested in Mr Percy because he knew a good deal about moorland plants. I much prefer to be with you, for all that," she said, as candid in her explanation as Robert had been.

"I am very glad to hear it. Now let us dismiss this unfortunate misunderstanding, shall we?" he asked, kissing the inside of her fingertips.

"Yes, but Robert . . ."

"No more buts, Charlotte," Robert decreed firmly. "It is finished. Stop being a dunderhead by going on and on."

"Whatever happened to 'quick-witted'?" Charlotte ribbed; and on that cheery note they parted company.

Chapter Seven

When he returned home on Friday morning, Robert heard Mrs Treleaven's voice from the drawing room. He assumed Charlotte was with her.

"Where's Charlotte?" he asked, looking around.

"She did not come today," Sophie replied. "I believe she may be engaged upon a special sewing task." Her eyes twinkled merrily.

Robert frowned in chagrin. "Uhm. I particularly wanted to see her." He turned to Mrs Treleaven with a questioning rise of the brow. "I'll pop down to Crane with your permission, Aunt Alethea."

Assuming an affirmative, he set out immediately, taking the short cut across field. There was no sign of Charlotte in the garden, only Morley at work wielding a leisurely hoe. He entered the house and called: "Charlotte? Hallo?" several times.

Charlotte was not expecting to see Robert before he left on his fishing weekend. Accordingly, her morning tasks accomplished, she went upstairs to work on his shirt, daydreaming of him as she sewed.

When she first heard his voice she thought it was only her imagination. When he called again she realised he was truly there. Her heart filled with elation, all the greater for being unexpected.

"Robert!"

She jumped up, scattering the contents of her workbox heedlessly, and ran to the head of the stairs. She saw Robert look up when he heard her answering call; her face alight with happiness she flew down the stairs to meet him.

As Robert, in his turn, caught sight of Charlotte and saw the revealing joy on her face, he felt a dizzying surge of the blood. Even as she began her descent he was moving towards her, his arms held wide in welcome. She flew into his embrace and he saw that her lips were already parted invitingly in surrender. Unthinkingly his mouth came down on hers, hard and possessive. He groaned softly as an abrupt and deep intimacy sprang to life unbidden. He crushed her to him, his finely tuned senses responding instantly to Charlotte's powerful lure. She struggled in his hold, but only to raise her arms about his neck . . . and then there was no barrier between them to conceal the building pulse of his desire.

Heart pounding, Robert kissed her harder, demanding more and yet more of Charlotte, feeling as though he were drowning in her sweetness, fevered almost beyond bearing and wanting nothing except to surrender to the overwhelming tide. However, he was not entirely lost to the voice of reason which, as yesterday, cautioned him to draw back, even though all his responses so far had been an automatic slide into the intimacy growing between them unseen these past months.

Robert eased away from Charlotte and drew a shuddering breath. They looked at each other in shock, both surprised by the intensity of the sensual feeling they had shared. Trembling, Charlotte released her clasp on Robert. He let her go slowly, striving for normality. To gain time he made some trifling adjustment to his waistcoat, looking anywhere but at Charlotte.

Breathless, feeling boneless, she said: "What a lovely surprise, dear Sir. I did not expect to see you today."

"No, I was not planning to come but I have a small present I wished to give you before I go away." Robert was aware he sounded quite unlike his usual self.

"A present for me? How lovely." Charlotte tried for a light tone, to distract her from the stunning revelation of a mind and body tingling with awareness; awareness of sharp hunger for the man who stood before her. This was Robert, who teased and treated her by turn, who ordered or cajoled her as he would. Now, she realised, he was also a man whose physical power was able to command or cajole her responses in much more precise and intimate ways. Her heart raced, she still seemed to feel the imprint of his body on hers, its warmth and its masculine shape.

"Are you proposing to keep me in the hall?" Robert asked lightly. Charlotte recognised in his tone the same stratagem she had used.

"It would be churlish when you come bearing gifts; would it not?" she asked with a smile and led him into the drawing room.

Robert shut the door and stood immobile for a moment, aware of returning intimacy when they were closed in the room together. He fought against it and walked to the fireplace, to take up a favoured stance, leaning one shoulder against the mantelpiece with hands thrust into the pockets of his pantaloons.

"Or, at least, one gift," Charlotte prompted. How graceful he was, how manly. She moved closer, drawn irresistibly.

He smiled and nodded. Charlotte's heart turned over as she observed how his mouth curled up at the corners when he smiled, the upper lip, slightly shorter than the lower, making the attractive curve more pronounced. His was a beautiful mouth, so alluring, a little wicked and so very tempting. How irresistibly it drew her.

Robert took a small package from his coat pocket and offered it to her. The wrapper concealed a book. It proved to be a volume on wild flowers and Charlotte drew a breath of pure pleasure.

"Robert! Oh, my dearest, kindest Sir . . . how wonderful you are," she exclaimed and reached out to him on an upsurge of heartfelt delight.

"You approve, then?" Laughingly softly, he caught her up and rocked her in his arms, as always her spontaneity bringing him a lilt of elation.

"How could I not when you are the very best gentleman in all the world?" Charlotte sighed with happiness, her head coming to rest on Robert's chest. "You really are so kind, dear Sir," she murmured.

Robert felt her breath through waistcoat and shirt, vibrantly aware of her as he was. He was also highly conscious of her embrace and beginning to surrender to it.

"This is a peace offering for my churlishness of yesterday," he murmured. His hands were caressing her of their own accord. Tremors were shaking him. "I got it from Launceston this morning and it is my earnest hope that it will serve to exorcise the ghost of the unfortunate Mr Percy."

As he spoke, Robert's mind was working on two separate levels. Consciously he gave attention to their conversation. Beneath, he listened to the prompting of his senses, which pointed out with sharp clarity that the light touch of Charlotte's body against his was producing a definite response in him, frissons of heady delight vibrating to every extremity. Somewhere else a warning note sounded but it was very faint. Of its own volition his body began to curve about Charlotte, his arms tightening around her possessively.

Robert's silence drew Charlotte's gaze upwards. He spoke softly. "I was so disappointed yesterday, dear heart." His eyes were a smoky blue, his gaze somnolent.

"How?" Charlotte asked, already knowing, for there was that in Robert's eyes, in his body and the way he held her, that communicated a great deal on an instinctive level.

"You meant to kiss me and I so much wanted you to; but then you drew back." In tone and temper this was Craddock Moor reprised.

Robert's hands slid down her back. Charlotte could feel his legs pressed to hers. How strong he was and how persuasive the light pressure of his hands in the small of her back as he urged her closer to his burgeoning desire, for the consummation of which Charlotte hungered achingly.

They gazed at each other for long moments pregnant with unspoken but sharply felt persuasions. Slowly Charlotte rose on tiptoe. There was the tiniest pause while Robert waited, every nerve tensed expectantly . . . and then she kissed him, her mouth soft and warm and tasting of honey under his. Moreover when he parted her lips with his tongue, there it was again, that shy incursion which was more exciting, more enchanting than any caress he had ever known. Robert closed his eyes, drowning in the heady sweetness of her surrender, that first ardent kiss given to him of her own volition. Unconsciously, he sucked on her tongue, echoing the desire which was now very much in evidence, upthrust against Charlotte's body.

***

When the long kiss ended, Robert drew Charlotte down to the sofa. There they sat, absorbed in each other, Charlotte resting against Robert, her mind filled with the wonder of loving and wanting him. She found it hard to remember a time when she had not known the joy that he was, nor had the substance of her whole world altered by his nerve-tingling kisses. She was *so* happy.

Robert was equally content. He leaned his chin on the top of her head, a hand caressing her arm lightly. He felt at peace with the universe, his happiness having much to do with the pleasure engendered by the sweetness of Charlotte's tender, untried mouth, and the yielding confidence with which she now lay in his embrace. She had kissed him and he knew that if he tilted her chin she would do so again. To know this was to be filled with power, strong and satisfying. She might lead him a merry dance at times but she could be enchantingly submissive at others. He was tempted to put his power to the test and the thought made excitement leap. It erupted as laughter and Charlotte looked an enquiry. He pressed a swift kiss to her lips and jumped up.

"Dear love, I must go," he said with obvious reluctance. He took her hands and pulled her upright. "Now, you *are* to miss me while I am away," he commanded, a man sure of himself and his world, sublimely confident.

"You may be certain I will, dear Sir," she promised. He squeezed her fingers and then was gone, with a springing step. He felt marvellously alive and jubilant. Life was truly fulfilling.

***

For the rest of that day Charlotte went about in a haze of happiness, almost afraid to believe what a singing heart told her. Robert loved her! He really loved her! He had not said it but his ardent attentions, the desire he had not scrupled to reveal, all pointed that way. It was a miracle!

However, one thought pierced her happy daze. If she were to finish

Robert's shirt for his birthday, next Tuesday, she must get down to it this very day. She could do little tomorrow, Saturday, as this was the busiest of her week. It was market day in Launceston town.

Launceston market provided all the requisites of Crane Lodge which were not home-produced. Additionally, Charlotte sent her surplus garden and dairy goods to market, thereby accruing some ready money, not so vital now that the pension had been restored but very useful nonetheless. It was Morley's business to make the trip into town and as he left very early, perforce, Charlotte was also up before dawn to help him pack the donkey shay.

Consequently, when Charlotte roused her mother with a breakfast tray (this was Alethea's Saturday treat), Morley had already departed with a well-laden shay; the cows were milked and returned to pasture; the milk was separated; cream was being prepared and the bread was already proving. Moreover, Charlotte had laid out baking utensils to make a plum cake for Robert's birthday. It says much for the power of love that she still had energy for some sewing, in spite of all her busyness that day.

Sunday saw Charlotte and the two mamas in church at North Hill. Mr Treloware asked after Robert. When told he was away on a pleasure trip the elderly cleric expressed a hope that he would enjoy it.

Equally, so did Charlotte but she also longed for his return with an intensity that produced a physical ache in the most intimate parts of her body. Never having experienced such before she was a little disturbed, finding these sensations unsettling and difficult to contend with. Was Robert feeling the same, she wondered? She could soon ask him as it was but one night before he came home.

However, Monday saw only a letter from Mr Hattenbury postponing his return. He sent a funning message, saying he would bring the fruits of his fishing catch for Charlotte to make a stargazey pie.

He went on to regale her with a tale of his Sunday morning at Stoke Climsland church saying: "Mr Lethbridge has not Mr Treloware's more laissez faire attitude to church attendance: no-one is excused, no matter the reason. I overheard it said outside church, by one of the mine workers of the parish, that backsliders might expect to find themselves rounded up on the end of a shotgun if they were tardy of attendance! However, this was not the case in the matter of the Call family and their guests. I saw no shot gun. But then, we all trooped into the family pews meek as lambs, to listen to a very robust sermon. Afterwards, the Reverend Lethbridge was invited to break his fast with us at Whiteford and I found him entertaining although as robust in his eating and drinking as in his preaching of sermons. They tell me he also runs his own pack of harriers for hare hunting, so he is not in your usual style of parsons by any means."

Robert's letter was very amusing but in no way compensated for his absence. Indeed, for no reason she knew, Charlotte began to wonder if he would return in time for the birthday dinner which had been planned in his absence. Surely, he must?

Mrs Hattenbury was staying at Crane prior to the party, to help in its preparations. She too wondered why Robert had not come as promised. She saw Charlotte's deep disappointment and momentarily caught her disquiet. It was clear that Charlotte adored Robert and he loved her in return; did he not?

Yes, of course! The disquiet passed as she thought over the happy weeks her son had been home. Only think how different he was with Charlotte, making no attempt to dissemble his affection. Indeed, he was sometimes rather *too* proprietorial but that also spoke volumes because he would never indulge a flirtation with Charlotte, as metropolitans did so readily. He knew it would not serve here, in the Western peninsula, where things were conducted quite differently; manners might be freer but morality was not. He was probably being cautious and that was no bad thing.

Cautious! Had Sophie but known!

Robert was missing Charlotte and longed for her, that was true, (how much only he knew), but now he was away from her he wondered, with a deep unease that twisted his gut, how he had come to forget all the circumspection he had decided upon at Twowatersfoot? Further, how had he managed to go so far, and so quickly, in a contrary direction without being aware of it? How was it he never remembered Charlotte's immaturity when he was with her?

A wave of shamed heat engulfed him as he recalled the last occasion he had been in Charlotte's company. This was when he stepped over that clear line between affectionate kisses and making love to her as though she were nubile, which she wasn't yet; here was the sticking point. To reveal so openly the extent of his desire, as he had done; to court her response, as he had done; to cajole her into kissing him, as he had done; and, further, to have thrilled in her submission, as he had done, was unforgivably heinous.

And yet . . . and yet . . . when he remembered their lovemaking, the feel of Charlotte in his arms, the exhilarating delight experienced in the press of her body against his aroused thighs, and the seducing honey of her lips, he experienced again the power-filled excitement which consumed him then, in spite of his shame.

Thus stood Mr Hattenbury revealed to himself: a very confused young man.

He wanted to be with Charlotte and acknowledged it freely but the reasons which prompted him to seek her out were the very ones which brought him up short. She was too young yet and had not even been into society. She did not look mature when compared to the young ladies in whose company he was presently spending time. He should not think of Charlotte as he did, nor treat her with the extreme possessiveness he used towards her. It would not do.

Sombre thoughts: but in his heart Robert kept recalling the adoring candour of Charlotte's grey eyes, her spontaneous affection towards him, the warmth and taste of her responsive mouth, and his throat ached with unbearable longing. The mature young ladies of Whiteford paled to insignificance. Despairingly, he wished he had gone to Brighton, for if he had not come to know Charlotte so well he would not have been subject to this turmoil. There would have been other diversions to occupy him at the seaside. Too late for that now.

No, he must look to make an orderly retreat. The path down which he had been leading them was fraught with danger. She was not ready at this juncture. It must stop otherwise . . . he was reluctant to acknowledge what was in his mind. Nor would he contemplate the problems which would have to be faced if he allowed Charlotte's attraction for him to deepen. The London salons? No, that was impossible! Finishing school first and then . . . maybe . . .

Interestingly, in all his confused heart-searchings, Robert never once stopped to consider Charlotte's part in their dealings, or remember that she *had* succumbed to his persuasions. She had known his mind, the symbolism of what he asked. She had understood the message of his body and not drawn back. She had kissed him freely and with passion. She had chosen. Perhaps, for Charlotte, it was already too late.

***

Robert returned Tuesday morning, to be greeted with a shower of gifts.

"Happy birthday, darling," Sophie said. "I am so glad you are home in time to celebrate the day with us." She linked arms with Robert and lead him to the drawing room. "Look, here is your present from Charlotte and several from London ~ Aunt Jane's writing is unmistakable ~ and here is one from Alethea." She gave him the latter and Robert laughed.

"On past experience this will either be a book of moralising tales or handkerchiefs," he guessed. His mama looked impish.

"Not a book. The parcel is too soft. Clearly, she thinks you too old for improving stories now. Do you remember," Sophie asked, as Robert unwrapped Alethea's gift, initialled handkerchiefs, "the unfortunate tale of the greedy child? How incensed you were." She laughed anew as she recalled the famous occasion. "It took all my powers of persuasion to convince you that she was not pointing a moralising finger of accusation at you."

Robert's shapely mouth curved in a reminiscent smile as he remembered the story of the greedy child, in the book called Robert alas, who took the best of everything for himself but was invariably disappointed, the largest fruit proving to be maggot-eaten, and so on. He still remembered his indignation at the time.

"How could I forget?" he said, "although, I must confess, the morality was lost on me. The only thing that book did was to make me think ill of Aunt Alethea at the time."

This exchange produced a good deal of laughter and Sophie was obliged to dry wet eyes. While she was doing so Robert opened Charlotte's gift. When the shirt came into view he held it up and silently rubbed the smooth cambric between his fingers. There was a strange, hard to define expression on his face as he examined the garment, sewn with such love by Charlotte. His mother waited for him to comment. He said nothing.

"Do you like it, darling?" she prompted at length.

"Yes," he responded slowly. "Charlotte has great skill with a needle . . ." he stopped, his thoughts clearly winging, but to where Sophie could not guess. "How quickly she has made it."

"Ah, that is for a special purpose. She means you to wear it today, for your birthday dinner at Crane."

Robert cast his mother a sidelong glance. He still had an odd look about him but he smiled suddenly and said: "Then I better had."

"Shall you visit Charlotte this morning?" Sophie asked.

"No," he answered, a quick frown replacing his smile. "There are some several things I must do today. I shall see her at dinner. If you will excuse me, Mama?" Robert gathered up his presents and was gone.

Again, Sophie experienced unease on hearing that Robert was not to visit Charlotte. He usually did. Why not today? She decided to wait upon events, as she had been obliged to do many times before. Life had taught her to be philosophical.

***

The carriage arrived at Crane Lodge promptly at six, to a door held wide by a smiling Megan, proudly wearing a new white pinny. She ushered the visitors into the drawing room. Here, Alethea and Charlotte waited to greet their visitors.

Robert never even saw Mrs Treleaven, nor anything else. As he walked through the door he was brought up short, his breath stopped on a sharp intake of awesome delight when his startled eyes beheld Charlotte.

She was poised by a wing chair, one hand on the skirt of her gown, the other resting on the chair's curved top. She was facing Robert, waiting for him, her face radiant with expectation. But this . . . this was a Charlotte he had never before seen!

For the first time her hair had been put up, dressed high upon her head, revealing her slender neck and smooth shoulders. She was wearing a beautiful, rose silk evening gown . . . and, astonishingly, heart-stoppingly, she seemed to have grown up overnight! Here before him stood the veriest miracle, the Charlotte of his dreams!

Robert was wholly stunned. He could only stare at her, taking in her appearance in one single glance, and in that glance encompassing all that now was Charlotte.

How beautiful she was, how perfect, how desirable, making reality of every dream and every dream a possibility! He released a long-pent breath and in a daze moved slowly towards her with outstretched hands.

"Charlotte!" he exclaimed in incredulous delight, when at last he could speak. Still he stared, unable to keep his eyes from the vision she was in her new low-necked gown, one fitting her to perfection, like nothing else she had ever worn. Robert saw how lovingly the rose silk clung to her dainty breasts, revealing them to his enchanted eyes for the very first time. Looking at her, his mind in turmoil, his body a powerhouse of thunderous emotion, he scarcely dared to believe what he saw.

"Charlotte," he said again. Her hands went out to meet his and she laughed in delight to see him so entranced. "Beautiful, beautiful Charlotte." His voice was low and husking with desire.

He took her hands and then, abruptly, she was in his arms, pressed close to a thudding heart. Unbidden his mouth sought hers and it was only at the last-ditch moment that discretion came to his aid. He remembered the watching mamas and drew back, to gaze down at an adorably blushing Charlotte, her cheeks as rosy as her gown.

"Goodness! What a stranger you have become," he said, his voice uneven as he tried to make light of the situation. "I swear that in five days you have quite grown up. I hardly recognise you in your new finery." Slowly he released her.

Still blushing, she responded in kind. "What, Sir! Are you saying this how you greet all strangers?"

"Not all, that is true, Charlotte, but certainly the prettier ones," he answered more smoothly, recovering his savoir faire to a degree.

"Ignore Robert's graceless remark, dearest," Sophie said to Charlotte, smiling as she came forward, "and allow me to compliment you upon your looks. The dress is perfect and suits you admirably. When did it arrive?"

"This morning," Charlotte told her. "What luck it came so soon."

Her answer was mechanical. Her attention had been drawn back to Robert, a vision almost to equal her own, in his new cream shirt and cream kerseymeres. He wore a blue waistcoat and a deeper blue jacket, one which accentuated the cerulean blue of his eyes. He looked adorably handsome but, Charlotte saw, for some reason his blond curls had been ruthlessly subdued tonight.

"How was your stay with Sir William, Robert?" Mrs Treleaven asked. Robert was grateful for her intervention. It gave him an opportunity to school his shaken perceptibilities.

"It was fine, thank you, Aunt Alethea. One day we took a boat out on the Tamar, courtesy of Mr Tillie Coryton who is an acquaintance of Call. Coryton showed us over his castle, a word I use advisedly. Pentillie makes our house look like a shippen, in size if not splendour. It has all the attributes of a Gothic cathedral, with battlemented roof and fluted pinnacles everywhere, very similar to Falmouth's home, Tregothnan. It is clearly a Wilkins design. Why, I wonder, is he *so* popular in this part of the country?" Robert mused.

"I would not care to live in a cathedral," Alethea observed placidly.

"Just *think* of the cleaning, dear," Charlotte observed, in an amusing imitation of her mother's manner that drew laughter on all sides. On this note the company repaired to the dining room.

"How are the Misses Call, Robert?" Sophie enquired as they made their way thither. "I have heard that Miss Georgina has been unwell of late."

"Indeed, Mama, one would have to say that she did not look hale, although her sister, Augusta, was blooming." He added, with a smile: "I suspect this may have something to do with the attentions of a certain Mr Hornby."

"Is there a match in the offing?" Sophie asked with interest, weddings having been somewhat on her mind recently.

"I believe so," Robert said absently. Arriving in the dining room at this point, his attention was caught by the table. It was laid with Crane's best silverware and napery. In pride of place was a plum cake, with Robert's initial picked out in sugared violets, and in the place laid for their principal guest Charlotte had placed a candle in honour of his birthday.

Robert was immeasurably moved by the trouble Charlotte had taken to please him, (clearly it was her work), and all his hastily erected defences crumbled. He turned to her, his face perfectly expressive of all he was feeling.

"Charlotte . . . what can I say but thank you."

"Nothing else is needed, dear Sir," she responded softly, her tone so evocative of love Robert's heart turned over. He stood gazing down at her and because she was close he could see the shallow vale between her breasts, could smell the perfume of her body and his pulses hammered anew.

It was as well Charlotte stood between him and the mamas, for not until it was done did he realise that his fingers were stroking round the neckline of her bodice, dipping towards the perfumed valley it exposed to his gaze. He quickly transferred his touch to a beautifully draped beret sleeve, saying, in an effort to appear normal: "This really is the prettiest gown, Charlotte. The colour becomes you so." His hand slid down her arm in a tantalising caress, unwitting, unknowing and instinctive.

Charlotte was as affected by his touch as he in touching. She could not resist kissing his cheek, leaning into him as she rose on tiptoe to reach. Inevitably, then, she was once more in Robert's arms; and so attuned to her was he, his body responded to her nearness with an immediate and betraying manifestation of desire, upthrust and hot. His heart laboured, he felt panicky, wondering how he was to manage himself socially, or even if he could decently face the two mamas. He was sure of nothing in the tip-tilting world he had entered on first sight of Charlotte that summer evening.

Blushing, as a heat in her own body acknowledged the seeking of Robert's, she eased away from him, leaving him to feel isolated and vulnerable.

He ate his dinner automatically and could not afterwards have said what it constituted, absorbed as he was in the sharpest awareness of Charlotte, conscious of her on every plane; the words she spoke; each movement she made. When she plied a fork to her mouth, he swallowed; when she made the smallest gesture, his own muscles responded alike, so vibrantly open were all his senses to her. He could not keep his eyes from her, feeling sure his clamorous disturbance must be obvious to all. Yet it was only Charlotte's gaze which rested on him frequently and that, clearly, was for a different reason.

At meal's end they withdrew to the terrace for coolth, since the house was hot in spite of tall Venetian windows standing wide, and only the smallest zephyr rippled the languid air.

Robert, suffering more than atmospheric warmth, shed jacket and waistcoat for the informality of shirtsleeves. The two mamas plied their fans. Charlotte, alone, seemed untroubled by the heat. She offered to fan Robert's face but that was a provocation too far and not to be borne. He wrested the fan from her and laid it down, pulses racing when he touched her. Time after time he felt the strongest compulsion to embrace her; each required a palpable effort to resist, becoming ever more difficult.

"You are quiet, Robert," Charlotte murmured.

He shrugged and got to his feet. He crossed the terrace to lean on the stone balustrade, aware of the heady scent of the flowers, the somnolent drone of bees still at work upon them, and the seductive summer air.

Restlessly, he stirred and went back to Charlotte. She was talking to Alethea but he interrupted without ceremony. "Come and play chess," he said peremptorily.

For the next hour Robert brooded over the chessboard but played an indifferent game. Charlotte beat him twice. The third game looked to be going the same way until, abruptly, he swept all the pieces from the board.

"I am playing like an idiot," he said irritably.

Charlotte gently touched his wrist. "What is it? What is wrong, Robert?" she asked in concern.

"Oh . . . nothing." He shook his head. His wrist was burning from her touch. "The heat is making me bad tempered. Come, play the piano for me. Perhaps that will sweeten my mood."

Charlotte agreed, happy to accommodate him in every way open to her. "What shall it be, Sir?"

"Something soothing. Bach or a Beethoven sonata, perhaps," Robert said, as Charlotte sat down to play. Prudently, he kept his distance.

The two mamas came in, attracted by the sound of music, but Charlotte's recital did not last long. She changed from Beethoven to Krieger, playing Robert's favourite Menuet which she knew he loved, but not on this occasion apparently. He jumped up and crossed to the piano.

"No, not that," he said forcefully, pulling her hands from the keys. To him the music was unbearably haunting and plaintive that night, filling his already overburdened senses with a sharp longing, too painful to bear.

"I thought you liked it." Charlotte was surprised to be stopped so abruptly.

"I do, sweet love, but not now. I am too restless to listen." Suddenly, the need to be alone with her was overpowering and could no longer be resisted. "Walk with me in the garden." His voice was low, the look in his eyes pregnant with pleading.

Charlotte's heart missed a beat. She knew exactly the portent in his voice because, as with Robert, she had wanted to be alone with him all evening, hungering for his kiss. Without a word, she took his hand.

"We are going to stroll in the garden," she explained simply.

They left the mamas exchanging smiles of happy significance, Alethea whispering to Sophie: "Do you think Robert will ask for Charlotte tonight? They seem so much in love; do they not?"

Walking out to the terrace, Robert asked Charlotte if she had ridden while he was away. Without realising it he held her hand in a crushing grip.

"Very little, Sir. I was too busy making a present for a charming gentleman of my acquaintance." She was teasingly demure.

"Not much charm in evidence tonight," he said wryly. His longing for her was a fierce physical ache. He was hurting from head to toe. He *must* hold her. He must!

"I do not complain," she replied, unjudgemental as always, especially in his regard. She sighed dreamily and leaned against his arm, anticipation quickening her senses.

Robert's hand tightened further over hers. He drew a deep breath. "Come and renew acquaintance with Dulcima since you have not ridden her lately."

Awaiting no agreement, he took Charlotte to the stables. He held open the door and watched as she crossed to Dulcima's box. For a moment longer he stayed at the door and then, with a feeling of pre-ordained inevitability, he too crossed the rough floor to stand behind her, with not so much as a glance for the horse.

Slowly, his arms settled about Charlotte's waist. Giving a long sigh he drew her back against him. At last! He was holding her, as he had longed to do these interminable hours past, the contours of his body instinctively shaping to hers. His lips found the nape of her neck, her throat, her shoulder, and the relief of submitting to the urgent prompting of the senses, which had been riding him so hard all evening, was formidable, so much so he was dizzy from its sudden intoxication, his whole body flushed with an awareness of Charlotte that was pain as well as pleasure. His arms tightened, crushing her to him fiercely; but she seemed not to mind.

"At last! Charlotte, my beautiful, beautiful, darling Charlotte! Oh, God . . . you are so lovely," he breathed, shaking so much he was barely intelligible. "It has been sheer torture this evening . . . to be near and not touch you. I cannot . . . I simply cannot resist any longer. I have tried, indeed I have tried, but I cannot bear this torment. Oh, Charlotte, believe me, I cannot."

She drew a sharp breath and turned her head. "Robert, I know. It is the same for me. I missed you so much when you were away. Indeed, I ached for you." Their lips came together, fusing magically, heat upon heat.

So it began, the irresistible, spiralling loss of themselves to love.

His arms loosened their tight hold, hands rising slowly until they settled upon her breasts, holding, shaping and searching, as he had wanted to do all night and, in truth, many nights past. In some recess of his mind he knew he was committed, that there was no going back, but this knowledge was as nothing in the face of overwhelming need and . . . and the stunning revelation he was experiencing at that moment!

With blood singing and the breath stopped in his throat, Robert felt Charlotte's breasts respond to his questing hands, a response that could not be mistaken, and heard her soft sounds of pleasure as she pressed herself back against him.

She wanted him!

'I ached for you,' she had said and now he knew how. With these words, every improbable desire of the last soul-torturing weeks was vindicated, transformed into wondrous possibility. The girl in his arms was a woman, a vibrant woman, whose body came alive under his smallest touch, whose clinging lips echoed every hungry nuance of his own.

Charlotte wanted him!

Restraint abandoned, Robert's caresses became ever more overt, squeezing her breasts, stroking her budded nipples, his kisses more demanding. But Charlotte's response was unequivocal and Robert's mind flooded with a wondering sense of the rightness of what was happening between them. How could he have doubted?

With a shuddering sigh their mouths parted; she turned in his arms. He cupped her face, murmuring her name as he kissed her eyes, her nose and lips, and the sweetness of making unrestrained love to her was freedom and such relief, after the hungry, arid weeks which had gone before.

All the while, desire, and a feeling of joyful destiny, was mounting in him. He could fight it no longer. This, with his darling girl, was meant to be. Now she would be his, his for always, close held in his arms . . . but not yet close enough.

Robert pushed her back against the box, completely unaware of the gently blowing animal behind them, and held her there with exigent thighs, his arousal urgent and demanding. His hands left her face and pulled out the pins which held her hair in place. They fell to the floor with an unheeded clatter as Charlotte's hair tumbled down. He leaned forward to bury his face in the silky, scented masses, breathing in the scent of the provocative curtain, intoxicated, kissing her wildly.

No tentative kisses these. They were the explicit, possessive kisses of a man gone far beyond the delicate. He was lost to everything except the powerful ardour surging in him, power which was manifested in a compulsively rhythmic appraisal of Charlotte's body, held thigh to thigh. He made no attempt to keep the strength of his desire from her; indeed he had long passed the point where it would have been possible; nor did he stop to consider where that desire was leading them. Nothing mattered except to make love to Charlotte.

As he kissed her ever more wildly, he could hear himself repeating a litany of hunger. "Charlotte, I want you, I want you, oh, God, I want you so much."

"Robert, darling Robert, I love you too," she responded fiercely and wound her arms tightly about his neck, as his lips, parted and importunate, found hers in a thrusting kiss that was a deeply intimate prelude to the intense hunger he felt for her; a kiss such as Charlotte had never dreamed of; a kiss which emptied her mind of everything except an awareness of Robert; in his person, in his hard body and each separate part of him where they clung.

"Charlotte."

He spoke her name, his voice harsh and tortured. His ardour increased, the movements of his thighs becoming more open and demanding. He tugged at the buttons of her bodice until her breast rose, free and unfettered, into the rough caress of his palms. He was too exigent to be gentle but she did not mind. Each caress, gentle or not, was welcome to her. But still it was not enough to assuage the consuming hunger; not for Charlotte; not for Robert.

"Oh, darling, I long for you. I want you so much it is torture." He took her hands and brought them to the source of the driving need, his erect, scaldingly hot shaft. Startled by this first touch Charlotte gasped and instinctively drew away.

"Charlotte, no!"

He repudiated the withdrawal, speaking her name urgently, demandingly, pleadingly, his own hands urging hers to compliance, showing her what he wanted from her.

By small, yielding degrees she came back to him. Tentative and a little fearful she touched him, skin to skin, so very gently. Yet such a touch as it was, the merest whisper at first but with all the power to bring this arrogant young man to his knees.

Robert groaned, his pleasure so intense it was almost unbearable. Blindly, he sought for her mouth and, kissing her, stood abandoned to the rule of her sweetly seducing touch, her fingers stroking up and down the length of his shaft, to induce heart-stopping ecstasy.

"Charlotte!"

The burning need was relentless and mounting, silken skirts too much of a barrier. Under the persuasion of importunate hands, without resistance, they began to rise. For a long moment there was silence in the stables, as Robert and Charlotte sought to sheath and be sheathed. Even the gentle Dulcima was still.

Suddenly the silence was broken by the harsh intrusion of a voice.

"Master, Master; what h'ever be doin', boy? You can't be adoin' this to Miss Charlotte! What h'ever be thinkin' of? Tidn't right. You got to stop this minit."

Charlotte gasped and jumped with shock, frightened to awareness by the abrupt intervention.

"Charlotte, no!"

It took a good deal longer for Morley's voice to penetrate Robert's erotic daze. He was too much absorbed in Charlotte and the achievement of his union with her. Such was the urgency of his physical arousal, and the need for its assuagement, he did not immediately understand what was happening. He was so close, incapable of releasing Charlotte because he had gone too far down the road of desire to retreat easily.

"No, Charlotte, do not leave me," he protested, unbelieving. "Charlotte! You cannot stop now, you cannot." He gave a strange, mewling cry.

Of protest? Of despair? It was impossible to say. All Robert knew was that what was being asked of him was insupportable. He could not stop, he *could* not. He had come too close to be denied. "No!" Robert's chest heaved as he gasped for breath. Morley's voice sounded again.

"You got to, boy. Tidn't no good. Tidn't right, what you'm doin'," the old man went on in scolding vein. "Miss Charlotte be a maid. You shouldn't 'arm 'er like this. Think, boy, think. She be a maid . . . a good little maid."

At last, as Robert stood mutely with eyes closed, the sense of Morley's diatribe began to penetrate his passionate trance but he still held Charlotte in a crushing embrace. He could not let her go. It was impossible. He held her enfolded, her face hidden in his chest, feeling sick and miserable beyond belief, the pain of the withdrawal being forced upon him an agony not to be contained.

Yet, it must be. Somehow, it must. He had to release Charlotte with the consuming need unmet. There was no help for it. Oh, God, how could he?

"Come on, then, boy. Tha's better," Morley said. "Come you on, then. You'll be all right. You see. There now, Master . . ."

With the admonishing, and strangely reassuring, text flowing over him Robert was given sorely needed time to adjust. It took a long while, a time of drawing resolutely upon inner reserves, of taking strength from Morley's encouragement, but he did eventually come back to a semblance of social normality, accepting the old man's scolding dictates without protest, thinking nothing of the familiarity with which he was addressed in this instance. He knew Morley would think it his duty to look to Charlotte's welfare, no matter the consequences, for was she not his pride and joy, as much the child of his heart as any sprung from his own seed?

At last, Robert was able to speak, though even to his own ears he sounded horribly strained. "You are right, of course, Morley, but I . . . I am sure you understand . . . when a man is . . . is with the lady who has promised to be his wife, he sometimes . . . sometimes forgets the proprieties. I am thankful you chanced by when you did. Be assured that I shall not be so careless of Miss Charlotte's wellbeing again. You may safely leave us now."

Morley studied Robert and then nodded his head. "Well, Master, that be good news but you'd best get on up and tell they ladies afor they do come alooking for 'ee."

Morley started for the door. Charlotte's voice, unheard since he had entered the stable, arrested him. "Morley," she called urgently, and then seemed not to know how to continue.

The old man smiled. "Do'n 'ee worry, maid. You'm all right with the Master. He be the best of boys. He jus' bin a bit froward, tha's all."

Chapter Eight

How they got through the rest of that dreadful evening, Robert never afterwards recalled. He did remember the awful silence when Morley left, Charlotte still in his arms, her hands yet holding him; and even then he was not completely passive.

Avoiding his eyes she disengaged her touch, an awkward business in itself. In doing so she unwittingly hurt Robert and it took him a few minutes more to regain composure. Charlotte waited silently while he made himself presentable.

Unsurprisingly, she was shocked and close to tears. Robert understood and did his best to comfort her, but it was difficult such was his own sensitive state.

However, worse than the physical pain was his mental anguish. Having been forcibly sobered to awareness of what he was about, Robert felt most terribly ashamed of having exposed Charlotte to the odium of censure, of hazarding her virtue; and of himself that he should have been so lacking in control as even to *contemplate* what he had been on the brink of doing. Only by the grace of God, and Morley's intervention, had Charlotte been reprieved.

He had forgotten entirely the sober reflections of Stoke urging him to discretion; forgotten, equally, his resolution to respect her innocence. With the first exchanged glance of the evening he had swung from intended retreat to burning, compulsive commitment, no matter the cost, in a fever of desire, able to think of nothing but the driving need to make love to her.

How, then, view his taking her to the stables, except as an act of criminal obduracy? He had cautioned himself, only that morning, to be guarded in Charlotte's company. Did he not recognise, only too well, that the caution was warranted?

He had known almost from the beginning, although mortified to acknowledge it, the dangerous attraction Charlotte held for him. He had also been aware of his own unaccountable weakness in the face of that attraction, a weakness which made him behave towards her with uncharacteristic lack of reserve. Yet, none of this crossed his mind tonight. Left to himself he would have plunged them heedlessly into disaster.

Seeing Charlotte's distress now, he was filled with self-disgust. He felt he should take her into his arms and soothe her distress but shame held him back. Additionally, if he were truthful, the abrupt cessation of their lovemaking had left him physically very uncomfortable and he was unsure of control.

He took her hand, diffidently. "Charlotte, I'm so sorry," he apologised. "Please forgive me, won't you?" He drew a harsh breath. "I realise that contrition is useless but what else can I say? I have no idea what possessed me to constrain you as I did. I cannot tell you . . . I really cannot say how ashamed I am." His shame was plain to see and hear. "However, Charlotte, this dreadful situation is easily retrieved."

Even in the present, wounding circumstances Charlotte was truthful. "Constrained? No, I was not constrained, Robert," she said, shaking her head. "There is nothing to forgive on that score."

He laughed mirthlessly. "Is that to relieve me of all guilt?" he asked, his manner constricted. "I think not. I ought to have known better. But, as I said, we can right this easily."

"Do you mean the saving grace of marriage, Sir?"

"I mean exactly that, Charlotte. However, we must leave this discussion for now and go up to the house before our absence occasions comment." Robert began drawing her to the door. "I shall come to you early tomorrow. We can make plans then. For now it is essential we return to the mamas. Come, Charlotte, smile. We must look happy when we break the glad tidings." Robert's tone was drier than he intended.

Charlotte tried to do as he bade her but it took all her resolution, and the strength of Robert's assurance, to carry her through the remaining hours of the evening. When she saw two pairs of astonished eyes register her wildly tumbled hair, and Robert's annihilated neckcloth, her spirits sank. Seeing Charlotte's instinctive withdrawal, he urged her forward with a defensive arm around her. Then he made the announcement of their engagement without delay.

"Well, Mama, Aunt Alethea, you must excuse me for demolishing Charlotte's delightful coiffure." Smiling, he took the bull by the horns before they made mention of it themselves. "It occurred when she accepted my proposal of marriage. In the circumstances, I am sure you will agree that I should be forgiven this once."

Charlotte gazed at him in amazement, wondering how on earth he could behave so normally, how talk so easily of proposals and weddings. Little did she understand the cost to Robert of his charade.

It was successful, however. Two very happy mamas were completely disarmed, this news so welcome to them everything else was forgotten. They even began tentative wedding plans. Robert was swift to close off that avenue.

"Plans are for later. My dear Charlotte is quite exhausted by all the excitement and so am I. Tomorrow is soon enough."

Naturally, Charlotte's welfare came first with the mamas. They contained their excitement as best they could, contenting themselves with warm hugs and kisses as Charlotte was ushered off to bed.

Bending over to kiss her hand as she went, Robert was conscious of leaving Charlotte uncomforted but he felt too drained to do anything more. "I will see you tomorrow," was he all he could say.

He did not kiss me goodnight, Charlotte thought. She might have slept better had she known why.

***

Unusually Robert was slow to wake, his eyes opening reluctantly. His whole body felt stiff and heavy, every muscle protesting its unwillingness to stir. A nebulous unease fretted at his mind's edge. He heard the dogs clamouring and concluded that their barking had woken him. They were obviously ready for their morning run. He would call to see Charlotte on the way back.

Charlotte!

At once the vague unease took shape, the events of last evening crowding in upon him. God in heaven! Charlotte!

All lethargy gone, he sat up and threw back the bedcovers. Dear God, what time was it? Why had he overslept, on this, of all mornings? He rang for his valet and dressed with haste before going, breakfastless, to Crane, where he found Charlotte in the dairy separating the milk ready for butter making. When she saw him she ceased her endeavours abruptly and the separator came to a clattering halt.

She did not welcome him with her customary unaffected manner, nor were her lovely eyes alight to see him as they usually were. She only gazed at him uncertainly; of course he knew why. He gave her a smile of conscious good cheer.

"Good morning, Charlotte. I am sorry to be late but, dashed nuisance, I overslept. How perverse is life that it must happen today of all days?"

"I thought you were not coming, Sir." Her troubled look pained Robert, shaming him anew.

"Why would I not?" He smiled. "We have plans to make." Robert tried to take her hands but Charlotte repulsed him, anchoring them together at her breast.

He frowned. Then remembering the difficulties his behaviour had created, and thinking she might be wary of him as a result, he said gently: "Charlotte, do not push me away." He reached for her again. "Dear heart, I know I gave you the most dreadful shock last night but it is now my earnest wish to make reparation in every way possible. Nothing of . . . of that same shocking nature will occur again, I promise. You need not fear me."

Robert's chivalrous effort was wasted. Charlotte would have none of him, nor his fair words. How could she with what was on her mind?

He, knowing nothing of her thoughts, only saw the alacrity with which she put the width of a churn trestle between them, and his frown deepened. Not surprisingly he was finding an antipathetic Charlotte difficult to handle, tired and teasy as he was, and feeling guilty, especially as he had been expecting to find his usual loving and welcoming companion. Riding to Crane, minutes earlier, he had pictured her running into his arms, had seen them exchanging sweetly forgiving kisses.

"What *is* the matter, Charlotte?" He paused, head at an enquiring angle to study her. "Well?" His voice sharpened a little. "You are not usually so silent. Why now? It is not helpful." Charlotte's grey eyes were riveted to his face but gave him no clue to her thoughts.

Robert drew a quick sigh, and said carefully: "I see that you are still upset." It was a reasonable assumption in the circumstances. "I understand of course but Charlotte . . . I know I behaved abominably . . . I was . . . I was not thinking clearly last evening and I am sorry, truly I am. I had hoped you would feel better after a night's sleep. Was I wrong? Do I expect too much? Were these hopes no more than a reflection of my own desire to feel better? Or, worse, are you so disgusted with me that you cannot even bear me to touch you?" Robert's voice and face alike were extremely wry. He still wore a tired frown.

"In no way do you disgust me, Sir." Finally Charlotte responded, shaking her head; which was better than nothing.

"Then what is it? Why won't you talk to me?" he asked, shoulders lifting irritably. He had neither patience nor energy for maidenly skirmishing this morning. Why could not Charlotte be her normal, straightforward self? Alas, she only continued to give him an uncertain look, which did nothing to dispel Robert's growing exasperation. "For God's sake, Charlotte," he snapped, "sit down, do. We *must* talk. Can't you see that? What *is* the matter with you?"

He began to lose his temper in earnest, the sympathy he'd felt for her position overlaid by irritation at her uncharacteristically obtuse behaviour; he had his own troubles, after all. He moved swiftly around the trestle. Taking a firm grip on Charlotte he sat her down forcibly. "Now," he said grimly, "what have we here? What is toward, Charlotte? Tell me."

She gave a barely discernible sigh of resignation and met his eyes. "I have been thinking," she said.

This simple statement covered much that had troubled Charlotte since Robert's departure last evening. She had gone to bed with the mamas' joyful exclamations ringing in her ears but they sounded no echo in her own heart. In fact she had felt miserable, at first believing this was because of her culpable behaviour with Robert. Gradually she came to see this was only part of the cause.

What troubled her more, she realised eventually, was the manner of Robert's declaration. When he spoke to Morley of marriage it was as though of an existing contract; but Robert had not previously mentioned marriage, nor given any indication of meaning to. Inevitably, since Charlotte was not unintelligent, this led her to the conclusion that he only declared for marriage because the old man found them in a compromising situation: which meant Robert was offering for her because he had to, not necessarily because he wanted to. Therefore, she must suppose, his offer was, perhaps, only an expedient to protect her reputation.

This painful supposition was anathema. Charlotte did not want a husband on those terms, not even Robert; particularly not darling Robert. She wanted him willingly and joyfully. She needed him to love her as completely as she loved him. Nothing less would do for her.

In truth he had never said he loved her. All he *had* said positively, and that in the heat of passion, was that he wanted her. This brought her back to where she had begun, the painful truth being, that in spite of her fear she would have done whatever he wished, gone wherever he led, for love of him and the accomplishment of his happiness; and, it must be said, her own. Perhaps such an admission made her a wanton but it did not alter its essential truth. If lovemaking was all Robert wanted he could have had it, with no mention of marriage . . . if Morley had not come by.

These thoughts were odious and humiliating. Therefore, before making wedding plans, she had to know the truth and how was she to find out except by asking Robert? Which now, by painful degrees and long silences when words would not come, she brought herself to do.

"And?" Robert prompted impatiently.

"Do you really want to marry me, Sir, or is it that you feel obliged to offer for me because of what Morley saw us doing?" she asked at length.

The question took Robert completely by surprise. It was not at all what he had been expecting. His thoughts had taken an entirely different direction and he was nonplussed momentarily.

"What?" he asked sharply, adjusting to this new turn. Uneasily, he realised that with her usual clear-sightedness Charlotte had put her finger on the pulse of truth. It shook him considerably and his reactions were slow to come.

She repeated the question word for word, watching him all the while, her eyes questing, examining his face, seeking reassurance, willing him to give her the answer she wanted. Naturally, he did.

"Of course I want to marry you. I said so," he stated baldly. Where now was the smooth-mannered Mr Hattenbury of cosmopolitan days? "I *do* want you," he reiterated, seeing her unconvinced.

With a sinking heart, knowing him as she did, Charlotte knew he lied. She had pinned her hopes on his reply. What she heard was their death knell. Robert saw it mirrored in her eyes.

"Believe me, Charlotte," he said emphatically, leaning forward to grasp her arm. He shook her lightly, to underline his emphasis. "Believe me," he repeated. "I have long wanted you and you could not help but know this. Have I not shown my feelings from the outset and with a lamentable lack of reticence at times? Would a man otherwise behave towards you as I did last night? Charlotte . . ." he paused, trying to be more conciliatory, speaking more gently, "I know I have often been less than chivalrous with you but the very fact that I could so far forget my honour, and the respect which is your due, must prove that I speak the truth."

"Perhaps," she agreed, "but that is not to say you want me for your wife."

"I have *told* you I do."

"Yes," she assented quietly, "but you lied, Sir."

Again Robert was caught off balance by Charlotte's directness. Not yet recovered from recent happenings himself, he reacted with anger to a situation that was fast getting outwith his control. He swore.

"Damn you, Charlotte! Have done with this nonsense. I am not lying and I *do* want to marry you. What else can I say?" He threw up his hands. "Why am I here?" he challenged, glaring at her furiously, his look scarcely that of an ardent suitor. Charlotte held his gaze.

"You are here to do your duty," she responded in a colourless voice.

At this, Robert lost his temper completely. "For God's sake girl, will you stop being so damnably stupid? I am here because I wish to be but with you in this ridiculous mood I am beginning to wonder why," he thundered.

He jumped up from the bench and began striding about the dairy, flicking at the sills and churns with his riding crop. He was fulminating, his face a tight mask of controlled anger.

Eventually he reined back on the explosive temper, reminding himself that Charlotte had experienced a great shock because of him. She was not herself. Neither was he for that matter, so how could he expect Charlotte to behave as though unaffected by what had happened?

He swallowed a residual chagrin, which lingered despite reasoned argument, and went back to her. She sat unmoving upon the bench where he had left her. Crouching down on his haunches he made a conscious effort to smile.

"See here, poppet," he began in coaxing tone, "we are getting out of stride and if it continues we shall end by quarrelling." He took her fingers, gave them a cuddling shake, and said: "Let us start anew. Here I am, upon one knee before you, and I ask: Miss Treleaven, will you do me the honour of becoming my wife?"

Charlotte gave a small, anguished cry. Her eyes closed. "No," she said.

This was his answer, soft-voiced but final. The single word, coming without embellishment, was the final straw for Robert. He had tried hard to be gentle and understanding but this further laceration to churned up feelings was too much. He jumped to his feet and grabbed Charlotte by the shoulders, pulling her up with him, shaking her in his fury.

"Are you totally senseless?" he grated between clenched teeth. "What matters it *why* I am here? There is no question of a refusal. We *have* to marry, whether you will or not, whether *I* will or not."

He flung her away and turned his back, arms folded, chin sunk to his chest. He was breathing hard, fighting for control. Behind him, Charlotte stood where she had been thrust, well and truly shaken and much discomposed.

"I cannot marry you," she cried. Robert swung about.

"In God's name, why not?" he demanded furiously. "You appeared happy enough at the prospect yesterday. Why have you changed? Has my unbridled behaviour given you a disgust of me? Does that bring us to the truth?"

"No, it does not, as you well know," Charlotte denied, her voice rising in agitation. She covered her eyes to shut out Robert's distorted features. "It is not I who lies, it is *you*, Sir."

Roughly, Robert dragged her hands from her face. Charlotte gasped with shock and her eyes flew open. She pulled her hands from his grasp. "I am not lying, damn you," he raged, glaring at her, head thrust forward aggressively.

"You *are*, I know you are," she cried wildly and, quite without meaning to, she slapped his out-thrust face as hard as she could.

Robert reared back in outraged stupefaction, utterly scandalised that she should *dare* to strike him. He went white with fury, so that the mark of her hand showed livid against his pallid cheek. He was speechless with rage, nostrils flaring, hands clenched into tight fists.

Hugely shocked at what she had done, Charlotte thought for a moment that Robert was going to beat her and knew she deserved it. That he did not, was a matter of the most iron self-control. She could see his whole body shaking with the effort to quash the violent impulse. Trembling hands rose to cover her mouth. She was frightened of the devil she had roused in him. She had gone too far and knew it.

"**How dare you**!" he spat. He grabbed her arm, jerking her towards him as she cowered in fright. "Insolent girl! Have you run your length?" he demanded rigidly, his throat constricted with wrath.

"I am sorry, Sir, I did not mean to strike you. I'm so sorry," she whispered, recoiling from the cold fury in his eyes. He let her go abruptly, as though he could no longer bear to touch her.

"*That* I do not doubt," he said with bitter, lip-curling hostility, breathing hard, "but I have not yet done with you, mannerless brat. So . . . you want the truth of me, do you? Very well, you shall have it. I would have spared your feelings but if you will not have it thus, so be it.

"Yes, madam, you are right. It was not my intention to ask for your hand at this stage. Circumstances, not least my own execrable lack of control, force me to this step. Having taken it, I must now be content and, I might add, so must you, bearing in mind your contribution to the situation."

Upset as she was, the injustice of this cruel remark was lost on Charlotte but she did feel the unkind reminder deeply.

"The truth is, Miss Treleaven, you are as yet unfitted to be my wife. You are ill-prepared, knowing nothing of the outside world and too immature by far. I have always known this and many times, in saner moments, told myself I should retreat. But I allowed myself to be blinded to the difficulties by my admiration for you. In reality, you know little of me except what you have seen here; but I spend only a few weeks, at most a few months, at home each year. The greater part of my life is spent in London or abroad and of that, my friends, my mode of living and activities, you know nothing. You are not even acquainted with the duties and obligations expected of you as my wife in society. How should you be?"

Never had he addressed Charlotte so coldly. Never had he looked at her with such acute dislike.

"You have not been correctly trained, notwithstanding the responsibilities life thrust upon you at an early age. You are not yet sixteen and ought still to be in the schoolroom, not going to your wedding." He gave a rigid shake of the head. "It is useless to repine. The thing is done. I was heedless and negligent to thrust you into this awkward situation, one which can only hold us both up to ridicule. But . . ." another adamantine shake of his shapely head, "the responsibility has to be accepted. In honour, we can only go forward together. Propriety and convention demands it. We must make the best of things." When he finished speaking Robert's face was as bleak as winter, clearly not one whit relishing the picture he painted.

Charlotte grew pale and paler as she listened to his diatribe, hurt beyond bearing by Robert's harshness, unable to believe her ears when he said it was against his better judgement that he admired her. Saner moments?

It seemed impossible when she remembered all the affectionate passages between them, the demonstrations of what she had taken to be love. How could she have been so mistaken? How could Robert have deceived her so well? Even last night, when tortured by doubts, there was a part of her which believed he would lovingly dispel them. There was to be no dispelling of anxiety. Far from it. Each word he spoke betrayed him further, destroying all her cherished illusions.

How coldly, how harshly, he addressed her. How slightingly! How *unfairly*!

Gradually, Charlotte's hurt was replaced by anger at the unjustness of his disparaging dismissal. When she answered him her voice was clearly indicative of the pain and anger she felt. There was no hint of the vulnerable droop her lips sometimes showed.

"You are insulting," she denounced him contemptuously, without appellation. "How dare you stand there, so grand and haughty, and tell me I am too immature to be your wife after the passion with which you made love to me last night? How deceitful of you to do so, thinking as you do." Charlotte did not mince her words and Robert's tight face showed the thrust had gone home. "You tell me I am a child and will make you look ridiculous. Allow me to say that you do not need *my* help in that enterprise. It is your own shabby behaviour that makes you ridiculous.

"As to my being unfitted to be your wife, pray cease to disturb yourself. You are not obliged to take me. I will not hold you to a promise so unwillingly given." She tossed her head in proud disdain. "You speak of affection but yours is clearly a paltry thing." Her lip curled disdainfully. "You clearly believe you do me too much honour in asking me to be your wife; equally, you care more for your standing in society than you do for me. Therefore I repudiate you and your miserable affection. You may think as highly of yourself as you choose, but don't expect me to join you in that business because I despise you. You are a *sham*, Sir, and I am done with you."

Shaking visibly, close to tears now, Charlotte made to push past

Robert. His hand shot out to fasten on her arm, tightening harshly when she resisted.

"Idiot! Are you completely without sense?" he thundered as she struggled to release herself. "Be controlled!" His voice was like a whiplash, each cutting word he spoke a further wound to Charlotte's lacerated feelings. *How could he speak so to her?*

"Leave me be! Leave me *be*!" she cried, still struggling.

It took several minutes to subdue her but Robert's superior strength told eventually, although he was obliged to retain a hold on Charlotte to keep her in control. Nostrils flaring, he demanded: "By what right do you address me in this disrespectful way? What pray, is the meaning of your simpleton's speech? There is no *question* of a refusal. I made that clear. We are committed and you will do as you are told. Are you too stupid and obdurate to see that?"

"You do not own me, and *I will not marry you*," Charlotte cried passionately, standing rigidly under his duress. "I despise you for your duplicity. You are not the man I thought you. I made a mistake." A sob escaped her; the threatening tears fell.

Once more, Robert thrust Charlotte away. He turned his back on her, so incensed he could not trust himself near her.

Was it for this he was prepared to give up his freedom? How dare she be so insulting? How dare she treat him as though he were of no account? He knew a round dozen of women who would fall over themselves to accept an offer from him. How dare Charlotte impugn his honour as she did?

How dared she?

The anger fountained again and again; Robert was obliged to fight for control, breathing hard, eyes closed, head sunk on his chest. He stood perfectly immobile, hands bunched into fists at his side. He heard Charlotte crying behind him but it left him unmoved. The anger was all-consuming.

After several, highly charged minutes he was sufficiently in command to speak but he spat his words at Charlotte icily. "You made a mistake, you say. Well," his lip curled derisively, "you are at liberty to think so. Permit me to point out, however, that your discovery has come too late to be of practical use. To be helpful it should have come twenty four hours ago. It would then have benefited us both. As it is, I can only counsel you to remember the events of last night, which bind us irrevocably together. You cannot change your mind now."

As he fully intended, the cruel irony of his observations was not lost on Charlotte. She flushed painfully but would not be moved from her stand.

"I *have* changed my mind. I will not marry you; not now, not ever." She was shaking so hard she could scarcely speak.

Robert felt the choking anger rise again. "Indeed. Are you, then, so fickle a creature as to change your mind overnight?" he ground out with a biting sarcasm which increased the shamed flush on Charlotte's face. It also completely disregarded the fact that the same criticism might, with equal truth, be levelled at him. Charlotte was in no state to appreciate his lack of logic. She shook her head dumbly.

"I am not fickle, Mr Hattenbury, but I will not marry you now," she reiterated, the niceness of her distinction lost on Robert. At the time Charlotte was unaware of having made it.

For a very long moment, there was silence in the dairy. It was tangible and menacing, Robert's face unreadable as he stared at her with fixed, unseeing eyes but the absolute rigidity of his body added to the menace.

Suddenly, his gaze snapped into focus and Charlotte saw cold hostility in their blue depths. She stepped back instinctively but he made no move to touch her. He turned on his heel and strode away without another word.

Charlotte sat down abruptly, her legs weak and trembling. Then she began to cry in earnest. She cried for lost love; she cried for the misery of disillusion and the shattering of her secure world, the world in which she and Robert had shared warm companionship. Where was he, the Robert of that world, the man she had loved, the sound of whose step could send her running in eager anticipation? What had happened to him, he whose presence and person had so wonderfully altered her life?

Unbelievably, he had disappeared in the space of an hour, leaving in his place a cold angry man who thought of her disparagingly; a man who did not want her, deny it though he may; a man who was marrying because he must, not because he would. He spoke of admiration for her and in the same breath added biting criticism. But love took no account of fault so how *could* he have loved her? It seemed the love had only been in her imagination. She had made the most shattering mistake.

Charlotte cried for a long time but gradually, out of all the pain, some comfort emerged: she still retained her pride and determination. Now, in the place where love once stood, there was fierce antipathy. Although she had nothing else, these were left to her and they helped harden her resolve.

Let Mr Hattenbury remove himself to London and his fine friends who were too good for her. She wanted nothing of him. She felt only hatred for the brutality with which he had destroyed her illusions, feeling diminished by his catalogue of her failings. She despised him for the deception of their relationship. He had betrayed her, where she had willingly been giving him all her love. She could not, and would not, trust him again as long as she lived.

Sadly, Charlotte wished with all her heart that she had never seen his sparkling blue eyes, nor tasted the honey of his persuasive mouth.

***

Twenty four hours later Robert was back at Crane Lodge. His normal polished front was very much in evidence; so too was his reserve. He was once more in command, the shock of Charlotte's repudiation having been absorbed. If anything it had hardened his attitude, the sympathy he felt for her position dissipated by the insults she had offered him, particularly the ultimate one of rejection. He returned with grim determination to brook no opposition. He knew his duty, even if Charlotte refused to acknowledge it, and was immovably determined to carry it out.

He walked into the hall, to be met by Mrs Treleaven who, by her looks, already knew of the broken engagement. Robert cursed inwardly.

"Oh . . . Robert, dear . . . how lovely to see you," she greeted him nervously.

He ignored this pleasantry. “I take it Charlotte has told you that she wishes to terminate our engagement?”

“Well, dear . . . yes,” she confirmed unhappily.

“You will appreciate, Aunt Alethea, that I want to change her mind. I wish to see her . . . alone if you please,” he said crisply, never doubting an affirmative response. Mrs Treleaven hovered indecisively looking flustered, her hands clasped nervously and, after several false starts, told him Charlotte would not see him.

“Oh dear, Robert . . .” Mrs Treleaven broke off on an exclamation of distress. “What has got into Charlotte? I never knew her behave so capriciously. Such vacillation . . . such disappointment. I am quite at a loss . . . so great the chagrin for you. What is to be done?”

Robert allowed her to run down before repeating his request to see Charlotte. He was polite but very determined. Mrs Treleaven did not know how to answer him. With all her heart she wished to give the reply he wanted. There was nothing she would like better than for Charlotte to change her mind but, in refusing to see him, Charlotte had been as determined as Robert.

Alethea wrung her hands in agitation; she made soft exclamations of dismay; at the same time she shook her head. “Charlotte will not see you,” she cried.

Robert’s hands covered hers. He calmed her to stillness. “I must and *will* see Charlotte,” he said quietly. “Tell me where she is and leave the rest to me.”

His firm handling did the trick. This was something to which Mrs Treleaven, from long training, instinctively responded. Indeed she was thankful, relieved to have the responsibility for her daughter’s wilful behaviour transferred to Robert.

“She is in the kitchen,” Alethea revealed simply.

“Thank you. Now, Aunt Alethea, may I suggest you go upstairs? It might be more comfortable for you in the circumstances.”

Unaware that Robert’s motive was not purely altruistic, Alethea thanked him heartfeltedly and went away.

Robert found Charlotte preparing vegetables at the big deal table in the kitchen. She looked up at the door’s opening. On seeing Robert, she set down the knife she was holding and dusted off her hands, her expression tart.

He opened coldly, without preamble. "I wish to see you, Miss Treleaven. Now, if you please." This was Robert at his most remote but still addressing Charlotte politely from ingrained habit.

She gave him no such consideration. "I, however, do not wish to see you. I am busy." Her tone suggested that he should also be busy and that his busyness should he occurring elsewhere.

He wasted no time in fruitless argument; gripping Charlotte by the upper arm he propelled her to the door, watched by an open-mouthed Minna.

Charlotte gasped at the unexpected move, protesting at every step, as a hard-faced Robert frog-marched her to the drawing room. He released her only when he had closed the door behind them.

"How dare you use coercion upon me?" Charlotte flared, rubbing a painful arm. "Who are you to force me to your will?"

"I was given permission to see you by your mama. You will not question her right to dispose your time, I believe?" A haughty arrogance of tone matched the elevation of Robert's brow.

"Did she also give you leave to mistreat me?" Charlotte demanded, pressing her lips together angrily. He ignored this.

"Listen to me carefully. I shall not repeat myself, nor allow for pawkiness . . . and there will be *no* refusals this time."

Charlotte's face flooded with colour at the dismissive way he spoke to her, his offensive words and their implicit assumption of right. "There is *nothing* I wish to hear from you except farewell. Leave my house," she retorted furiously and started for the door.

He was much too quick for her. Before she was aware of his intention he had forcibly set her upon a chair, and there she was held by iron hands in which there was no shade of the tenderness he once used towards her.

Hard blue eyes boring into hers, he opened: "I have said you will listen and that is precisely what you *will* do, Miss Treleaven." He spoke slowly, very, very quietly but there was no mistaking the menace behind the softly uttered words. Chilled, wide-eyed and just a little frightened,

Charlotte stared up at the stranger Robert had become. When he was sure she had been subdued, he stepped back.

"You were kind enough, yesterday, to call me a sham," he began and there was no sign on his face of the outrage *that* remark had called forth when he first heard it. "You also declined my proposal. Under normal circumstances I would be only too happy to accept my dismissal, but our circumstances are not normal and I cannot take this course. However, since neither of us is anxious to assume the burden of matrimony at this time, I have formulated a different plan for discharging my duty to you. I mean to postpone our conjoining until such time as you have learned obedience. Instead I shall make you my ward."

Charlotte listened to this autocratic disposal of her future with growing ire. "Learned obedience, indeed! Certainly not to *you.* Have I nothing to say to these fine plans of yours? Or Mama?" she demanded angrily.

He gave her a measured, disparaging look. "Aunt Alethea will approve them and *you*, Miss Treleaven, will do as you are told."

Charlotte gasped. "Indeed!" she exclaimed, swelling with indignation. "If that is what you think you are much mistaken, Sir!"

He was unmoved by her defiance. He seemed almost amused. Charlotte could not imagine why, yet had an awful premonition that his amusement boded her no good.

"Oh but you will," he decreed arrogantly, looking down the length of his high-bridged nose, "unless you wish me to regale our parents with the tale of . . . well . . . shall we call it . . . recent happenings? You understand me?" He pressed home the point. "Naturally I do not wish to take this course . . . so distressing for the mamas. But if you are intransigent, *make you no mistake*, I shall do so without hesitation."

Threat made, the smallest of cold smiles lifted one corner of his shapely mouth. He raised a sardonic brow and his eyes were as icy as Arctic seas.

Charlotte felt as chilled. Her heart sank. She stared at him in numbed disbelief. "You would not dare," she cried.

Robert's tiny smile died. "Do not put me to the test," he warned frigidly.

She stared at him despairingly. Surely, *surely*, he would never relate what had occurred on his birthday? It would disgrace them both! Would he? By his looks, all too clearly he could, but . . . oh, surely, he would not?

Continuing to stare at him, she realised that she could not predict what this new Robert would do. In spite of this, she was tempted to throw his highhanded plans back into his autocratic face and defy him to do his worst. Almost, almost, Charlotte did send Robert to the devil and the impulse showed in her stormy face. But only for the time it took to realise the selfishness of such an act. She thought of the numbing heartache it would bring to those whom she loved the most; to lose their esteem? Oh, no. She could not do it.

But equally, to give in to Robert without the least demur? How galling! How humiliating. How totally against all resolution! Yet what else could she do? She wracked her brains for an alternative.

Robert watched her, saying nothing. He knew she must come to it in the end. He was determined she would. She would *not* best him again.

"Well, Miss Treleaven, having searched your mind for other solutions, you find none. Am I correct?" he asked coolly.

She stared at him with an acute dislike amounting almost to hatred, feeling trapped and thwarted at every turn by this horribly unlovely man towering over her, he whom she had adored with all her soul only a day ago. How hard his face now. How different from other times.

"Well?" he repeated more sharply. "Do you intend to sit mumchance hour upon hour? Or shall I call down your mama? Come, I have not all day to waste on this matter," he added, cruelly indifferent to her feelings.

In her heart Charlotte knew she had no choice, but the words of surrender stuck in her throat, too difficult to speak. "Wardship," she said finally, in a flat voice. This was her tacit admission.

"As I have already stated," Robert responded coldly.

Again Charlotte was silent; but as Robert watched every nuance of emotion playing across her face, he could almost hear her thoughts and knew exactly when she capitulated. He had broken her resistance and an ignominious satisfaction creamed through him. He cleared his throat and put up a hand to smooth already immaculate hair. His moment of triumph was brief. Charlotte burst his small bubble of self-satisfaction with her capitulation.

"So be it, Mr Hattenbury. I shall count wardship as punishment for the wrong-doing in which we shared. *You* may take it as penance." Robert gave no sign her thrust had gone home.

"To continue," he said shortly; and now she had accepted his dictates he was more gentle, "I shall go to Italy as planned, first making you my ward. You will go to finishing school." Clearly, he had already given this thought. "It will be a useful preparation for the life we shall later share, giving you polish and self-assurance, teaching you all you will need to know."

Life we shall later share? Charlotte stared at him in disbelief. Could he truly think that possible, after his cruel and disparaging treatment of her?

"Then a London season next spring," he was saying, "something you will enjoy, I believe. At the end of this you will be rather older, of course." At this point Robert's peroration came to an end. He was lost in thought.

Not pleasant ones, judging by his expression, Charlotte assumed. She herself felt crushed by all the upheaval of recent days and was thinking, with a great deal of resentment, that in a short space of time Robert had brusquely destroyed her past life. Now, as brusquely, he disposed her future.

He sighed suddenly and asked:" Is there anything you wish to contribute to this discourse, Miss Treleaven?"

"There is." Charlotte got up decisively and crossed to where he stood. Looking up at him, her antipathy was obvious, as also that her spirit had not been broken even though forced to surrender. "I am pawky, you say, fit only to do as I am told. I am unpolished and *dreadfully* unsuited to be your wife." She mimicked the tone he had used to her and saw his expression harden. "You do not want to marry me and I *certainly* do not wish to marry you. Yet, Sir, you are as perverse as you say I am, for you will not accept a way out when it is offered. What is the matter with you?"

Looking down at Charlotte, listening with growing ire to her denunciation, Robert could have spanked her for the insolence of her manner and lack of respect.

"Cease to try my patience, Miss Treleaven," he warned frostily.

And yet . . . and yet . . . with Charlotte close to him and he being enveloped in the subtle perfume of her presence, even now something lurked unacknowledged within him, which, with the offering of her mouth or a loving touch, might still have brought him around her thumb again if she chose; but she did not know this.

However, standing before him, Charlotte *did* see an odd flicker in his eyes, a hint of her old, adorable Robert, very small it is true, but it was there. It evoked in her a keen, piercing regret and such a longing for her erstwhile loving companion that her antipathetic feelings underwent an abrupt change. The anger and resentment died, leaving only a poignant tristesse for the loss of her parfait knight.

Charlotte gazed at him, shaking her head in perplexed angst. "I really thought you loved me. How could I have been so wrong?" she asked, the words drawn out of her against her will.

She stepped back and turned away but had not taken two paces when she felt Robert behind her. His arms fastened about her waist, he pulled her back against him and all hint of frostiness was gone as he said gently: "No, Charlotte, you were not wrong in thinking thus, I assure you."

For an unbelievable moment of wondering delight Charlotte did not register Robert's words, experiencing only the ineffable joy of his loving and much loved nearness. No anger or hostility, only warmth and caring in his touch, his arms strong and protective about her, his mouth now caressing her nape.

Could this be true? Was it possible that her dear companion had miraculously been restored to her, after all the wrongness that had passed between them these last days? She leaned back against Robert, willing him to continue with the heavenly kisses, wanting him never to stop, except only to press his mouth to hers

Then she realised what he had said and whirled about, standing back to gaze up at him gladly. "You do love me, Robert?" she asked tremulously, her mouth curving to a smile. "Are you saying that you did not mean all those horrible things you said yesterday? Is that possible?

Do you truly want me for your wife?" The eager questions tumbled from her parted lips. "Oh, how wonderful that would be. Robert?" Almost, she could not believe it.

Robert took a deep breath, wanting to give Charlotte the simple yes she so ardently desired, but knowing there were things he must first make clear to her, situations he must make her understand. He did not pull her into his arms, although he felt her impetus to be back within his embrace, because he knew that if he did his thought processes might very well be suspended. Instead, he held her face to face, placing his hands on her upper arms, leaving a small space between them. Charlotte's hands were clasped at her waist against their need to be about Robert's person at a time when, clearly, embraces were not his intention.

"Charlotte . . . " he began hesitantly, "yes, of course I want you for my wife. I have already told you that. Do not question it." He took a breath. "As to yesterday . . . I know I was unpardonably intemperate but I was tired and teasy because I had not slept well the previous night, from guilt at my unbridled behaviour towards you and, I'm afraid . . . the truth is I lost my temper. However, that does not, I know, excuse the unmannerly way in which I addressed you and for this I ask your indulgence."

He waited a moment, looking down at her unsmiling. Charlotte's euphoria began to die as she recognised in his expression a consciousness of something held back. It prompted her to say: "And? Or should that be a 'but', Sir?" A small kernel of doubt, almost a dread, had settled in her breast.

After another moment of silence, Robert drew breath and said carefully: "It was very wrong of me to plunge us into this hasty marriage. It cannot now be helped but we must think our course through carefully. As I pointed out to you . . . and it is still true, Charlotte . . . you are not yet ready for the London salons. This has to be faced before we can go forward."

Charlotte's steady grey eyes remained fixed on his face but she did not respond, except with the smallest flicker of an eyebrow, which in no wise reflected her inner feelings. For she realised, listening to Robert's careful exposition, which sounded so horribly familiar, that nothing had really changed and that she was almost certainly facing a second death of joyful expectation, because she knew in her heart, with dreadful certitude, what Robert was about to say next.

He went on: "Your life in Cornwall has not fitted you for a role in the wider world. You have a great deal to learn before you are ready to be . . ." again Robert hesitated, "to . . . to . . ." he seemed unable to find the right words, he who was usually so smooth of tongue and manner. Charlotte came to his aid.

From a stony heart, she said: "To be your wife is what you mean, I believe. What you are trying to reiterate politely, although there is no way it really *can* be expressed politely, is that I am not up to snuff; I am not good enough to be the wife of Mr Hattenbury, society gentleman."

"Charlotte, no!" Robert protested, his face tightening "you wilfully misinterpret me."

Grey gaze steady upon his face, Charlotte said carefully: "I think not, Sir. The truth of the matter, which is not in doubt since it was made quite clear to me on your birthday, is that you would very much admire to lie with me, just as long as your friends and high-born acquaintances know nothing of it; but marriage is a horse of a different colour; is it not? And in your heart you have no desire to ride it."

Robert drew breath sharply, shocked at Charlotte's deliberate, and very exact, summation; indeed, he was goaded by it, as much as if she had struck him again. "No, no!" He would not have it such and protested again: "*No*, I say to you. What are you about here, Charlotte?" he demanded harshly. "We are coming to terms. Will you now plunge us back into disorder?"

Charlotte did not answer him, but carried on as though he had not spoken, making her final pronouncement from a leaden heart though it cost her dearly to do so. "When I marry, Sir, it will be to a gentleman who loves me as I am, without reservation; one who is not ashamed of association with me. That man will not be you, Robert, for you do not pass *my* test. *You,* alas, are not quite good enough for me."

Her hands came up to his chest and exerted the lightest pressure to indicate that she wished to be free. Robert let her go unresisting, but still with that goaded look upon his face. For a small space they looked at each other and what passed between them, unspoken, wiped Robert's features clean of all expression, making of it a mask to hide the maelstrom of feeling he was experiencing; his fury at Charlotte's intransigence; his anger at her repeated, insulting rejection; the conviction that she had bested him again. And too, there was a discomfort that would not leave him, a nebulous feeling not understood, which held that he was rightly bested.

Thinking thus, he retreated into cold hauteur. Face still impassive, he said frigidly: "Again, and without regard to the feelings of others, you have made your sentiments abundantly plain. So be it, Miss Treleaven. Wardship it is then."

Ignoring Charlotte completely, he took another moment's sombre contemplation, before continuing: "There are still some mundane questions to be settled. Our families conjoin for the Solstice celebrations tomorrow. I shall send the carriage for you shortly before six this evening. Is this agreeable to you?"

Charlotte did not answer directly. "Does Aunt Sophie know?" she asked diffidently.

"I did not tell her because I expected to reverse your decision. May I?" Robert was nothing if not steadfast to his resolve, no matter his inner reservations.

Charlotte's reply was unflatteringly emphatic. "Never," she said, without even the conciliatory appellation of a 'sir' to soften her rejection.

"As you wish," he responded, even more distantly. "I shall inform Mama when I return home. I leave you to explain your reasons as best you may."

The sting in his last comment struck Charlotte acutely. She drew sharp breath. "You are unchivalrous, Sir," she said flatly, looking him straight in the eye, her own accusing. "You need not enjoy my discomfiture. The fault is yours as well as mine."

As on so many previous occasions Robert was astonished, and affronted, that Charlotte read him with such acuity. He was reduced to furious angry again, not only because she had seen what was in him but that she had the temerity to denounce him for it. Equally, he was afraid that she might, with comparable ease, recognise the emotion which had prompted him, so untypically, to spite. That was something he was not prepared to face. He need not have worried. Such was Charlotte's turmoil, she could not analyse her own feelings at that point, never mind his.

He rounded on her furiously. "*I* was ready to make amends. This turn of events is all *your* doing, not mine. You must learn to live with it, even as I," he said savagely and strode away.

His is always the last word, thought Charlotte. *Robert has always bested me but I did not mind when I thought he loved me*.

Once more, the scalding tears fell as Charlotte, with a breaking heart, surveyed this second shattering of her precious dreams, their fragile beauty reduced to piercing shards.

Chapter Nine

Robert went straight to his mother and told her his engagement was at an end. Her face was redolent of shock at this extremely unwelcome news. He invited her to sit, kindly considering the state of his own feelings, while he explained.

"Robert, why?" she murmured in distress and stretched out a sympathetic hand. "You and Charlotte were so happy when you told us you were to marry. What happened?"

Sophie could not believe it. No engagement? Was this why Robert had been so withdrawn yesterday? It had been clear something was wrong, but she would never have guessed at this. What could possibly have chanced to terminate the loving contract so soon?

Robert took the proffered hand and urged her to a seat but did not sit down himself. He went to the fireplace and hitched a foot over the fender. He leaned a forearm along the mantle and gazed at the hearth reflectively, speaking over his shoulder.

"Charlotte has changed her mind."

"Changed her mind?" Sophie echoed, dismayed and disbelieving.

"I fear so, Mama."

"Robert, why? Charlotte wants to marry you, I *know* she does. She was so happy when you made the announcement," she wailed. "I cannot credit it."

"It is true, I assure you," Robert said dryly. "As to her reasons, no doubt she will tell you in time." He went silent, leaving his mother little the wiser.

She looked at him, struggling to make sense of what he was saying. She still could not take it in. How had this situation come about and when? She thought back to first intimations of something amiss. It had been yesterday morning, the very next after his birthday party.

So soon? Could it be . . . she had thought briefly on the engagement night that . . . well, they had been gone rather long, and both looked dishevelled when they returned, but . . . no, no, it was impossible; was it not?

"Robert?" Hesitantly, she attracted his attention. "Did you . . . did you do anything? To upset Charlotte . . . I mean . . . to set her against you?"

He turned his head, and the look on his face caused Mrs Hattenbury to rush into speech. "In truth, darling, this kind of behaviour is so unlike Charlotte. She is usually so steady and reliable."

"What sort of upset had you in mind, Mama?" he enquired, extremely cool. He turned fully to face her.

"It was only that I thought, perhaps, that . . . that possibly you might have . . ." There was a long pause while she tried to formulate an awkward thought inoffensively. It could not be done. The pause stretched out into uncomfortable silence.

Robert knew well what was in her mind. He squared his shoulders, stiffening perceptibly. "Should you wish to pursue this conversation, Mama, you will have to be more explicit. If, as I suppose, the difficulty in expressing your thought stems from the nature of your suspicions, it might be better to desist."

His bearing was one of absolute and icy remoteness. That he presented it to *her* showed Sophie how greatly she had transgressed, how much she offended him. Filled with guilt at the crass nature of her suspicions, she retracted immediately and rose to go to him.

"Darling, do forgive me. I don't know what I was thinking of. It is only that I cannot bear to believe your dream of happiness is dashed. Is there no possibility of Charlotte's reconsidering? Have you asked her?"

"I have, and shall continue to do so, fully expecting to change her mind in due course." He looked at Sophie straightly and added, with measured deliberation: "I would go so far as to say that I mean to have her, come what might. Now, Mama, I would prefer not to discuss it further."

"Of course, dearest," she assented automatically, her mind sifting Robert's last, extraordinary statement. What did he mean by it? "But, Robert, what is to happen about the weekend party?"

"It will go on, naturally. Because Charlotte declines to marry me is no reason to suppose we may not engage in social intercourse. She and her mother are coming to dinner this evening, as you wished. I also invited the Tregodicks to make up our party. This should ease us over any trifling awkwardness, although, personally, I expect none. However, I do think it best not to mention the engagement since there no longer is one."

He spoke with all the assurance of any well-bred young man, the disappointment of the broken engagement well hidden, but Sophie knew he must be concealing a full heart. Only he knew how full, and from what cause.

"As you wish." She pressed his hand in quick sympathy. He gave silent acknowledgement and drew away.

"If you will excuse me, Mama?" He bowed gracefully and was gone, leaving Sophie to think over the dismal news and wonder afresh how it had come about.

She thought of every possible reason, but none seemed to fit. She even returned to her inexcusably presumptuous suppositions briefly, but dismissed those too. However, on reflection, she realised that Robert had not *denied* them. He had only made her feel she had no right to question him.

***

Charlotte's explanation brought no more enlightenment. She simply said she felt unequal to the life Robert offered and thought it best to admit her mistake, feeling certain Mr Hattenbury would come to agree with her eventually. There was no time for more because of visitors in the house.

Saturday evening was taken up with the bonfire party, and the assembly broke up after church on Sunday. By then the engagement had been relegated to the background. Without pre-knowledge, no-one could have guessed at the trauma of a disengagement.

From Monday onwards, Robert called on Charlotte punctiliously. They exchanged a few guarded phrases each time and then he took his leave. On Thursday he left for London with Richard Tregodick, promising to return on Saturday of the following week. Charlotte watched him go with relief.

To see him daily was misery, his behaviour so chillingly correct, and in such stark contrast to his previous warmth. It brought her sharp pain, which had to be subdued after each visit. She was thankful to be relieved of the strain for a while.

She felt desperately unhappy, and the disappointed bewilderment of her mother and Aunt Sophie was a constant, if unintended, reproach. At least, with Robert away, she could begin to come to terms with the turmoil into which he had plunged her. He may have dashed her hopes for happiness but she still had to think of the future.

Mrs Treleaven noticed, sadly, that her daughter had become quiet again, and had developed a reserve not apparent before. She spent long hours alone, working in the garden. All the brightness of blossoming personality, which had come with the advent of Robert's brilliant star on her horizon, was quenched.

***

On Robert's return to Cornwall, he went to Charlotte and made her a formal declaration. She looked at him in a surprise bordering on amazement.

"Why do you keep proposing?" she asked. "You do not want me for your wife."

Thankfully, Charlotte would never know how true that was at this time. Robert had just come from his own milieu, and the sojourn there had reinforced his every objection to marriage with Charlotte. She would never have coped with the management of Meva House, or the social arrangements of London society.

There was also an ignominious voice in the corner of his mind, which reminded him starkly that some part of his reluctance had nothing to do with Charlotte's ability to cope, but stemmed from knowing that this marriage must expose some very private desires to public speculation. Being an extremely reticent young man, that thought was anathema to Robert.

He had always been aloof, unable to reveal more than an accepted social veneer to all but a few close companions, (a legacy of his father's licentiousness, perhaps), keeping his most deeply felt emotions well hidden. He rarely allowed people to come close. Even with his own mama, he was reserved and disinclined for confidences. Only with Charlotte had he allowed the mask to slip, more by accident than design, and look how disastrous it had been. The shock had certainly cooled his ardour. However, his sense of responsibility was in no way diminished. He might not *want* to marry Charlotte right now but knew that he must do, and take the consequences.

"Because we are obligated," he answered without enthusiasm, his voice plainly reflecting the tone of his thoughts.

"You are outwith your senses, Sir," Charlotte said dismissively. "Why force yourself to do what is clearly distasteful? You are nonsensical."

Infuriating girl! Why must she goad him so? "What, then, of Morley's knowledge?" he asked sharply.

Charlotte gave him a look of unmistakable disdain. "You need not fear for his discretion," she said with a hint of contempt.

Robert froze absolutely; his eyes filled with such icy fury Charlotte went hot with shame and alarm. "You do me less than justice, Miss Treleaven. It was of you that I was thinking," he said, with a frigidity which quickly chilled her flushed mortification.

For a long time Robert was silent, giving Charlotte no indication that her contempt had pained as well as angered him.

She was uncomfortably aware of having maligned him, realising that her ill-considered remark had worsened the situation between them. She scarcely knew how to conduct herself under the bane of his arctic gaze, and very much wanted to leave the room but was reluctant to seek permission.

Robert eventually indicated that she should be seated; he sat also. "Very well, Miss Treleaven, it shall be as you wish," he said. "Since you will not accept the protection of my name, having illustrated beyond doubt in what light you regard me, we shall go forward on the wardship course." His voice was bleak. "Now I am certain of the way, I shall take the necessary steps, in this way discharging my duty towards you. I shall confer with Aunt Alethea immediately. Meanwhile, hold yourself in readiness to leave for school. This comes first."

Charlotte was alarmed by the speed with which he proposed to move. "I cannot leave Mama to cope alone," she protested vehemently.

"Do not concern yourself. Previous difficulties no longer exist. I have already engaged staff to look after your mother's interests while we are away. This was always part of my plan, no matter how things transpired. It is definitely fixed."

"But she will be lonely without me," Charlotte objected quickly.

He demolished that hurdle with equal ease. "Certainly, she will miss you, but she will not be lonely. I intend to close Hattenbury while you and I are away. Mama will take up residence with Aunt Alethea for the duration. This will prove a satisfactory solution, one much to their taste, I believe."

She stared at him in frustration, feeling trapped in a situation outwith her control, reflecting dismally that he appeared to have thought of everything.

"Have I nothing to say to all your fine plans? Are my feelings of no account?" she asked resentfully.

"They would have been, had you chosen differently, but that time has passed, Miss Treleaven," he answered without in the least dissembling. Charlotte's heart sank still further. "And I need not remind you who gave me jurisdiction over your affairs," he added coldly, reducing Charlotte to silent humiliation.

After a moment he continued: "The new staff arrives on Wednesday. Your labours will cease from that time. *You* will devote yourself to gathering a school wardrobe. While on this topic, were you pleased with Mrs Buckingham's work?"

"Yes, Sir," she replied colourlessly.

"Then engage her for your school collection."

"As you wish," she agreed, but with a heart full of rebellion.

He got to his feet. "If you please, send Aunt Alethea to me now. I shall acquaint her with what has passed."

It was dismissal. Politely, he held the door for her, relenting not one jot of his inimical attitude. Feeling much subdued, Charlotte accepted her congé and went in search of her mother.

When this unhappy lady heard what was to happen, she could not take in the news. Charlotte was to be Robert's ward and not his wife? Nothing need worry them. Everything was taken care of. Staff had been engaged. Wardrobes were to be collected, and Charlotte . . . Charlotte was going to school!

It all seemed too wonderful to be true. However, Robert assured her that it was so, and Alethea felt dazed by the immensity of their good fortune. Despite the broken engagement, here was an end to all difficulties. Her relief at this astonishing turn of events was so great Mrs Treleaven broke down and wept. Robert comforted her briefly, and then went on to say that he intended asking his mama to take up residence at Crane while Charlotte was at school. "I know that little persuasion will be necessary," he said, with a gentle smile.

This further proof of good fortune caused Alethea to break down again, but her tears soon dried as she listened to the rosy picture Robert was painting. Silently, she thanked God for His kindness in removing the heavy burden she had been forced to carry these last few years. Dear, dear Robert. Again, thank God for sending him.

"Leave everything to me," Robert was saying; and that short phrase was music to Alethea's ears, the best she had heard in many a long day.

Robert brushed aside her thanks and asked to see the accounts. He would need to know what funds to put at their disposal when Sophie moved into the Lodge. This sounded perfectly reasonable to Mrs Treleaven. Still in a joyful daze, she led him to the escritoire where they were kept. Robert then suggested that she take a glass of wine while he cast an eye over the books. Alethea agreed happily, thankful to sit contemplating their wonderfully changed future.

After only a cursory glance at the accounts, Robert saw how ably and courageously Charlotte had coped with the problems of living on an extremely restricted income. He saw her egg and butter entries; the market accounts; rent from the cottage, all pitiful sums to offset the expenditure of a large house. He observed how she had saved a little here and sold a little there. One item was particularly expressive: she had entered last year's birthday money from Sophie and none, he saw, had been spent on Charlotte herself.

There were entries: 'to seed for the garden; 'repairs to the cottage'; but none for their own house. There were items speaking of new uniforms for Megan and Minna, but no new wardrobe for Charlotte until her recent excursion to Mrs Buckingham's establishment. No wonder her clothes had been so shabby.

Every detail was there, written out in Charlotte's hand. Reading on, Robert's hostility to her lessened as he realised the problems laid on her youthful shoulders. He reflected that it was as well that fate, in his own shape, had intervened to lift the impossible burden. Indeed, he rather thought that in sending Charlotte to school he had chosen the best answer after all. It would give her a chance to be carefree for a while. He had been more right than he knew, Robert thought comfortingly.

He did not linger over the accounts; there was no need. Once he had the main picture, he took his leave and rode across the moors. He felt drained by the medley of emotions he had experienced that morning, and needed to slough off their residue before encountering his mother. So saying, he stopped for a meal at the Manor in Rilla Mill, where he lingered with a tankard of ale until ready to face his mama.

Sophie's astonishment and joy equalled that of her friend and, as expected, she was delighted at the prospect of living in Crane. Here, it seemed, all difficulties were taken care of even without marriage.

"How was Charlotte persuaded? Are marriage plans now abandoned?" she asked.

Robert chose his answering words carefully, since he knew his mother would not accept any pronouncement with the same facility as Mrs Treleaven. Sophie's was a more questioning mind.

"No, Mama, I still intend to make Charlotte my wife, but she is not ready yet. She should have some freedom and social pleasures first. I am simply giving her that opportunity. At the same time, the situation at Crane cannot be allowed to go unchecked. Wardship makes it easy for me to rectify matters sensibly."

Robert paused and smiled pleasantly, his face unreadable. "As to how Charlotte was persuaded, I do not intend to tell you," he said coolly. "Suffice it to say that she was amenable and knows I mean to propose again at a later date. I am not without hopes of changing her mind but I am in no hurry."

Sophie thought, ruefully, that Robert had told her much, but also nothing. However, she was so happy at the retrieval of a dismal situation she was not inclined to question further. One could only go so far with Robert. Perhaps the solution was not the ideal she had hoped for, but it did remove many difficulties and had fallen out particularly well for herself and Alethea.

If only things could have been different for Robert. Charlotte was not the only one to have lost her glow. His brightness was also dimmed. He had retreated back behind his old hauteur. The openly affectionate young man of summer was gone. He had disappeared into his shell again and Sophie grieved for his loss. These past months he had been perfect joy, lighting up all their lives. However, all was not lost. Robert said he still hoped, so it *could* come right.

***

The following month flew in a whirl of activity. It saw Charlotte's preparation for school; it saw the upheaval of Mrs Hattenbury's removal to Crane; it saw the comings and goings of Roddick Sampson, who sorted out the legalities of wardship. Finally, before Charlotte's departure to Bath, it saw the wedding of her friend, Julia, to Richard Tregodick.

During this time, Robert was not much in evidence, but the speed with which he made arrangements left them gasping. Within one short month, their lives were altered beyond belief. Each was set on a new course, and it happened so quickly there was no time to think or repine.

This applied particularly to Charlotte. In theory, she had become a lady of leisure since the servants were installed. In reality, she had never been busier because there was so much to do and all at speed. It was a pleasant relief to relax when they went to Twowatersfoot for Julia's wedding.

Mercifully for Charlotte, the visit was short. It was painful to think how nearly the joy transfiguring her friend's face had been her own. She put away such thoughts. Despair was not appropriate at a wedding. She would not look at Robert, nor let her thoughts dwell on him. At which, unbidden, her gaze was drawn to her erstwhile fiancé. As though aware of her glance, he turned his head and their eyes met. His face was impassive, revealing nothing, not even the smallest consciousness of his once cherished Charlotte.

No, it was not to be, she thought with an aching heart. School lay ahead. "Think of that," she muttered bleakly, as she later watched the new Mrs Tregodick drive off on honeymoon to Penzance.

***

However, when settled at Miss Lacey's Seminar for Young ladies, in Bath, Charlotte was most agreeably surprised. It was not at all bleak and she became accustomed to her new life with remarkable ease, after the first few homesick days.

For one thing, it was extremely pleasant to have the companionship of girls her own age; a pleasure so far denied her. For another, the tiresome lessons she had expected did not materialise. Lessons there were but they were a joy.

How could needlework be regarded as tiresome, or drawing? Whenever had the pianoforte been a bore; or deportment, when one was taught the art of graceful movement and the wearing of good fashion? Who could not enjoy dancing and learning how to hold interesting conversations? Further, what was more enthralling than to see the historic sights of Bath, and learn of King Bladud, the city's originator? Some of the older girls might yawn and protest languidly that it was all too boring, but not Charlotte Treleaven.

It was completely different from the restricted life she had known before, and she embraced each new experience eagerly, throwing herself into everything with such energy there was no time to brood over recent events. She allowed no leisure for thoughts of Robert, and if she sometimes cried with longing for him at night, no-one knew of her tears and she despised herself for them in the morning.

Gradually, as week succeeded week, marching into golden autumn, Charlotte achieved tranquillity, the aspiration to which she could not have contemplated when her dream world crashed in the blaze of summer. She no longer saw Robert around every corner, or thought of him in all contexts. His image was still clear and she could conjure it at will, if she chose, but the pain he had inflicted on her heart was still so deeply engrained that she could not think of him without hostility. Her senses might respond, involuntarily, to memories of him but it made no inroads on her antipathy. She could not forget his base deception.

However, truthful as always, when she began to acquire the town polish Mr Hattenbury desired for her, she saw, if only reluctantly, that his viewpoint on marriage between them was not totally unsympathetic. It did not excuse the brutality with which he had expressed the view but went some way to explain it. After all, he was a man of the world and she a gauche schoolgirl with everything yet to learn.

Additionally, Charlotte realised, without the training she was now undergoing, she would have floundered ignobly in the drawing rooms of polite society, and thereby diminished Robert's standing. She quite saw that he could not have welcomed this possibility. She would have managed better in Cornwall because the social life there was simpler, with *de rigueur* manners not so much in evidence; the country life, in fact. Moreover, knowing her, everyone would have made allowances for her youth.

Not so in London; she would have been judged as seen. In the metropolis, she would have been unfamiliar with the protocols of the social round. She would have found it difficult to run Meva House, the Hattenbury town residence, despite her experience at Crane, which had little relevance to that expected of Robert's helpmeet; just as he had so infuriatingly said! Her life would have been a trial and she was fortunate to have escaped the ordeal. Only a few short months in Bath had shown her this, and Charlotte no longer resented being sent to school.

Indeed, she knew she should thank Mr Hattenbury for his foresight, but thinking and doing were two different things. She might send home long letters full of her doings to the mamas and Julia, but letters to Robert were short and dutiful.

He was in Italy and Charlotte had not thought of writing to him at all when she arrived at school but, some weeks later, she received a letter from Venice, his first port of call. He expressed the hope that she was enjoying her new life or, at least, profiting by it. This remark aroused her ire at once but the irritation disappeared as she read further, for Robert went on to describe *La Serenissima*, indulging her passion for the historic and picturesque.

He wrote that Venice was made up of some hundred and twenty islands, joined by four hundred bridges, a number he had not checked personally (Charlotte's mind boggled) but saw no reason to doubt; and it was very wet, the city being no more than a foot and a half above sea level. The famous Piazza San Marco was frequently flooded. Native Venetians were obliged to go about their business with the waters swirling round their ankles, but they seemed not to mind; inured to it probably, he ventured to think.

Charlotte could see Robert's very expression as she read this, the curve of his smile, the sardonic glint in his eye, and could not help but enjoy his style of writing, in spite of her reservations. It was just as though he spoke to her. She wrote back rather later than was polite.

Robert next wrote from Milan, talking of Milan's cathedral, which had so many flying buttresses it reminded him, comically, of Tregothnan. He went on in this amusing vein for several pages more, which Charlotte enjoyed enormously. No more letters came for some weeks.

Meanwhile, there was a new arrival at school, a Miss Xanthe Dean, who was a year older than Charlotte. She was tall and blonde, almost the exact antithesis of Charlotte, which was probably why they formed an immediate liking that quickly blossomed into friendship. Apart from liking each other, and being new girls, they had nothing else in common.

Where Charlotte came from a small family, Miss Dean was one of eight, four of whom were older brothers. Her parents were political socialites, known for the brilliance of their entertainments. Other relatives shone with equal brightness, being able to count such as the Duke of Wellington as a friend. Two of her brothers, Hadley and Spencer, were in politics; Simon was in the army, and Philip was still at university. The younger children were either at home or school, according to sex.

To Charlotte, her new friend appeared sophisticated and dazzlingly self-assured. Charlotte wondered why she needed to be at school.

"I am at an awkward age," Xanthe explained, with cheerful insouciance, "too old for the schoolroom, but not polished enough for Mama's drawing room. She declares that unless one can balance plate and cup in one hand, whilst drying one's lips on a napkin, preparatory to holding forth to the charming young man at one's shoulder ~ he, incidentally, who thoughtlessly filled both one's hands and mouth with comestibles ~" she paused here to draw a necessary breath, before ending in a drawl, "unless one can do all this, my dear, one is simply not ready for the drawing room."

Charlotte was reduced to giggles by this animated description; Xanthe laughed, too. Then Charlotte explained that she was also at school to be polished off.

"You make it sound as though via the churchyard," Xanthe observed, which produced more girlish laughter.

"No, but I have lived secluded in Cornwall, and Robert thought finishing school necessary before my going into society," Charlotte explained.

"Robert? Your brother?"

"Again, no. I speak of my guardian, Mr Hattenbury. I have neither father nor brother; only one sister and she is married and resident in Scotland."

"No family? Oh, poor darling," Xanthe exclaimed sympathetically and gave her a hug, "you shall have a share in mine. So . . . your Mr Hattenbury is next in responsibility, is he? Incidentally, Charlotte," Xanthe paused, looking alert, "your Mr H would not chance to be *the* Mr Hattenbury, would he? It is an unusual name."

"What do you mean?" Charlotte asked, perplexed.

Xanthe looked conspiratorial. "Well, if it *is* he, your guardian is just about the most eligible bachelor in town, wildly fashionable, divine looking, and with mistresses by the *score*. They say he breaks hearts without even trying. Every match-making mama is on the catch for him."

Charlotte's face was a study as she listened to these artless revelations. Could this be their Robert of whom Xanthe spoke, her erstwhile dear companion? Had she really rejected the most eligible bachelor in town?

He was certainly beautiful and fashionable, and the mistresses seemed all too probable. Robert was so attractive many women must fall to his charm; as she knew from bitter experience. No wonder he hadn't wanted to marry her when he could have his pick of all these other, far more eligible women seemingly fawning over him.

"It is possible," Charlotte agreed, reluctantly. "Mr Hattenbury is certainly handsome and distinguished. He has blond hair, like yours."

Xanthe clapped her hands in wicked enjoyment. "It *is* he. Lucky you to have such a guardian. Well Charlotte, I shall assuredly cultivate your friendship now. Imagine how elated Mama will be if I managed to attache that darling Mr 'H'. What an opportunity; and I may be his type from all I hear."

Charlotte took Xanthe's teasing in good part, but the conversation gave her food for thought. "How come you to know so much about my guardian?" she asked.

"Darling, *everyone* has heard of Mr Hattenbury," Xanthe declared extravagantly. "He is so beautiful, and rich of course, there is not a drawing room from which he is excluded if he chooses; as with his papa before him. *He* you know was said to be the most delightful rake imaginable."

"Uncle Francis?" Charlotte was astounded. "But he died ages ago! You must still have been in the schoolroom then. What can you possibly know about him?"

"Oh, he is still talked of fondly when his son is mentioned. One hears that all the old ladies in town cherished a tendre for him at one time or another; and, of course, there is the *family*," she said knowingly. At Charlotte's look of incomprehension, she added: "The illegitimate offspring."

"Illegitimate offspring?" Charlotte echoed blankly. "Of Uncle Francis?"

"Yes, my dear. They are quite accepted, you know, although not everywhere naturally," Xanthe responded, very blasé, her manner and tone suggesting she parroted a phrase heard elsewhere.

"Do you know them?" Charlotte could scarcely believe her ears. What unthought-of revelations she was now hearing; and never a word of them at home, where, surely, they must be known!

"I have certainly *seen* some of them but, to be perfectly honest, that which I relate is mostly hearsay; although, from the way she speaks of him, and Papa frowns, I quite believe Mama also sighed over Mr Hattenbury's papa in her day."

"Your Mama?" Xanthe's continuing revelations left Charlotte stunned. "I am quite at a loss. Is Robert's family on every gossip's tongue?"

"Perhaps not to the extent I may have led you to believe. But, *this* much is true . . . that I, personally, know about Mr Hattenbury from my brother Hadley, who is a friend of Mr Knox, who, in turn, is a friend of your darling Mr H. They all move in the same social circles, you know," Xanthe looked mischievous, "which is how I come to hear some of the gossip about their paramours."

Charlotte ignored this very interesting aside for the moment. "My guardian is in Italy with Mr Knox," she said.

"Really?" Xanthe was diverted. "Then you know Mr Knox. What do you think of him?" Before Charlotte could answer, she went on: "He is, perhaps, a little old for my taste but with such dashing good looks; don't you think?"

"I have never met him," Charlotte said, when she could get a word in. Then, blushing slightly, she asked: "Do you know who is my guardian's latest flirt?"

"Oh, indeed, yes; it is Mistress Lerpiniere, who is utterly beautiful and with *such* a figure. Gentlemen swoon at the very sight of her and the ladies die of envy. She is married of course, but . . . you know . . ." Xanthe gave Charlotte a confidential 'nod and a wink' look, " she is one of the 'available' ladies. They say she has Mr 'H' at her feet," Xanthe sighed enviously. "Imagine, Charlotte, having the divine Mr 'H' at one's feet."

"Imagine," Charlotte echoed faintly, as she mentally relived a time when the divine Mr 'H' had been at her own feet, literally as well as figuratively.

From the preceding conversation, she had expected to hear something of the sort Xanthe related in regard to Robert, but to have one's suspicions confirmed, and to know the name of the lady in question, was a different matter. She felt sick. *'He has not taken long to find another love,'* she thought.

Xanthe was laughing, and speaking again. "My brother, Philip, calls her 'buxom Barbara' but his tastes do not run to the voluptuous. He prefers dainty creatures such as you. When we are out I shall introduce him. He will adore you, I know, and would it not be heavenly if we were sisters?"

Charlotte agreed sincerely that it would.

Shortly, they were called to the hall, ready for their weekly visit to the lending library and reading rooms in Milsom Street. Miss Lacey had previously explained: "While not appearing blue-stockings, young ladies must be au fait with what is current in the literary world. It also makes a pretty picture when a girl is seen, reposefully, with a suitable volume to hand. It is not absolutely essential to read the whole volume."

Walking decorously to the library, two by two, Charlotte was quiet, wondering if Robert had taken his inamorata to Italy. The pain of this thought was unbearable. *Voluptuous, was she? No wonder he lost interest in me,* Charlotte thought miserably. Tears stung her eyes but she willed them not to fall. Let him enjoy his fat ladies. See if she cared. Why, then, did she spend so much time later, looking into a mirror and agonising over her lack of curves?

When Robert's next letter arrived she viewed the pressed sheets with hostility; but once she began to read she found her usual pleasure in his literary style. He spoke of Florence, describing its many splendours.

"This is a most literate city. If one is unwise enough to be found gazing at the Palazzo della Signoria, even the waiters begin quoting large chunks of Dante at one. Imagine, Charlotte, Dante must often have seen the builders at work upon the Palazzo. Does this not make history more immediate?

"Incidentally, here is a little gossip for you. Were you aware that Dante only saw his beloved Beatrice four times in all, as with Petrarch and his Laura? I am inclined to Byron's view that we would have had less ecstatic poetry if Dante and Petrarch had not been the victims of thwarted passion; and I quote: 'think you if Laura had been Petrarch's wife, he would have written sonnets all his life?' The sentiment is somewhat cynical but truthful, don't you think?"

Reading this comment, which seemed hurtfully apropos, Charlotte experienced such bleak feelings she was obliged to put down the letter for a while. However, interested in spite of herself, she finished it later.

In her next letter to Robert, Charlotte mentioned Miss Dean, speaking of the connection they shared through Mr Knox.

Robert's reply came more quickly than usual, but Rome was described in very perfunctory fashion. He had seen St Peter's and the Coliseum, both enormous; the ruined baths of Diocletian left too much to the imagination; the Cemeterium and Catacumbas were gloomy. Robert's grumpiness may have been explained (Charlotte laughed to herself) by his following comment that Rome was so noisy he had scarcely managed to close his eyes in sleep since arriving!

Robert seemed more interested in discussing Miss Dean, saying he knew Spencer Dean well, and that if Charlotte liked her new friend, maybe she would care to invite her for Yuletide at Crane. If so, he would acquaint Miss Dean's parents with what was mooted.

Charlotte was delighted, as was Xanthe, and Mrs Dean was more than willing when approached by Mr Hattenbury on his return to England, looking tanned and fit, after an absence of three months. It was an unheard of accolade to receive an invitation for a family visit from Mr Hattenbury. Mrs Dean knew of no other young lady so distinguished. Additionally, Spencer Dean was invited for the festive season, and Charles Knox was also to come. It promised to be a lively party.

Large too, Robert discovered when his mother wrote to say Charlotte wanted to invite the Tregodick families, and that she, herself, had asked the Langfords to join them. He began to wonder what he had let himself in for by proposing the holiday, but reflected philosophically that it was too late to repine.

At all events, it would be a useful experience for Charlotte, allowing her to pursue a friendship with Miss Dean, who could then be a companion for her when they were out next year. To invite a select circle of town company would also give Charlotte a necessary taste of entertaining.

Incidentally, but no less important, he wished to keep himself in the forefront of Charlotte's mind. She had to be reminded that they were contracted. On a loose rein, ad interim, maybe, but it would be drawn in at the appropriate time. He still intended to marry Charlotte.

The three month sojourn in Italy had done Robert a great deal of good. During that healing time, his shattered self-esteem and sang froid were restored. He had also experienced a considerable change of view, vis-à-vis Charlotte. He no longer felt the alienation her antipathetic behaviour had roused at the unseemly termination of their halcyon summer. With hindsight, he saw it as a predictable reaction to his own questionable attitude. They had both been off balance and said unpardonable things to each other, but now he was confident of bringing his relationship with Charlotte to a satisfactory conclusion.

He was also more at ease physically in her regard, and could think of her without a clenched fist of tension knotting his stomach, his mind no longer flinching away from memories of his birthday. He did not actively court their return but if, as sometimes happened, vagrant impressions stirred him, he did not feel obliged to suppress them so rigorously. In point of fact, he realised, most of his aversion to marrying Charlotte had disappeared with the postponing of their nuptials. With one hit, his objections were demolished. Even before that, whilst still in London, he had decided that if Charlotte did accept his offer, he would take her to Jacinta, allowing time for the inevitable interest in their conjoining to die down. Already, he saw in retrospect, he had begun the process of adjustment.

That process was now complete. He had absorbed the unpleasant shock of self-discovery the whole course of events had given him, and now understood his previously inexplicable behaviour towards Charlotte.

It was as simple as this; he loved her, and was therefore vulnerable to a compulsion which had not existed before. Now, he saw, that from Charlotte's first inadvertent kiss, what happened subsequently had been highly predictable. First there had been the rapport of mind and companionship, followed swiftly by a physical desire for closeness. He had not recognised it initially because he had been too taken up with outward appearance and impression. Everyone at home had seen him falling headlong in love with Charlotte and found it perfectly acceptable. Only he had been blind; in more ways than one.

However, in realising this, he had discovered a profound truth; that burned bridges might make life hazardous, requiring a certain courage or foolhardiness, but they also brought positive relief. Translated into personal terms, it meant he could now think of Charlotte in any context, sexual or otherwise, without feeling guilty.

All things considered, he was content. Charlotte was growing and learning, if her letters were good indication, and a few months in society would enable her to take her place confidently at his side when the time came. Then he could begin his courtship all over again, but this time within the safe limits of accepted protocol. Truly, it had all turned out better than he had the right to expect. It had turned out very well.

Observe: Mr Hattenbury in sanguine mood . . . for a while.

Chapter Ten

Charlotte and Xanthe arrived at Crane Lodge, escorted by Spencer Dean and Charles Knox, on the Tuesday before Yule. Mr Hattenbury was already at home preparing for his guests. He, it was, who stood at the door to greet them. Charles and Spencer Dean got down first, to a barrage of benevolent hand shaking and back slapping. Then Xanthe stepped out, preceding Charlotte.

Robert welcomed Miss Dean warmly, agreeably surprised, as Charlotte was not slow to notice. Xanthe moved forward with her brother and Robert turned to offer Charlotte assistance. She put her hand into his and stepped down lightly.

"How good to be home, Sir," she remarked pleasantly.

Robert held Charlotte hand-fast and smiled. "Welcome home, my love," he said and raised her fingers to his lips.

Instantly, all Charlotte's hard-won poise deserted her. She snatched her hand from his grasp, her skin burning where his lips had touched. Her heart was bumping erratically, her body creaming with desire.

No! It could not happen again! One touch? Was that all it needed to make her tremble afresh? No, no! It must not be allowed to happen again. She would not fall victim to his charm a second time.

Heavens! What was she thinking? Only one kiss, and already the months at Bath might never have been. Mr Hattenbury was simply being polite. She should not read more than social grace into his behaviour. She had made that mistake before and at what painful cost?

But the months at Bath proved useful after all. Their training helped Charlotte to recover poise, concealing the inner turmoil admirably. “Thank you, Mr Hattenbury,” she said graciously.

Crossing the terrace to enter the house, she left Robert to look after her pleasurably. A smile lifted the corners of his mouth. He noticed, analytically, that his pulse had quickened, and he experienced a sudden rise in temperature which made nothing of the crisp winter air.

Inside the house all was excitement, as Charlotte was greeted ecstatically by her mama and Aunt Sophie, ‘darlings’ and ‘dearests’ sounding on all sides.

Xanthe Dean was not alone in noticing how Charlotte blossomed under the affectionate barrage. So did her brother. In the coach coming from Bath, Spencer had thought Miss Treleaven charming, if somewhat quiet. Now he saw her come to life, sparkling joyfully, and Mr Dean was not averse to being dazzled as he helped her off with her fur-edged, mulberry-colour Polish mantle. Sportingly, he also fielded her large muff.

Mr Knox performed the same service for Miss Dean before the company trooped into the drawing room, rubbing chilled hands and making polite conversation. Welcoming glasses of hot punch soon had hands and faces glowing. Shortly, the visitors were shown to their rooms and left to settle in until dinner.

Charlotte was accompanied to her room by the two mamas, who wanted to know all about her time in Bath, and to exclaim in surprise at the change in her. “How grown up, how smart!” they said in unison.

“It is still the same me underneath,” she assured them cheerfully, hugging both at the same time. “It’s wonderful to be home again. I *did* miss you, darlings. Tell me, is everything the same or all changed? Is Morley looking after my beautiful garden? Talking of which . . . oh, Mama, Aunt Sophie, you would adore the new parks at Bath. They are full of the most glorious monkey puzzle trees like the ones at Trebartha, with magnolia, cherry, and rhododendron in abundance. I have yet to see them in blossom, of course, but from the variety of species planted the parks must be a mass of colour in season. I’ve heard that the Sydney Garden is also beautiful in bloom.”

"Maybe we shall see them later, darling," said Mrs Hattenbury, her interest fairly aroused. "We must ask Robert to arrange a visit. However, enough of that. We have much better things of which to speak now. Come along, Alethea, let us act lady's maid to Charlotte."

"Oh . . . certainly, dear," responded Mrs Treleaven, a little flustered by Sophie's brisk tone but bustling about willingly.

By the time Charlotte was dressed for dinner, most of the urgent news had been told and there was still time for the older ladies to make their own toilette.

Charlotte descended to the hall. From the dining room she could hear low voices and the chink of cutlery. She made a way to the drawing room which, being empty, was quiet except for a crackling fire that lit the room with a cheerful glow. She sighed contentedly. Home again.

Looking about, she noticed how the familiar room had altered. The window drapes were new; missing crystals had been replaced in the chandelier; the ceiling plaster was repaired, and the upholstery recovered. There were pieces of furniture from Hattenbury dotted about. Everything looked fresher, and Charlotte thought happily that this was how she remembered it from earlier times.

Behind her the door closed. She turned, to find a smiling Robert watching her. "Do you approve?" he asked.

"It's lovely," she said contentedly. "I was thinking that this is how I remembered it when I was younger; or so I believe."

"I don't recall it precisely but I imagine you are right. I *do* know the mamas are happy living here together. It is they who made the alterations. From all I hear," he went on in amusement, so clearly it did not trouble him, "this is only the beginning. They are planning enough to keep them occupied for years to come."

Charlotte frowned. That sounded permanent enough to give her pause. "Should they be? Their living together is only pro tem, is it not?"

"Long-term, I would have thought," Robert corrected mildly. "You will not return here on a fixed basis, Charlotte, and it was always our parents' hope to live combined in their declining years."

"Why should I not return to Mama?" she asked, startled and wide-eyed.

"Because you will marry in the fullness of time, and take up residence with your husband." He crossed the space separating them and took her hands. "The husband I have in mind is me. Will you marry me, Charlotte?" Robert asked softly, giving her his heart-turning smile.

The touch of his hands set Charlotte's pulses racing. They were cool and as familiar as the scent of his body. She was suffused with glowing warmth, an awareness of Robert that made her long to be near him. The effort not to move closer was painful. She had to step back to prevent it, anchoring her hands at her breast to disguise their trembling. She hoped Robert would not notice how much he disturbed her, but once was enough. She would not be trapped in the mesh of his dangerous attraction again.

"Why do you keep proposing, Robert?" Charlotte asked, agitated, forgetting her practised formality towards him.

Robert did notice her trembling, of course. Aware of her in every fibre, how could he not? He also took pleasure in hearing her call him by name. She had not done so in a long while. "You know my reasons," he said.

"They are no longer valid," she objected. "You said we would go forward on a different course."

"Only as a temporary measure. Guardianship does not entirely discharge our obligation to each other," he countered.

"It does," she insisted stubbornly. "I do not wish to marry you. You do not wish to marry me. Why persist with so universally unpopular a scheme?"

"Charlotte Treleaven, what a little doubter you are," he mocked. "I fear you should have been called Thomasina. It is not unpopular with me, I assure you. No matter. When I convince you of my honourable intentions you may safely say yes."

Her head snapped up at his mocking arrogance and she answered him sharply. "Quite possibly, Sir," she said, her tone cutting, "but it will not be to you." Having retaliated, she would have turned away, but Robert caught her quickly and held her in a painfully firm grasp.

"Indeed? But have you considered, Miss Treleaven, that as your guardian I have right of veto in the matter of your marriage?" he asked softly, his blue eyes glittering dangerously. He gave a lazy smile and released her, giving no further indication of how accurately her thrust had struck home, leaving Charlotte to seethe with anger. When he spoke again it was on a different topic.

"I have arranged for you to meet the servants in the morning. The new staff will naturally wish to see you, and the established ones to welcome you home. There are one or two fresh faces which may give you a surprise. Mrs Penrose, the new housekeeper, is also anxious to receive your instructions."

Charlotte looked at him sharply, her anger overlaid by this new start. "Why does the housekeeper wish to see me?"

Robert feigned surprise, although well aware Charlotte had not been expecting this development. "You are accustomed to directing Crane, are you not?" he asked. "You will naturally continue to do so."

"Hold hard, Sir. Mama is the one to be consulted, not I," she rejoined.

"How so?" Robert raised his eyebrows. "She is conditioned to your being in charge," he pointed out. "It would be selfish to slough off your responsibility when the house is filled with guests. I cannot believe you capable of such unkindness, Charlotte. You must know that your refusing to take charge will completely spoil the festivities for Aunt Alethea. Her peace will be quite cut up. Forgive me . . . she is the sweetest creature in the world but not best fitted to have the ordering of the house at this time. No, Charlotte, it must be you," Robert said firmly.

As he spoke, Charlotte watched him intently. When he ceased, she felt bound to agree, although far from happy at the prospect.

"You are right, I suppose. I had not seen it in that light. However . . ." her chin rose on a challenge and Robert guessed, from quite a few past experiences, that she was about to deliver him a broadside, "do you really feel me competent to instruct the housekeeper? Only recently you pointed up all my shortcomings in this regard, Sir." That still rankled bitterly.

"Of course I think you competent," he replied mildly, "and Crane Lodge, being your home, must be directed as you will, regardless of my opinion. Additionally, your accusation is wrong. I never denied your competence in any sphere. I only pointed out a single inadequacy; your social inexperience, which is remediable. Incidentally, it pleases me to hear that my opinion counts with you."

He was at his most gently satirical; Charlotte could have slapped him. This was a course not open to her, but she was not yet done with him for all that.

"Mr Hattenbury, as your ward it is my duty to listen to you. That is not to say your opinions count for aught." She tossed her head disdainfully and Robert laughed with unaffected amusement, thereby arousing Charlotte's ire further.

"Oh, my adorable, venturesome angel, you do like to have the last word, don't you? So be it. This time I allow it but . . ." he dabbed a gently admonishing finger on the tip of her nose, "do not be *too* venturesome, will you? I might bite," he said softly, eyes aflare with provocation. Charlotte jerked away, bosom swelling with anger, and made no answer. "Come," he spoke caressingly, "cry truce. Our guests will descend shortly. Why not play the piano to welcome them? It will soothe your irritation with me at the same time."

Still eyeing Robert with cordial dislike, Charlotte went to do his bidding because there was truth in what he said, as was soon proved. Yet, when the anger passed, she was left feeling melancholy.

Was it always to be like this when she was with Robert? Would he always have the power to disturb her? Last summer, she thought he had killed all her feelings for him. Now she was not so sure. He had killed her love but not the physical attraction, she realised with unwelcome surprise. Part of the difficulty was that she knew him so well. If he chose to be caressing, as he *was* being, though heaven alone knew why, it would be fatally easy to let him under her guard again.

The thought horrified Charlotte. It must not be allowed to happen. She would do well to remember the last time she saw him, when he had been all coldness and chilling correctitude. That too was Robert, an aspect of him not to be forgotten. She must watch herself and be alert at all times. Alas, how difficult it made life when one was obliged to catch up on every thought and word; and where was it to end?

Robert still seemed to think they ought to marry. After the dreadful things he had said to her, the unflattering sentiments expressed? He might conveniently deny them now but she remembered, only too exactly, what he had said. It had destroyed all her respect for him, and any marriage not underpinned by respect was impossible. *He* might be driven to something he did not want, by considerations of honour or convention, but not she. What of the years of living together after the ceremony? How was that to be got through without mutual respect? How would it be possible to open her heart and mind to Robert again, knowing how he thought of her? Even to imagine it made her shrivel inside. She would not follow this course of action simply because he decreed it. It was still anathema to her and as far as she was concerned Mr Hattenbury could whistle down the wind.

The melancholy train of Charlotte's thought was reflected in her playing, as she presently became aware. She made an effort to change mood by changing the music.

Her efforts were helped by the admiration in Mr Dean's eyes, when he saw the charming picture she made, sitting at the piano and wearing a highly fashionable dress from the Ackerman's Repository collection, a gown of rose velvet which, with its close-fitting bodice, and décolleté neckline extending into beret sleeves, flattered her dainty bosom delightfully. When she stopped playing, Mr Dean came to the piano to compliment her on the beautiful gown and her glowing looks.

Charlotte smiled and thanked him demurely, thinking that Mr Dean had noticed the care taken with her toilette even if Mr Hattenbury had not. Thereafter, she devoted much of her attention to Mr Dean, while mindful of Miss Lacey's precept that one should endeavour to engage all one's guests in conversation at some time during an evening's entertainment; but this evening Mr Dean was her defence against Robert and she made full use of him.

***

Their party was unwieldy since they were seven in number, but the next day brought the Langfords and their niece, Mary Fleming, who had come to live with them after Julia's marriage. The newly-wed Tregodicks and the Tregodicks senior were also expected, bringing the full complement to fourteen, a number more easily seated at table; as Mrs Penrose remarked to Charlotte in the morning, at close of an hour going over the menus.

Before consulting with the housekeeper, Robert escorted Charlotte to the kitchens. There she met the servant retinue lined up to meet her and was amazed at the length of the line. Gone were the days of Megan and Minna alone, although the two girls were still there, beaming happily.

First to be introduced was Mr Penrose, the steward. Next to him was the footman, a familiar figure from Hattenbury House, and by his side a new under footman. They were followed by housemaids, upstairs and down, and two kitchen maids, plus Megan's sister Nancy, who had also come up from the big house. Next was the laundry maid, the dairy maid, and sundry other maids before, right at the end of the line, Charlotte encountered a small, dark-haired boy. Seeing him, she smiled widely.

"Hallo, Charlie," she greeted warmly. This was Megan's youngest sibling and Charlotte knew him well. "What is your job?"

"I do's the boots, Miss Charlotte," he replied with a grin.

"Do you like the job, Charlie?" she asked.

"No, Miss," he answered with cheerful insouciance and Charlotte laughed.

"Why not?" she wanted to know.

"Me arms bain't long ennuf to reach down 'em, Miss."

This practical answer brought discrete laughter from some of the servants. Charlotte laughed too, putting back her head to share the enjoyment with Robert quite naturally, as she would have done of old.

"Stuff the boot with dusters first, Charlie," Mr Hattenbury advised.

At close of the introduction ceremony Charlotte thanked the staff for their welcome, and they were dismissed about their duties. Leaving the kitchen with Robert, Charlotte asked how he managed to house all the domestics.

"With difficulty," he replied laconically. "I bought back one of the estate houses for Michael Penrose and his wife. Young Charlie goes home each day. Later, we plan to extend the servant quarters, but all in good time. This suffices for now."

Charlotte came to a halt and stared at him. "Where is the money coming from for all these additions, Sir?"

Robert touched her cheek lightly. "Later, dear heart. We cannot stand in the hall discussing finances with guests milling about. By the bye, you look charming this morning, but these gigot sleeves are the outside of enough, for they keep one at such a distance; a disadvantage; don't you find?"

"That rather depends on who the 'one' is, Mr Hattenbury," Charlotte replied, perfectly cool and composed.

"Not Mr Dean, of course," he murmured confidentially but with a wicked smile lighting his eyes; which remark made Charlotte self-conscious when Mr Dean engaged her in conversation at breakfast.

She forgot Robert's teasing later because she was busy looking to the comfort of the new arrivals. This took time because there was a mutual budget of news to catch up. There was also the introduction of Julia's cousin, Mary Fleming. She was a pretty girl but rather deaf. Introductions made, the guests were shown to their rooms. Julia lingered behind, her purpose being to share a small, but growing, matter of interest. Charlotte exclaimed with delight and kissed her friend.

"Julia! I am so happy for you. When is it to be?"

"Next July we think, but I'm not perfectly certain. We've told Richard's Mama and mine but no-one else, except you," she reported shyly.

"I am honoured, Julia. Now I shall set to and make baby's first layette," Charlotte said warmly. Julia looked amused.

"When will you have either time or energy for sewing, Charlotte? What with balls and late night parties, your eyes will be too dimmed to thread a needle."

"You underestimate my stamina, Julia. Mama says my energies have always been inexhaustible, and Mr Hattenbury that he feels enervated simply to watch me," Charlotte riposted cheerfully.

Looking contemplative, Julia said: "I always thought you and Mr Hattenbury would marry, Charlotte. I was surprised to hear you were his ward."

Charlotte coloured, looking uncomfortable. "Good gracious, no!" she denied emphatically. "Mr Hattenbury is quite above *my* touch."

Julia was not convinced. She knew her friend had been in love with him, no matter what she might say now, and he had returned her admiration, of that there was no doubt, but if Charlotte wished not to speak of it there was no more to be said.

However, at dinner, Julia noticed that Charlotte seemed more interested in an attentive Mr Dean, while Mr Hattenbury devoted his time to her cousin Mary. Julia also noticed Miss Dean quietly flirting with Mr Knox, but decided that was not her business either.

Bedtime was early that night in deference to the new arrivals. As a natural corollary, the house was astir at a correspondingly early hour next morning. Immediately after breakfast, the gentlemen decided on a rough shoot, walking up game with the dogs, which had been brought up from Hattenbury. Alas, though they were out nearly all day, they bagged only a brace of pheasant. This inadequate bag produced derisory comment from the ladies. The sportsmen excused themselves by saying the game had gone to ground because of a sharp hoar frost.

"What! All day?" Mrs Langford asked her husband, feigning surprise while clearly intending her comment for general hearing. "I declare, I had not noticed the fields still white after noon."

A gust of laughter greeted this sally, to which Mr Langford returned promptly: "My dear, if frost is not evident in the fields it certainly is upon your tongue, which is as sharp as a knife. Take care you do not cut yourself upon it," he advised jovially.

As might be expected, this thrust drew roars of laughter from the gentlemen.

Richard joined in the repartee. "I think not, Sir. After such an outrageous remark, I fancy that *yours* will be the first blood drawn."

"Quite so, for it is all bravado," Richard's mother put in. "Gentlemen are all much the same . . . brave as a lion in company, but who is to say that they are not more mouse-like at home?"

"I am afraid of mice," Miss Dean commented artlessly, with a mischievous glance for Mr Knox.

"Only because you are little acquainted with them, my dear," came Mrs Hattenbury's assured voice from the nether end of the room. "When you are, you will realise they are easily tamed. It takes but a modicum of resolution."

Throughout this banter Robert said nothing; he was observing

Charlotte. She sat opposite him, at the other end of the table, her eyes alight with amusement at the conversational exchanges. He watched her bend forward to catch a low-voiced comment from Mr Dean, who was at her left hand. They were too far away for Robert to hear what was said but he saw Charlotte laugh and blush faintly. He called out to her.

"Charlotte? Have you no contribution to make to this conversation? Judging by the sharpness with which you address me at times, I cannot believe you have nothing to add," he challenged.

She eyed him reproachfully. "Sir, why must you mention such regrettable lapses now, when Mr Dean has only just commented flatteringly upon my remarkable forbearance in the face of male provocation? Alas, I did not undeceive him; now you have exposed me."

"Charlotte," Robert exclaimed, equally reproachful. He tutted. "Do you tell me you were acting the sham?" he asked sorrowfully, with a touch of malice, only he knowing why Charlotte's eyes sparkled suddenly. Her reply was demure, however.

"I must confess that it was so, Sir. Such is human frailty, is it not? I wished to look well in the eyes of the world. Vanity! That is a consideration which would never move you, I am sure. You are too superior for such failings."

"You flatter me, Charlotte. Still, I am bound to agree with your last comment for I am a man and . . . are not all men superior?"

Affording much amusement, the light-hearted argument continued to fly back and forth, neither side giving ground. After dinner there was less talk and more action. The drawing room carpet was rolled aside for dancing, which went on until past eleven since all were enjoying themselves, so the tea tray was sent for much later.

During tea, Robert was heard to mention that he intended going down to Hattenbury the following morning. Xanthe claimed his attention

"Oh, that sounds delightful, Mr Hattenbury. Might we not make an expedition to your house, Sir? I am sure we would all be interested to see it."

"Certainly," he agreed amiably.

***

After breakfast, next morning, the party wrapped up warmly, there being another hoar frost, and trooped down the lane, stepping out smartly to keep the cold at bay.

They were first taken on a tour of the gardens and Miss Fleming exclaimed to see the pool frozen over. Charlotte wondered whether the lake was similarly clothed. Evidently Robert did too, because he suggested going to check.

He had wanted to accompany Charlotte on their walk but Miss Fleming fell to his lot. He noticed, with an amusement more wry than he cared to admit, that Mr Dean was recipient of Charlotte's dainty hand. The minx. She was thumbing her nose at him. But would she remember, as he did, that she had been in his arms for the first time at the lake? With equal clarity, he remembered the last time he had held her but closed his mind to that.

Robert devoted his attention to Miss Fleming, but as she was rather deaf conversation was necessarily loud, which was limiting, and he longed for the relief of Charlotte's agile tongue. It was not granted him.

He saw little of her either that day or the next, Saturday, which was Christmas Eve. Only when carriages were called out, to take them to midnight service, did Robert get within hailing distance of Charlotte. Then, by judicious arrangement, he sat beside her in the carriage.

Charlotte was very conscious of Robert's nearness as his body warmth began to permeate her mantle. He was equally aware of her, contentedly so. His brain had been sending out definite signals of need which her presence was satisfying. He could feel her and her scent was all about him; for the moment that was enough.

After service, no-one lingered because it was extremely cold. A spanking pace was set for home, and a warming punch before bed.

Breakfast on Christmas Day was followed by a further visit to church. As the day had warmed a little, the congregation exchanged seasonal greetings and news, when gathered at the lychgate after the service.

Mr Treloway peered at Charlotte short-sightedly, observing that she had grown. To Robert, he remarked: "It is unusual to see you at this time of year, Mr Hattenbury."

Robert replied "It is an omission I intend to repair in future." As he spoke, his hand descended lightly on Charlotte's shoulder.

The rector did not notice the proprietorial gesture. Charles Knox did and wondered at its significance, as he had wondered to see Charlotte hostessing Robert's table. Did it point in a certain direction?

He and Robert had been friends since school days, at Queen Elizabeth's Hospital in Bristol, and had gone through university together. They were not alike in looks or manner but their friendship was strong, Charles being one of the few people who had been allowed to see what lay beneath Robert's aloof exterior. It was this knowledge which had set him thinking.

He had been surprised when Robert did not join him in Brighton last summer. It was unlike him not to keep to an arrangement. Clearly, something of importance held him back, but Robert's letters gave no hint of things untoward. This intrigued Charles, making him suspect the influence of a lady, because Robert was invariably reticent in affairs of the heart. He was never one to discuss his love life.

Suspicion was laid to rest, when Robert told him he had been detained in Cornwall on business of wardship. At first a surprise, it was understandable when explained further. Thereafter the matter rested and it had not crossed Charles' mind again until now, when he had begun to notice how frequently Robert's eyes rested upon Miss Treleaven; not precisely lover-like, but with a certain un-guardianish consciousness. Interesting speculation, and the best of luck to Robbie if it were so. For his own part Miss Dean's charms held more allure.

Charles watched the lively young blonde, thinking that Spencer's sister had grown into a pleasant surprise, very pleasant indeed. She was still young, but that would not matter when she was brought out.

'Brought out.' For no good reason the phrase struck him amusively. It had overtones of a good port unexpectedly come to light; *'and no bad simile at that'*, mused Charles.

Meanwhile, the young lady who prompted his musings stepped into the carriage. Charles came to himself with a start, realising he had lost his opportunity to sit beside her. He found himself with Miss Fleming and reflected that it was as well. It would not do to single out Miss Dean too particularly.

***

Christmas Day dinner was put forward to two o'clock. This left the company free to listen to the carollers, who always came to sing at dusk, complete with coloured lanterns to lighten the gloom.

Robert, of course, was known to the carollers and was greeted jovially when he invited them into the hall for the customary mince pies and punch, followed by the giving of a monetary gift. After this the singers moved off to serenade other houses.

With their departure Crane Lodge assumed a somnolent air, everyone being slightly overfull of good meats and plum pudding. For some, the fire's warmth was an added inducement to a peaceful doze. Others played quietly at cards until tea was brought at nine. After tea they drifted off to bed in ones and twos.

Robert escorted Charlotte to the bottom stair. "I have scarcely seen you the whole day, Charlotte." He leaned forward and kissed her lightly. "Happy Christmas, dear heart. You will find a gift under your pillow," he murmured against her ear.

He returned to the drawing room without looking back. Had he done so, he would have seen Charlotte touch one trembling hand to the cheek he had kissed, the other to a breast disturbed by racing heartbeats. Why, oh why, must he be such a darling? It was much easier to dislike him when he was being horrid.

Under her pillow she found a gold filigree neck chain set with sapphires, the very colour of Robert's eyes. She fastened the chain about her neck, admiring herself in the mirror for long minutes. Then she fetched Robert's gift from her dresser. She had made him an embroidered, blue satin waistcoat.

Stroking the fine fabric, fingers tracing the embroidery, her mind returned involuntarily to previous times, the satin's touch evoking sweet memories . . . of Robert's magical lovemaking; the silken smoothness of his hot skin under her hands that birthday night; the acute ache of disappointment that he had not been made hers. Oh, how painful to dwell upon that lovely interlude; her body was on fire with a shameful hunger for its repetition; indeed, not just its repetition but its full completion. Oh, Robert, Robert.

Her indulgence cost Charlotte dearly. She ached with renewed longing for the golden knight of her dreams, a man who existed only in her imagination. That Robert was not real, she knew, and was ashamed of wanting him so passionately. She chided herself for fruitless agonising and resolved not to think of him again. If she could do that a peaceful heart must return, given time. She had to stop this foolishness, stop it instantly. Because Robert gave her a lovely gift was no reason to soften. It probably meant little to him, only one of many gifts he had given. She must show him how little it meant to her too. It was just another cadeau.

She rose decisively and took Robert's gift to his chamber. His valet took the parcel, assuring her that his master would receive it upon retiring. Charlotte nodded and returned to her own room, thinking that Mr Trevor was every bit as high in the instep as his autocratic master. They were a well-matched pair.

That night she wore her necklace to bed; it was a little like touching Robert himself; but she removed it before going down in the morning. She thanked Robert for his gift and saw him glance in surprise at her bare neck. He was wearing her present.

He raised his brows, and since they were not alone enquired softly: "Did my gift not please you, Charlotte?"

"It is beautiful, Sir," she replied truthfully.

"You do not wear it?" The rise of his brow was more pronounced.

"I will fetch it now if you wish," she offered dutifully.

"It is yours, to do with as you will," he answered shortly, annoyed by her equivocal responses, and hurt that she disparaged his gift; but there was no time for more.

Mrs Treleaven indicated that the staff was ready for the traditional Boxing Day gifts. Charlotte and her mama went to follow the happy annual custom of handing out fruits, nuts and money to all the servants.

Young Charlie was more interested in the comestibles. Prudently, Megan took his money in charge.

For the rest of the day Robert was sombre, withdrawn from Charlotte, which was a painful experience but not entirely new. It was salutary, helping to enforce her resolution. At holiday's end, when he showed no sign of relenting his coolth, Charlotte was glad to be returning to Bath. There was, however, one ordeal remaining before she departed.

On Wednesday after Christmas, the Langford and Tregodick families left for home. Charlotte and Xanthe were due back at school on Friday. Mr Dean and Mr Knox remained at Crane to provide an escort for the return journey.

The evening before departure, Robert told Charlotte he wished to see her alone. With guests in the house this was not easy to achieve, but eventually the spense proved adequate. The spense, a room peculiar to the Cornish, where the correspondence and lumber of many lifetimes was collected in the smallest possible space, held a leather-topped desk, and a chair which Robert cleared for Charlotte. He rested his weight against the desk edge and gazed down at her, his expression enigmatic.

"Before you return to school, Charlotte, I must compliment you on the excellence of your household arrangements. You did well and we all enjoyed the festival as a result. I know I speak for both mamas in commending you."

"Thank you, Mr Hattenbury. I did no more than my duty. The responsibility was mine, as you pointed out," she replied, as cool with Robert as he had been to her. He acknowledged her response with a slight nod of the head. Then he was silent, gazing at her. "Is that all, Sir?" she asked.

"Not quite," he replied, his face remaining impassive. After a moment he continued abruptly: "I caution you, Charlotte, not to encourage Mr Dean. It can only lead to his disappointment if you do."

Charlotte stiffened. "What *can* you mean, Mr Hattenbury?"

His answer was deliberate. "You know well what I mean. You have been flirting abominably with Spencer Dean, but you are not to lead him on. You are contracted to me. I advise you not to forget that." As usual, his apparent calm assurance infuriated Charlotte and she answered him sharply.

"I am *not* contracted to you, Sir! I am only your ward and that under protest, as well you know. Think what you will, I am not going to marry you, now or in future. I once made the mistake of thinking I wanted to, but only because I was too young to know better, as you yourself told me. Now I do know better. You may coerce me in some matters but you will not coerce me into marriage. It is the *last* thing I would contemplate . . . at least with you."

This hurtful and determined answer brought a savage look to Robert's face. Goaded by fear he reacted with anger and ground out: "You will do as you are told." His hand shot out and seized her crossed arms. He jerked her near and brought her face close to his. Charlotte's eyes dilated with shock.

"You are hurting me," she protested.

Robert was breathing hard, a maelstrom of emotion coursing through him. "Then do not ride me so recklessly," he warned. Without another word he kissed her, parting her lips and commanding her mouth as he would. When he let her go, Charlotte's breath came in gasping sobs. Blindly, she made for the door but Robert's arm reached over her shoulder to hold it closed.

She bowed her head. "Please let me leave," she whispered, shaking.

"No, not yet. You cannot emerge from here looking as though I have beaten you." There was a long pause. When Robert spoke again he was more controlled. "You must not push me so hard, Charlotte. I am not a man of iron, without feeling." One hand curved under her chin. He turned her face up to his, palm against her cheek. She found herself gazing into lustrous blue eyes, awash with emotions she did not recognise. Her own eyes were brilliant with unshed tears.

"Lead me and I will go wherever you wish, but do not goad me," he said softly, his mouth so close Charlotte could smell the sweetness of his breath. She knew he was going to kiss her again, but had neither the strength nor will to defy him further.

"Robert, why do you persist?" she whispered despairingly.

Robert's face was sombre. "Because I must," he said with careful emphasis. He did not tell Charlotte he was savagely jealous, or that her persistent rejection hurt and alarmed him.

Instead, he solicited her forgiveness with gentle lips and hands which caressed her tenderly; until treacherous senses betrayed Charlotte. She became murmurous and taut with love, her involuntary responses balm to Robert's troubled heart, an assurance that she was still his, despite all the harsh words she threw at him.

"Robert." Charlotte's carefully erected defences were breached entirely, in total disarray. Her trembling was renewed. She leaned back against him bonelessly, and he held her tight, one arm banding her body, a hand resting beneath her breast.

"Robert." She made soft, mewling sounds in her throat. He could feel them under his mouth. "Oh . . . Robert." His name was an unconscious plea, a plea she was not aware of making.

Gently, Robert unlaced her gown and lowered its beret sleeves, sliding them down her slender arms. The gown's bodice, perforce, came with them, and her bosom was rendered into his hands, the sweetly focused caresses leaving Charlotte mindless with hunger, aware of nothing but Robert, totally enthralled by his love-making. Starved of him for long months, she sought for his mouth.

A single movement turned her in his arms. Their bodies clung, each to the other, with Robert's strong arms lifting Charlotte so as to achieve the contact most urgent to both. Then, somehow, they were sitting, with Charlotte upon Robert's lap.

So it was that haughty Mr Hattenbury, who never bent the neck to any woman, bowed his head to Charlotte's breast for their mutual pleasure. Startled exclamations of ineffable joy escaped her parted lips, at the wondrous havoc Robert's mouth was creating and her hands crossed behind his head to hold him fast. Her mouth caressed his hair; she felt as though drowning in this, his first wondrous cosseting, its haunting sensitivity a thing which returned to her repeatedly later, remembrance tormenting her with echoes of heady delight, and a deeper, more fundamental need.

She was so enchanted, so blinded to all else, she did not understand at first when Robert desisted his lovemaking and murmured thickly, his forehead resting between her breasts: "Charlotte, I cannot sustain this. If I do not stop now, I shall not be able to stop at all. There is no Morley to come by this time. Charlotte?"

When she did understand what he was asking, becoming aware at the same time that beneath the skirt of her gown his free hand was being most shockingly intimate with her limbs, frissons of alarm jolted every nerve-ending. The enchantment began to fade and reality to step in. No! No, no! What was she doing? What madness had possessed her?

"No!" Her hands unfolded from his neck. "No, Robert. We cannot, we should not. It is not right!" She pressed down on his arms.

"For us it is. You are as ready to make the final commitment as I," he said, his arms holding firm. His breath fanned hotly over her skin, his mouth reluctant to leave the solace, the comfort and pleasure of her bosom, his body still tensioned with need; but when Charlotte continued to deny him he did not persist.

Although reluctant, he released her without demur, even though he was stretched and aching, because his heart was easy. Nevertheless he felt reassured, knowing from her responses that she still loved him, no matter what she might say. "So be it. I will not press you. But you *do* want me, Charlotte. You cannot say me nay to that."

Hearing him say this aloud, Charlotte knew she had betrayed her unmaidenly desires to Robert again, and shame swept over her. She covered her face and once more denied him. "No, whatever you say, it is not right."

For a moment longer Robert watched her broodingly. Then he drew a deep breath and said: "As you wish." He drew up the sleeves of her gown until they rested once more at the curve of her shoulder. He smoothed the lace-edged neckline over her breasts; he knelt at her feet to make her skirts decorous.

"How are the mighty fallen," he said, looking up at her, his lips twisting into a wry smile at the crumbling of his erstwhile pride. Then he rose gracefully and bowed over her hand. "Goodnight, Charlotte. Sleep well."

Chapter Eleven

It took weeks for Charlotte to overcome the effects of the last encounter with her guardian, and many a night she cried hopelessly into her pillow.

All the pain of summer was back, the outrage too, that Robert could tear down her defences so easily, with heartless disregard for her feelings, concerned only with enforcing his will. 'You *will* do as you are told,' he had said.

What kind of man was he to treat her as he did? One moment he was charming enough to melt the heart, the next he was brutally dictatorial. He *would* be obeyed, come what might. The slightest opposition made him exert authority with crushing savagery. And for what? Ironically, it was for a marriage he did not want. But *he* had made up his mind they must marry, and marry they would, entirely without reference to her own wishes. With frightening clarity, Charlotte saw there could be many more such clashes ahead, because Robert did not mean to give up. She knew that now.

So be it. Neither would she; not for anything. He would find his cruel jibe at her yielding to him, 'how are the mighty fallen', sufficient goad to stiffen her will. She would not fall again, and meant to dent his dictatorial complacency if it were the last thing she ever did.

Yet, Charlotte knew, it would not be easy. The Yuletide holiday had shown something unpalatable to her pride, revealing that Robert was still irresistible in caressing mood. His mouth, tasting faintly of brandy that last time, he in his person, was as persuasive as ever and he was right to say she still wanted him. Despise Robert she might, but he still had the power to sway her beyond the limits of discretion and even morality. No wonder he had such a reputation as a heart-breaker, but he would *not* break hers again. She would find the will to resist him if it took every ounce of her determination.

As with all journeys, however, she had to make a start. The first thing was to stop thinking of him and put all her energies into learning. She would show that snobbish man just how polished and well-bred she could become.

Xanthe noticed the determination with which Charlotte attacked every task and jokingly accused her of becoming a 'high riser'. "You will be dining at the palace in no time. Are you aiming for a Duke, or will a lowly Marquis do?"

Charlotte made a laughing disclaimer. "Neither. I simply want my guardian to be proud of me. I wish to be au fait with all social situations, so that when I marry my husband will admire my accomplishments and be fond of me."

Xanthe looked puzzled. "Charlotte, what a goose, you are," she said, hugging her affectionately. "Husbands are fond whether one is accomplished or not, otherwise who would ever find a spouse? At all events, you are already accomplished, silly creature. You play the piano divinely; sit a horse well; sew a fine seam and draw. As for your domestic talents, they are legion! My dear friend, you make the rest of us look positively *shabby*. Incidentally, I know a gentleman who is already impressed with you." She smiled mysteriously. "You may suspect who it is."

"I would not presume to 'suspect' any gentleman in this context," said Charlotte, smiling demurely. Xanthe ignored that irrelevance.

"I refer to Spencer, of course. He would make a splendid husband for you and you an excellent political hostess for him. He could try for a seat at Launceston, or Newport, which is in the Duke of Northumberland's gift I believe. Spencer knows him quite well, fortunately."

"How do you know all this?" said Charlotte, surprised at her friend's knowledge.

Xanthe explained: "I heard it mentioned when Spencer and your darling Mr 'H' were discussing the Reform Bill debate. My brother Spencer thinks the bill must get through eventually, despite having brought down the Duke last November because he would not put it through parliament then. It *has* to be a goer, apparently.

"Later, Mr Hattenbury laughingly told Spencer that Mr Brogden had been Launceston's member since the last century, and looked set to go on into the next, so Spencer should settle for Newport. I quite think that you, Charlotte, could do worse than settle for Spencer. Unless you have other plans of which I know nothing?" There was a plain enough hint.

"Plans?" Charlotte queried lightly.

"Yes. I fancied to see the teensiest bit of interest in that lovely guardian of yours." Xanthe's thumb and forefinger came together. "Think how convenient it would be. Your mamas already live together."

Charlotte shook her head and kept smiling. "I am not Robert's style and," she shrugged a shoulder, "convenience is not everything. Now enough of this nonsense, Xanthe, let's fetch our mantles and go to look at the crocuses," she ended crisply.

"Charlotte, are you quite mad?" Xanthe protested strongly. "There is a blanket of snow covering the garden!"

"Yes, but the snowdrops and crocus are showing through in the most cheering way. It is a sure auger for spring. Do come, Xanthe," she coaxed. "You know Miss Lacey will not allow me to go alone."

"Oh . . . if I must," Xanthe agreed grudgingly. "Any sensible person would keep close to the fireside in this bitter weather."

Charlotte laughed. "Think of our glowing complexions when we return."

Her friend remained unenthusiastic. "I prefer to be pale and languid."

"You?" Charlotte hooted in amusement. "That is the most ridiculous thing I ever heard. You are much too healthy and robust."

Arguing amiably, they went into the garden. True, it was cold, but Charlotte was heartened to see tender snowdrops struggling to push through their frozen cover. She knelt to lift the tiny heads clear of the crystalline carpet, smiling with pleasure.

"Get up Charlotte," Xanthe urged, "or your knees will be too rheumaticky to dance."

"Poetic justice, you could then say with perfect truth, as you observe me in my Bath chair, sitting among the wallflowers while you dance by."

Xanthe giggled at the picture Charlotte painted but her advice was sensible. The wind was blowing keenly from the South East and grey skies were leaden with snow. Temperatures had not risen above freezing for days past. The nights were really cold, and the girls were finding ice in their wash jugs on rising.

The weather was colder than anything Charlotte had experienced in Cornwall, where temperatures were several degrees warmer at all times of year. On the journey back to school she had noticed the temperature dropping considerably when they reached Exeter. By the time they arrived at the Old Down Inn, on the outskirts of Bath, it was snowing heavily, which made thoughts of school very welcome.

Going back into school now, Charlotte and Xanthe had time to warm themselves at the fire before the breakfast bell. After breakfast, letters were passed out to those whom the mails favoured. Then it was down to the serious business of the day, their mentor saying, with a genteel clap of the hands: "Now, young ladies, to work." There was no time to peruse letters until they stopped to drink a dish of soup at midday, which practice occurred only in winter. At other times of the year no refreshment was taken between breakfast and dinner.

This was most unwelcome news to Charlotte when she first arrived at school. They were much heartier trenchers in Cornwall, and she was accustomed to having an informal meal at midday, the interval between breakfast and dinner being too long for those passing their day in strenuous labour. To discover Miss Lacey's establishment did not serve a meal that her mother called luncheon came as a distinct shock, only slightly alleviated by the news that dinner was served earlier, at five o'clock. It was still a long interval, however, and the bowl of soup was very welcome, as was the opportunity to read letters.

Charlotte had two letters from home; the first from her mother, the second from Aunt Sophie. So far this term there had been no communication from her guardian. She knew he was still in Cornwall and still, it seemed, directing their affairs. In different style, both letters related that Mr Hattenbury was bringing the two mamas to Bath prior to Charlotte's birthday on February the fourteenth. They would stay at the White Hart hotel for a few days before travelling to London, where Charlotte was to join them after Easter.

This news was delightful to Charlotte, but it also caused some apprehension since her guardian would, of course, be with the mamas. What if he proposed again? How could she cope with it? Her heart sank at the thought.

She could not go through another such as that last scene with him. It had left her drained and utterly miserable, because it seemed that no matter how spiritedly she opposed him, he always won the day by some means. In truth, the more spirited she was, the more determined he became to crush her. Only when she had been overborne did he show his gentler side.

'Lead me but do not goad me,' he had said. What he meant was 'do not oppose me'. But he must be opposed for she could not, and would not, marry him. She had gone his way too many times before and it led to heartbreak. Was she to spend the rest of her life on a dreadful seesaw between Robert's approbation and his anathema, simply because he said so? No, no! She neither trusted nor respected him, and would die an old maid rather than be forced into this spurious contract of Robert's proposing. She *would* recover from her feelings for him because she *meant* to.

However, after nearly a sennight, during which Charlotte's mind was much occupied with her guardian, she began to feel better. She had thought about Mr Hattenbury's advice, that he might be led where he could not be pushed, and began to believe that light-hearted persuasion could prevail where spirited opposition had not. With this in mind she planned accordingly, determined that 'darling Mr H', as Xanthe called him, was not to have everything his own way this time.

Of course, Mr Hattenbury had other ideas.

***

Several days before her birthday, Charlotte was called to Miss Lacey's room and informed that she had been granted the privilege of a birthday outing at her guardian's request. She was to be ready at twelve o'clock on the appointed day.

"Lucky you," Xanthe commented blithely. "I, too, would admire to spend the day with Mr Hattenbury. What shall you wear?"

Charlotte cast a mind over her wardrobe. "My crushed raspberry velvet will be suitable, I think."

"Yes, it suits you divinely, and Mr H will love it."

"I meant for warmth," Charlotte said repressively, but Xanthe was unrepentant.

"One need not object to being fashionable as well as warm."

Charlotte tried on the dress on Tuesday, turning to the mirror for a critical side view. It fitted perfectly, high-necked, tight-waisted and bosom-shaping, with a beautiful flowing skirt. Alas, nothing short of padding could add to the sum of inches inside the gown. She sighed and continued her toilette.

Exactly at noon, when Charlotte and Miss Lacey were sitting composedly in the reception room, a carriage was heard. Shortly, Mr Hattenbury was shown in. He bowed gracefully over the principal's hand and expressed his thanks for his ward's day of freedom.

Miss Lacey inclined her head graciously, as befitted a respectable school principal, but heightened colour revealed that she, too, was not immune to Mr Hattenbury's charm. "Not at all, Sir," she said, and drew her pupil forward.

This was a tacit signal for Charlotte to go through the oft-rehearsed paces of a polite greeting, so that her guardian could observe for himself the value and efficacy of Miss Lacey's training.

Charlotte performed perfectly, her curtsey of just the right depth, the extension of her fingertips at precisely the correct angle, the warmth of tone and expression exactly what should be accorded one's guardian. In the event, Miss Lacey's expectant smile was entirely justified.

Mr Hattenbury's answering smile was tinged with amusement, but he nobly commended them both, very much in his guardian's manner.

"My dear Miss Treleaven that was beautifully executed. It shows how well you have benefited from the excellent tuition on offer here."

"Thank you, Guardian," Charlotte murmured dutifully, just as she ought, and was told to run and fetch her mantle.

When she returned, Robert and Miss Lacey were conversing in the hall. Seeing Charlotte descend the stairs, the principal bustled forward to straighten her bonnet a smidgen. She did not actually remind her pupil to be good, but it was implicit in her matronly attitude.

Charlotte was handed into the carriage; Mr Hattenbury climbed in after her; the door was shut and away they went: upon which Robert's avuncular manner dropped from him like a cloak.

"Hallo, darling, darling, Charlotte," he said softly, and smiled, his eyes asparkle.

"Hallo, Sir," she replied with a collected smile of her own. "Where is Mama and Aunt Sophie? I expected to see them with you."

He continued to observe her for a moment, examining every feature of her face, as he went on smiling his lovely, lazy smile. It was as though, seeing her, he could not stop his mouth curving with pleasure. She would be foolish to believe that, of course, though it might once have been.

"They are taking the waters," he said eventually. "Now *that* has surprised you, I warrant," he added with an attractive flare of sparkling blue eyes.

Charlotte *was* surprised and could not help laughing. "What on earth for? Neither suffers from the rheumatics or gout."

"No-one who drinks your mama's wine could possibly contract gout, Charlotte, no more than a confirmed teetotaller," he replied with feeling, and she laughed again, beginning to feel alive and full of birthday joy.

"Now that is unkind, Mr Hattenbury, since you know that I make most of Mama's wines," she reproved cheerfully.

"Yes," he agreed musingly, "which ought to make them taste like nectar. I wonder why it does not?"

She took him up promptly. "Because, Sir, the situation here is similar to the circumstance of 'beauty is in the eye of the beholder', in which case one sees with the inner eye what is not apparent to others. Now, Mama thinks my wines delightful because she expects them to be. On the other hand, you, Sir, have no such expectation and so are disappointed," she expatiated wisely, straight-faced.

Robert's rejoinder was immediate and pithy. "Rubbish!" he asserted. "What you mean is that Aunt Alethea's palate is uneducated."

"Well . . . yes," Charlotte agreed demurely, and they both collapsed with mirth.

"Oh, Charlotte, my dear heart's darling, how much I have missed your nimble tongue," he said caressingly, when they were more sober and he could speak again.

"Only because of your immurement in the country, Sir, but when you are back in London's social throng you will be in your own element again," she replied lightly.

This he denied vigorously. "No. My sentiments are not mutable, Charlotte . . . ah, no!" His eyes lit appreciatively and he laughed hugely, so great was his pleasure in her. "I see what you are about! What a slow top I am. *You*, of course, will be part of that throng. Oh, Charlotte, you are adorable." He leaned forward as though to kiss her. Unwisely, Charlotte's heart leaped in anticipation. Fortunately, he did not.

"Mr Hattenbury!" she exclaimed, blushing, and not only from his teasing. Heat from the pleasure of Robert's nearness was creaming through her, but admirably concealed. "How could you think me so vain? I would not dream of making such an allusion. What *would* Miss Lacey think of me? Fie on you for teasing me. Let us change the subject if you please."

Charlotte's demure expression made for indulgence. Indeed, Robert was so pleased to be with her she could have asked anything of him that day. "Granted, my heart's darling, since, as always, it is my aim to please you."

"Charmingly said, Mr Hattenbury. I could quite think you one of Miss Lacey's star pupils," Charlotte responded dryly.

They continued their lively badinage until reaching the spa, where Robert was seen to be in excellent spirits by the two mamas. They saw him leaning over Charlotte in his old, absorbed way, while she looked upon him with attentive warmth. The former happy rapport between them seemed obvious.

Sophie and Alethea exchanged speaking glances when they beheld their offspring. Each knew the other's mind but the moment was inopportune of comment, and soon overlaid in pleasure at seeing their darling Charlotte again. Happy birthdays sounded and kisses were exchanged on all sides.

"Thank you, thank you. Oh, darlings, how lovely to see you again. Now, tell me, what is this I hear of you taking the waters? I could not believe my ears when Mr Hattenbury told me. Are you both in fading health?"

"No, dear, of course not, but it is frightfully fashionable. Shall you try some?" her mother asked. "It is extremely good they say, and that must be true because it tastes quite horrid." Mrs Treleaven looked to Sophie for confirmation of this remark.

"On the assumption that all things bad are good for one and vice versa, I presume," Robert observed mockingly.

"Naturally darling, everyone knows this to be a universal truth," his mama agreed with comfortable assurance. "If you are enjoying something it is almost certainly not good for you."

Robert laughed. "Be that as it may, I intend to enjoy my dinner and, equally, I intend not to drink that abominable liquid. Make what you will of that. Shall we go?"

Half an hour later they arrived at Round House in Kelston, the home of Charles Knox's parents. The house was so called by reason of its proximity to Kelston Round Tump, an ancient promontory with a fine stand of trees at its crown.

The visitors were warmly welcomed and sat talking and drinking coffee with their hosts for a good part of the afternoon. Charles was not at home but his married sister, Amaryliss Norris, was staying with her family for the birth of her first child. On this account she had been unable to travel with her husband, James, a diplomat who was presently abroad.

Charlotte was struck by Robert's tender manner towards Mrs Norris, and her heart contracted jealously, just for a moment. When she spoke to Mrs Norris a little later, Charlotte mentioned their mutual acquaintance, Miss Dean.

"Xanthe has lately grown up, my brother tells me. He appeared quite taken with her but I could be mistaken. I would have thought her too much the ingénue to appeal to Charles," Mrs Norris said.

The remark was not malicious, but it gave Charlotte food for thought. "She will be seventeen after Easter," she pointed out.

"And comes from a family politic, so Charles' interest may not be so unusual, when one thinks a little. I should like to see her again. Possibly, something can be arranged before I become too elephantine to move," Mrs Norris said, with a rueful glance at her figure. Charlotte promised to pass on the message.

Shortly, the visitors took leave. Before their departure Mrs Knox pressed them to come again, suggesting that the two mamas might stay for a few days, on their way up to London, a suggestion which was taken up with great pleasure.

***

Mr Hattenbury's carriage arrived back at the White Hart at five o'clock. The three ladies retired to repair their toilette before sitting down to an excellent table.

"Even the wine is tolerable," Robert averred, with an oblique glance in Charlotte's direction. She was still in sparkling mood, such was the effect of the indulgent encouragement she received on all sides.

Watching her contentedly, Robert noticed how well she was responding to his overtures. He felt happier than he had done for some time; he very much liked having Charlotte's attention to himself.

After dinner he dropped the bombshell.

So far, no mention had been made of a birthday gift from Robert. Charlotte received a handsome shawl from her mama and a gold locket from Aunt Sophie, one she had been given on her own sixteenth birthday. Now, Mr Hattenbury withdrew a small box from an inner coat pocket and snapped it open. The two mamas watched with interest when he extended the box to Charlotte. Inside, nestled a ring of dainty sapphires in a gold filigree mount, an obvious match for the necklet he had given her at Yuletide.

On first seeing the box, Charlotte's heart began to thump alarmingly, thinking Robert was about to make her a declaration. *In public*, she wondered incredulously? The heavy thump subsided when she saw the sapphire ring and realised her mistake. This, clearly, was not a betrothal band.

"How beautiful, Sir," she exclaimed. "It is a match for my lovely necklet." She reached for the box but found her hand stayed by Robert's. He delved into his pocket once more.

"That is no more than a trifle, Charlotte," he said, with a nod towards the first box. "This is what I really wish you to have of me."

The second ring was a blaze of diamonds, flashing brilliantly in the candle light. Charlotte's heart thumped anew and she blushed crimson. Startled eyes flew to Robert's face. He smiled and spoke again before she could utter a word. "Charlotte, will you be my wife?" he asked.

"No, no, Robert!" She was all beautiful, rosy confusion, adorably so, thought all three persons watching her. She withdrew her hands and pressed them to flushed cheeks, scarcely knowing where to rest her eyes. "What are you thinking of, to speak of this here?"

He answered without a moment's pause: "Of the old adage, 'he who would the daughter win, must with the mother first begin'. Since I have two here to support me, I thought . . ." with a laughing catch to his voice he allowed the rest of his remark to hang in the air. He turned to Mrs Treleaven, giving Charlotte a space for composure. "What say you, Aunt Alethea? Don't you think this would be a splendid match?"

"Oh, Robert, dear, yes, I do," Alethea replied earnestly. "There is nothing in the world I would rather see, as you are aware, but if Charlotte . . . if Charlotte . . ."

Mrs Hattenbury made an interpolation to rescue Alethea. "Robert, darling, you are behaving quite sans-gêne, you know. Charlotte is dreadfully embarrassed."

"You don't think it a good stratagem to bring the big guns to bear? And it does, of course, save me the task of relaying all the relevant information to you both at a later date. Very tiresome that." He turned lazily to Charlotte. "What do you say, my dear, lovely Miss Treleaven?"

Charlotte was more composed, the hectic flush in her cheeks dying down, and she was able to reply in a reasonably collected manner. "I thank you for the honour, Guardian, but I cannot marry you."

"Why not?" he asked coolly, not looking at all put out. His casual tone annoyed Charlotte. She was obliged to remind herself not to become embroiled in confrontation with Mr Hattenbury, particularly not in public.

"I am much too young and silly for you," she said lightly, "not at all a suitable wife for so elevated a gentleman." There, she thought with satisfaction, that was carrying the war back into his camp, and she was only repeating what he said to her last year, after all.

"Is one permitted to offer comment?" Mrs Hattenbury asked. With a graceful wave of the hand, Robert indicated that she might. "In that case, Charlotte, if suitability is your only objection to marrying Robert, I am bound to say that I believe you are wrong. It is apparent to me, and your mama, that you are eminently suitable."

"Oh, it is true, dear," Alethea agreed earnestly. "I always thought that."

"Yes, and I know why," her daughter replied. "You are both biased in my favour, but what about poor, darling, Mr Hattenbury? Is he to go through life saddled with a liability simply because it is advantageous for us?"

Charlotte turned to Robert, smiling and calm-faced, although far from calm inwardly. "I see what you mean about the big guns, Sir. You were very wily."

"Not successful, though," he observed with cool regret, concealing his disappointment. "Incidentally, my dear liability . . . I only quote you, please note . . . if anything were needed to make me think twice about marrying you, it would be your last ill-advised speech. I never heard such rubbish in all my days." He was laughing at her in his inimitably annoying way. Charlotte's irritation began to surface.

"In speaking of marriage, Sir," she observed, assuming a thoughtful air, “if you *are* bent on it, you could do worse than look to Miss Dean. From hearsay, she is more to your taste than I, and just think how angelic your offspring would look, with both of you having blond hair.”

Robert’s deep blue eyes widened, holding an arrested look. When he spoke it was with great deliberation, and he effectively silenced Charlotte, their mamas also.

“My dear Miss Treleaven, I cannot imagine what you have been hearing ~ by the bye, sweet heart, should one listen to gossip? ~ but allow me to tell you that, angelic or not, my sons will be yours or no-one’s.” His lips curved to a gently sardonic smile, and Charlotte was very glad, suddenly, that they not alone.

He closed the lid on the diamonds. “For the moment let it be the sapphires,” he said.

There it ended. Nothing further was said until they were in the carriage returning to school. Wardship having some privileges, Robert was once more alone with Charlotte, she sitting circumspectly in a corner opposite him. When the carriage stopped Charlotte waited for Robert to hand her down. He did not do so immediately. Instead he watched her, but in the half light she could not make out his expression. He came to sit beside her and took possession of her hands.

“Charlotte . . . look at me.”

“There is little point, Sir. I can scarcely see you in this dark,” she objected. Nevertheless, she conceded a small turn towards him.

Robert gave a sigh. “Shall you never willingly do as I ask?”

“You do not always ask, Guardian. Often you constrain.”

“As you say, Charlotte,” he acknowledged, adding softly, “but this time I am petitioning you.”

“For what, Sir?”

There was a tiny pause, and then he said: “I am hungry for the taste of your lips. Will you kiss me, Charlotte?”

She denied him instantly. “No, I will not.” ‘*No, no, never again,*’ Charlotte thought. *‘It must not be. Let there be no more talk of hungers. I will not listen.’*

Robert drew breath harshly. His hands tightened over hers, and Charlotte fully expected him to override her rebuttal, bending her to his will as always. She felt the impulse, the air between them vibrating with tension. Mr Hattenbury did not care to be thwarted.

There was a very long moment of silence before Robert let out his breath. Broodingly, he gazed at this slip of a girl, little more than half his age, she who had him in thrall, whose smiles or frowns held the power to dispose his happiness and dictate all his actions.

He was, it has to be said, almost resentful of her sway over him, as he recalled the insouciance with which he had bedded a good many women over his adult years: but none, he acknowledged, had touched the central core of who he was as Charlotte did, or made him feel incomplete without her. Yet, resentful or not, here he was, pleading for a single kiss, he, who usually commanded! What now of his vaunted independence, his need to be inviolate, or his self-satisfied ability to charm?

Infuriatingly, Charlotte seemed to best him at every turn, and though he knew it was his to bend her to his will as he decreed, both physically and legally, he had the feeling that even if he did, she would remain shiningly beyond him.

That had not always been so. He had once known the joy of basking in her adoration, but that happiness had been lost to him by foolish pride, and he now had only cold comfort in exchange.

Robert had the nastiest conviction he had been an idiot in his dealings with Charlotte last year; that his present predicament was his own fault entirely. To know this was cold comfort indeed, as he realised that, once again, Charlotte had brought him uncomfortably face to face with himself.

So strong was the feeling of need for Charlotte, he felt urgent to press his face between her breasts, and plead with her to comfort him; only pride held him back.

Had he sent his pride to the devil, he might have saved himself months of despair, but pride had not yet done with him. Perhaps, therefore, he needed to know despair for his soul's sake.

Finally, he spoke. "It seems not to occur to you, Charlotte that last summer was a shock for me, also. You slapped my face; you called me shabby, and rejected my proposal, all in the space of five minutes! I have never been so insulted in my whole life! Of *course* I was discomposed. What did you expect? You cannot challenge everything a man believes himself to be without expecting *some* repercussions."

From pathos to bathos: Robert's recital of his woes made him sound like an aggrieved child who has lost his treats. Charlotte burst into giggles.

"*Now,* in addition, I am risible to you," he exclaimed, affronted.

"No, Sir, oh no," Charlotte gasped, still giggling. She leaned towards him, pressing his hands lightly, drawn in spite of herself, by an instinctive need to console him and smooth his ruffled feathers. "Please forgive me. I am not laughing at you, only the amusive way in which you spoke. I *am* sorry." She was still having trouble suppressing the cascading laughter.

"Humph!" he said. The affront subsided, but he could not raise a smile. However, as conscious of Charlotte as she of him, he registered her softening, and asked: "Will you not relent and kiss me?"

"No." Charlotte reiterated. Kisses with Robert always led to less innocent excursions, and she had willed never to follow that path again. To do so when she had thought he loved her was, if not morally defensible, at least, understandable. To do so without love would be shameful sin.

Robert sighed, recalling that Charlotte had rejected his proposal with that single word. He pressed a lingering kiss into her palm, the tip of his tongue tasting her, caressing her skin, and Charlotte's emotions underwent an abrupt change.

"Might you not be more forgiving if you thought on what I have said?" he asked broodingly.

***

That night, Charlotte could not sleep for thinking of it, but her reflections led nowhere. For a wild moment she thought . . . well, what had she thought? She scarcely knew and, not being privy to Robert's thoughts, was afraid to conjecture. She had been wrong too many times before. He was so difficult to understand.

But . . . suppose his enigmatical phrases meant . . . did he mean to imply that . . . oh, if only he would be plain! And what was *his* shock? Her rejection? But he had not said he was pained by it, only that he was insulted, no doubt expecting her to fall on his neck in gratitude that he deigned to offer for her at all! His pride was hurt, that much was certain, but that was all. Yet, he *had* wanted to kiss her.

Perhaps, she *could* bring him back to her, if she wanted to . . . but, then, it still did not mean that he loved her, did it? Want was not love. And if he did not love her, the situation remained unchanged. Or . . . maybe he would come to love her in time. Perhaps, after want came love, and . . .

Round and round went the thoughts in Charlotte's head, toward and froward, until she developed a headache, but had still found no solution. Finally she concluded, sighing, that Robert was only using a different way to pursue the same end, to whit: bending her to his will. As the commitment he cherished, in spite of everything, was all on his side, and she no longer loved him, it really made no difference.

Yet . . . he *had* accepted her denial this time. He had allowed her to choose.

In the morning Charlotte looked wan and dispirited after a sleepless night, but was cheered by a visit from the two mamas. The following day Miss Lacey allowed Charlotte and Xanthe to take tea with the Cornish visitors. By this time Charlotte was more herself, able to view the departure of her dear ones with equanimity, and remark, with only slightly counterfeit cheer, that their reunion in April was not far off.

As it happened, she spoke no more than truth. Once settled to work again the time flew. She even wondered whether the sum of school days left was sufficient to accomplish all that she wished; but by the time Miss Lacey's farewell speeches were being made Charlotte knew herself to be a very different person from the confused and unhappy girl who had arrived at school in September.

She also saw a measurable difference in Xanthe, although she had seemed so sophisticated initially. Now, Charlotte recognised, she moved with greater assurance and poise. The same could be said of herself.

Miss Lacey had richly fulfilled her promise to make ladies of her pupils. Mr Hattenbury's money had been well spent.

***

Both Charlotte and Xanthe were posting up to town, so what more natural than that they should travel together? First, they visited Kelston for a few days.

Mrs Norris had kept her promise to call on Xanthe at school, and letters had been flying back and forth ever since. The visit now underway promised to be enjoyable, because Mr Norris' younger brother, John, and his sister, Andrena, were also visiting Kelston, as was the elder of Xanthe's political brothers, Hadley. Being a particular friend of James Norris, who was now home from abroad for the birth of his child, it had been appropriate to invite Hadley as he could then provide an escort to London for the girls.

The visit was fortuitous for Hadley in another way. He cherished a penchant for Miss Andrena Norris, which Charlotte and Xanthe were not slow to notice. "Mrs Andrena Dean! It does not sit well at all, does it?" Xanthe whispered naughtily, rolling an eye at Charlotte, and was quite properly hushed for her pains.

Further, Hadley was interested to meet Charlotte, of whom his brother had spoken at length. Meeting her, he could see why she had aroused Spencer's interest. She was just such a lively girl as would attract him, but she was also rational and had careful assurance. Too many young women were without sensible conversation; but Miss Treleaven was not of their ilk.

One could envision her entertaining Spencer's intellectual friends with ease. This was an important consideration for men such as Spencer and himself. They could not be wholly free of choice if wanting to advance in the political sphere. In his own case, fortunately, he believed he had found the ideal.

Hadley's eyes travelled over Miss Norris appreciatively, observing the sway of her skirts as she glided over the parkland. She walked with her brother, another young man destined for the diplomatic service, although not yet old enough to take an active part. Evidently, he was not too young to enjoy feminine charms.

John Norris was enjoying himself hugely, in the company of two ladies as diversely entertaining as Miss Dean and Miss Treleaven. Acting as a foil for each other, it was difficult to know which one preferred. Better to enjoy both equally, he decided; which goes to show how very well suited he was to his chosen profession.

Soon, it was time for the London bound party to take leave. Bowling along the Marlborough road towards the capital, Xanthe sighed contentedly. "Home, Hadley."

"Not for long if Mama's plans come to fruition," he remarked.

Chapter Twelve

In London, the two mamas awaited Charlotte's coming impatiently. They were not alone in this. Robert, too, longed for her coming; he had so missed her, the weeks since he last saw her having passed excruciatingly slowly in spite of busy preparations for the season ahead. Life without Charlotte now felt incomplete to him, and he keenly anticipated her arrival on the appointed day, Thursday the fourteenth of April, two months exactly since her birthday.

The evening of the thirteenth Robert dined with the Styneleys. Gerald, Lord Styneley, the Marquess of Hinton, was known to him through their club and shooting at Manton's. He also knew Styneley's scandalous cousin, Lord Darel John, who held the Barony of Fittleworth, and had often seen him about town before he settled to domesticity last year, with a beautiful new bride.

Of Styneley's wife, Lady Caroline Styneley, Robert had known little previously, only becoming better acquainted with her through their recent, mutual interest in the debutante rounds. This year, Lady Styneley was bringing out the second of her Yorkshire nieces, Miss Mary Williams, younger sister of Emily, the new Baroness Fittleworth, daughters of her long-dead and still mourned sister, Barbara.

Robert found the Marchioness charming, in a stately fashion, and not lacking in sal atticum, but she was a little repressive for his taste. Notwithstanding, they would be useful to each other in the coming months, their common interest providing ground for communication.

Speaking now to her ladyship, Robert accepted an invitation for Charlotte, the mamas and himself to join a river boating party the following week. He, in turn, extended an invitation to Charlotte's first soirée.

Shortly, there were sounds of further arrivals. Lady Styneley excused herself and went to greet her other guests. Robert glanced at the newcomers and found himself staring straight into the limpid green gaze of Mistress Lerpiniere.

He saw her draw a full lip down over perfect teeth in a familiar, provocative gesture, before greeting Lady Styneley. At Barbara's side, unusually, was her husband, a Huguenot, whose family had come over from France at the time of the persecution. As her husband bowed over the hand of their hostess, Barbara cast another smiling glance at Robert.

Against his will he was stirred. It was the first time he had seen his erstwhile paramour since last summer and he saw that her beauty was undimmed. Her breast jutted as proudly, her mouth was as inviting and her eyes held the same promise.

Sardonically, Robert thought that his reaction betrayed how long it was since he had last known the pleasures of love, but he was committed to Charlotte now and it kept him celibate. Indeed, Barbara had been the last woman to share his bed, her present effect upon him a learned response which he recognised with wry amusement.

Introductions made, Robert was soon exchanging bows with Peter Lerpiniere, a man of nondescript colouring, whose balding head barely topped his wife's shoulder, but he was extremely rich, which explained the alliance between the ill-matched pair.

The banker moved on and Robert bowed over Barbara's hand, raising it politely to his lips. Adroitly, she turned her hand so that he found himself kissing the inside of her fingers. Much more intimate.

"How do you do, Mr Hattenbury. It is long since we last met. You are well?" Her smile was brilliant, her tone the correct mix of politeness and studied interest, any undertimbre for Robert's ear alone. He smiled and responded with his own brand of cool assurance.

"How do you do, Mrs Lerpiniere. Thank you, yes, I am. Permit me to comment on the felicity of your own looks. I hear you were in Europe this winter."

To observe them, no-one could imagine they once sported in bed together. Robert wondered if the lady's husband knew of her extra-marital activities, and concluded that he must, a thought which had not occurred before. If Lerpiniere loved his wife, it must pain him to see her enamoured of other men. Belatedly, Robert felt guilty, knowing from family history the misery infidelity could cause.

"Yes, such a bore, but family obligations must be fulfilled. However, we contrived some amusement and later managed several weeks in Paris, which was enjoyable. And you, Sir, how did you pass winter?"

"I was at home this year, after an autumn trip to Italy with Charles Knox. It was a delightful visit and we returned feeling able to cope with the inclement English weather. Now here we are, at the start of another season. How quickly time flies."

"Indeed," Barbara lowered her voice, "but I hope it will not be another year before we meet again, Mr Hattenbury."

She moved off with a provocative flick of her skirts. With a cynical smile on his beautifully shaped lips, Robert was left to make what he would of her invitation.

Directly, the company went into dinner and Robert found himself seated with Miss Mary Williams. On her other side was Spencer Dean, who enquired after Charlotte at the first opportunity. Robert replied lazily that he imagined Mr Dean knew as much as he, since Charlotte was spending a holiday with his sister in the West Country. He went on to point out consolingly, that both ladies would be in town next day. Here he paused, with a certain malicious amusement, as an expression of swiftly veiled disappointment flashed over Spencer's face. He relented his awkwardness, and saw a dawning smile, when he suggested that Mr Dean might wish to call and renew acquaintance with his ward. His suggestion was taken up with flattering alacrity.

Mr Dean was more his sensible self when the talk turned to politics. The Reform Bill was, of course, on every tongue, with opinions divided for and against. Spencer Dean said: "Wellington will oppose. What else?

He did not resign last November to approve it now. No, the government must fall, I believe."

"How is the Duchess of Wellington, Mr Dean?" Lady Styneley asked solicitously. "Our whole household prays for her. Is she at all improved?"

"I fear not, your ladyship. Her Grace was sadly ailing when last we saw her. She has been obliged to take to a sofa on the ground floor of Apsley. Miss Edgeworth says it is a comfort for her to be in the presence of the Duke's trophies."

"That must be consolation in the absence of the Duke, himself. He seems busier in opposition than when he was Prime Minister. The Duchess can scarcely have seen her husband lately," Mary Williams said earnestly; which was perfectly permissible comment for a young lady.

But a few eyebrows, including Mr Hattenbury's, were raised when she went on to add: "But it is a pity His Grace opposes the bill, Mr Dean, because reform must come in time. It is only justice that it should. It is common knowledge surely, that as far back as Eighteen Twenty the Black Book described parliament as ~ and I condense a little here ~ 'unconstitutional . . . glaringly absurd and ridiculous . . . founded on no rational principle of either population, intelligence or property'. This, I feel, is an exact summation of the present situation and obviously needs righting."

Lady Styneley immediately recognised Samuel, her brother by marriage's influence in his daughter's opinions (he being a man of liberal thought who had educated his three daughters as though they were sons) but frowned down her niece. Westover's dining room was no place for their expression: at least, not from a young woman.

"Miss Williams, no more radical talk, if you please." A smile alleviated the plainness of the Marchioness's words; but it was plain for all to see that Miss Williams did not care for the reprimand.

Mr Hopkins, across the table from Miss Williams, had been looking at her animated face with undisguised admiration while she spoke. Plainly not sharing Lady Styneley's stance, he now leaned forward and said: "I sincerely applaud your zeal, Miss Williams," which remark took some of the sting out of her aunt's rebuke.

Robert, however, made a mental note to keep Miss Williams and Charlotte apart. He did not want another little radical residing at Meva House, and Charlotte was quite capable of becoming one just to tease him.

***

In his bedchamber, that night, Robert was thinking of Spencer Dean's interest in Charlotte. He spoke aloud, suddenly. "Much good it will do you, Mr Dean." His valet looked an enquiry.

Robert dismissed him and got into bed, but lay sleepless thinking of what the morrow was to bring, filled with pleasurable anticipation. Charlotte of the nimble tongue and graceful carriage; his lovely Charlotte, with her clear gaze and total lack of affectation; Charlotte with her intelligence, her warmth and love, the embodiment of his every desire, she who, one day soon, would be his wife. Forward that joyful day.

He turned over, impatient for the dawn, with never a thought for Mistress Lerpiniere.

***

The occupants of Meva were up early on Thursday morning, although Charlotte was not expected before noon. Mrs Treleaven was distracted with excitement at the thought of her daughter's return; she had missed her sorely. Even Mrs Hattenbury was less than her normal collected self.

Robert himself went to the market, buying armfuls of flowers to welcome Charlotte home. He came back laden with tulips and narcissus which the two mamas arranged in great bowls throughout the house. He also brought masses of Convallaria, which he knew Charlotte adored, and placed them all over her suite. In every room she would see them and know he had thought of her.

At last the impatient inhabitants of Meva heard a carriage approach. Even before it drew up at the portal, the front door was flung wide, and

Charlotte stepped down from the carriage into the loving embraces of mother and titular aunt.

Hadley Dean and Xanthe descended after Charlotte. They saluted Robert over the heads of the warmly embracing trio between them. He gave them only a cursory acknowledgement, before his gaze was drawn back to Charlotte. Excitement was riding high in him.

She turned from hugging the mamas and saw Robert standing in the doorway. Impulsively, borne on a tide of welcoming affection, she ran up the steps separating them and stretched up to embrace him.

As she swung towards him the subtlety of her body's honeyed scent enveloped Robert and his eyes went blank. For a moment, he saw nothing of the scene around him. He was back in the stables at Crane, Charlotte in his arms and desire riding him hard.

In a flash the vision was gone and he returned to the present. He drew away from Charlotte abruptly, face stiff with the shock of his mind's betrayal. It had come so sharply and unexpectedly he was totally unprepared for the strength of feeling which assailed him. His whole body was tingling from head to toe. He was stretched by instant and urgent arousal, obliged to turn away in quick confusion.

Damn! Oh damn! Idiot! What a fool he must look if it had been observed that he was outwith control! Abominably rude though it was, Robert turned his back and spoke over his shoulder, calling everyone into the house. During the intervening bustle he was able to subdue his errant flesh.

The Deans stayed only long enough to make arrangements for further meetings. Then they were gone, leaving a pool of expectant silence, which was immediately filled by the continuation of the excited conversation their departure had interrupted.

For the most part, Robert was a withdrawn spectator still feeling vulnerable. He spoke when called upon but did not engage in his usual teasing with Charlotte.

She noticed his aloofness, as she had noticed his sharp recoil from her kiss. Not knowing the reason, she felt hurt and rejected; but there was no time to brood. The mamas showed her all over the house, which she had not seen before, pointing out the beautiful flowers. As if she could have missed them! Charlotte was then conducted to her own suite, where each room had been freshly decorated in her honour. She had been given a bedroom, sitting room and bathroom, each interconnecting, all light and airy, in the new style. Not the smallest strip of dark panelling in sight!

The bedroom was decorated in shades of cream and blue, both colours prominent in the washed Chinese carpet covering the floor from wall to wall. The sitting room continued the same theme, but with warmer shades of amber introduced in the brocades of furniture and window drapes. Between two long windows was a Chippendale table with cabriole legs. On its surface was Robert's flower offering, in cut glass bowls whose brilliance was reflected in the table's highly polished top.

When she saw the flowers Charlotte gave an exclamation of pleasure. "Oh, how lovely! Lily-of-the-valley!" Her hands reached instinctively to cup the dainty blooms, fingertips caressing the delicate petals as she bent to drink in their scent.

Robert strolled forward, his face lightening as he smiled. "You are pleased by our welcome, and your suite, I trust?"

"How could I not be, Sir? The rooms are delightful. Nothing could be better."

"Reserve judgement, Charlotte. You have yet to see your bathroom. I venture to think . . . that is to say *we* venture to think," his smile included the two mamas, "you will be even more pleasantly surprised. At least, we hope so; otherwise the banging and dust clouds we have endured will have been in vain. Do come and see." He held out a hand but only to usher Charlotte before him.

When Charlotte stepped into the bathroom, her eyes widened in astonishment. What! Had she stepped into a fairy tale? She could do nothing but stare. In truth, had the fashionable Miss Treleaven been less of an elegant young woman, one might have said she gawped!

The beautiful room had walls of ivory decorated with a gold leaf frieze. A luxurious ivory and crimson Indian carpet covered the floor. Beneath the window was a vanity table with a crimson ruffled skirt covering its legs. The table was set with bottles and bowls filled with soaps, powders and perfume. Beside the table was a cheval glass, and standing against the adjoining wall was a superb chaise-longue. It had an expandable screen of gold embroidered silk curved around one end, and a carved ivory towel rail, holding pristine white towels, at the other.

All this, however, was as nothing to the bath itself, which stood on elegant scroll legs, on a raised dais. It was a cast gilded shell, hung about with a cloud of shimmering gold net curtain which descended from a gilded coronet in the ceiling. The curtain was presently caught back by gold tassels on each side, but it could be let down for privacy if the bather so desired.

Charlotte stared at the dazzling spectacle, open-mouthed with astonishment. Whose imagination could have conjured up such splendour? And all for her!

"Is this for *me*?" she squeaked, after speechless moments of wonder.

"You can hardly think it to my taste, infant," Robert commented dryly, smiling to see Charlotte's pleasure.

"I shall be afraid to use it. It is so . . . so grand," she replied, still eyeing the gilded bath entranced, her fingers trailing around its petalled edge.

"Of course you won't. It is an appropriate setting for our very own Beauty of Bath," Mrs Hattenbury quipped brightly, a play on the name of an apple indigenous to the Bath area. She was as thrilled as Robert with Charlotte's joyful reaction. Mrs Treleaven beamed happily.

Still dazed, Charlotte asked: "Who planned all this?" holding out her arms to encompass the room, the like of which she could never have imagined in her wildest dreams, all white, crimson, and shining gold.

"I must confess it was I," Robert acknowledged in self-deprecating tones. He was in typical stance, with arms folded across his chest, one leg before the other. With the room's light gilding his blond curls and finely moulded features, he looked perfectly angelic, and Charlotte's breath caught painfully as she turned to him. There was a feeling as of a knife pressing into her breast and she could easily have wept. Why, oh why, must he be so beautiful and so disinterestedly kind, as, clearly, he was in this?

Robert returned her regard but she could not tell what he was thinking, or indeed what had prompted him to create such an exotic setting for her. She could have thought his surprise a lover-like gesture, except for his frigid reception at the front door earlier. Then, he had never looked or acted less the lover. He was so confusing.

He had planned all this for her pleasure, yet recoiled when she gave him a spontaneous kiss of welcome. He turned his house upside down for her, and then stood back aloofly, disassociated and looking as though he positively disliked her.

Charlotte gazed at him in perplexity. Would she ever understand him?

Mrs Hattenbury placed a hand on her son's arm. "Who would have believed you so romantical, Robert?" she asked gayly.

"I thought it would be a divertissement for Charlotte," he said coolly.

"It is very beautiful and I thank you, Sir," Charlotte responded. She spoke sincerely, but there was a catch in her voice from an overlaying of pain, for reasons felt though not perfectly understood.

"I'm glad you approve," Robert said, shepherding the two mamas towards the door. "Come ladies. We will leave Charlotte to settle in."

Alone in her new domain, Charlotte wondered why she was not happier when Robert had created all this beauty for her. His thoughtfulness should have made her ecstatic. Instead, she felt deeply heavy-hearted, realising that for her the beauty meant nothing, when all too clearly Robert's was a disinterested gesture.

She had not seen him since her birthday, nor had he written, although when she thought of his last words in the carriage, as he had urged her to do, both had seemed a possibility. Thinking over what he had said, Charlotte believed she must have misinterpreted him yet again. Frustrated, tortured by doubt, she wondered why he could not be plainer.

For a while, it seemed Robert was inferring he had not meant the terrible things he said last year, that he spoke only from the shock of what had happened. Looked at from another viewpoint his 'I, too, had a shock last summer' might imply that his fall from grace with her had brought Robert to his senses. However, this seemed not to fit the case either . . . until his abrupt withdrawal at the door today. He had not been able to hide his dislike of her impulsive show of affection. Yet, why had he recoiled? He had not found her repulsive before; even at . . . well, when he had been in such a fury with her at Yuletide. Shaming to admit, Charlotte knew Robert's purpose in the spense had been to bring home a certain lesson to her, because he had not been outwith control then. That said, he *had* been aroused; he *had* wanted her and would have possessed her had she allowed it. She knew this absolutely; she had not been anathema to him that night whatever his purpose. And too, he had asked her to kiss him on her birthday day, had clearly wanted her to. What had changed since?

A dismal thought struck forcibly.

Maybe, Robert had found a new love, or resumed with his old paramour. That would account for his silence since her birthday and his reaction today; but if this were so, why was she now living in his house, set for a season of pleasure at his expense, the whole house turned upside down for her pleasure?

Even more dismally, and beyond doubt, Charlotte knew the answer to this question. Mr Hattenbury's perceived duty. That would be a motivation, no matter his personal feelings. When honour was involved he would do what he must, whether he wanted to or not. As his ward she had been promised a season, and that is what she would get. Thank heaven she had not let him know she had begun to believe he wanted to marry her after all. How humiliating if he had known.

Charlotte had not dreamed it possible to feel more miserable than she already was but, ounce for ounce, she felt sure her heart must be heavier than lead.

So . . . what now?

Nothing had changed, except that if Robert had a new love there would be no more proposals. That was a problem solved. They could, each of them, get on with their separate lives, her own thrust now to find a husband and quickly. The sooner she did that, the sooner she would be free of Mr Hattenbury and he of her. Yes, that was it. A husband must be her aim.

Resolutely Charlotte drew back her shoulders and sighing, in spite of stern resolution, she moved to the window drawn by the scent of the Convallaria beneath it. She pulled a dainty flower from its bowl and brushed the velvet-soft bells against her lips, enjoying their coolth, taking comfort from their fragrance. Standing quietly, her eyes were drawn to the garden outside and, suddenly, all melancholy thoughts were deliquescent in flooding joy as she saw the vista spread below her.

Blooming magnificently were early azaleas, japonica, and rhododendron ready soon to burgeon. There were beds of beautiful red tulips nestling in a haze of lacy fern, muscari, primula, and wallflowers beginning to burst. Everywhere there was form and colour to bring a wondering sense of awe at the perfection of nature's beauty. How wonderful it was! Robert must have a veritable regiment of workers, to keep his grounds in such ideal condition, especially here, in the heart of London. She must congratulate him and ask to be made known to his gardener. Spirits miraculously uplifted, she went to convey her compliments to Robert.

Unfortunately, he was dining away from home. How selfish on her first night. She did not see him until next morning, when he was before her at the breakfast table.

***

They breakfasted alone and in silence, Robert engrossed in the newspaper. Presently he laid it aside and addressed Charlotte.

"Well, Charlotte," he said pleasantly, "here you are at the beginning of your season. I expect the house will soon be swarming with young bucks sending you flowers and poems tied up in ribbons. What say you?" His manner was decidedly avuncular, patronising too, it seemed to Charlotte.

"I hardly think it appropriate, Sir," she replied, at her most unsmilingly polite. "One would not care to be designated a flirt, as one must be if unwise enough to encourage the hordes you envision."

"Naturally," he responded with equal gravity. His equivocation irritated her.

"Naturally what?" she asked directly.

"One would not wish to be unwise," he answered forthrightly; but something in the set of his eyelids made Charlotte think he was not sincere, and his mouth was lifting slightly at the corners. Mr Hattenbury was amused? He glanced up and caught her watching him. "There would be safety in numbers, of course," he added conversationally. "However, that is not what I want to discuss with you, nor is this the place. Come with me to the drawing room."

Once there, he began without preamble. "Tomorrow we are giving a soirée to introduce you into society. A few friends and acquaintances only are invited, but it will start the ball rolling."

"Do I take it that today is my single holiday from pleasure, Guardian?" Charlotte asked whimsically.

"Probably, so make the most of it," he advised, smiling. He resumed: "Next week you are going on a boating expedition with Lady Styneley's party. I accepted on your behalf since I know your predilection for water. Also . . ."

"Am I going alone?" Charlotte interpolated with a shade of anxiety.

"Naturally not. The mamas and I have also been invited." He paused and gave her the glance direct. "On the subject of aloneness, I must make clear to you that it is absolutely forbidden for you to go anywhere alone, aloneness in this case meaning by yourself, or with a gentleman. London is very different from Cornwall but even at home I was not happy when you walked out unattended. Here, in the metropolis it must never happen. It is not safe for ladies to go abroad unaccompanied. You understand this?"

"Yes, Sir." Charlotte raised no difficulty.

"If you wish to shop you may take your maid. I trust you like Eliza, by the bye. She is a relative of Mrs Penrose and we brought her up from Saltash especially, thinking her Cornish accent would make you feel at home," he said in a smiling aside.

After pausing deliberately, he continued with emphasis: "The question of being alone with a gentleman is different but no less important. Simply stated . . . you must not do it. You may enjoy the company of gentlemen as much as you will, as long as you *are* in company. Is this clear to you, Charlotte?"

Robert felt some inner discomfort at this juncture since he, himself, had spent many an hour alone with Charlotte, engaged in just such pleasures as those of which he now warned her, but it had to be said.

"Quite clear, Sir." Charlotte was at her most docile and did not raise her eyes from the carpet. Her mind held thoughts similar to Robert's, but what could usefully be remarked?

"Good. Back to the itinerary. Thursday we dine with the Deans. Saturday is Miss Dean's coming-out ball. Your official debut will be made on the thirtieth, the following Saturday. This is all we have planned definitely, but other invitations will inevitably follow. One must leave time for them.

"I shall not attend every function with you and you are at liberty to accept invitations, subject to my approval. If you want to go to a theatre or opera house I will take you. Concerts will figure high on your list, I know, and I shall be happy to escort you to musical functions. But, Miss Treleaven, do not ask me to take you to the wild beast show," he ended jocosely. By then Charlotte's head was spinning.

"Robert, shall we get any sleep in London? You appear to have made a disposition for every minute of day and night," she said, bemused.

He noticed Charlotte's unconscious use of his name and was moved to pleasure although his face remained impassive. Unobserved, since her thoughts were clearly elsewhere, he watched her.

She sat in relaxed attitude, one cheek resting on clasped hands as she gazed out of the window. How beautiful Charlotte was, how graceful. His eyes took in the gentle curve of brow, still uncluttered by curls in spite of current fashion, and the long sweep of eyelash. His glance travelled to her tender nape, where small tendrils of hair curled against smooth skin, and on down slender arms. His gaze lingered on the bodice of her green silk gown which revealed breasts still small but growing into tempting womanly form. He had once tasted her breast, known the pleasure of a dark rose nipple nestled on his tongue. He thought of other places to nestle and cosset for Charlotte's pleasure but closed off that avenue. It was too soon and he should not be thinking such thoughts.

He looked his fill, with pleasurable anticipation creaming through him, but not with yesterday's disastrous results. His responses were well regulated this morning, the shock he had received putting him very much on his guard.

He recalled how, after Christmas, he had believed Charlotte safe in his keeping, that at some unspecified time in the future they would marry. He had pictured a light-hearted courtship, wooing her by sweet attrition, believing himself safe from the riveting compulsions of last summer.

Yesterday had shown him instantly the foolishness of his complacency. Desire, subdued to dormancy by the traumatic events of his last birthday, and the absence of Cornwall's propinquity, had sprung to life fiercely, his senses responding to Charlotte's unconscious lure, as hunger, the more potent for long denial, swept over him wildly. He wanted Charlotte *now* not in a sometime future. With hindsight he marvelled at his Yuletide restraint. She had been his, pliant, in the palm of his hand, and he had let her go! He must still have been in shock, for had he felt at Christmas as he did yesterday Charlotte could never have been reprieved.

Last night panic had sent him to his club for refuge, no matter the astonished look on his mother's face when he told her he was dining away from home.

"On Charlotte's first night with us?" When he reiterated, rather woodenly, that he was so engaged, she objected: "Oh, surely not, Robert?"

He had sat in the club with a glass of brandy, eschewing all company, wondering how to cope with this renewed threat to his peace of mind. However, only a little reflection had shown the irrationality of his fears. His present situation was very different from Cornwall. Now they were in busy, busy London, where one was constantly surrounded by others. He would not have unlimited seclusion with Charlotte, as at home.

Nor was she the naive child she had been, ergo, there was no reason to doubt his control. There were too many safety checks. All he had to do was wait for the wardship to end. Then he could take her to wife and, thankfully, longingly, to bed. If, as he now suspected, the waiting proved more difficult than anticipated, it served him right for the arrogance of thinking himself immune from the exigencies of desire. *Pride does, indeed, go before a fall*, he thought with wry humour. Last year's experience should have taught him that.

He sighed unconsciously, thinking, as with Dr Johnson, that while marriage indubitably had many pains celibacy was quite without pleasures. For Robert the time of choice had long passed.

The sigh caught Charlotte's attention. "You sound despondent, in spite of the rosy prospect you paint," she chaffed.

"I imagine the rosy prospect is more to your taste then mine," he responded, sounding dismissive. Charlotte bit her lip to hold back an irritated retort. It was not pleasant to be the object of duty.

"How could you know, Sir? You never asked my opinion of this metropolitan venture. The plan was all yours. If you do not like it the blame is also yours."

"I have no doubt of your enjoyment once the adventure gets underway, Charlotte," he replied evenly. "See at season's end if I am not au fait with your tastes. I may know you better than you think." Robert's ears caught the bustle of an arrival. "I hear a carriage. I did not think Mr Dean would fail," he ended on a derisory note; and he was right.

Spencer Dean called with a message from his mama, requesting the pleasure of Miss Treleaven's company at an informal party, that very afternoon, in honour of his sister's homecoming. The party was for the younger people, but Miss Treleaven's guardian was welcome to attend, he added.

Mr Hattenbury declined the dubious honour and, with a sardonic twist to his lips, said he felt sure Mrs Dean would provide adequate chaperonage.

Mr Dean then transferred his gaze, warmly appreciative of her charms, to Charlotte. He waited for her answer and his pleasure in her acceptance was evident.

Charlotte wondered at her guardian's sang froid over Mr Dean, recalling that at Yuletide he told her she was not to encourage him. Now it seemed not to matter.

Spencer Dean stayed ten minutes, quite long enough for the purposes of his call. Robert showed him out. Turning back into the house, he met Charlotte as she was crossing the hall.

"Bon Voyage, Miss Treleaven," he said soberly, his face shuttered.

What did he mean? wondered a perplexed Charlotte. Was he speaking of the season or referring to Mr Dean? She sighed, thinking that there had been a time when she could more readily read Robert's mind. Since last summer, he was a closed book.

***

Charlotte put the problem of Robert behind her and prepared for enjoyment that afternoon. She was introduced to the three youngest Deans, but not Philip who was still up at Cambridge. She would meet him when he played in the annual inter-varsity cricket match at Lord's the following week. Politely, Charlotte expressed pleasurable anticipation.

Xanthe told her that Philip looked like Anne, their younger sister. They were both dark-haired, unlike the rest of the family, and had the same carefree attitude to life. However, all the Deans shared one characteristic; open, friendly manners, an obvious inheritance from their parents.

Charlotte envied their warmth of family feeling, and thought fleetingly that it would be a good family to marry into. Looking up, she saw Spencer Dean regarding her and blushed, hoping he had not read her thoughts. With a hand he mutely invited her to join him in the garden. She went happily as there were others already walking the lawns. They were accompanied by Elizabeth Clement, Mrs Dean's niece, a shy young lady of nineteen, and Mr Knox, the four of them spending a pleasant half hour together before going in to tea.

The assembly broke up soon after and Charlotte was handed into the carriage by Spencer Dean. He pressed her hand and said he hoped to see her again shortly. She returned the hope. First, there was her soirée to be faced the following evening.

It was a small party to which Robert had invited Charles Knox and Charles' cousin Francis. The Styneleys were coming, together with their ward Miss Williams: Mr and Mrs Dean were bringing Xanthe. Robert had also invited a young couple called Fitz-Bassett, known both to him and Charles, thinking that Charlotte would enjoy the company of the gamin Mrs Fitz-Bassett. This couple were also acquainted with the Styneleys and Deans.

All things considered, the evening held few terrors for Charlotte and she enjoyed it immensely, the happy outcome a commendation from Robert on the excellence of her social poise, and several invitations for the following week. The invitation to join the Dean family in watching Philip play cricket at Lord's, and afterwards take dinner with them, was confirmed, as was Mr Francis Knox's suggestion of a visit to the Zoological Gardens.

Charlotte, remembering Robert's strictures about the wild beast show, could not resist a glance at him when the idea was mooted, but he gave back the blandest of smiles and said: "Excellent." Later she taxed him with mendacity.

"No such thing," he denied. "The Zoological Gardens are quite unlike the wild beast show. Besides," he added with a grin, "the gardens are no more than a mile hence ~ one can hear the occasional roar at night, if the wind is in this direction ~ so I can always sneak home if I am bored. *You* will enjoy it tremendously, Charlotte."

This conversation took place in Charlotte's sitting room, where the mamas gravitated each evening before retiring. Robert was also with them this night. Before they went to bed he told Charlotte, with more warmth than he had so far shown that he and the mamas were pleased with her.

"You behaved beautifully this evening, your deportment a credit to Miss Lacey's good example and to us, your family, who bask in the reflection of your excellence. Our visitors were as impressed as we. Well done, Charlotte."

"Yes, dear, such a credit," Mrs Treleaven agreed, moved to tears on hearing her darling daughter so warmly praised. She took a lace-edged handkerchief Mrs Hattenbury offered, in lieu of her own, for which she searched in vain, dabbing it happily to her eyes.

"Thank you Mama, and thank you Guardian." Charlotte felt warmed by Robert's approval and smiled. He returned the smile, bowed and said goodnight. The two mamas left shortly afterwards.

Alone, Charlotte went into the bathroom to prepare for bed. The bathroom still amazed her but she was no longer overawed by its opulence. Indeed, she was most appreciative of its wonderful conveniences, knowing few other people, either in the metropolis or at home, enjoyed such luxury. She wondered who would use it when she left Meva House. Robert's wife, presumably.

She made this supposition on discovering another door into the bathroom. It was in the corner, concealed by the ivory silk screen and not immediately apparent. This locked door connected with Robert's rooms. What was now her bathroom had previously been part of his dressing room, the part which looked onto the garden. The other end, abutting the bathroom, was all that remained of his once spacious dressing room. It had been reduced by over half, and Charlotte thought it typical of Robert's kindness to give up so much space to her; a kindness he had dismissed as a nothing when she tried to thank him. His attitude made her feel as though snubbed.

Tonight, in the bathroom, she realised Robert had gone straight to bed, because she heard sounds of movement and the murmur of voices on the other side of the wall. It was reassuring to know he was close.

Similarly, Robert could hear Charlotte, but she had not thought of that. He heard soft singing and the splash of water. Later, came the sound of laughter from her maid (he was glad Charlotte liked her), then all became silent.

Robert remained seated for a few minutes more, aroused by the intimacy of hearing Charlotte prepare for bed, thinking of her in a nightgown, wondering what it was like. It would not be all lace and gauze, the kind meant to seduce, but something pretty, possibly embroidered by one of the mamas; this he knew. With a small spurt of excitement, he imagined divesting Charlotte of the said gown when they married. He allowed the pleasure of his thoughts to wash over him, knowing it was safe to do so. But when the desire subsided, he felt, not without a touch of wry humour, that he would do well to avoid too frequent a repetition. It could prove dangerous to Charlotte's virtue, not to say uncomfortable to him ad interim.

***

Sunday morning saw them at All Souls', where prayers were offered up for the Duchess of Wellington. Thereafter the day was spent quietly, Robert alone dining out that evening, at the Cornish Club in Thatched House. The mamas and Charlotte settled down to sewing after dinner. Charlotte was working on the promised layette for Julia's expected baby and was already well ahead with it, gaining great pleasure from seeing the tiny garments forming under her hand.

After a good night's sleep Charlotte was full of energy and happy to receive visitors next morning. Xanthe came with her brother Spencer, and Mr Knox. They invited her to ride with them. Mr Hattenbury not being at home, the two mamas gave permission, sure that Robert would not object.

Off they went to Hyde Park and Charlotte saw for the first time where the fashionable gathered in concourse. Few were abroad at that hour, except genuine horsemen, but this was no bar to enjoyment, possibly the reverse.

Mr Dean made the most of his time with Charlotte, slowing his mount behind the other pair, but only a little since he took the chaperoning of his sister seriously.

"You look perfectly charming this morning, Miss Treleaven. May I say how pleasurably I look forward to seeing you during your sojourn in our capital city?"

"Indeed, you may, Sir. I have not the least objection to your uttering such pretty sentiments," she answered demurely.

He laughed with amusement. "I understand our families are conjoining tomorrow for a visit to the Zoological Gardens."

Charlotte was surprised. "Are you coming, too, Mr Dean? I would have thought it too juvenile a treat for you."

"Mama thought I might like to be included," he said, a trifle self-consciously.

"I have never seen such a thing before. Have you, Mr Dean?"

"Several times, but it never loses appeal. There is something fresh to see at each visit. You will like it, I believe."

"My guardian said the same," Charlotte revealed, "but I do not think he shares the anticipation." She told him of Mr Hattenbury's aversion to wild beast shows. Mr Dean was amused. However, when conversation resumed, he spoke thoughtfully.

"You have a high regard for your mentor, it seems," he said, on a questioning note.

Charlotte agreed without hesitation. "Indeed, yes. Mr Hattenbury is ever attentive to our comfort and so kind." She was truthful in her praise.

Spencer Dean hesitated before continuing delicately: "The ties between your families are strong, it seems."

She considered this remark. "Well, of course, we are near neighbours at home, and Mama and Aunt Sophie have been best friends since childhood. They spend a great deal of time together and, as a consequence, so do we all. It sometimes seems we are one family but with two mamas instead of a parent of each sex." Charlotte began laughing. "Robert says that as he is surrounded by women, it is a jolly good thing he has always been used to it, or our chatter would drive him mad. He and my sister were playmates in early days, you know."

Mr Dean nodded his understanding. "I see. One could not have a better brother than Mr Hattenbury." Charlotte had not thought of Robert as a brother before, but now she took up that theme enthusiastically.

"Of course, he knows all about the latest fashions and is perfectly able to tell what suits one or not. He is always ready to act escort, arranging all manner of treats for us. Do you know, Mr Dean," she said, confiding her discovery, "I have only now realised how fortunate I am to have such an agreeable guardian. I quite took him for granted and did not realise until you pointed it out."

"I am glad to have been of service, and would be equally happy to serve you in any other way. If, for example, Mr Hattenbury fails as escort, you may rely on me, Miss Treleaven," he offered gallantly. Charlotte accepted his offer graciously, while doubting that Robert would fail; not, at least, in the field of which Mr Dean spoke.

Robert was back when they returned to Meva. He strolled to meet them and invited the visitors in for refreshments. He surveyed Mr Dean and his ward lazily, moving without hurry to help Charlotte dismount, forestalling the other man. Then, indulgently, he took a hand of each young lady and led them into the house, saying: "You must both attend me since I am host. Other gentlemen must look to their own desserts," he said, over his shoulder.

"Crafty dog," Charles Knox said cheerfully, "up to every trick in the book."

"It is known as a coup de maître, don't you know," Robert agreed blandly, with a warm smile for Miss Dean, who dimpled attractively. He also smiled at Charlotte, not to distinguish her companion, but it was too late. She had already experienced an uncomfortable restriction in her breast. She withdrew her hand as soon as possible.

She tried not to think in terms of Robert favouring her friend and put on a cheerful face, talking to Mr Dean of the Zoological Gardens and telling her guardian, when he looked an enquiry, that Xanthe's brother was also going. Underneath the bright exterior her mind worked on another level. It reminded her that instead of feeling upset, she should be glad to see Robert taking the gratuitous advice she had given him in regard to Xanthe. Was this not what she wanted, to be free of so disinterested a suitor, a man who clearly did not want her and who favoured others before her? Let Xanthe have him if she wished.

However, later that day, Charlotte was not sure Xanthe stood any better chance than she did. They were dining with the Misses Jane and Constanza Wyvern, Mrs Hattenbury's maiden stepsisters, offshoot of a second marriage. Being unmarried, the elder Miss Wyvern was interested in the children of the family. She particularly liked Robert but still took a malicious delight in recognising his illegitimate siblings, to her favourite nephew's discomfiture.

Robert never acknowledged their existence by look or naming. His late father's penchant for producing illegitimate offspring was not something Robert viewed with equanimity. It was a characteristic he found most unpalatable, that, and Francis's unfaithfulness to Sophie. Neither was something Robert would contemplate for himself. Charlotte would have his undivided loyalty and his children would be hers alone. Mistresses he may have had aplenty, but none had carried his child.

The rooms were crowded, the Wyvern ladies being noted for their hospitality, but there was no-one to whom Robert objected. Not even Mistress Lerpiniere, who was there with one of the Neville boys in tow, a doting youth of some nineteen summers.

When Charlotte heard the name, followed by a low, husky voice addressing Mr Hattenbury, she turned slowly to look at his mistress and her heart stood still. Sick with jealousy, she knew instantly why she, herself, had lost Robert's interest. In the face of such formidable opposition she doubted even Xanthe could succeed, for Robert's lady love was every bit as alluring as she had been painted.

Her eyes were an astonishing shade of green, her skin that enviable, matt whiteness which often accompanies red hair. Her 'neck', current euphemism for bosom, was perfect, and perfectly revealed by a décolleté bodice. Her waist was no more than a hand span. Oh, thought Charlotte, how unfair that so much loveliness was encompassed in one human frame. It made her feel hollow, only to gaze upon the woman at whose feet Robert worshipped. Who would blame him except, possibly, her unfortunate husband?

All this went through Charlotte's mind in the time it took Robert to draw her forward. "You have not met my ward. Mrs Lerpiniere . . . Miss Treleaven."

"I am happy to make your acquaintance, Miss Treleaven," Barbara Lerpiniere greeted, in the same husky voice she had used to Robert. It was natural apparently, not designed to ensnare. Even in this she was perfect.

"How do you do," Charlotte responded politely, before Robert moved on. From the corner of her eye she saw Mr Neville drift after the green-eyed charmer.

Robert also saw because he murmured, to no-one in particular: "chacon à son goût".[1] With an upsurge of rage Charlotte silently agreed with him.

Later, sitting with Aunt Jane, who scooped Charlotte out of the crowd, saying she wanted to hear all about her nephew's ward, she saw Robert with his paramour again. His blond head was bent forward as she

*Everyone to his taste.

spoke close to his ear. Her hand rested on his arm possessively. Evidently Mr Hattenbury agreed with what she said for he nodded and presently both left the room. Charlotte would have given anything to know where they went. This was knowledge not afforded her but she was certain she knew why they had gone. Chacon à son goût, indeed. She could have killed him.

On the way home she had no word for her guardian, but he seemed not to notice. Once home, she gave him the shortest of goodnights, before going upstairs with head high. Inwardly, she was screaming with pain and frustration at not knowing what had been toward, but Robert's demeanour gave nothing away. He said goodnight as briefly as she and watched her out of sight. As he turned into the library, where a bottle of brandy awaited him, Robert saw his mother watching him in her turn. Impulsively, he kissed her cheek; to her surprise.

When he went to bed, an hour or so later, there was no sound from Charlotte's rooms to disturb his peace; but she only cried for a short time.

Chapter Thirteen

Robert was before her at breakfast. The mamas were not yet down.

"Good morning, Sir." Charlotte was civil, if cool.

He looked at her over his newspaper. "Good morning, angel," he replied equably. Immediately, Charlotte let out an exclamation of annoyance.

"*Must* you call me by inappropriate names? It is so undignified. You *could* call me Miss Treleaven, if all else fails," she objected strenuously.

Robert raised an eyebrow. "Who minds dignity at the breakfast table?"

"As long as it is not yours, one presumes, but that is scarcely to the point. *I* mind, Sir." Charlotte was quite impassioned. Robert made things infinitely worse with his next cheerful remark.

"Oh dear, who got out of bed on the wrong side this morning?" he asked.

Charlotte's look of smouldering dislike should have wiped the cheer from his face. It did not have that effect, but her accompanying words did, at which she experienced a brief surge of triumph.

"Oh, I see what it is. You are in your insufferably patronising 'humour the child' mood, are you not, Sir?" She spoke with a proudly lifted head.

Robert was silent for a brief moment, watching her. She stared back defiantly.

"That was extraordinarily rude, Charlotte, and quite uncalled for. It is no part of a guardian's duty to pander to ill-temper. Apologise, please." His voice was level.

"Indeed, I will not! Clearly, it is perfectly possible for you to address me howsoever you will and I to have no redress. Is that right? Humph, I think *not,*" she flung out at him boldly.

Again he was silent, tapping a thumb nail against his lips. When he spoke it was with a snap. "I will not bandy words with you, Miss Treleaven. Apologise now, or else go to your room."

"What?" Charlotte demanded, a humiliated red tide mantling her cheeks at his tone. "Who are you to tell me what I must or must not do? Go to my room, indeed. And if I say I will not?" she challenged, head high.

"I shall make it my business to see that you do," he returned with cold emphasis. He rose and came towards her.

"Oh . . . how I hate you! You think you can do anything you wish," she stormed, fury clouding her brow. She jumped to her feet, longing to fly out at him. He barred her way with an iron grip on her arm, staring down at her.

"Do you tell me I cannot?" His voice was icy, body hostile. "Well?" he ground out, his face a mask of chilled hauteur.

Charlotte had seen Mr Hattenbury in this dangerous mood several times before. Only once had fear of ill-considered action not held her back; now it did, in spite of her fury. She glared at him, her expression a compound of rage and trepidation, her breast heaving against an arm which barred her way but would not hold her. The impulse to strike out at the implacable face above her was so strong Charlotte's hand rose of its own volition. When she realised what she was about to do the punitive hand wavered. She breathed in gasping sobs, not knowing how to channel the violent surge of energy propelling her to aggression.

Robert did not say a word, nor did he move to avoid the threatened blow, but glittering blue eyes bored implacably into hers until, by sheer force of will, Charlotte was subdued.

Furiously, she struck his hand from her arm, and ran sobbing from the room. In her bedroom Charlotte, astonishingly, cried and beat her fists against her pillows in an almighty temper tantrum, the very first of her life.

Hearing her screams, the mamas would have run to her instantly. Robert forbade it. He told them Charlotte had been sent to her room for unpardonable rudeness. When she apologised they could go to her, or she could come out.

As he was explaining, the whole situation suddenly got the better of Robert. He felt the beginnings of irrational and highly unseemly mirth bubbling up, and was obliged to leave the mamas immediately. He could not allow it to emerge in the face of their distress. He came back later with reassurances, but on his return both ladies were still upset, his own mother every bit as much as Charlotte's.

Alethea's lips were trembling as she looked unhappily at Robert. "Robert, dear," she began, "I know you must be right if you say Charlotte was naughty but, surely, it would be perfectly in order for *us* to see how she does? I do not understand. She is *never* bad, is she, Sophie?" she appealed, verging on tears.

Mrs Hattenbury instantly agreed. "Indeed, I never knew her to be so. What has she *done* to incur your anger, Mr Hattenbury?" It was a measure of Sophie's concern that she addressed her son so formally.

"One moment, if you please, Mama," Robert said. He turned and took Mrs Treleaven's hand, and spoke to her gently. "Aunt Alethea, do you think I have ever before treated Charlotte unjustly?"

Her eyes searched his face in the same way Charlotte's did. She shook her head, although tears still trembled. "No, dear, you have been kindness itself."

Robert dismissed that, with a shake of the head, and said: "Then you must know I am not simply being overbearing, when I insist Charlotte stays in her room until she has apologised. As to what has brought about this unpleasant state of affairs," Robert's glance included his mother, "I will not discuss it outwith Charlotte's presence."

"What of the visit to Regent's Park?" Alethea asked, gazing up at him hopefully, willing him to relent. Robert pressed her hand sympathetically.

"She will miss it, I'm afraid," he said gently, regretful but firm.

Miss it she did, because she would not make reparation. Mr Hattenbury's depleted party went without her. Charlotte was left at home, to sob in outrage at being locked in her rooms. Mr Dean looked for her in vain.

The afternoon's party was not a success. Three of its members went home earlier than planned. On reaching Meva all was silent, much too silent for the concerned mamas. They lingered at the base of the stairs, casting anxious glances at the silent regions above. Robert said he would look to see how Charlotte did.

"Go to the drawing room and ring for tea. Hopefully, I may bring her to you."

Robert unlocked the door to Charlotte's suite and entered the sitting room. There was no sign of her and, it must be admitted, he felt a twinge of alarm. He crossed to the bedroom and opened the door. He was about to call Charlotte's name when he heard a sob; then another; and yet another. With pain twisting his heart, he realised that Charlotte, his dear, difficult love, was sobbing in her sleep. Without any hesitation, he entered the bedroom and sat on the bedside, gathering her into his arms.

"Charlotte . . . oh, darling, my dear angel, you must not cry," he murmured, hating himself for reducing her to such distress.

She came awake slowly, but it took only moments to realise Robert was holding her and she responded immediately. She clasped him tightly and turned her face into his shoulder, crying anew.

"How could you leave me?" she sobbed, each word broken by a shuddering breath.

"Darling, dear heart, don't cry." He held her close, stroking her hair and caressing her tenderly. He kissed her tear-wet face. "Dear one, you are right. I should not have left you. It was my fault entirely. Hush, dearest. Stop crying now. You will make yourself ill," he comforted softly, his heart aching with love.

How disarming was Charlotte in her anguish, how very dear; and why had he been so harsh with her? He knew the cause of her anger. Had not his irrational mirth stemmed from the same source?

"Robert," she whispered, "I am so sorry. I did not mean to be rude. Please forgive me." Her cheek was pressed to his, her arms about his neck clinging as though she would never let him go.

"There is nothing to forgive, Charlotte. It was a stupid

misunderstanding, nothing else. Think of it no more." Robert continued his gentle caresses and subdued murmurings, until Charlotte was lulled into relaxing her convulsive hold.

When he kissed her, with the first touch of his mouth, her world was set to rights. With Robert's hands gentle upon her, his lips warmly caressing, she was at peace with herself for the first time in many a long day. She felt secure again, relieved of the weight of anxious churning which had been her constant companion so often lately.

After a moment Robert drew away. "I was too harsh, Charlotte. I should have been kinder but I lost my temper," he murmured against her brow.

"No, Sir, the fault was mine, I know it was." She gazed at him with longing, not wishing to be outwith his embrace, wanting, indeed, to be very much closer. It was such balm to feel his body close to hers. "I was perfectly horrid and I am so ashamed." The enticing curve of Robert's mouth drew her irresistibly. She wanted more of it and would have taken what she wished for but that he spoke first.

"Charlotte," he said more firmly, his arms tight around her, "enough has been said. Let us agree we were both at fault and begin again."

She moved closer under the persuasion of his clasp and rubbed her face against his throat, her parted lips savouring the familiar taste and texture of him. "As you wish," she murmured; anything to prolong the comfort of contact with him.

Robert held her a moment longer, then sat her up gently, saying, as he smoothed back her tumbled hair: "The mamas are terribly anxious, and have been giving me reproachful looks all day. None of us enjoyed the Gardens, I must confess. Shall we go down to them?"

"Yes, of course." Obediently, Charlotte began to rise. Robert stayed her.

"Tomorrow will be a better day, Charlotte," he promised softly.

There was no need to go to the mamas. Anxiety getting the better of them, they were even then outside. A gentle tap at the bedroom door heralded their arrival, and Charlotte was handed over to their loving ministrations. Robert went away to change a neckcloth which had been reduced to a ruin by Charlotte's tears.

It was many hours before she slept that night, in spite of feeling exhausted. Her mind kept reliving the dreadful day, still finding her behaviour incomprehensible. Why had she behaved so outrageously? Why conceive such a violent dislike for Robert simply because he tried to coax her out of a sullen mood? What was in a single remark to cause such immediate and robust offence? In her heart, Charlotte knew as well as Robert, but how could she acknowledge it?

***

Charlotte came awake to the sound of her name. She opened sleepy eyes to see the two mamas at her bedside. "What . . . what are you doing here? Have I overslept?" she asked, yawning.

"Yes. It is high time you woke, sleepy head," her mother chided lovingly.

"Oh, dear," Charlotte lamented placidly. She stretched and sat up.

"Oh dear, indeed," said Mrs Hattenbury. She piled the pillows at Charlotte's back. "Sit up properly. Breakfast is here," Sophie handed Charlotte a napkin, "and every morsel is to be eaten." Charlotte folded a corner of the napkin over the neck of her robe and Sophie settled the tray across her lap.

"Now, Charlotte," Alethea said, straightening the bed covers, "I have a message from dear Robert. He said you have one hour to present yourself in the drawing room. Or else . . ." Alethea gazed in mock severity, saying no more. She turned to Sophie. "Come along, dear." The two mamas made for the door.

"Or else what?" Charlotte called after them with just a scrimmet of anxiety. Smiling faces turned towards her.

"Or else you will not know of the treat Robert has planned." The small anxiety disappeared, leaving Charlotte bubbling with anticipation. Robert had planned a treat for her!

She flew through breakfast, bath and dressing. Ready in less than the stipulated hour, she ran downstairs to the drawing room where the mamas and Robert awaited her.

He was his usual elegant self in silver grey pantaloons, (not for

Robert, these new-fangled drainpipe trousers), and a velvet jacket of deep violet, the colour enhancing his blue eyes. Beneath the coat, he wore a white kerseymere waistcoat, and beneath that a white frilled shirt; an altogether elegant ensemble. He was so handsome he quite took Charlotte's breath away.

"You are commendably prompt, Charlotte," he greeted her.

"Good morning everyone," Charlotte responded sunnily. "Isn't it a lovely day?" For her it would have been no matter what the weather.

"It is," agreed Robert, "and now we're all here, let us be away."

"Where are we going?" Charlotte asked, drawing nearer.

"Our destination is a secret. However, I am perfectly certain you will like it. Is that not so?" he asked the two mamas. They chorused smiling agreement.

"How tantalising!"

Charlotte was gazing at Robert, every impulse urging her to him. This morning he drew her as irresistibly as candlelight draws a moth, and just as dangerously. She wanted to be close, touching him, forgotten her resolve to keep him at a distance. She was too happy to think of depressing resolutions, and it was only fear of being repulsed that held her back.

Something in her demeanour must have revealed the impulse, because Robert held out a hand. Charlotte needed no more encouragement. She flew to him immediately, both hands outstretched to clasp his. She leaned against the length of his arm, shivering with the pleasure of touching him, feeling safe, happy and carefree.

Robert looked down at her upturned face, framed in a pretty straw bonnet trimmed with gold ribbons. "You look most fetching today, poppet," he complimented. "Come along, then. Let's go."

Charlotte walked with Robert, regulating her step to his longer stride, while the mamas following more sedately. She felt vibrantly alive. This was like Cornwall last year when they had all been happy together. Robert was smiling and approachable, as then; given up to their company completely, as then; and for the moment everything was right, as then. She refused to think beyond the desire for Robert's attention. She was happy and that was enough for today.

Outside, in gleaming pale sunshine, the carriage awaited, ready to carry them off to an exciting destination. Charlotte stepped out eagerly.

Their objective proved to be the Botanical Garden in Chelsea. When Charlotte realised where they were going her cup was filled to overflowing, because she knew that with such a treat in mind Robert could have planned it only for her.

What a wonderful day! The two mamas showed their approval at every turn and Robert indulged her slightest whim. What more could she desire?

***

In the carriage, going home, Charlotte was tired but utterly content, leaning her head upon Robert's shoulder, bonnet discarded and her hand tucked up in his.

After an early dinner she went to bed, so tired she could scarcely keep her eyes open. Robert came to say goodnight before he went out, and she thanked him for her lovely day, a sentiment endorsed by the mamas.

"I am glad you enjoyed it," he said, smiling at Charlotte. He took her face between his hands and kissed her brow. "Goodnight, angel." He did not say where he was going and she would not allow herself to wonder.

Alone, contentedly reliving the day, she could not help remarking how different Robert had been. He had neither mocked nor patronised her. He had been exactly as of old and what a difference it made. In her vulnerable state, she could not help wishing he could be like this all the time, although the promptings of reason told her these hopes were not rational. Charlotte put such wistful thoughts away, resolving to be happy as she was, with the joy of having Robert back . . . even if it were only for one day.

***

There was no time for breakfast in bed for Charlotte next morning. They were up betimes, engaged to spend the day at Lord's with the

Dean family. Refreshed, after a good night's sleep, Charlotte was her usual sparkling self and overjoyed to find Robert still in harmonious mood.

At the cricket ground, Robert stayed with her. She spent the first hour sitting between him and Spencer Dean, gratified to have *two* such handsome gentlemen attending her. Once the match got under way, of course, their attention was taken up with the play, but she did not mind this. It was enough to be where she was, close to Robert, able to touch him discretely, if she chose.

During the interval, a lively discussion developed over the vexed question of round arm bowling. As long ago as Eighteen Sixteen, Marylebone cricket club had outlawed the practice as too dangerous. However, up and coming bowlers were pressing for its introduction because the skill attendant upon playing a higher delivery, one which lifted after pitching, obliged the batsmen to exercise more ingenuity in their return, thereby affording a greater variety of playing strokes which, said those in favour, made for a more interesting game.

Robert favoured the new proposal, as did Spencer Dean. Indeed, the latter gentleman went further. Why not over arm bowling, he suggested but Robert inclined to the view that this was taking things a little too far.

Philip Dean joined them in the interval and was introduced to Charlotte. He was as appreciative of her charms as his brother, but more juvenile in expressing it. He addressed her thus, his eyes alight with mischief: "Miss Treleaven," said he, a hand clasped to his heart theatrically, "such beauty! I see my sister did not exaggerate in describing you. Miss Treleaven, you must be mine . . . at least, to the extent of allowing me to escort you in to dinner this evening."

"Sit down and stop being such a gudgeon, Sir" his father admonished lightly.

Charlotte laughed and responded to Philip in like vein. "Alas I can give you no answer, Mr Dean. Modesty forbids. You must ask my guardian," she said, turning aside her face and lowering her eyes with maidenly decorum.

Robert was amused, and said to Mrs Dean: "Two of a kind, I fancy; precocious infants, both."

"Eat up, dear boy." Mr Dean's robust advice brought Philip to descend ravenously on the picnic basket, all pretensions forgotten.

Spencer Dean asked Charlotte if she would care to perambulate the grounds. Mr Hattenbury gave permission and off they went. They were soon joined by Xanthe and her cousin, George Clement, whose sisters, Elizabeth and Amalia, were approaching from the opposite direction in company with Mr Knox.

The two parties conjoined and started out again. To Spencer's annoyance, his partnership with Charlotte was usurped by George and he found himself with Elizabeth Clement, his cousin, while Charles appropriated Xanthe.

They soon returned to the main party, the purpose of the walk not having been accomplished for Mr Dean. He had wanted to talk to Charlotte of the imminent dissolution of parliament and sound out her political interests. He also thought it best to separate his sister from Charles, because she was exhibiting a tendency to flirt with his friend. It would need to be checked. Perhaps a word in his mother's ear?

Later, in Xanthe's bedroom at the Dean family residence, Charlotte remarked on Xanthe's seeming partiality for Mr Knox. "Are you drawn to him?" she asked.

Xanthe was slow to answer. A secretive smile played about her lips. "He's frightfully amusing and sophisticated," she conceded, "but . . . drawn to him?" She shrugged. "It is too early to speak in those terms and, of course, there is also the question of whether he is drawn to me."

She tossed her blonde curls dismissively and clasped Charlotte's hands, whirling her around, skirts flying, until they were breathless. They collapsed upon the bed and hugged each other affectionately, laughing almost until they cried.

"Oh, Charlotte, may not we simply enjoy life? Everything is so perfect now."

Was it? Charlotte wondered. *Perhaps not for all.* She gave an even-handed reply. Nevertheless, she was pleasantly aware of drawing several pairs of admiring male eyes that evening, including Mr Hattenbury's, but his glance might only have been avuncular interest, of course.

No such thing. Avuncular was not in Robert's vocabulary where

Charlotte was concerned. His easy smile was nothing but a social mask. He was far from the luxury of ease, his indulgence towards her costing him dearly. His nerves were exacerbated from a constant need to keep watch upon his treacherous body, which insisted on drawing his attention with subtle reminders of desirable outcomes with Charlotte. Robert's fear was that the subtle reminders might become overt, as on her first arriving at Meva.

Darling Miss Treleaven, kept at a distance, he could live with in relative comfort. Charlotte, on terms of intimacy, he could not. But what was he to do?

After Tuesday's disastrous quarrel he could have done no other than comfort her. Every instinct urged him to it. Loving her as he did, mind and heart alike dictated that he restore her to well-being. Unfortunately, the restoration of Charlotte's happiness brought its own problems. Kissing and holding her, even briefly, had catapulted him back into the fevered state of arousal he was trying to avoid. Being aroused, he wanted much more of her than was permissible. Even to watch her captivating Spencer Dean sent his blood spiralling. Remembering how yielding her slender form, as she had lain in his arms on her bed only days ago, there came another of those less than subtle reminders, and he barely suppressed a groan.

She could not know what she did to him, when she held his arm between her breasts, as she was wont to do without realising it. She did not see, when she clung to him with unconscious need, what it cost to return her loving gestures without succumbing to thunderous desire. The hunger for her was upon him. Feeling as he did, he could not be casual or dispassionate with the girl who dominated his every thought and longing. It had to be all or nothing. In their present circumstances it could not be all. Common sense, not to say morality, dictated it so. Although, speaking of morality, per se, Robert was less and less inclined to observe its dictates in Charlotte's regard. As far as he was concerned, they were already committed. However, it still couldn't be; he had to accept that. Therefore, it must be nothing. There was no other choice.

As if it needed definition, the problem of Charlotte was brought home to him clearly when they went home to Meva.

He took a glass of brandy after the ladies retired, but did not linger over it because he was tired, having slept badly the past two nights on Charlotte's account. In the upstairs corridor his steps slowed as he neared Charlotte's suite. Thinking the two mamas would still be with her, and tempted to see her again, he tapped the door. When she called he went in. The room was dimly lit by a single branch of candles on the mantelpiece . . . and Charlotte was alone.

She was in her night gear, standing by an open window, looking out over the garden. An absurd scrap of lace, serving as a night cap, covered the top of her head. Seeing Robert, she came to him instantly, giving him no time to withdraw. Her face lit with a smile, and she said: "I hoped you would come to say goodnight, Sir. I waited in case you did."

Robert stood looking down at her, his blood beating thickly. He tried to keep his face impassive, showing nothing of what he was feeling. He said lightly: "What is this thing perched upon your head, infant?" With a separate part of his mind, he noted that he had been right about Charlotte's nightgown; it *was* prettily embroidered.

Charlotte gurgled with laughter. "My night cap, Sir. Don't you like it? Is it not time I took to my caps now I am grown up?"

He said next: "Did you enjoy yourself today?" Without thinking he picked up a strand of her hair and rubbed it between his fingers. It was silky soft . . . and he had done this before.

"Yes, it was lovely," she said, and went on to comment on the day's highlights. Robert was not listening. He was enjoying, and being tormented by, the entrancing aura that was Charlotte. "Did you?" she asked.

For a moment he was uncomprehending. "Oh, yes," he said presently.

Charlotte's hands were fluttering between them. She wanted to be in his arms as much as he wanted to hold her, and he knew it. Danger signals flashed as his thighs, sensitive to the light touch of Charlotte's body near his, registered the quick rise of desire. He took a breath, opening his mouth to say goodnight, but in so doing breathed in her scent and was caught. Suddenly she blushed and blurted: "Shall you kiss me goodnight, Robert?"

Robert's heart began to pound, his nerve-endings ascald. Playfully, trying to ease the tension between them, he asked: "Another treat for a good infant?"

"Yes, if you please," she replied, as simple and direct as ever.

Robert hesitated. Oh, God, this was too unwise. Perhaps he could safely kiss her hand, or . . . He paused too long; Charlotte's blush deepened and he knew he had shamed her. Hesitating no longer, he took her into his arms.

She clung to him immediately, stretching herself to his length, satisfying a deep-held need to feel his hard-planed, but wonderfully accommodating body, pressed close to the yearning places in hers. She wanted him to snuggle her, warm her, surround her. She desperately craved his kiss, hunger greater than discretion. How did Robert know all this? Because it was everything he wanted, too, and when she offered him her mouth he could not resist.

Robert meant only to kiss her lightly but their mouths fused, in a white heat of passion, when Charlotte drew his nether lip into her mouth and began to suck. He groaned with tortured pleasure and his desire was made manifest between them, nudging Charlotte urgently. Immediately sensitive to his arousal, she murmured softly and moved to chime with him. When she did, showing clearly that both minds and bodies were in accord, he became a welter of conflict, rational thought urging retreat, the starved compulsion to lose himself in Charlotte frantically urging him on.

He was on fire for her, heart beating heavily against Charlotte's breast, its laboured thump shaking them both. He was drowning in her, sick with desire, his whole body sensitised to her. It would be agony to leave her now but leave he must. If he did not go immediately, he knew he would not go at all that night.

He wrenched his mouth from hers. His hands began to loosen their hold, but Charlotte was as urgent as he and reluctant to be put away. Her hands reached round the back of his neck; she pressed herself to him and clung.

"No, Charlotte. This will not do," he said, his voice strangled. She made soft sounds of protest, trying to keep him in her embrace, and it was unbearable to hold her off. Oh, God, how much he wanted her!

"No, Charlotte, it will not do," he repeated, and pulled her hands from his neck, pushing her away so firmly as to be almost brutal. Then he was obliged to turn his back on her distress. There was no other way he could have left her. Even so, it took all his resolution to walk away. "Goodnight." He left her without another glance.

Charlotte went to bed and cried, with arms crossed over her body for comfort.

***

Although neither was aware of it in the other, Robert and Charlotte spent a poor night and both woke to a sense of shame.

Robert was angry with himself for his weakness. Dammit, he was a man, not a schoolboy with a schoolboy's uncontrolled impulses. He knew very well what Charlotte could do to him, even if she did not. If he could not touch her without behaving like an untutored yokel, he should not touch her at all. Charlotte *had* to understand. If she were old enough to want him, she was old enough to see she must stop tantalising him. Oh, God, she *must* stop! How else could he stand this torment?

Such was the urgency of Robert's longing, equally the need for its assuagement, he saw no ambivalence in his angry reflections.

Charlotte's self-disgust came from a different source. She was uncomfortably aware of having been extremely forward, of putting Robert in the position of having to repulse her. To have asked for his kisses when, clearly, he had not wished to give them . . . why, oh, why had she done it? She had forced herself upon him. He must be despising her for a hussy! Why *did* she do these shameful things which left her burning with humiliation? How was she ever to face Robert again?

Of the two partners in guilt Charlotte's case was the worse, for she had more than shame to contend with. Her bubble of self-delusion had burst; that false illusion of no longer loving Robert.

Even on her birthday, Charlotte had reluctantly acknowledged that he could still move her to passion when he chose, while knowing she despised his shabbiness of character. But what he said to her then had softened her attitude over the intervening months, because his words seemed to imply he liked her better. She had begun to think of him more kindly and, still wanting him, also began to think she might welcome his next proposal, accepting his imperfections, as he must accept hers. Love could, surely, grow again?

This, of course, had been before the deeply depressing arrival in London, followed by an equally numbing introduction to Mistress Lerpiniere. It had shown the folly of her hopes, for how could she compete with such allure? Robert had been right when he told her that, as he was in London, she knew him not. Last night, she had solicited his love openly, betraying herself to him and again he had repulsed her. Oh, she had aroused his passion, that was true, but it had not been enough to hold him. He had not wanted her enough. Once more, in spite of proud resolution, she had read more into his behaviour than he intended. Worse, she knew she still loved him. This was Cornwall reprised and there seemed no escape from the trap. Would she never learn?

Charlotte was in despair.

***

For their differing reasons Robert and Charlotte were reserved with each other on Friday. Charlotte took her guardian's reserve as a sign of contempt. Shrivelling with shame and self-disgust, she avoided him as much as possible.

In Robert's case it was a need to have Charlotte out of temptation's way. When they joined Lady Styneley's boating party that afternoon, he was relieved to see her go off with Philip Dean and John Neville, knowing that the Marchioness's companion, Miss Bartholomew, was chaperoning them.

The Neville family had long known the Styneleys, which was why Mr Neville's younger brother, Oswald, came to be one of the party. With a besotted smile, he was escorting Mrs Lerpiniere.

When Charlotte saw the lovely Mrs Lerpiniere she could have cried. Of course, she did no such thing. Instead, she responded to the flattering attentions of her admirers with a degree of animation Lady Styneley privately designated flirtatious. John Neville, however, was very appreciative; as he made plain. Mr Hattenbury was rather taken up with Mrs Lerpiniere and did not notice what Charlotte was up to at first.

The green-eyed charmer was giving Robert clear signals to advance and, it must be said, he was tempted. It would make life much easier, relieving him of certain problems as it would. When she said her husband was away, remarking subsequently that it was a long time since Mr Hattenbury last visited, he actively contemplated it.

"When?" he asked, as casual as she. As he spoke, he looked up and caught Charlotte's glance. She looked young and lovely, laughing at something Miss Dean had said. Seeing her fresh countenance, Robert was filled with self-disgust. How could he think of betraying his love for Charlotte? No, convenient or not, that was not the way forward.

By an odd quirk of fate, Charlotte caught his question. She was too far away to hear Robert's voice, but saw his mouth frame the single word. She knew what they were discussing beyond doubt and felt sick, but was then even more determined to conceal how much she cared and became frenetically gay. This drew her guardian's attention.

Frowning, he excused himself to Mrs Lerpiniere, and made a way to Charlotte's group. He drew her aside and was then obliged to give John Neville a quelling glance as he looked set to follow.

Looking at Charlotte, Robert saw she was flushed with heat and wondered what she had been about. Upon reflection, he realised he had not seen her for several hours except distantly. He had been negligent of his duty, but comforted himself with the thought that the mamas would have kept an eye on her. This did not make his dereliction excusable.

"You are hot, Charlotte. Come and sit with the mamas until you are cooler."

"Indeed, Sir, I am not in the least hot," she told him brightly. "The last thing I wish is to be sitting down. I am enjoying myself *far* too much."

"I insist, Miss Treleaven," Robert said equably. He put a hand under her elbow. "Come. It is rather warm." It seemed she would still resist him, but she yielded suddenly and went to sit quietly with the two mamas.

At home she was equally quiet, becoming animated only when

Robert rose to quit the drawing room. He was off to White's with Charles, but Charlotte did not know this. She began asking about arrangements for the following evening, when they were going to Xanthe's coming out. She wanted to know all manner of things and he dealt with her patiently, until Alethea remonstrated with her daughter.

"Charlotte, dear Robert is ready to go out and you are holding him up."

"Are you holding me up, angel? I thought my own two legs were doing that," he quipped lightly.

Charlotte apologised for detaining him, and then watched him go with eyes which showed an agony of despair. She *knew* he was going to Mrs Lerpiniere and lay awake long hours listening for his return.

Consequently, she looked wan in the morning and was promptly despatched back to bed, to regain her looks for the ball. She managed to sleep briefly, but for the most part brooded with sick jealousy on Robert's association with his paramour, hating them for it but hating herself more for caring so deeply. However, it would not always be so. She was going to put them out of her head, and Robert out of her heart very soon. She would find another love and be done with him. Oh . . . if only she could go home and escape this stupid, frivolous season.

***

At Xanthe's ball, that evening, Charlotte wondered at the malignity of fate. The first thing she saw on entering the ballroom was Barbara Lerpiniere's flaunting beauty. Surrounded by admirers, she looked superb in a jade satin gown whose beret sleeves and low-necked bodice showed her magnificent bosom to perfection.

Charlotte was wearing a ball dress of white crepe, embroidered all over with knots of flowers, with satin festoons at the hem. Her bodice was also quite décolleté, with a deep *pelerine en coeur*, but beside the older woman she felt dowdy. This feeling was not allowed to show. She put up her chin and advanced into the ballroom, flanked by Robert and the mamas.

The two parties gave greeting. Several of the younger gentlemen in

Barbara's court defected to Charlotte. She chatted to them composedly while distributing the favours of her dance card. Robert put down his name, saying he had better do it quickly otherwise he would be outwith any hope. Since he said much the same to Mrs Lerpiniere Charlotte was not flattered.

Looking at Charlotte, Barbara remarked to Robert, entirely without malice for she was not a spiteful girl: "And a little child shall lead them."

In a flash, Charlotte responded: "But not into temptation, Mrs Lerpiniere." She kept smiling, in spite of the fury aroused by the condescending comment.

For a fraction there was startled silence until, led by Barbara, everyone laughed at Charlotte's sally. Who could think Miss Treleaven harboured anything but pleasant thoughts of Mrs Lerpiniere? Robert, perhaps? But then his appreciation of Charlotte's wit had always been keen.

She danced indefatigably that night, but when Robert came to claim his dance after supper, she was nowhere to be seen. He found her eventually, in a conservatory which opened off the ballroom. She was drinking fruit punch with John Neville, Miss Williams and Mr Hopkins.

When Charlotte saw her guardian she exclaimed in dismay, apologising for her forgetfulness. Mr Hattenbury forgave her easily, saying that his peace was not cut up by the loss of one dance. He sat down to join the quartet. Sad to say, his presence seemed to cast a damper over the gathering and they soon returned to the ballroom.

A little later, Robert retired to the card room and there he remained until it was time to depart. Even then Charlotte was still bubbling with life. Once home she sighed and stretched luxuriously, remarking how much she had enjoyed the ball.

Robert's eyes took in the lissom grace of her body but he had nothing to say. Charlotte kissed the two mamas and tripped off to bed lightly.

No kiss for Robert which, in view of his thoughts regarding their relationship at that time, was right and proper, Charlotte's behaviour exactly as he had wished.

So why did he feel excluded?

Chapter Fourteen

Mr Hattenbury's household slept late the morning after the ball. As a consequence, they were not seen in church. Mr Neville, who also worshipped at All Soul's, was unable to further acquaintance with Miss Treleaven as he had hoped.

He did see her that afternoon in the park and she smiled at him so sweetly he was encouraged to join her circle; it availed him nothing. She was flanked on either side by the brothers Dean, neither of whom showed the slightest inclination to give ground to John Neville.

Philip Dean told him cheerfully that he must wait his turn. "Until tomorrow Miss Treleaven's time is mine."

"Perhaps you should consult Miss Treleaven as to her preference," suggested Spencer with a glancing smile for Charlotte.

"Of course she prefers me. Do you not, Miss Treleaven?" Philip coaxed.

"Oh dear, you put me in a difficult position, Mr Dean," she answered sorrowfully, but with a face full of mischief. "How am I to respond without giving offence? No matter what I say I must offend someone, if only my guardian, per adventure."

"How so your guardian, Miss Treleaven?" asked Mr Neville, puzzled.

"Mr Neville, he would think me a shocking flirt if I said I preferred you all equally," she replied demurely, to the amusement of her three escorts, who burst into appreciative laughter. It drew attention to their group.

"Charlotte is being amusing, evidently," Mrs Hattenbury commented to Robert. Her look was a little anxious.

"Evidently," he agreed evenly, appearing not to mind that Charlotte was surrounded by admirers, and giving every sign of enjoying their admiration. After a moment, however, he suggested that Alethea walk forward with her daughter.

Charles Knox arrived presently. He asked after Miss Dean and was told she was elsewhere in the park. Very shortly, he rode away.

Later, they met Lady Styneley with her son, Lord Nicholas, and her niece, Mary Williams. Miss Williams walked with a hand tucked into the elbow of a certain Mr Hopkins. Both looked happy with the arrangement. Her ladyship confided that a match was in the air, one of which she approved as Mr Hopkins was of sound character. She spoke with a force which suggested she was thinking of her other niece, Emily, who married Lord John of Fittleworth, (Robert met them in Paris, on their honeymoon, when he was coming back from Italy) and the gossip their conjoining had caused. How little Lady Styneley approved *that* marriage.

Charlotte liked Mary Williams and promptly accepted an invitation to ride with her. Robert was also invited but declined. At home, later, he remarked that Miss Williams was charming but, like her aunt, was a little too managing for his taste. Charlotte could not resist the opening this gave her.

"Chacon à son goût," she remarked and had the satisfaction of raising her guardian's eyebrows before she ran upstairs.

***

The following week they were never at home. Charlotte had callers every day and floral tributes arrived constantly. Daily, she rode with one or other of her admirers. Several times, she danced a large part of the night away with them. Robert looked on.

She enjoyed an opera with Mr Neville and his party. She spent an evening at Sadlers Wells in a gathering of young people, hosted by Mrs Clement, Mrs Dean's sister. She went to a soirée and sat with Spencer Dean the whole evening.

During one interval, they discussed the king's dissolution of parliament on the twenty second, which came about because (what with the general unrest and some extremely stormy debates in both houses of parliament) he was forced to this measure, although he was himself opposed to the bill. Possibly, the street rioting helped to concentrate his mind, particularly after last year's uprising against the king in France.

Spencer said: "I am a Tory by upbringing and inclination, but I cannot help thinking that our present electoral system is not sustainable now that the provinces are expanding so rapidly. Manchester for example, has no representation in parliament whereas your own county of Cornwall has forty two members; a great disparity of interest there. Thinking thus of course, I am in opposition to the Duke of Wellington." He gave a wry smile. "Hadley, being on the Duke's staff, sees me as being a radical in this, I'm afraid."

"You do not strike me as a radical, Mr Dean," Charlotte responded with a smile. "As to vexed question of the Reform Bill . . . I cannot say that I fully understand it. Miss Williams ~ now she *is* inclined to be radical, I think ~ and I were discussing it one morning when we rode together: she was saying that the Duke is too die-hard in his attitudes here. Since I am not acquainted with His Grace I cannot comment on that," Charlotte said, with another smile, "but it does seem to me only justice that voting rights should not be reserved to a powerful few but should be extended to all. But, as I said, I do not fully understand the business and would need to study it further before commenting sensibly.

"But as to your other point, I find it quite reprehensible that the Duke of Wellington should have his windows smashed by the mob, because he would not show a candle in solidarity, when it was common knowledge that his wife still lay in the house after her sad demise on Sunday. As if he had not enough to contend with already, poor man," Charlotte remarked sympathetically."

Mr Dean was struck, both by Charlotte's good sense in matters pragmatic and her kind heart. Unconsciously, he echoed Hadley's thought that Miss Treleaven would make a good political wife. He was very conscious of her, close by his arm, and of her perfume. He wished she would be more encouraging. Plainly, she enjoyed his company but not to the exclusion of others it seemed.

Charlotte saw the admiring glow in his eyes and was torn. She wanted to encourage him, as she had planned, but something held her back. She meant to marry, obviously she must, but she was not sure it could be to Spencer Dean. He was a fine man who deserved a fine wife. Charlotte had a lowering presentiment she did not quite fit the bill because of what had happened with Robert last summer. Maybe Mr Neville would suit her better.

He was younger than Mr Dean but equally taken with her. Further, his admiration was not as measured as Mr Dean's, but nor was his intelligence so keen. This was a disadvantage in some ways, of course.

Inwardly Charlotte sighed. It was so difficult and confusing; all Mr Hattenbury's fault. Had he not . . . complicated things, none of this anxiety would have arisen. She could have made a choice without the odium of comparison to blur decision. He was insufferable, she thought resentfully.

Her resentment of Robert was never allowed to show. She kept a firm watch on heart and mind alike, intent on not falling from grace again. To the contrary, she went out of her way to show how little she cared for Mr Hattenbury, guardian and erstwhile lover, demonstrating her pleasure in the attentions of her admirers.

Robert watched her antics with a degree of indulgence, not liking them but knowing exactly what she was up to. As he had said, there was safety in numbers. If it kept her amused and made his life easier, so be it. Time was passing. His birthday approached. After that the rein could be drawn in. Let Charlotte run her length while she might. Thus, Mr Hattenbury, in quietly confident mood, which received a nasty check on the night of Charlotte's ball.

She looked perfectly adorable, on presenting herself downstairs, in a white gown with an amber sash, and Robert's susceptible heart began its usual uneven tattoo. Only stringent mental strictures enabled him to resist the temptation she presented. After a moment, he was sufficiently in command to kiss her cheek, telling her how beautiful she was. Without hurry, but quite definitely, Charlotte removed herself from his clasp. Robert's smile went awry.

"Is one no longer permitted to show pride in you, Charlotte?" he asked, piqued.

"You do me too much honour, Sir," she replied formally, giving him a curtsey.

In the following hours Robert was too busy to think of anything but the needs of their guests. It was only with the back of his mind he noticed Charlotte's vivid animation. He was brought up short when he saw her going down the dance with Wesley Neath and looking very pleased with life.

The Neath family was socially prominent. Unfortunately, an old scandal linked his father with Mrs Neath. Her second daughter, Ariadne, the only blonde in the family, bore an undeniable resemblance to Robert. He could never look at her without feeling uncomfortable. However, there was no doubt of Wesley's paternity. Evidently, the cuckolded husband had brought his erring wife to heel, and to bed, in no uncertain measure. Even so, Robert wanted no connections with that family.

After supper, Mr Hattenbury's savoir faire received another jolt. Spencer Dean asked permission to pay his addresses to Charlotte. Robert gave him a sharp look and invited Mr Dean to join him in the library. Once seated, they took a glass of wine, while Mr Hattenbury made his position clear to the would-be suitor.

"Spencer, I must warn you that I believe Charlotte feels no more than friendship for you," he began.

"I am aware of that, Sir," Mr Dean addressed him formally, "but she does like me; ceteris paribus, her interest could be channelled in my direction."

Mr Hattenbury was silent, in something of a quandary. Then he asked: "Do you love her, Spencer?"

The other man answered openly, if a trifle stiffly. "I admire her a great deal and have done since Yuletide. I believe Miss Treleaven might make an excellent wife for a man in my position, and I think I have much to offer her."

Robert's brows rose fractionally. "Might make an excellent wife?" he queried, gently satirical. "We, of this household, think Charlotte perfect as she is, Mr Dean." Robert's smiling manner concealed considerable ire.

Spencer Dean made an equable return, although Robert's tone left him uncomfortable. "I was referring to the forms of political practice to be learned, Sir. Of herself, Miss Treleaven is a delight."

Robert inclined his head in acknowledgement. He continued to study the other man, after some deliberation saying: "I am sorry, but at this stage I must tell you no, Spencer. I think you too precipitate." He smiled. "If Charlotte means to have you she will, never doubt that. Let's see what happens. If you still wish it, approach me again in a few months."

"As you say, Sir." Spencer accepted his congé with good grace, and left Mr Hattenbury in the library.

Robert stayed on for five minutes or so, angry with Spencer Dean for putting him in an ambiguous position. He was also a little angry with Charlotte, wondering what encouragement the other man had received to bring about so previous a declaration, and whether he should tax Charlotte in this regard.

Eventually he decided against it. For one thing, he did not want to set her back up. In such case, she would most likely go against him for devilment. For another, once he had absorbed the initial shock, he did not feel threatened, especially when he recalled how Charlotte had clung to him during their last embrace. Her eyes had been clouded with love, her body quick with desire. No, he did not question her love. She was leading him a dance from pique, but he never doubted that she would submit to him when the time was right.

For all his confidence, Mr Hattenbury could not resist the lightest probe at evening's end. He had not meant to but there was a flicker of something inside him which acted of its own volition.

"Well, Charlotte, my love, you are launched," Sophie said contentedly.

"And quite the success, dear," Alethea added with motherly pride.

"It is all thanks to you, darlings, if I am." Charlotte yawned and stretched.

Robert came up behind and slipped his arms about her waist. He pressed a kiss under her ear. "Am I not to share in your approbation, Charlotte?"

Charlotte went still. Robert made no move to release her. After a moment she stepped out of his embrace. Turning, she said: "That is quite understood, Guardian. None of it could have happened without you." She kissed Sophie and went upstairs with Alethea.

Noticing that Charlotte had twice been unwelcoming to Robert that evening, Mrs Hattenbury was disquieted. He still seemed confident of marrying Charlotte but what if she no longer loved him? Sophie had seen Charlotte's friendliness to Mr Dean, and her other admirers. What if she loved another? She would be lost to them.

Robert saw his mother's anxiety and took her hand. "You should not worry, Mama," he advised with a reassuring smile, "all is well."

"Darling . . . are you perfectly sure?"

"Yes," he said gently. As she still looked anxious he added, with a wry twist of the mouth: "I shall not suffer you to lose your beloved Charlotte, believe me."

"Robert, no," she said with a dismissive shake of the head, "that is not my concern, but . . . she seems to have taken a liking for Mr Dean. If this is so, how will she marry you? And, darling, do not mistake me, it is *your* happiness that I want, not just mine, to keep Charlotte with me."

Out of the blue Robert spoke a thought he had not been aware of entertaining. "You certainly love her better than you ever loved me."

There was a moment of absolute, stunned silence. Sophie was so stultified by what Robert had said she could utter not a word. They stared at each other, she in horror that he should believe such a thing, he stupefied to have revealed it.

"Robert, no," Sophie found voice, "that is simply not *true*! How could you even *think* such a thing? Darling, oh . . . you must know I love you more than anyone in the world!" she exclaimed. "How could it be otherwise? You are my dear son, my darling boy! Oh . . . Robert . . ." Sophie put her arms about him tightly, "you must not think this dreadful calumny of me." Tears were in her eyes as she looked into his face. "I want you to marry Charlotte so that y*ou* can be happy. Do you not know that? *You*, Robert, for all your life to be happy with her, as you were last year at home, because you *were* happy then, I *know* you were."

Robert's expression was a strange mixture, hard to define, as he returned her embrace. "I was a fool not to marry her when you advised it," he said, for once speaking without reserve. "I should have listened to you, Mama. Unfortunately, it is only these last months I realised that Charlotte is the only person who can make me happy . . . she, and she alone. I am not like Papa in that, you see."

Sophie gasped! What a night of shocks! But . . . how to respond to this one? Before she could even begin to think Robert drew back from her, apologising.

"I retract that remark absolutely, Mama. Please forgive me." He would have turned away but she quickly prevented him.

"No, no, dearest, wait. Robert, wait. There is no need to apologise. I . . . I was taken by surprise, that is all, but I am perfectly willing to speak of this if it is your wish. Indeed, perhaps it is time for you to know, but . . . do you think, a glass of wine, to help us marshal our thoughts?"

Robert took his mother to the library. Once settled, Sophie began to speak of what had caused the tragic separation from his father, her quiet voice, at this late date, revealing very little of her feelings about it. Looking at her, it was not hard to trace Robert's coolth to its source, for both of them concealed deep emotion beneath a composed exterior.

"You see, darling," she concluded at length, "only those who cannot know the truth blame your papa. His was a very hard choice to make."

Robert listened intently, frowning, digesting all he had been told. His first instinctive reaction as a virile young man was to be appalled at what his parents had been called upon to face. Following swiftly on this was pain that he had been its unwitting cause. "You say you love me, Mama, but I wonder you did not detest me!" he said wryly.

"Darling, how could I? It was not your fault," Sophie said gently.

Robert continued to gaze at his mother, shaking his head in disbelief as other, more fundamental and deeply felt emotions rose to the surface.

"I find your forbearance remarkable, Mama, both to myself and Papa. But . . . did he truly deserve it? How *could* he have left you solitary at such a time, and for such reason? Did he never once consider that your loss was as great as his? Why did he not stay with you?" At this point, Robert, shocked out of his usual reticence by the nature of

Sophie's revelations, said: "Surely . . . do forgive my indelicacy, Mama, but, surely, mutual solace may be provided in ways other than conjoining? What of his vow to love and cherish you, to be faithful unto death? If he loved you, must not this come first? I find his selfishness incomprehensible and totally unforgivable."

Sophie blushed faintly but was equally candid. This was a night for honesty it appeared. Never had mother and son spoken so plainly to each other. "Your father wanted children, Robert. We planned a dozen, at least. And as to your . . . conjecture, Francis did make me such an offer, but knowing that if he wanted children he must prefer other women before me, I could not bring myself to accept."

"He wanted children! That is to excuse him?" Robert shook his head in disgust. "No, Mama. I make no doubt, so did *you*. Do I not myself? Though mistresses *I* have had aplenty, you will find no bastard of mine gracing society in years to come. One falls over Papa's everywhere!" Robert was bitterly impassioned.

"Hush, darling boy. It is useless to repine now. Whatever you think of Papa, of what he did, you must remember that he always loved you dearly," Sophie said gently.

After a moment's silence, while he became calmer, Robert nodded slowly. "Yes, I always knew that, though I had little enough of his society. Others had much more," he said, showing his resentment at this circumstance.

Sophie ignored that, not prepared to engage in further difficult issues this night. Instead, she declared stoutly: "And *I* love you, Robert, so let there be no more nonsensical talk of my loving Charlotte better. What you must do is marry her quickly, so that I may take pleasure in you both," she paused, "and in your children, of course," she added mischievously.

He smiled. "I will do my best to fulfil expectation, Mama."

There the conversation ended, yet both were easier with each other afterwards. The shared confidence brought mother and son closer. In time, it enabled Robert to speak to her openly of his love for Charlotte.

There was another, slightly curious effect. Breakfasting en famille, and very late, the morning after the ball, Robert began addressing Mrs

Treleaven as mater. Naturally, it was noticed. With cheerful insouciance he said she was like another mother, so he may as well address her as such. Mrs Treleaven was delighted and showed her pleasure in a confused speech which ended, incoherently, with a kiss planted on Robert's cheek. Charlotte had nothing to say.

Shortly after breakfast, a thunderous knock heralded the arrival of a boisterous Charles Knox, in company with Miss Dean, Miss Clement, the two Misters Neville and the Fitz-Bassetts. There was no sign of Spencer Dean.

"*Avanti*, Robbie, old chap, *avanti*. How often did we hear that on our travels?" Charles hailed him loudly.

"What had you in mind?" Robert queried, unruffled.

"Riding. Come, lovely Miss Charlotte. We are off instanter. No time to lose on this heavenly morning."

"Such exuberance," Robert commented mildly, as Charles caught Charlotte by the hand and hurried her away. He followed at a more leisurely pace. Thankfully, the two mamas subsided into the abrupt peace left by their departure.

Charlotte became infected with Charles' gaiety and her excitement set the douce animal beneath her to prancing. Robert brought his horse alongside to quiet her, but Charlotte waved him away: with that the mare plunged and galloped off. Robert was left watching anxiously for Charlotte's safety. Mr Knox showed no such anxiety and galloped after her with a wild hulloo, followed by an equally exuberant Miss Dean.

The rest of the party came on, but it was some time before they caught up and then only because Charlotte turned back. She pulled up in front of them, breathless and laughing. Miss Dean, and Charles, was right behind.

The whole time they were out Charlotte bubbled with life and laughter. Robert was torn between irritation at her provocative behaviour and pleasure in her vivid loveliness. Had he been the focus of her attention he would have felt only the pleasure, he knew. Nothing of these feelings showed, however. He gave his partner, Miss Clement, all the attention which was her due.

Back at Meva, the party trooped into the house to take refreshments, disrupting the older ladies' peace once more. During coffee Mrs Fitz-Bassett mooted an evening at Vauxhall Gardens. It was enthusiastically seconded by Xanthe. Her cousin Elizabeth was not sure of gaining approval. Xanthe said airily she would fix it and provisional arrangements were made for the following Friday.

After refreshment, Mr Neville asked if Charlotte would show him the beautiful garden, at which there was a general exodus into the fresh air.

Robert walked with Charlotte and her escort. This had not been Mr Neville's intention but there was nothing he could do to prevent it. Only at visit's end did the frustrated young man get Charlotte to himself. He created the moment by pausing to point at a bush. "What is this plant, Miss Treleaven?" he asked.

She turned back and told him its name. He put a hand over hers, where it rested on the top rail of a rustic seat. Charlotte looked an enquiry and tried to draw her hand away. He tightened his grip.

"Miss Treleaven, please wait a moment," he whispered. "I cannot get you to myself, even for a minute and there is so much I would like to say."

"Mr Neville, I am perfectly happy to talk to you but do release my hand. My guardian will not look upon this constraint with favour." He apologised and released her at once. Charlotte sat down with him. They were in full view so there could be no objection. Mr Neville wasted no time.

"My sister is shopping at the haberdasher's in Bond Street tomorrow and I am escorting her. Would you care to join us?"

As she had yet to go shopping, Charlotte was delighted and said she would ask Mr Hattenbury.

"Pray, do not speak to him in front of the others. They will all want to come and that is not what I wish," Mr Neville said anxiously. "Ask him when we are gone. My sister and I will call in hope of gaining a positive response tomorrow." Charlotte agreed, laughing.

***

Mr Hattenbury raised no objection when the idea was put to him. In fact, he gave Charlotte some guineas to spend and told her lightly not to flirt too much with her new beau. He also waited in to greet Mr Neville when he called.

For a wicked moment, when he saw the young man eye him with trepidation, Robert was tempted to include himself in the expedition. With some regret, he decided he could not be such a cur as to destroy all Mr Neville's careful planning. He contented himself with waving them off. He lingered in the street after they had gone, enjoying the morning freshness and, as he stood there, a chaise approached. In it were Xanthe and Spencer Dean.

Robert sighed. Charlotte's beaux were beginning to weary him. However, he greeted the pair civilly and invited them in. However, when he said Charlotte had gone shopping Spencer declined, thinking Xanthe might also like to go to the shops. She was not keen at first but was eventually persuaded. Unregretful, Robert saw them go.

He was not destined for a peaceful morning. Shortly, Charles Knox arrived. Robert began to think he was living in the middle of Piccadilly Circus. He also recognised the source of Miss Dean's disinclination for shopping.

"How-de-do, Charles," he greeted blandly. "I fear you have missed your target. The lady has gone."

"Damn!" Charles grinned unashamedly. "When do you expect Miss Charlotte's return? Soon, I hope."

Robert eyed him sardonically. "Come, Charles. You can do better than that."

Charles threw down hat and crop. He settled in a chair, and told Robert to get out a bottle. Robert made no demur. With the bottle between them Charles spoke again. "What do you think of her?"

"Charlotte? I think her delightful, of course." Robert feigned surprise.

"No, you fool, I meant Xanthe Dean. Do you think her too young for me? Eh?" Charles looked at Robert obliquely.

"Are you serious?" Robert was really surprised this time.

"I think I am," Charles answered, slowly. He was pensive, twisting the stem of the glass between his fingers. He went on: "The thing is . . . do I go ahead? The sweet darling likes me, I know, but is she old enough to know her own mind, or am I simply a passing fancy? That is the question but I'm damned if I know the answer. Am I just an old fool, Robbie? What say you? What should I do?"

"My dear Charles, I can't advise you. You, alone, know what you should do."

"You are right of course, and commonsense inclines me to retire but ~ and it is a damnable but ~ she fires me. There's the truth on it. She fires me, damn it." He tossed off his wine in a gulp while Robert watched him through narrowed eyes.

"Think of an alternative, something a little older, perhaps," Robert suggested.

Charles' mouth twisted wryly at Robert's suggestion. "It has no appeal."

Robert shrugged. "Here. Drink up and drown your sorrows." He replenished their glasses liberally.

"What think you of marriage, Robbie?"

"I?" Robert laughed shortly. "I am all in favour. It beats celibacy any day."

Something in his tone caught Charles' attention. "What! You, too? Who is it? Charlotte! It has to be," he hazarded.

"Yes," Robert said laconically, after a long moment of reserve.

Charles stared at him, and burst out laughing. He laughed until the tears stood in his eyes, and then hooted: "My God, Robbie what a pair of cawkers we are. Oh . . . damnation to all women! Old Harry take the lot of them! Let's pledge ourselves to wine instead."

"Here, here," Robert agreed. The effects of wine were predictable; the effects of love were not. So far it had brought him more trouble than joy. Strange that he should echo Charlotte's sentiments so nearly.

***

Meanwhile, the sprightly damsels of whom they spoke were spending money lavishly, together with Miss Neville and her brother.

John Neville eyed Mr Dean with cordial dislike, fulminating at the uninvited addition to his party. But, as had happened so frequently before, there was nothing he could do but endure his misfortune and try his luck again that evening at the theatre. He prognosticated gloomily that he probably would not succeed there either.

Alas, Mr Neville's expectations looked all too probable. The enchanting Miss Treleaven was knee deep in admirers when he arrived at Mr Hattenbury's box during the first interval. He could only bow over the adored one's hand.

He fared better at the second attempt because all the Deans, thank heaven, were in their own box for once, and he had the foresight to take Mrs Lerpiniere with him. She, miraculously, drew off Miss Charlotte's guardian. Even so it was a close run thing. Mr Hattenbury was setting out to take a stroll with his ward. Thoughtfully, John Neville fell into step with the lovely Miss Treleaven.

She welcomed him warmly and graced his arm with her fingertips. He was in seventh heaven. Walking with Charlotte, he mentioned an outing his mother planned to Somerset House, to see an exhibition of pictures and view the painted ceiling panels by Cipriani. Would she and her mother care to join them?

Charlotte smiled and said she was sure her guardian would agree. "Why not ask him now?" she suggested and turned back to the others. Coming up to Mr Hattenbury, whose arm also supported an elegant hand, she adopted a coaxing pose. "Dear Mr H," she began, at which he put up a haughty brow.

"Dear Mr H, indeed. Unless I miss my guess, *you* are about to ask for something, infant," he drawled.

"How did you guess, Sir? Mr Neville has invited me to a picture exhibition with his family and I would *so* like to go. May I?" Charlotte asked, her warmth of tone thrilling to John Neville's ears.

Mr Hattenbury's reaction was rather different. He gave his ward an extremely level glance before asking: "Is the invitation for you alone?"

"Oh, no, Sir," Mr Neville interjected hastily. "Mrs Treleaven is also invited."

"Very well," Mr Hattenbury agreed brusquely, at which the party moved on, Charlotte's beau ecstatic, as she responded to his overtures with melting warmth.

Robert, on the other hand, was furious. What the devil did Charlotte think she was up to? Family parties indeed! At this rate, young Neville would be declaring himself as precipitately as Spencer Dean. He could cheerfully have throttled Charlotte as he watched her lead the unsuspecting John Neville up the garden path.

As a relief for exacerbated feelings, he entered into a light flirtation with his erstwhile mistress, allowing his gaze to linger, quite definitely linger, on her charms. When Charlotte saw this she, of course, felt obliged to flirt even more, just to show how little she cared for Mr Hattenbury and his activities.

She salved her conscience by deciding that she would definitely accept Mr Neville if he proposed. Yes, certainly! He would make an excellent husband. Further, his family lived in Sussex, so she could be entirely separate from Mr Hattenbury once she married, and the sooner the better. What he saw in that . . . that . . . woman she would never know!

At evening's end, Mr Hattenbury hustled his family into the carriage and home. Charlotte protested his cavalier treatment. He told her savagely to be quiet and she subsided, overcome with sudden misery. Robert was conscious of two pairs of enquiring eyes directed at him. He was too angry to care and made no explanation.

Sophie knew very well what ailed him. She had seen Charlotte's provocative behaviour with Mr Neville. What a worry! First Mr Dean, and now this! What had got into Charlotte? She was not normally wayward. If Robert allowed her to run the length he would lose her for sure.

Robert had no intention of allowing any such thing. He did some thinking after his womenfolk had gone to bed that night. In the morning he was ready. Before Charlotte stepped out he called her to the library.

"Charlotte," he commenced without preamble, "I would be failing in my duty if I did not point out that you are behaving unwisely with Mr Neville."

She put up her brows in an unconscious imitation of his style. "Indeed," she remarked, every bit as haughty as he could be.

"Yes, indeed, my angel. It ought to stop," he went on evenly.

Charlotte tutted irritably. "Sir, I have already asked you not to address me by inept titles. I am neither angelic nor infantile. Call me Miss Treleaven, if you please." She was angry and, with one glance at her stormy face, everything fell into place for Robert. This was familiar ground.

"I beg your pardon, Charlotte," he sued. "It was not my intention to patronise you. If that is how it seemed, you are perfectly right to object. Truthfully, I meant only to express affection." Robert was mild and conciliatory. His approach took the wind out of Charlotte's eye and her poker back relaxed visibly. He went on: "But that is side tracking. The point is that it is unkind to encourage Mr Neville, unless you mean something by it, otherwise, you could break his heart," he said straightly.

"Who is to say what I mean?" she responded evasively.

"Only you, Charlotte," he replied gravely.

"What if I am happy to encourage Mr Neville?" she asked, raising her chin.

"I would caution you to search your heart. If you continue as you are, Mr Neville will ask me for an interview. What do you wish me to tell him if he does?"

Charlotte opened her mouth to speak but closed it again, word unspoken. She was confused by her guardian's directness. Suddenly her eyes flashed, and up went her head. She rose, to stand before him defiantly. "As my guardian, what do *you* advise, Sir?" she challenged.

Robert also rose, in leisurely fashion. Surprising Charlotte, he drew her near, putting one hand under her chin, the other at the back of her head. Then he kissed her, his mouth moving with infinitely skilled sweetness on hers, until her lips parted and she gave herself up to him. When she did, triumph manifestly surged through Robert's body. He took his hands from her face and slid them down her back, to nestle her closer to the desire Charlotte always roused in him when she was close, as now, and she did not resist.

Reluctantly, Robert brought up his head and drew breath, pressing his cheek to Charlotte's throat, rubbing his mouth against the silken skin of her shoulder.

"If you feel like this when John Neville kisses you, I would advise you to take him, Miss Treleaven," Robert whispered huskily. Charlotte leaned into him weakly, her body flooded with acute, anguished desire, tormented by a hunger for that which she could not have.

There was a tap at the door and Mrs Treleaven bustled in. She stopped short, to see Charlotte in Robert's arms, his mouth pressed to her throat.

"Oh, Robert dear, I do beg your pardon," she said in confusion, "I did not know you were . . ." She hardly liked to express her thought in words.

Robert straightened. With perfect composure he said: "No doubt, Mater, you have come to tell me Charlotte's visitors are here."

"Yes, dear, that is it exactly," she responded in relief. She turned to her daughter. "Are you ready my love?"

"I am, Mama," Charlotte murmured, very subdued as she left the room. She did not look at Robert again, but he was never outwith her thoughts the entire day.

Her reflections were sombre indeed, concerned with his cruelty, (there was no other word for it), in diminishing her as he did by reminders of her weakness for him. Why must he do it?

Why?

***

They did not meet again until evening when they dined with James Norris. He was in London to bring glad tidings to his widowed father of the birth of a son to Amaryllis. He brought his brother and younger sister, Andrena, home with him.

The dinner, a large affair, was by way of celebration. Charles Knox, the new uncle, was there; most of the Deans were invited, as was Robert and his three ladies; and numerous other family connections.

Robert behaved quite naturally when he saw Charlotte again, and she with him, giving no hint of what she thought of the morning's love making. Indeed, to observe them together, it might never have happened; *and what did it matter anyway*, Charlotte thought? There were other interesting gentlemen aplenty.

Spencer Dean was back in town. He presented Charlotte with a flower. Fortuitously, it matched her gown. She would not allow him to pin it to her sleeve himself but she did wear it. Mr Knox commented pleasingly that it gave her eyes an amber tint, agreeing with Robert who had remarked it first, unknown to Charlotte.

As Charles spoke his glance strayed to Xanthe. She also was wearing a flower, one he had given her, and his face revealed everything he was feeling. Xanthe blushed and returned his heart-melting look.

Charlotte intercepted the exchange between them and pain knifed through her sharply, but she would not allow it to take hold. She *would* be happy. She would! With whom, though? There was the rub. She could not make up her mind between Mr Dean and Mr Neville.

It was so difficult a choice Charlotte cried herself to sleep and woke with a severe headache in the morning. She felt heavy and lethargic. After breakfast Mr Hattenbury despatched her back to bed with an injunction to stay there until she felt better, in spite of Charlotte's assurances that there was nothing wrong with her. Still, it was pleasant to be comfortably in bed, being cosseted by the two mamas, and when she got up for dinner she was restored to her usual vivacity, as her guardian observed, taking her face between his hands and giving her a searching look.

"Better, yes, but I think we should not be late tonight all the same," he remarked judiciously. Charlotte moved restively and he released her.

"Certainly, Sir, if you think it best," she said, surprising Robert with her docility. The sting came in the tail. "I would not hazard my day out with Mr Neville tomorrow. You had not forgotten, I hope."

He laughed. "No, darling, I had not forgotten. Pray don't worry. I am watching you every step of the way, little Thomasina."

Charlotte blushed with annoyance and began remonstrating with him over his arrogance, but he hushed her because their guests were arriving, leaving her to another evening of fulmination over her insufferable guardian. She was glad to retire at evening's end, to be outwith the constant goad of his presence.

However, next day all unpleasantness was forgotten. The Neville family was so affable and welcoming Charlotte liked them immediately.

John Neville himself was courteously attentive which she also appreciated.

After a leisurely visit to Somerset House, they returned to the family home, where refreshments were laid out in the garden. Here again, Charlotte's spirits were rejuvenated, for now that John Neville had achieved his objective, having Charlotte to himself, he was more relaxed in his manner and Charlotte opened to him.

There was a river at the bottom of the garden. Mr Neville asked Mrs Treleaven's permission to take Charlotte out in a boat. Permission granted, Charlotte was settled under a parasol. Her escort took to the oars and rowed industriously for some minutes. Then he shipped oar and allowed the boat to drift while they talked of general things, finding themselves in agreement on many points.

They were not out long. When the boat nudged bank, John Neville helped Charlotte on to dry land, his hand trembling as he touched her. He was shaking, she saw, as he put her fingers to his lips. He raised bemused eyes to her face and she knew, as though he had said it aloud, that though he kissed her fingers he was thinking of her lips. She drew back in confusion for no man but Robert had ever kissed her. Mr Neville stepped away at once and apologised for his presumption.

Later, as Charlotte and her mother were leaving, Mr Neville's father kissed the hand of both ladies in farewell. John Neville followed his father's example and Charlotte found she was no longer confused by his touch. When he said he looked forward to seeing her at the opera that evening she echoed the sentiment truthfully.

Charlotte enjoyed his company but not, alas, the opera. To her ears, the music sounded raucous and ended by giving her the headache. She was not sorry to go home, the thought of bed blissful.

At home, about to go upstairs, she paused reluctantly at Robert's bidding. He studied her searchingly and touched the faint shadows under her eyes. "Are you not feeling well, Charlotte?" he asked kindly.

"I have a headache, that is all, Sir," she replied, unmoving under his light duress. She had a sudden longing to be in his arms, to rest her head upon his shoulder. He was comfort and she so wanted to be comforted.

"In that case, off to bed with you. I will send Mater up with a relieving powder. Sleep well, Charlotte. You will not want to be tired for your visit to Vauxhall."

Charlotte went to bed wearily, for once taking no pleasure in the morrow's prospects. Tucked up in bed by her mama, she soon drifted off to sleep. In the morning her headache was completely gone.

Xanthe called with her sister Anne. The girls repaired to Charlotte's suite, to spend an enjoyable hour discussing their toilettes for that evening. Anne was too young to go to the party but was still interested in their gowns.

While they were abovestairs another visitor arrived. Predictably, it was Charles Knox. Robert took him into the garden, where they were presently joined by the girls, who discovered them deep in serious talk.

Charles abandoned Robert without a backward glance as soon as Xanthe appeared. After a few minutes general conversation they drifted off.

Robert watched them go, face enigmatic, before turning to the other girls. He then entertained Miss Dean amusingly for the next quarter of an hour, while Charlotte sat in the shade of a magnolia absorbed in sewing, the smallest of droops to her lips. She was frowning, Robert noticed, and wondered if she had another headache. There was an air about her which brought him unaccustomed anguish that day.

To banish the feeling he called to invite her for a walk around the garden with Miss Dean. She looked up and the drooping lip curved into a smile. Robert's anxiety disappeared, in spite of Charlotte's refusal to go with them, saying she preferred to stay where she was. He took young Miss Dean alone. When he returned, Charles and Xanthe were with him. Xanthe wore the dreamy look of a girl who had been thoroughly kissed. Robert hoped her sister was not a tale bearer.

Charles was no less thorough when he kissed his lady at Vauxhall Gardens that night. They slipped away for precious moments of privacy. He could scarcely leash his desire for Xanthe, body afire, heart beating frantically. He was desperate to have her to himself and the unreservedly passionate kisses he pressed upon Xanthe kept her mute in his arms. She trembled but held to him as tightly as he to her, returning his kisses with an unmistakable hunger that went to his head completely.

"Oh, God, Xanthe, I love you. I want you so much I am in a fever night and day," he groaned, his mouth pressed to her throat. "I know I should not say these things to you, dearest love, but my first thought when I wake in the morning is of you. You are my last thought at night. I long for you unceasingly. Can I ever hope you would love me in return? Do not play with my feelings, Xanthe. Put me out of my misery. If I ask the impossible tell me, but tell me quickly for I can bear this torment no longer."

"Oh, Charles, darling Mr Knox, I adore you," she breathed tremulously.

Charles' body jerked with glorious shock. For a moment he could not quite believe what he had heard. "Do you? Do you, truly? Oh, my lovely Xanthe, my darling, darling girl!" he exclaimed feverishly. "Do you know how happy you make me?"

"Dear Charles I have loved you this age," she murmured, "and felt sure you must know, for I cannot be calm when you are near. I look for you in every place I go and *long* to be with you."

There was a moment of wondering silence, pregnant with yearnings and hopes as yet unexpressed. Then Charles asked: "Enough to spend the whole of your life with me, darling?" He was holding her ever more tightly, to which she made not the smallest objection, clinging to his ardent body in return, drowning in the pleasure his touch induced. Too overcome to speak, she could only nod her consent and draw down his head until their lips met; at which Charles kissed her; and he went on kissing her.

Mrs Dean drew her husband's attention to Xanthe's absence. When their daughter returned, more than an hour later, Mr Dean was on the watch for her, frowning when he saw she was with Knox and giving him a repressive glance. He looked even more repressive when Xanthe's escort requested an interview. He told Charles he would grant him ten minutes on Monday morning.

Charles was prompt and nervous as he asked for Xanthe's hand in marriage. Mr Dean calmly declined to give it. Charles drew a sharp breath, his disappointment profound. White about the mouth, he asked why.

"My daughter has been out only a few weeks, too short a time to make an informed choice. She is not ready for marriage," Mr Dean answered.

Although he refused Charles, he was not quite as repressive as at Vauxhall. Seeing that Charles was genuinely distressed, he added: "Mr Knox, I see you feel true admiration for my daughter but you are some years older than she and know your own mind. She is young, with many opportunities ahead."

"I know that, Sir, and was myself cautious of advancing. I said nothing until I was sure of Miss Dean's feelings for me. But . . . she does love me and our affection is not solely of a few weeks standing. We fell in love at Christmas and we do deal well together," Charles said quietly, composed but still rather white.

Mr Dean observed Charles keenly, hands steepled, forefingers to his lips. After a moment's deliberation he spoke again. "Mr Knox, I must reiterate that I believe Miss Dean too young to marry although, I will tell you, she does speak of loving you also."

"What if she speaks truly, Sir?" Charles asked, as calmly as he could. Again he came under Mr Dean's penetrating eye. He held the keen gaze while hoping his inner turmoil did not show, finding it difficult to gauge Mr Dean's thoughts.

"If so you are at liberty to approach me again, but there will be no talk of a match yet, Mr Knox."

This response did much to dispel Charles' anxiety, if not quite the whole. "Thank you, Sir," he said. "I shall be back."

Mr Dean rather thought he would.

Chapter Fifteen

Charlotte knew nothing of Xanthe's fortunes for some time because she was seriously ill. At Vauxhall she developed another violent headache. It was so bad, and her throat so sore, she felt sick with pain. Eventually it became insupportable and she looked for Robert, too ill to dissemble. She desperately needed the comfort only he could give her.

"Robert," she whispered. He looked up sharply.

"Charlotte, what is it?" he asked, frowning in concern at her white face.

"Pain . . ." she touched a finger to her temples, wincing convulsively as the hammer blows struck again and again. "I feel so ill. Please may I go home, Sir," she supplicated, with outstretched hands.

Mr Hattenbury waited for nothing and no-one, nor even excused himself to their party. He lifted Charlotte in his arms and supported her to the carriage, holding her until they reached home. On arrival he carried her up to her rooms.

This was when the nightmare began for Robert and the mamas.

Charlotte was got to bed and the physician sent for. Until he arrived Robert held Charlotte close, even when she vomited from the raging pain of head and throat. He soothed her with meaningless phrases of comfort, wiping her face and stroking her hair. When she began to lose consciousness, fear ate into him.

She rallied briefly and entreated: "Please stay, Robert. Do not leave me."

"I will never leave you, my darling," he promised calmly, hiding his fear.

His face, and the comforting sound of his voice, went with Charlotte into the void which presently claimed her. They were her last recollections for many days; and Robert was left in deepest dread as he listened to the sound of her laboured breathing. In his mind was one, deathly word.

Cholera!

This mortal scourge was already in the city, as it was in many other towns. At Falmouth, in their isolated county of Cornwall, there was the worst outbreak for many years. Now, Charlotte was exhibiting all the symptoms of cholera. Was it for this he had brought her to London, Charlotte's life the cost of his pride? Dear God, let it not be! Oh, please, let it not be!

The physician arrived. He examined Charlotte, shaking his head gravely.

"Well!" Robert demanded sharply. "Is it cholera?"

"I fear it could be, Sir. We shall not know for several days. Meanwhile, you will need a nurse to care for the patient. I know . . ."

"No!" Robert's tone brooked no argument. "In this house are three persons who love her more than life itself. We will care for her."

"As you wish, Sir," the man agreed, looking most surprised. "So then . . . you must keep the patient warm and dry. Let her drink wine and water mixed, if she can keep it down, but nothing else. I shall call again tomorrow."

***

Charlotte was deathly ill for a sennight, with the physician calling every day. The first week was a living nightmare for those in Meva House because they did not know if she would live or die. Their anxiety was only slightly relieved by the physician's eventual pronouncement that she did not have cholera for there was no bloody flux. What she had was a putrid infection of the throat[2] a less dread disease, but still fatal more often than not.

Tonsilitis.

There were seven days of delirium during which time Robert never left Charlotte's bedside, not even at night, although his mother urged him to rest.

"I cannot leave her, Mama, I cannot. I promised Charlotte I would stay." He looked at Sophie with eyes dark-hollowed from lack of sleep and fear.

"Darling, she would not want you to make yourself ill. Truly, she would not," his mother reasoned. Robert shook his head doggedly. He would not be moved.

"If anything happened when I was not with her, I could not bear it." His burning gaze returned to Charlotte. "She knows that I am here, Mama. She rests more easily when I hold her."

Sophie had to acknowledge that this was true, having watched Robert help Charlotte drink, or hold her when the fever was high and she rambled, calling for him constantly. She had seen him sponge the streaming perspiration from Charlotte's face and body, changing her soaked nightrail, caring for her as selflessly as any parent for a child. Indeed, at first, she had been moved to protest at the intimate nature of Robert's attentions to Charlotte.

"I should be doing this for her, not you, Robert," she said.

He ignored her strictures. "No," he said with finality, "*I* will do whatever must be done. Nothing matters, Mama, except that she lives."

Poor Mrs Treleaven was too distracted to notice what Robert did, her mind numbed with fear that she might be about to lose the last and best of her dear babies. Surely, oh surely, God would not be so cruel? Was nothing to be left her?

On the fourth night there was no change; nor the fifth and six. On the seventh night of fever, in the darkest hour, so great was Robert's exhaustion he was overcome by the fear of Charlotte's dying. She already looked like a wraith and he knew her fever-ravaged body could not continue the battle much longer. *But if she died what would he do?* Oh, such anguish: the thought of a world in which there was no Charlotte.

Robert wept, in an agony of despair, head bowed over Charlotte's prone form.

Shaking with fear, he kissed and stroked her face repeatedly, telling her how much he loved her, that he could not live without her, imploring her not to leave him. Then, with terror numbing his mind, he lay with Charlotte and took her in his arms. He opened her nightgown and pressed his face to her breast for his own comfort, because it might be for the very last time.

Never again to hold Charlotte in his arms, or know her kiss? Never again to hear her voice or see her smile? Oh, God in heaven let that not be!

***

Had this been the turning point of her illness? Robert did not know. He only knew that after the night's events he woke, at the touch of his mother's hand, and found Charlotte sleeping peacefully, her skin cool, the fever broken.

He looked up at Sophie with tears in his eyes. "Mama, feel." He transferred her hand to Charlotte's brow. "The fever is gone, praise God. Oh, dear, darling, lovely Charlotte, my plea was heard." Robert gathered her close and pressed a tear-wet face to Charlotte's. Sophie held them both in a thankful embrace.

After a moment she spoke. "Let me look after Charlotte now, darling. You *must* go to bed and rest. Give her into my keeping," Sophie urged, "I will watch her for you."

"A moment alone with Charlotte, Mama, then I will do as you ask."

So it was, that on the eight day of Charlotte's illness, Robert consented to retire to his own chamber, where once again he thanked God upon his knees before falling into bed exhausted. He slept the clock around and was not seen again until Sunday evening.

Charlotte's first, brief return to wakefulness came at Saturday noon. She recognised her mama and asked for a drink. Then she closed her eyes and drifted away. This happened several times during that day. She slept the whole of Saturday night through and, as dawn was breaking, she awoke to full consciousness. It was the first time in nine days, and a miracle she had survived so long and ravaging an illness.

Opening her eyes she saw a carafe on the bedside table. It was an irresistible draw but Charlotte was too weak to reach it. She only succeeded in knocking over the glass. Sophie, dozing in a chair, was roused by the noise. Seeing that Charlotte was awake, a smile lit her tired face.

"Dearest . . . you are awake at last," she murmured, smoothing the tumbled hair from Charlotte's brow. "Were you trying to reach the flask?"

"Please," Charlotte said, her throat so dry she could hardly speak, but it was no longer intolerably sore and closed.

After drinking, Charlotte did not go back to sleep immediately but watched as dawn's pearl light drifted into the room. Outside, bird song was beginning to disturb the quiet. She listened and dreamed of Cornwall, of dawn breaking over Hawks Tor, of kestrels wheeling above the rocks, of pheasants silently strutting the lanes, and of the abiding quietude of the moor. Her heart longed for its solitude and austere beauty. She closed her eyes and was transported back into that secure world of home.

Next time she woke it was after noon. Her mama sat with her, looking every bit as tired as Mrs Hattenbury, and equally joyful to see Charlotte wake.

She took her daughter's hand. "My dear love, we have been so worried. How glad I am to see you looking better. Can I get you anything, dearest child?"

"A drink, please, Mama."

Alethea hovered solicitously while Charlotte drank. "Oh, my dear, how relieved I am to see you awake." Thankful tears were in her eyes. "This last week has been a nightmare. Without dear Robert's constant help and encouragement we would all have despaired." Her voice shook with emotion. Charlotte was obliged to press her mother's hand for her comfort.

When Robert emerged from his rooms he ate first and then returned to Charlotte. She was sleeping again. He sent Alethea away to rest and stood gazing at his beloved. She was his world and now he knew, beyond question, that he was hers; for so she had shown him the last night he was with her. Never again would he doubt. He sat beside Charlotte and took her hand. She did not stir.

***

From Monday onwards, Charlotte began to improve in earnest. She was not strong enough to get out of bed that first day but she did eat a little. Robert saw her much improved when he visited that evening but she was very tired and dreadfully wasted. Not wanting to tire her, he stayed only half an hour.

"I will relieve you of my presence, Charlotte. I am dining at the Cornish Club with James Norris," he told her as he went away.

He left Charlotte tearfully resentful. Robert had not seen her for more than a week and when he did come he stayed only half an hour. She supposed he was busy with the lovely Barbara. He'd been in her party at Vauxhall when Charlotte went to him.

Next morning Charlotte stepped out of bed, on very wobbly legs, to be bathed and have her hair washed. When she first saw herself in the looking glass she cried with misery. Her dainty figure had all but disappeared. She was unbelievably thin and white-faced, her eyes nothing but huge, dark hollows. She quite saw why Robert had not been attracted to visit her.

However, she cheered up when brought evidence of Mr Neville's constancy. He had prayed for her recovery and called with flowers every day. Mr Dean had done the same until duty called him away. In fact, a good many friends and acquaintances had called to enquire after her health or send tokens of esteem. To hear this made Charlotte feel much better.

Tuesday afternoon saw her being carried down to the drawing room, to receive a visit from Mr Knox. He kissed her hand and commiserated with her, his expression sympathetic. Charlotte almost expected Xanthe to be with him but, Charles told her, the Deans were out of town, after which he set out to cheer her with deliberately amusing stories. He did not stay long and promised to call again.

When he was gone, Charlotte lay upon the sofa and drifted, neither sleeping nor waking, the two mamas murmured conversation a comforting backdrop to her reverie.

The budget of her thought was Robert, as he so often was. He was always in her mind for one reason or another, as he was in her heart, as he had been, she realised, for a very long time. Until seeing him again last summer, she had not remembered quite how much she adored him when she was small; but, during this illness, drifting in and out of a dreamlike inner world, she had remembered much previously unrecalled.

It had come to her in flashes while she lay comatose although why, at this juncture in her life, she did not know. At first, she wondered if the recall was real or dream but ultimately came to realise that some, thankfully, had been dream.

She remembered a time when she was quite small, with Robert home from Bristol, and formed a mental picture of herself standing before him, her arms upstretched. She wanted him to lift her, so that she could see what he and Jacinta were watching far above her head. He did not noticed her at once and to gain his attention she tugged his breeches, (to his extreme annoyance because he was entering his fashionable stage), at which he picked her up. She could not now recall what his focus of interest had been, but she clearly remembered him telling her: "Pray, baby, do not crush my neckcloth."

She could even see herself putting chubby arms about his neck, doing precisely what he bade her not to do, while thinking she had been carefully obedient, and his resultant irritated frown. Jacinta had laughed. After the shortest pause Robert also laughed and threw Charlotte high into the air, swinging her about when he caught her, and playing delightful tickling games which set her chuckling with pleasure.

During her illness Charlotte recalled many instances of Robert's good nature when she was a young child when, upon consideration, she realised she must have been a nuisance to him. How kind he had been, nevertheless; how warming to remember his kindness now.

Another recall was less comforting but this, she knew, must have been a dream. She blushed even to think of it privately, but in her dream she had lain with Robert in her bed, here at Meva. In the dream he had been distressed, wanting her kisses for comfort and pressing his face to her breast; at which, acting instinctively, she had introduced her hands to Robert's most private person, to hold him for reassurance; a giving and garnering of solace for them both.

Except, of course, that she already was asleep and dreaming, and he would never come to her with his distresses. He was too much his own man to demonstrate weakness, no longer the same person as the warm-natured youth of her dream recall. Kind he still was, but there was a hard edge to him not evident when he was young.

***

Charles Knox came again next morning. In fact, he was Charlotte's only visitor for several days. Robert turned away all the others because he thought her too frail for extensive social intercourse. Charles was encouraged to visit as he could cheer Charlotte when the rest of their household, Robert included, could not.

Charles was only too happy to play the buffoon for Robert's love. In more sober moments he spoke of Xanthe, and what balm it was to hear her name on Charlotte's lips. There were times when he could not hide the avidity of his interest in Xanthe, nor his longing for her.

Of her friend's feelings, Charlotte knew only what she had been told by the lady herself. Of Charles' there could be no doubt and she hoped sincerely that he was not to suffer a disappointment.

Alive to every nuance where Xanthe was concerned, Charles read what was in Charlotte's face, and suddenly the story of his love for her friend came tumbling out. "Do you think she cares for me, Charlotte? She is very young and may not know her own mind." Charles looked desperately worried. He alone knew why.

Clearly, Charles wanted reassurance. Charlotte could only say that she hoped as he did, and he appeared satisfied with this oblique response.

They were sitting in the garden when this conversation took place, Charlotte in a low chair, Charles leaning on an elbow on the grass at her feet. He took her hand and pressed it to his lips in gratitude. Charlotte smiled at him sweetly.

Robert saw them in this apparently intimate pose as he came out to the garden. The unexpected pain he experienced stopped him in his tracks. When they looked up and saw him approach neither looked awkward or guilty and the pain receded, leaving Robert to feel foolish at his unwarranted suspicion. "I am an idiot," he muttered.

Robert carried Charlotte indoors after Charles left. "It is too warm now to be outdoors," he said.

"I am perfectly able to walk, Sir," she protested. He responded that he would not be denied the pleasure of carrying her. He smiled as he spoke but Charlotte was unresponsive. He set her down upon the sofa and looked at her closely.

"Are you feeling well, poppet?"

"I am thank you."

"Well enough to receive a visitor?" he asked. Before she could reply he went on abruptly: "John Neville has been beating a path to my door near upon these past two weeks. I don't think I can hold him off much longer. Will you see him today?"

"I should love to," Charlotte responded.

Robert's lips twisted into a wry smile. "Possibly you *should,* but the question is, dear heart, do you?"

"Of course." Charlotte smiled at his quip. "What time does he call?" She put up a hand to her hair. "I must bathe and tidy myself."

Robert watched the feminine gesture with an unfathomable look. He hitched forward a stool and sat down beside the sofa. He was then looking up at Charlotte and the reversal of their usual roles showed him in so endearing a light it wrenched at her tenderest feelings. She was obliged to clamp down on welling sensitivity, tears pricking her eyes. He leaned against the sofa and rested his hand in her lap.

"John Neville is very fond of you." She made no reply, staring over his head. "Unless you mean to have him, he is in for a keen setback." For all he was so sure of her there was an echo of the same feeling in Robert's heart.

Charlotte was thinking of Charles Knox's unhappiness and of her own disappointments, reflecting that love, with all its attendant pain, was not worth the candle, could one but choose.

"I think I do mean to have him," she said slowly. In her lap Robert's hand tightened into a fist. His other grasped her arm.

"Has he passed the test?" he demanded harshly. He shook her lightly, a token only, to make her attend him. Charlotte's gaze came back to his face.

"Yes," she said boldly, which brought an ugly look to Robert's eyes and tightened all his muscles . . . until he realised she was lying. She had never been alone with Neville since the test was proposed. He laughed and relaxed visibly.

"My sweet Charlotte, you are still full of crochets." He was suddenly caressing. "Never mind. Let us wait until you are completely recovered before we speak of this again." He picked her up. "Come along, darling. You must prepare for the young sprig's coming."

He ascended the stairs lightly, for all that he carried Charlotte in his arms, and shouldered open the door of her sitting room. She expected him to leave her there, but he carried her through to the bathroom and lowered her to the chaise longue before allowing his gaze to roam over the room.

Robert had not seen it since the first showing to Charlotte and he noticed how her stamp had been set upon the room's exotic decor, her possessions everywhere, and her perfume tangible on the air. The whole aura spoke of Charlotte and he shivered as excitement coursed through him.

His glance came back to her and he smiled brilliantly, the curve of his mouth evocative of pleasure, his eyes sparkling in their old way. Charlotte looked at him, frowning. He came down beside her and leaned forward, touching parted lips to a smooth shoulder, caressing her with his tongue.

At this, Charlotte, so resentful of her guardian, nevertheless longed for Robert with the strongest of contrary impulses. How familiar he was, how known. An anguish that she stubbornly resisted beat at her heart. She told herself the weakness came from being ill and would pass.

He put a hand to her throat, caressing her lightly. "Do you know I can hear you when you are bathing, Charlotte?" he murmured. His free hand drifted down to her breast . . . so faint a caress, sweet havoc in its wake. She sat very still and would not raise her eyes, nor respond. There came another fleeting caress, at which Charlotte drew a small involuntary breath, pleasure creaming through her. Robert uhmed softly and straightened, reassured that her indifference was assumed; as he had known in his heart it was. He said equably: "You must not keep Mr Neville waiting."

Then he went away, leaving her to bitter thoughts of his careless disregard for her feelings, of his playing with her as a cat with a mouse.

***

Mr Neville walked with Charlotte in the garden. He offered her an arm for support and she took it, making no objection when his other hand closed over hers.

He stayed for an hour and she felt better for his coming. His was not particularly amusing company, as was Mr Knox's, nor did he stimulate her, as did her guardian, but his cherishing attitude was very soothing to a wounded heart. Charlotte was grateful for his solicitude and gladly agreed when he asked if he might call again.

As he left, she thought: '*I could love him, given time.*' If only Robert would get on with his own life and allow her to forget what had gone before. Why would he not? Why must he keep pointing up her weakness? Why must he tie her to him with ever increasing bonds when he did not want her? What was wrong with him?

***

After this first visit, Charlotte received callers daily and made small excursions out. Very soon she regained the lost weight, her blooming looks returned and with them her spirit. Seeing her bevy of admirers in attendance once more, confidence in the power to control her own destiny was renewed. She would *not* allow Robert to master her and demonstrated this to him daily.

Naturally, he noticed her antipathy but put it down to her illness. As the weeks went by however, observing her smile for others but not for him, he became increasingly uneasy despite his certainty of her love. His might know it with his mind but his feelings were still capable of wounding, and they *were*. He became even more worried when he saw how particular John Neville was becoming, with Charlotte giving no sign of repulsing him; far from it, in fact. Robert began to question, with incredulous disbelief, whether she really did mean to have the pup.

She could not, she simply could not!

Everything in Robert recoiled from the idea. Charlotte was his. How could she marry another man when she belonged to him? No! It was impossible. Charlotte could not do this. She could not possibly care for Neville when she . . . when she . . . Had she not shown, beyond all doubt when she was ill, that she was committed to him? What in heaven's name had got into her? Why was she leading him such a dance? What had gone wrong? There was something. He knew there was. He could feel it.

Robert was brought up short on a dreadful thought.

Could it be that his confidence was misplaced? What if she did mean to have Neville, in spite of everything? No, of *course* not; he was frightening himself needlessly. Think how jealous he had been of Charles, when Charlotte seemed to prefer his company, and how foolish his fears then.

Sensible reasoning or not, Robert remained uneasy. To add to his misery, the Deans returned and Spencer was once more on his doorstep. He was a little less attentive when he saw Mr Neville a frequent visitor, but his was still a goading presence to Robert. And Charlotte continued elusive, always just out of his reach.

Mr Hattenbury's sole relief, at this juncture, was that Charlotte spent a good deal of time with Xanthe Dean. At least, when the girls were together, he need not fear for unwanted declarations from amorous young men coveting his beloved, and it afforded him time to think with a brain unclouded by jealousy. Having deliberated, he came to conclusions which prompted him to call Charlotte into the library.

Unsmiling, he opened without preamble, as straightforward as she usually was. "Charlotte, have I offended you?" he asked, plain but polite.

"No, Mr Hattenbury. Why should you think this?" She was equally polite.

"I think it because you rebuff me constantly. You smile upon others but not me. Therefore, I conclude, I have offended you."

"Not at all, Sir. I will smile for you now if that is your wish," she said, her lips curving obediently.

Robert sighed. She did not mean to help him that was clear. He continued to look at her, himself unsmiling, wondering how to bring down the barriers she had raised and make her understand; more to the point, how to do so without courting disaster.

"Charlotte . . ." he paused, eyes closing as he stroked a forefinger across his brow, back and forth, back and forth. He let out another sigh and tried again. "Charlotte . . . I need your help at this time. Could you not be more patient with our . . . awkward situation? Please? Life would be so much easier if you were more understanding of my problems."

"What do you mean, Guardian? Since you have not acquainted me with your problems, how may I be more understanding of them?"

He gave a wry smile. "I think you understand very well what I am saying, Charlotte. It is perfectly plain. *You*, mostly, constitute my problems, that you are my ward chief among them. We both appreciate the difficulties this raises, do we not?"

Charlotte drew a quick breath. "It is a problem easily solved in a few months," she said stiffly, feeling as though she had been dealt a blow to the heart. Was Robert so eager to be rid of her?

"This is true," he agreed, thankful she had readily understood, "but, meanwhile, don't you see, the problem still *is*." He took her hands and kissed them. He smiled winningly. "Help me with this, won't you? Be my good angel, Charlotte. The time will pass quickly if we are more comfortable with each other."

Charlotte returned his smile, hiding the hurt, and the desire reignited by his lips upon her hands. "I will do my best, Sir," she promised, from a throat thick with unshed tears and the pain of unrequited love.

"Thank you, Charlotte." He leaned forward, to press his face into the curve of her neck, kissing her gently. He wanted to embrace her because when she was near, as now, need was far greater than discretion. Charlotte, however, removed herself to a safe distance.

"You must play your part, too, Guardian. You cannot have your cake and eat it. You may not kiss me whenever you choose. This arrangement must suit us both," she said sombrely, drawing herself to the fullness of her diminutive height.

Robert sighed, perfectly aware of her meaning. "It is certainly more prudent, a matter of sound sense," he agreed. "Why is it that sound sense is so often depressingly unappealing, Charlotte?"

Xanthe Dean's arrival being announced, Charlotte was not required to answer.

***

Immediate news exchanged, and Charlotte's illness talked over at length, Xanthe went on to speak of her own activities. Charlotte heard with dismay how popular she had been with the Newmarket beaux. *Where does this leave Charles?* she wondered.

"Mr Knox was a frequent visitor while you were away. He spoke of you often," she opened tentatively. Xanthe's expression became guarded. "He certainly missed you," Charlotte went on.

"Did he say so?" Xanthe asked.

"He did not need to. It is plain when he talks of you. Xanthe, do you remember the first time we spoke of him at school?" Her friend giggled as Charlotte quoted her words of that time: "Rather sweet and such dashing good looks."

"Oh, yes . . . which is true, of course," she agreed. Suddenly candid, she added: "If you are asking discretely am I in love with Charles, the answer is yes, Charlotte."

Xanthe deliberated a moment. What relief it would be to speak of Charles and share the wonder of her love with Charlotte. Her deliberation was brief, the urge to speak too strong. "Did he tell you that he had approached Papa?" she asked.

"No." Charlotte's eyes widened with surprise. Then she realised the implication of Xanthe's question. "Oh dear . . . he was refused; but why? Surely, his credentials are impeccable?"

Xanthe shrugged unhappily. "I am too young to marry, Papa says. I am simply flattered by the attentions of a sophisticated older man, he says. What nonsense! It absolutely is not true! I adore Charles. I always shall. Oh, Charlotte," she drew her friend to the sofa, "I cannot tell you how wonderful he is, everything about him . . . his darling smile, the way his hair curls about his ears, his touch . . ."

As she spoke, Xanthe unconsciously stroked the back of her fingers to a parted mouth, and Charlotte could see Charles' caress as though he were there. So clear was the image her own lips tingled, remembering how she also had known such a caress from a man with an equally darling smile.

No, she would not entertain these subversive visions. Listen instead to what her friend was saying. She drew a deep, sighing breath. "Charles thinks you wonderful, too, you know."

"Yes! Isn't it marvellous?" Xanthe's elation at her good fortune was plain. "He could have any girl he desired but he chose me . . . me! I could not believe it when he first told me but then . . ." her elation faded. "Why couldn't Papa have said yes? Why must we wait? I *want* him so, Charlotte," she said miserably.

The emphasis of her revealing remark was quite unintended, but Charlotte felt it immediately. Was not she, too, acquainted with the nature of want?

No. It could not be. Could it? No, of course not. Her thoughts were coloured by her own experiences, but this was Xanthe of whom they spoke. She was silent, no easy comment coming to mind.

Xanthe picked up the nuances of Charlotte's uneasy silence. As the girls looked at each other, something portentous, and shockingly vibrant, hung in the air.

"Charlotte." Xanthe spoke first. "Charles and I have already been as one," she whispered. Her eyes were wide, a little frightened but triumphant. "And I cannot tell you how . . . how . . ."

There were no words to describe that first, awesome coming together, how incredible it had been. Blank-eyed, Xanthe shuddered with pleasure as she relived the experience, as she had been doing constantly since it happened. Only to think of Charles, or mention his name, brought back every detail of his love making. Again, Xanthe gave a shuddering sigh. "You could not understand, Charlotte. It is impossible to explain. All I know is that I am no longer the Xanthe I was. Now I am one half of Charles and it is misery to be without him, as though something of me is missing." She became aware that Charlotte had still not spoken. She pressed her hands together anxiously. "You say nothing. Do you condemn me, Charlotte?"

"Indeed I do not, Xanthe," said Charlotte, coming to herself quickly. She gave her friend a reassuring hug. "I am honoured by your confidence," she looked at Xanthe searchingly, "but dear friend, *do* be careful, won't you?" she urged. "If it were discovered or if anything happened . . ." She did not need to say more.

"What need for care? I am not to see Charles," Xanthe said unhappily.

"Perhaps it is better to be out of temptation's way," Charlotte suggested prudently.

"How easily you pronounce on the benefits of separation, Charlotte. You cannot know what it is like. I so long to be Charles' wife and be with him always." Xanthe's trembling lips revealed her misery and the depth of her longing.

Could I not know, thought Charlotte?

She had almost been in the same position herself and knew very well, suffering for it ever since. What a bizarre coincidence that she and her friend were so similarly placed? There was a difference, of course. It was eminently reasonable to expect a happy outcome for Xanthe if Charles proved constant and he was so head over ears in love his constancy was unquestionable.

Constancy: here lay the difference. Robert was not constant. It seemed he enjoyed her adoration of him as a comfortable backdrop to his life; that he liked to feel his power over her, to know she would go to him when he wanted. He was caressing with her only when she was unresponsive. If, against all dictates of will, she *did* respond he turned cool and distant, resuming his complacent attitudes and, she must suppose, his affairs. Was this not the antithesis of constancy? Was it not cruel?

***

"You did not say you had offered for Xanthe," Charlotte taxed Charles when next she saw him. They had been riding but were now returned to the stable.

"Who told you? It is not yet known, even to Robert," Charles responded in surprise.

"Xanthe told me, but you need not to fear for my discretion, Charles."

For a dreadful moment, hearing the word discretion, Charles was almost surprised into asking if other confidences had been imparted. No, it was impossible. Even the thought made him feel hot with shamed embarrassment. He coloured under his tan.

Charlotte schooled her face to impassivity, knowing from Charles' heightened colour, quite otherwise to his normal self-possession, what was in his mind. She said: "Charles, Xanthe wants to marry you ~ she said as much to me ~ so your recent question is moribund, is it not?"

"Is it, Charlotte? She is so beautiful. How do I know that in the interval she will not find another and better man, someone younger, as her parents wish?" he responded anxiously.

"She will not be looking because she loves you. How do I know this?" Charlotte smiled and drew a letter from her pocket. "I know because she pleaded with me so eloquently to give you this. We are partners in crime on your behalf."

"Charlotte! You adorable angel! Oh, were I not already spoken for I would fall at your feet for this kindness." He quickly secreted the note in his pocket and raised her hands to his lips. "Will you do me the same service?"

"I ought not to collude with you but I dare say I shall," she agreed.

"Oh, you sweet darling!" said Charles and hugged her gratefully.

"Should you be squeezing my ward so affectionately, Charles?" asked a cool voice behind them. Mr Hattenbury strolled up, looking perfectly collected. "I suppose you will be next in line asking to see me."

Charles laughed. "I should be so lucky. Au revoir, Charlotte. As Robert is here I shall leave you with him. I have recalled a pressing engagement." He placed a hand over the letter in his breast pocket. He kissed his fingers to her and was off.

Robert watched him go through narrowed eyes, before turning to Charlotte. "Another beau?" he asked mockingly.

"Yes, Sir," replied Charlotte. Robert put up his brows. "But not at the end of my ribbons. Were you looking for me, Guardian?"

"Either that or I am spying on you," he said coldly. "You are wanted."

He strode off without another word, face like a thundercloud, leaving Charlotte to make her own way to the house. She did not see him again for several days.

***

Saturday evening Mr Hattenbury returned as unexpectedly as he had gone, strolling into the ballroom, where Charlotte was dancing with her usual vivacity, and ruthlessly using his privileged guardian's position to claim her hand for the waltz, although she did point out that her card was full.

"No-one will object to your dancing with me," he said equably, "not even you, perhaps?" he added, his tone slightly barbed.

While they danced Robert conversed pleasantly, asking what Charlotte had been doing while he was away and seeming interested in her answers. He did not say where he had been.

Nor did he tell the mamas when he took Charlotte home, even though they asked him directly. "It is a secret," he said blandly, looking pleased with himself.

Alas, as so often of late, his good cheer received a severe setback the very next day.

After church on Sunday, John Neville called, and asked permission to take Charlotte into the garden. Robert did not like his determined looks and watched the pair covertly, caring nothing for the dictates of good manners.

Robert did well to fear. On that lovely June day, in the garden at Meva House, Mr Neville ventured his all. He drew Charlotte down to the rustic seat, where grew the bush whose name he still could not remember, and pressed her hands.

"My dear Miss Charlotte!"

She recognised his pregnancy of tone at once and her heart began to beat faster. She had expected him to make a declaration, but now it came Charlotte was not ready.

"I believe you know I entertain feelings of liking and affection for you. I also believe you may be coming to return my regard. May I, therefore, approach your guardian for permission to pay my addresses?"

Charlotte allowed him to hold her hands, making no attempt at maidenly pretence. Nor could she be less than frank with him. His was too kind a nature to trifle with.

"Mr Neville, I like you very well, but I am not sure if this is basis enough for more," she said honestly.

"*I* am sure," he said eagerly, "for love must, surely, follow on from liking."

"As with your dog or horses, you mean," Charlotte commented with wry humour.

Mr Neville shook his head earnestly. "No, indeed, the cases are entirely different. Truly, Miss Charlotte, it would be my pleasure and honour to pay you my respects. Will you give me that right?"

Still Charlotte hesitated, looking at him searchingly. Then she said slowly: "I thank you for the honour you do me, Mr Neville, but we are both young yet and there is plenty of time for thoughts of this serious nature. Could you be content with friendship for now? I fear that is all I have to offer at the moment."

Disappointment clouded Mr Neville's face but he took his dismissal manfully. "As you wish, Miss Treleaven, but believe me constant if you will." He could not quite stifle a sigh before adding: "I am going out of town tomorrow. May I call on you when I return?"

Constancy, how poignant a thought; unwisely, it moved Charlotte to lean forward and kiss Mr Neville's cheek. He was greatly affected by the spontaneous gesture, and instinctively held her to prolong the sweet contact.

Watching jealously, Robert went cold with pain and fury. That his own, beloved Charlotte should willingly embrace another man was profound torture. To see her adored mouth, which had known no touch but his own, approached to John Neville's face brought Robert's most savage instincts to the fore. His temper flared dangerously.

And, alas, unkind fate had not yet done with him that day.

After noon, Charlotte went carriage riding with the mamas. She met up briefly with Xanthe and Philip. Xanthe looked blooming and whispered to Charlotte of glorious good news. Charles was invited to spend the summer with them, en famille, at Amberly. "Ask him about it when he calls on you later." Xanthe kissed her quickly. "I must fly . . . so much to do before we go."

Charlotte was left to possess her soul as patiently as possible until Charles arrived. When she heard him being shown into the drawing room, she ran downstairs immediately and went to him with hands outstretched in welcome. She did not see Robert coming in through the glass doors.

"Charles, I am so happy at the news," she exclaimed, her face showing all the pleasure she felt for him. She reached up to kiss his cheek. "Your fortunes are changing, it seems."

Before Charles could reply, there was a savagely explosive sound from Robert. Charles, having already seen him, was about to call out his good news, but the look on Robert's face stopped the words in his throat.

"Release her," Robert ground out, voice guttural. His face was white with rage, his blue eyes almost black with fury. Charles looked at him, mouth inelegantly agape.

"Robbie . . ." he began.

"Did you hear me?" Robert advanced, shoulders raised menacingly, arms hanging straight at his sides. Charles stared at him, uncomprehending. He could neither take in nor understand the change in his friend.

Charlotte knew instinctively and was frightened for Charles. She ran to Robert, thrusting herself in front of him so that he could not advance further.

"Mr Hattenbury, dear Sir, there is no need for anger." She spoke in a low, urgent voice, clasping his arms, pressing herself to him. She rose on tiptoe; she leaned into him, rubbing her cheek to his in a submissive gesture. "Mr Knox is not at fault, I do assure you. I would have explained, but did not see you."

Robert raised his arms, breaking out of her hold violently. Charlotte lost her balance and clutched him to save herself. The momentum swung her back to him heavily; he winced but caught her automatically.

He had completely forgotten Charles. Eyes fastened on Charlotte's face, he looked at her with total hostility, and so deep was his fury he was quite unable to understand what she was saying. He could have throttled her and the murderous urge was transmitted through his hands, which dug bitingly into her shoulders. Her brows contracted with pain and he was savagely glad. It was small recompense for the constant anguish she caused him. He tightened his grip. Charlotte winced involuntarily. Her head fell forward to his chest.

"Mr Knox is to marry Xanthe, Sir. He is going to Amberly with the family. I was congratulating him," she explained softly, for his ear alone.

Robert became totally still. Even his breathing was suspended. When he did move, after a moment, it was with startling suddenness. Grasping Charlotte's topknot, he jerked up her head, holding her with throat curved at a high angle. Glaring at her, his face only inches from hers, he ground out, through clenched teeth: "Were you also congratulating Mr Neville on his good fortune this morning? Is this a day for kissing your admirers? Surely, Miss Treleaven, it must be my turn now!"

Robert's breathing was so erratic he could scarcely bring out the accusatory words. Before Charlotte could reply, he took her mouth in a savage kiss which cut her lip on his teeth, bruising her. He was groaning deep in his throat, a man possessed, so much aroused he was nearly outwith control.

Abruptly, then, he threw her off, afraid of what he would do if she remained. He felt like beating her . . . wanted to beat her until she cried for mercy. He wanted to shake her until the teeth rattled in her head; he wanted, he wanted . . . oh, God, he wanted her so much it was agony. How could he bear it any longer? *Why* would she not love him? Why? Why? Why?

Robert drew a trembling hand across his mouth. He was still shaking with fury and staring at Charlotte as though he hated her. "Go to your room," he commanded harshly, at length.

"Yes, Sir," she murmured submissively.

Only when she was gone did Robert remember Charles. Their eyes locked across the room. Robert was first to look away. Slowly, he walked to the fireplace and leaned his arms on the mantle shelf, body slumped, head sunk to his arms. "Dear God, she is driving me insane!" he groaned.

Charles stirred and looked at Robert. "If you want her so badly why don't you marry her?" he asked incredulously.

Robert slewed round. "Because the stupid bitch won't have me," he cried wildly. "She means to have that fawning tripehound Neville. Christ help me, Charles, I cannot even bear the thought of it! What am I to do?" Without conscious volition, Robert's fingers were tearing his hair into furious disorder.

Charles considered him long and hard, taking in Robert's distraught state, the physical arousal he was hard put to conceal. He scarcely recognised his friend in this impassioned lover; but love, he had discovered, sometimes made man a stranger, even to himself.

"I suggest you mount her . . . or another," he said bluntly, "otherwise you will be carted off to Bedlam."

Chapter Sixteen

Charlotte was not allowed out of her suite for the rest of the day, in spite of the mamas' remonstrances. Robert was rigidly adamant, and such was his look neither mama cared to argue too forcefully.

Mrs Treleaven could not conceive of what Charlotte had done to upset dear Robert *this* time. She really was quite naughty recently. He did not deserve such disregard after his many kindnesses. Alethea's feelings of agitation were so great she was almost ready to speak sharply to her daughter. How could Charlotte be so ungrateful, after Robert had devoted yes, *devoted,* himself to her entirely when she was ill?

Mrs Hattenbury's thoughts were different but equally uncomfortable. She had seen the driven look her son wore many years before, in her husband Francis, and she was frightened. To watch Robert now, as Charlotte flaunted her suitors under his very nose, was to see disaster in the making, because Sophie knew well what her son's look betokened. In some things he *was* like his father. If Charlotte continued to drive him so recklessly. . .

The thought was too frightening to complete because Sophie knew, from his possessiveness towards her, that Robert had long been committed to Charlotte in some way. She would not go further than this, even in her thoughts, but there was a certain something about Robert in Charlotte's regard, which made so clear a statement to a seeing eye, it could not be missed.

Remembering the gentleness of her son's hands upon Charlotte's unclothed body during her illness, the unthinkingly proprietorial way he treated her, of how, indeed, she had found them closely entwined, like lovers, on the morning of Charlotte's recovery from the fever, fear rose like a bile in Sophie's throat. Robert thwarted was an awesome force to deal with and here, to all intents and purposes, it seemed Robert was to be thwarted.

What would he do? For a man of such indomitable will he would, undoubtedly, do something which was likely to prove extremely uncomfortable for all. She prayed it would not be anything *worse* than discomfort, at the same time knowing they were heading for disaster if Charlotte were not checked.

Robert's thinking was exactly the same as his mama's. He could have murdered Charlotte without regret. He hated her as much as he loved her. Above all he longed for her, with a compulsive passion which gave him no peace, and knew he could no longer bear the constant provocation of Charlotte's presence without at least the promise of her love. She *had* to come to him . . . and soon! God help her, and Neville, if she persisted on her wayward path. He would not answer for his actions.

He contemplated cancelling their engagement with the Styneleys, since even the thought of one more evening spent in Charlotte's company was insupportable, but the necessity of staying at home with her was even worse anathema. He sent a message telling his ladies to prepare for an evening at Westover and went to change.

Arriving in his chamber, he heard sounds of running water from Charlotte's bathroom. As on so many previous occasions, awareness of her, at the other side of his door, was a wrenching torment, even more so after the events of this day. He could feel impotent rage sweeping over him again and stood perfectly immobile, hands curled into fists. He stared at the door, eyes drawn irresistibly to a bright, shining key nestling in its own snug lock, as it had done since the bathroom was completed; such a tenuous obstacle.

Slowly, Robert walked towards the door. He leaned against it for a while and listened to Charlotte in the other room. She was not singing today. She had not sung for a long time. Maybe she was as unhappy as he.

Robert's mind began to wander as he leaned his forehead against the cool wood of the panelling, thinking of Cornwall, of the things they had done together, of their happiness last year, of the stables at Crane . . .

Only when the door opened under his hand did he realise he had unlocked it.

Charlotte heard the door open but could not quite believe her ears. She turned her head . . . and there stood Robert, on his face a look such as she had never seen before!

Slowly, slowly, he came to stand beside her, watching her as she sat in the golden shell of her bath, glistening droplets gliding over smooth skin, rounded limbs showing pearly through clear water. He moved closer. The shimmering net curtain caught on his hair and spilled over the shoulder of his jacket. He reached out to touch her, his hands cold against her warmth, his fingers trembling as they came to rest on her shoulder. Robert's mouth was trembling, too, Charlotte saw.

"Robert?" She breathed his name in question.

"*Charlotte*," he accented her name in the French fashion, his voice husky and redolent of longing, "*Ce n'est plus une ardour dans mes veines cachée. C'est Vénus toute entière à sa proie attachée.*"[3] Yearning eyes fixed on her.

After a long frozen moment, during which neither spoke, Robert turned and left, as silently as he had come, door clipping quietly shut behind him. Charlotte, unmoving, almost believed she had imagined his coming; only gently swinging gold curtains gave any substance to the reality of Robert's brief presence.

How strangely he had behaved. What had he said with such deep pathos? What had he meant? Why had he looked at her in that way, with longing it seemed, but with something else, too, the same something showing on Charles' face when his eyes rested on Xanthe, the look of . . . love?

Could it be that Robert loved her . . . really loved her? She hardly

It is no longer a heat concealed in my blood. It is Venus herself grasping her prey. Racine.

dared to think it, after all the mistaken beliefs and heartache which had gone before.

But what if he did? The wonderful vistas this thought opened up turned Charlotte to jelly. Robert her very own, as he once had been; Robert to love, and love her in return as before. Oh how glorious a thought!

But . . . what if he did not?

What if he were not to be *all* her own? What if she were wrong again? She had been wrong so many times before and each was a worse agony. If it were to be the same again Charlotte knew she would be utterly lost, because the weeks since her illness had shown her how much Robert still influenced her every thought and deed, no matter what he did. She would always respond to him, unless she kept tight rein on her feelings, because he had set his mark upon her indelibly.

More reason, therefore, not to grasp too eagerly at what might only be the nettle of illusion. Let Robert first show her what he meant.

He had the chance to do so in less than an hour, when he came to her room. Seeing him, Charlotte coloured, her heart beating violently. Face enigmatic, Robert walked towards her deliberately as she stood up to meet him.

"Forgive me, Charlotte. I was presumptuous," he said in a low voice. He brought up his arm; she felt his fingers warm on her skin, above the low neck of her gown; there was a quick chill between her breasts and his hand fell away. Robert turned and left.

Nestling between her breasts was . . . a bright door key.

***

Mr Hattenbury was not his usual charming self that evening. Rather was he silent and sombre in the carriage going to Westover. In truth, he was suffering deeply from fear and deprivation, both experiences new to him and therefore the harder to bear. Little sign now of the erstwhile, arrogant Robert of Cornwall, he who had known beyond doubt where he was going and with whom.

Robert still knew where he wanted to go; he still knew with whom;

but Charlotte, who epitomised everything he desired, was out of his reach, something in her remaining shiningly, tantalisingly beyond him. He felt like a child who cries in vain for the moon for, no matter what he did, she slipped more and more out of his grasp. He had been so sure of her but with each passing day his certainty faded a little more, leaving him lost and stumbling. He no longer knew what to do and was more afraid than he had ever been in his life. She meant to have John Neville. He was certain of it.

Robert was also certain of another thing. While he lived, it never would be! Charlotte belonged to him and him alone! There was no way in this world he would allow another man to touch her. Never! The mere thought of it turned him sick. Whatever the cost, she would never belong to anyone else. Never! She was *his*.

Robert clung to this single thought with grim determination, despite the frightened, impotent fury which made him want to lash out at everything around him.

The carriage drew up before Westover House with a jolt, bringing Robert out of his tormented reverie. When he moved to get down, he realised he was holding Charlotte's arm in a punishing grip. Until that moment he had not noticed. When the ladies shed their wraps a surreptitious glance showed a weal upon her arm, which Charlotte attempted to conceal in the folds of her skirt.

Robert backed away. He could not bear to look at her. He had the most awful presentiment that if he did he would cry out all his pain and bewilderment. *'Why will you not love me?'* he wanted to demand of her. The words persisted in rising to his lips. He was not sure he hadn't already spoken them.

He kept his eyes averted, listening gravely to Gerald Styneley's talk of horses, nodding his agreement now and then.

More arrivals were heralded and he heard Mr Neville's name announced. Robert's head jerked up, his stomach tightening with hate and revulsion. Fortunately, it was only Mr Oswald Neville and the tension drained. Then he saw Mr Neville's companion and the tension returned in force; but for quite a different reason. Mistress Lerpiniere was looking straight at him across the breadth of the room.

'Mount another,' Charles had said . . . and here was the perfect opportunity.

The message passing between two sets of eyes, one green and one a lustrous blue, was loud and clear. Relief ran through Robert's frame, like the coolth of water over a fevered brow; for the first time that day he smiled.

'Two can play at your game, my lovely Charlotte,' he thought vengefully, and made a way to Barbara Lerpiniere's side.

Seeing Robert smile at his mistress, Charlotte's hopes died, drowning in the bitter bile which rose in her throat. How *could* she have imagined he loved her when he looked at Mrs Lerpiniere with such open lust?

Charlotte never knew how she got through dinner that night. Luckily, she was seated beside Nicholas Styneley, the Earl of Cambourne, a young man who made few conversational demands. By turning her head towards him she managed to appear absorbed and was not then obliged to watch Robert's siren fascinate him.

Her guardian stayed with the green-eyed temptress until after dinner. Card tables were set up but he did not join the players. He sat across a small table from Mrs Lerpiniere, head inclined towards her, and when he raised a wine goblet to his lips he watched his companion over its rim.

The situation became unbearable. With a murmured excuse, Charlotte drifted out of the room and sought sanctuary in the library, wanting nothing but solitude.

She found it behind the curtain of a deep window embrasure. Here, she curled up on the seat, holding a bruised and throbbing wrist to the sore mouth Robert had inflicted upon her earlier. She dared not dwell on the day's events because she knew scalding tears would fall, and she must not be seen to have cried.

Time passed gently. Charlotte grew calmer. She was thinking to emerge, had gone so far as to begin opening the curtain, when the library door opened and two people came in: Robert and Barbara Lerpiniere.

"Darling, why have you waited so long to come to me? It has been months," Mrs Lerpiniere complained and went into Robert's arms, searching avidly for his mouth. She pressed Robert's hands to her breasts, pleasurable little cries escaping her lips.

Charlotte wanted to die.

"Come to me tonight. My husband is away," Barbara breathed at length.

"What time?"

"When you can get away; any time; I shall wait for you. Darling, do not make me wait too long. It has been an age and I am on fire for you," she whispered.

"A la bonne heure" said Robert, "but, come, we should return to the company before we are missed."

"One kiss more."

Merciful silence followed the closing of the door. Charlotte sat as though turned to stone. She was in a despair too deep for tears, a feeling which stayed with her all night, and in some strange way helped to get her through it.

Returning to the drawing room, she saw Robert was no longer with his paramour, but it meant nothing. She felt nothing, ergo, there was nothing to feel. She even spoke civilly to her guardian when he came to her side, looking at him dispassionately and realising, with some surprise, that he raised no emotion in her whatsoever. He was as nothing to her, he who had coloured all her days. How very odd.

Xanthe and Charles joined them. Charlotte listened with every appearance of pleasure when told that Mr Dean had relented his stern opposition to Mr Knox, because his daughter had been so patently distressed, hence the invitation for Charles to stay at Amberly for the summer.

"Pray, invite me to the wedding," Charlotte said. The happy pair laughed and assured her they would.

Once only did harsh reality break through Charlotte's blessed veil and that was when they reached home. About to go upstairs, Robert prevented her by placing his hand over hers on the stair rail. He lifted the edge of her wrap, revealing the still-visible mark on her wrist, frowning as though he too were in pain.

"This looks distressing, Charlotte. Forgive me, please. Is there something I can do to help?" he asked, a pleading note in his voice.

Agony knifed through Charlotte, harsh and grinding. "Do, Sir, do?

You have cut my mouth. You have invaded my privacy unasked. You have bruised my wrist and abused me most cruelly. Is this not enough doing for one day? No, Robert, no! There is *nothing* I wish from you . . . not now, not ever," she replied with loathing, and snatched her hand out from under his.

Charlotte half turned, then looked back over her shoulder and said, harshly: "As to forgiveness, what use is this? You are always regretful after the event but it has never stopped your cruel incursions into my life, has it?"

She walked carefully up the stairs, leaving him to gaze after her in a despair every bit as keen as her own. He would have given his soul for the right to be with her then, and have her welcome him into the fastness of her body with love. All the alluring mistresses in the world could not alter that fact. For him Charlotte was the staff of life. Tonight he had discovered an incontrovertible truth . . . that he could not satisfy his need for Charlotte by lying with another woman. It simply would not do.

Robert spent the rest of the night pacing the library floor, racking thoughts going round and around in circles, knowing he must find a road back to Charlotte. There was a way and he *must* find it. He could not go on without her.

With the coming of morning, an exhausted Robert had still found no solution. Sighing, rubbing sore and tired eyes, he went to bed finally.

In her bathroom, Charlotte heard him go into his rooms. She too had spent a sleepless night imagining Robert in the arms of his lover. She felt like screaming at the ghastly pictures her mind conjured. How could he do it? How could he?

She covered her mouth with trembling hands, to stifle the moans which threatened to erupt into raging protest against her dreadful knowledge.

If he truly wanted Mrs Lerpiniere why had he passionately embraced she, herself, only yesterday morning, in front of Charles, all uncaring what his friend may have thought? Why had he intruded on her in this very bathroom last night? Why use his strength to bruise and break her in such wild rage? What manner of man *was* he? What did he *want*?

Surely to heaven, it could not simply be that he wanted two women at once, could it? There were such men, witness his own father. Was Robert like him? And if he were, why, why, dear Lord . . . why had she to love him so?

Charlotte's torturing thoughts propelled her out of the bath and across the room in a single surge. Hands curled into fists knuckled her head as she panted her distress. Suddenly, one arm flew out and she swept everything off the table in front of her. A lovely flower bowl shattered against the wall, splashing water everywhere, spilling its tender flowers in a broken heap among splintered glass.

Charlotte slumped to her knees and began to weep hopelessly.

***

No-one appeared for breakfast. The food was removed cold and untouched. Comment was rife but, for once, no-one belowstairs knew what was toward. The only certainty was that the master was in a very ugly mood. Whatever was to come next?

The master's sentiments exactly; what did come next? When he woke after midday, he still felt tired and jaded, made utterly miserable by a situation outwith his control.

Bathed and dressed, he kept to his rooms and sat with fingers pressed to his eyes, inwardly contemplating a future bleak beyond bearing. Being alone brought no consolation, no solutions, only the unending goad of fear to exhaust him and exacerbate an already uncertain temper.

Thinking, thinking, thinking. What was he to do? He could see no way forward. His lovely Charlotte was no more than two chambers' width from him yet, so distant from each other were they, she may as well have been home in Cornwall, or on the moon.

Cornwall. Oh, what would he not give for the blessing of those halcyon months last year? How content he had been, each day bringing a surge of anticipation on waking because of Charlotte, knowing he would see her, that when he did she would run to him joyfully. Contrasting that pleasurable time, when love had been awakening between them, with the barren acrimony which now was all they shared, Robert could have wept. He was an idiot not to have married her when Mama urged him to it. They had been so happy, long hours spent alone together, no-one to interfere, no hordes of handsome young men eager to part him from his beloved, no endless round of futile engagements to keep them separated.

Alone with Charlotte; how blissful the thought. Alas, alone with Charlotte was precisely what he could not be. That had been the trouble all along. She was too much of a temptation to him, one he was less and less able to resist, and he must not give in to it, could not give in to it, he could not, he . . .

Could not?

A thought of amazing simplicity suddenly struck Robert. It raised such a tingle in all his nerve-endings, he felt as though clothed in a second, electrified skin. The burst of energy he experienced was so powerful, it propelled him from his chair in one bound. He began to pace the carpet in a fever of excitement, unable to be still.

Could not? Could not? Or . . . could he?

Robert took several deep breaths, trying to control his trembling, and school chaotic thoughts into some kind of order, as he examined the nature of what he was thinking in regard to Charlotte; for the plain truth was that he contemplated her ravishment no less. He drew sharp breath; such a thought: to lie with Charlotte at last!

Totally reprehensible; yes, yes, he admitted it freely; but did he care? No, in truth, he did not and anything, *anything* was better than to lose her. Indeed, he had nearly made love to her last year without benefit of banns. From exigence he certainly would have done so, but for Morley's intervention. What was different now?

Nothing, except in the matter of deliberate intent and who would know? There could be no damage to Charlotte's reputation if no-one knew. But, incontrovertibly, a seduced Charlotte could not then marry anyone but him! And she would not refuse him; he would see to that, making sure that he presented the gift of himself so pleasurably she would not even *think* of it. She had loved him once and he *knew* he could make her love him again; only let him get her into his bed.

Robert sat down again, abruptly, his trembling renewed as he acknowledged exactly what he was planning. He felt his energy leap once more as he realised that, yes, he really did not care. A bright banner of incontrovertible fact shone blazingly in his mind. Once Charlotte belonged to him she could not marry another! He would have her safe. It was brilliantly simple.

What was not quite so simple, however, was the manner of bringing the budget of this truth home to Charlotte. Robert's euphoria died a smidgeon as he thought about that, especially when he recalled his transgressions against her yesterday. In the light of her anger last night, not to mention her antipathy of recent weeks, it was probable that she would have other, quite decided ideas than to fall upon his neck. He would have to tread with great care, first mending the breaches.

Rejuvenated at the prospect of Charlotte belonging to him again, Robert immediately commenced the plan of action. He rose to his feet. Upright, he inspected himself in the mirror, determinedly pulled down on waistcoat and cuffs, and quit his rooms. As Charlotte's suite was next to his he was soon knocking on her door. He did not wait for her to bid him enter but marched straight in.

She sat before a window, gazing out over the garden, and glanced up on hearing the door open. Seeing her guardian she froze into deep hostility. Robert noticed her look only with the periphery of his mind, all his concentration centred on the need to bring Charlotte back to him. She belonged to him and he *would* have her because she loved him, *him* and no-one else.

"What do *you* want?" she asked and her tone was extremely hostile, not even the semblance of good manners. Robert did not care.

He brought a chair and stationed himself before her. "May I speak with you?"

"Have I a choice?" Charlotte demanded harshly.

Robert ignored that. "First, I would like to apologise," he said quietly. "My behaviour to you yesterday was quite abominable and I ask your pardon."

Charlotte's expression remained cold. "Why bother? You are always a law unto yourself and will no doubt continue to be so, pardon or not."

Robert's heart was beating thickly in his throat. Charlotte made a formidable opponent when she chose, as he already knew to his cost, and she was in a mood for battle now. He must go slowly, praying for help to choose the right words.

"I bother, Charlotte, because it matters that I gain your forgiveness and . . ."

"No, Sir," she broke in, "*you* matter to you. I do not. You go your own way."

Robert's lips twisted into the travesty of a smile. "If only you knew how seldom that has been true this last year."

Charlotte was cynically dismissive. "You are maudlin, Sir. What is that to the point?"

"Nothing, perhaps," he acknowledged, "so I ask again, will you forgive me?"

She conceded sardonically. "For what it is worth, you are forgiven." She rose to her feet. "Is that all?" The interview was clearly at an end.

"Not quite, Charlotte. Please sit down."

She did so unwillingly, wanting him gone from her. Robert could see that, as clearly as if she had said it. For a moment his heart quailed. He wanted to take her in his arms but knew it would be fatal at this juncture. Instead, he said: "I wondered if you would care to see the Diorama in Regents's park. I am sure you would enjoy it."

Charlotte gave him a look of unmistakeable disdain, her lip curling. "What? A treat in reparation for yesterday, Guardian?"

"No." He kept his tone equable. "I thought of it some weeks ago, but we have been busy. If we do not go soon it will be too late. We move to Brighton shortly."

Up went Charlotte's brows, her stance every bit as haughty and imperious as Mr Hattenbury's could be. "You said nothing to me of Brighton. Am I *never* to be consulted as to my wishes? No, of course not; how stupid of me to expect it."

"Charlotte." Robert began to lose his coolth under her goading. "I did not tell you sooner because I wanted it to be a surprise, but we need not go if you do not wish it. I would not constrain you in this."

"Why not?" she asked in patent disbelief. "You constrain me to everything else that suits you. If you mean me to go, no doubt I shall."

Robert took a deep breath, urging himself to be calm. He let it pass and leaned a little closer, as if to take her hand. Charlotte stiffened away.

"No. My sole desire in this is to please you," he said carefully.

"To please me?" she echoed contemptuously. "Do not insult my intelligence. You, Sir, have but one desire in life and that to please yourself. You do not hoodwink me with your smiling falsehoods." She seethed at his manifest dishonesty.

"Charlotte, no; you like the seaside, you *know* you do. *I* do not. I simply thought you would enjoy Brighton. If I am wrong you have only to say and the thing is undone. Charlotte, please." A tinge of desperation began to colour Robert's voice. He felt impelled to action and went down on one knee before her. This time he did take her hand and would not let it go although she resisted him.

Charlotte could see the gold-spiked tips of his long eyelashes, the dark blue eyes which seemed to be supplicating. Robert supplicating? Never.

"You coax me, Sir, but when you do there is always a price to pay," she said harshly. "What do you want this time?"

Her accusation hurt Robert; he drew breath sharply, his brows contracting with pain. "Is that how it seems to you, Charlotte? I assure you, that it is never my intention. I speak the exact truth when I say that I want to please you, in every way open to me. As to what I want . . . it is to have you back . . . because I am so unhappy without you." Indeed, his blue eyes looked full of misery. "I will do *anything*, Charlotte, anything you wish, if you will only be my dear heart again . . . love me again." He drew a shaken breath and leaned forward, his head butting into the curve of her neck, the need to touch her overwhelming caution. "Darling, please? I . . . I am so hungry for your companionship. Please," he pleaded.

Charlotte stiffened, not trusting him, hating his touch, yet still wanting it in spite of everything, the fresh smell of his hair, as she breathed in, as familiar to her as breath itself; but she would not give in to perverse, treacherous longings.

Robert felt her instinct to reject him and prudently moved back, clamping down on the need. "Charlotte, listen," he said quickly, taking a firmer hold on her hand, "there are so many things we could do together. We could travel to Tuscany, you and I. Oh, dear heart, you would love the marvellous gardens there," he said, inspired. "They are aglow with colour, flowers of such perfection as you can only imagine in dreams; tall trees with leaves shimmering in soft warm breezes, their soughing like a song upon the ear. I could show you temples like jewels and Umbrian palaces so magnificent they take your breath away.

"We could see Paris," he went on eagerly, "where Abelard's love for Eloise is perpetuated in marble. I could take you to where Dante first beheld Beatrix, and Petrarch his Laura. Remember how I wrote of them to you?" Robert's eagerness gathered momentum. "We could climb the Seven Hills of Rome, the snowy mountains of Switzerland, or lie beneath the stars of Andalusia, with a heavenly scent from the lemon trees rising on the air." He began to quote from Goethe:

"Kennst du das Land, wo die Zitronen blühn, Im dunkeln Laub die Gold-Orangen glühn?

Kennst du es wohl? Dahin! Dahin Möcht ich mit dir, o mein Geliebter zieln."[4]

As she listened, against her will Charlotte was torn, interested in spite of herself, not wanting to be but gradually drawn into the magical tapestry Robert's seductive words painted. In truth, she would love to do and see all of these things, as well he knew.

Seeing Charlotte's reluctant interest Robert continued to woo her, his voice dropping to a lower, huskier register. "I will read you Byron beside the Greek temple of his remembrance; and Donne, he who wrote to his wife:

'Come live with me and be my love, and we will some new pleasures prove . . .'

Unconsciously, Robert was caressing her wrist and she shivered. He came closer, his face brilliant with expectation, breathing shallow, parted lips moving as though already tasting hers. His eyes were limpid

---

"Do you know the land where the lemon-trees blossom,

Where the golden oranges glow in the dark foliage?

Do you know it perhaps?

It is there, there that I would like to go with you my beloved." Goethe.

and beautiful. Charlotte could see herself in their wondrous blue depths, which seemed to speak of all his heart.

"Charlotte, my adorable Charlotte, love me again. We could be so happy together if you would only marry me. Please, *please* . . . will you?"

He was within a hair's breadth of kissing her, his eyes closing in anticipation, when Charlotte suddenly gasped and jerked away violently. Her free hand flew out, slashing at his face, the ring she wore, the very same he had given her, gouging deep cuts across his cheek and opening up his lip.

"*How dare you! How dare you!*" she raged, lashing at him again and again. "You are utterly despicable . . . loathsome. You are *vile*. Oh, God, how I hate you!" She was beside herself with outrage, ranting, wide eyes filled with black despair. "Are you trying to seduce me again? Have you no *shame*? Are you *entirely* without honour?"

Her breast was heaving with the exertion of her impassioned outburst, drawing Robert's eyes, fixing them upon her. Again, she struck at his impassive face. How *could* he come to her straight from the arms of another woman and speak of love?

For a moment longer, Robert remained still, and silent, from the unexpected shock of Charlotte's violent attack. Then, bending away from the last blow, Robert wiped the blood from his cut mouth. He looked at the red smears, then at Charlotte.

"How is my honour in dispute?" he asked, shock keeping him calm. His very calmness made Charlotte the more incensed.

"Are you so lost to sensitivity you must be told?" she raged, and would have struck him again, but Robert had had enough and caught at her wrists.

"Stop this," he commanded quietly, "you are outwith control, Miss Treleaven." He rose, drawing her up with him.

Charlotte was a veritable fury, beside herself with hysterical rage; she could not be reasoned with. "Orders, orders, always orders: no, I will never again do as you say!" she screamed.

"Oh, but you will," Robert said, indomitable as ever, and slapped her sharply. The slap brought Charlotte to a stinging, sobbing halt. For a moment there was silence, except for her laboured breathing. "Be seated until you are in control," Robert commanded and freed her. "Then we will continue." He turned away, giving her time to recover composure.

Charlotte took several quivering breaths and closed her eyes. Trembling hands came up to her face, knuckles pressed to her mouth. After a long pause, she released pent breath in a deep sigh and subsided. When she could speak with any degree of equanimity, she said: "There is nothing further to discuss, Mr Hattenbury. I have told you, repeatedly, that I would not marry you if you were the last man on earth." Her voice was pregnant with feelings of revulsion.

Robert swung back to her but remained a few paces distant. He stared at Charlotte through narrowed eyes. "Why not?" he asked in measured tones.

"Why not?" she echoed, her voice rising again: she heard it and made a visible effort to hold herself in check. "You know why not."

"Do I? I think not, Charlotte. I only know what you have told me . . . which is that I am loathsome and you despise me." He leaned towards her. "Vile was another word you used, and shameless and, oh yes, I must not forget this . . . you hate me." He drew back again.

"This is what you have *said*," he paused, never relenting his hard stare, "but against that," he went on, "I remember how I stood in this very room with you in my arms. I was aching for you and you *knew* it, but did you repulse me?" He paused before answering his own question. "No, you did not. You pressed your body to mine passionately; you asked me to kiss you and protested when, from prudence, I ended our lovemaking." Again he leaned forward.

"I also cannot forget how often you have sought me out and tormented me with the touch of your body, the lure of your mouth. I remember how passionately you have always respond to my lovemaking. There have even been occasions when you were perfectly willing to surrender. You did not loathe and hate me then, I think."

Robert was breathing hard. *With pain? With arousal? He could not have said, only that something very primitive was rising in him.*

Listening to him, Charlotte went as pale as death. Robert made her sound like a harlot, shaming her with his recital; but the blame was not all hers and she repudiated him from the depths of her humiliation.

"But as you have said many times, and so rightly, Mr Hattenbury, I was a child when you first went about my seduction and children are easily deceived by those who ought to know better," she accused bitterly.

That was a punishing hit, and Robert flinched, shaking his head in an involuntary repudiation. "No! I have never deceived you, Charlotte. Do not say so!"

"Why not? Do you not care for the truth? Is it too painful to face? *I* have had to face it often enough this last year because of you. Think me dishonoured, if you will, but I am not alone in this."

"Charlotte, how is it dishonourable when I am offering you marriage? I know I have not always behaved to you as I should, but an offer of matrimony must, surely, *surely*, amend my unprincipled behaviour? *Why will you not have me*?" he cried, uncomprehending.

Incredibly, Charlotte realised, he really seemed not to understand. What kind of man was he? Could he spend the night with one woman and propose to another, only hours later, without feeling even a twinge of conscience?

"It is perfectly simple. I do not want you, Sir. Oh," her lip curled, "no doubt I should be flattered by your generous offer, after all I am something in the nature of damaged ware, even if only to *you*, so you must forgive me that I am *not* flattered. If you are still in a fog of misunderstanding, allow me to reiterate, yet again, that *I do not want you.*" Her voice pregnant with loathing, Charlotte spoke through clenched teeth. It was that, or scream.

"You are lying, Charlotte. You *do* want me, I know you do. I *know* it! I feel it whenever we are close, that electrical spark when we touch. I am right, Charlotte, you know that I am. Why do you persist in denying me?" he asked, white with pain at Charlotte's unrelenting rejection, she whom he loved most in the entire world.

"Why? I am tired of being treated like a thing you own, a casual possession to be picked up and put down on a whim, allowed no life of my own. I will not have it. Take your shoddy charms where they are best appreciated. They are not for me."

So dreadful was the finality of Charlotte's tone Robert scarcely noticed her insults. He felt as if the blood were draining from his body.

"I will not believe you, Charlotte," he said desperately. "Even if I am all you say, you belong to me and I to you. We need each other to be happy. I can make you happy. I *will,* I *swear* it. I give you my word. Charlotte . . . I cannot be without you. Please, I . . . need you." He spoke as though the words were wrung from him, his voice breaking as though on a tear. He reached out a supplicating hand.

Charlotte ignored it, her loathing of him reignited by his last words, remembered pain striking deep. "As you needed me last night?" she flung out at him in sick fury. "It seemed to me Mrs Lerpiniere sufficed you then. I suggest you apply to her again. Let her pander to your needs, if she chooses, but I will not." She looked at him with absolute disgust, the memory of last night sweeping over her in a nauseous tide.

Robert saw her swallow the bitter bile which rose to her throat, and something clicked into place in his mind. The library.

He became very still, silent, his eyes dark and unfathomable. "You saw us?" His question was no question. He already knew the answer.

"You were hardly discrete, were you? '*A la bonne heure*'," she mimicked with jeering accuracy. "You are fond of quotations, it seems."

"It is not what you think, believe me, Charlotte," he said quickly, coming near as though to touch her. "Listen and I will tell you." Defensive hands warded him off.

"Do not *dare* to touch me. I could not bear it; and as for explanations, no, I want no explanations of you; nothing!" She spat the words at him, filled with raging turmoil. "You disgust me."

"Do I? Do I, indeed?" he asked, "but what if your feelings are based on a false supposition? What then? And, Charlotte, no matter what you think, it is you I want and it is you I mean to have, whatever happens."

"Really?" she mocked, affecting a humourless laugh. "And again, I have no say in this? No, I think not this time, Mr Hattenbury. Sadly, you are about to be disappointed for once in your life, tantrums or not."

"No, Charlotte." Robert's nostrils flared on a sharply drawn breath, and he shook his head. "I *will* have you and to your great pleasure, I assure you. Oh, yes, I mean to have you if I must ravish you first, make no mistake about it." He spoke very quietly, white to the lips, but he was in deadly earnest.

"Bravely spoken, Sir!" she said contemptuously, her lips curling. "See how I am cowed." She threw up her head proudly, drawing Robert's eye to the beautiful curve of her throat and breast, tormenting him anew with memories of what had been, and what must, *must,* somehow, be again.

"Nothing to say, Guardian?" she goaded. "Then let me inform you, here and now, that you may ravish me as you will but I *still* will not take you. It makes no difference what threats you utter, or lures you throw out, marriage or *none*. It is all of a piece. I could not bear to have you touch me ever again. You are nothing but a corrupt dilettante and I will pardon you no longer. I am finished with you."

Though he listened to her intently, the sense of Charlotte's tirade escaped Robert completely because, suddenly, a feeling of déjà vu had come over him. That, and the shock of realising she had seen him with Barbara, cooled his brain.

It enabled him to see more clearly and he was able to take note of what his mind was urgently trying to tell him as he looked at Charlotte's storm clouded brow and rigid body contours. Robert, the thinking man, took over from the frustrated lover and, with wits unaddled by frustration, he began to see a different picture.

Could it be . . . could it possibly be . . . that . . .? Yes, yes, of course it was!

Comprehension slowly, but slowly, dawned and finally he saw in the light of understanding. Of course!

Of course! This impassioned young woman was one he recognised. He had been here before. Charlotte, his adored Charlotte, was in the wildest rage of jealousy because she thought he had bestowed upon Mrs Lerpiniere what was rightly her own!

Charlotte was showing him the way!

What an idiot he had been to lose it in the first place. Of *course* she loved him. She was madly jealous! That was what this was all about. She thought he had made love to Barbara last night!

Robert's mouth curved into a smile of profound relief because now he knew which way to go. So great was his relief he began to laugh aloud and his laughter made Charlotte ever more furious.

"Do you find me so vastly amusing?" she raged. "I will *not* be a source of amusement to you either; no, not even that! Get out of my room, you despicable cur. Get out, I say. Return to your lover and see if she will accommodate you for I never will again. Never! Do you hear me? I hate you with all the passion of which I am capable."

Charlotte's last statement bordered on uncomprehending desperation as Robert began to descend on her. Revitalised, he was laughing openly.

As he advanced she retreated, step by step, until brought up short by a sofa. She tried to go around it but he was too quick for her and used his body to pin her against it. His hands grasped the back rest on either side of her, so she could not escape, and then he stood looking down at her, eyes, so ravishing a blue now, filled with devilment, teeth gleaming white between parted lips. Watching him, frozen, Charlotte saw that laughter had reopened the cut she had made on his lip.

"Are you challenging me, Charlotte?" he asked softly, his eyes alive and dancing with violent excitement. He straightened his legs and the movement thrust him against her intimately. "Here, then, is *my* challenge. Resist me . . . if you can! I wager that you cannot and therefore pick up your gauntlet most willingly; but on your own head be it. Be warned. If this is the way you want to go, so be it. You shall yet be upon your knees pleading to me, for I mean to have you; come . . . what . . . may."

Grinning, he punctuated every last word with an overt thrust of his body against hers and Charlotte felt, unmistakably, how dangerously aroused he had become. He was teasing her with his body, gazing triumphantly at Charlotte's upturned mesmerised face and she drew a quick, shaken breath.

"Now what nonsense do you speak? Have you taken leave of your senses? Unhand me," she demanded, trying to regain control of the situation. But a shaking voice and her look, a compound of anger and misapprehension, betrayed her.

"Taken leave of my senses? No, I have come to them, my beautiful Charlotte . . . and as to that of which I speak . . . oh . . ." again he was laughing, unable to prevent the mirth erupting from deep in his chest, "you already know." He was totally alive, bursting with new awareness, every nerve tingling with anticipation.

His hands slid caressingly up the column of her throat, coming to rest with thumbs under her chin and spread fingers at the back of her head. She struggled against him uselessly. He was invincible in the power now flooding him. With the smallest turn of the wrist her head was tilted, and he kissed her, hard . . . and Charlotte had the taste of his blood in her mouth.

She stopped struggling, dazed and not understanding how events had come to take this totally unexpected turn. What she did understand was the uncurling heat of Robert's body as, murmurously, he made himself known to her, openly entreating her response, a knee pushed between hers, nudging her, something less than gently, to let him press closer to where he wanted to be. But Robert was taller than Charlotte and had to lift her to achieve his desire. When it was done, when she experienced again the heady delight of feeling his vibrant shaft, so very close, separated only by their clothing, heat flooded her body, her breasts tingling with remembered anticipation, and she was reduced to molten, unassailably shameless desire.

"No," she protested faintly, "no!"

"Yes, yes, my darling," he breathed. He was blatant in his advance, unyielding of hot, amorous persuasion where it was most likely to influence Charlotte, thrusting against her openly. Had their clothing *not* separated them, he *would* have been upon her, there and then!

Treacherous blood, treacherous heart, which now urged Charlotte to cosset his exigence, knowing that if she did he would become urgent with her, helpless with need, hers to command. How endearing Robert was then; and how powerful a thought, that she could assuage his need and bring this most arrogant of lovers to his knees. No! Oh, no!

What was she thinking of? No, no! It would all begin again.

She struggled to free herself, pushing against his chest, wrenching her mouth out from under his. He was breathing hard, like a man who has been running, his heart thundering under her hands.

"Oh, Charlotte," he murmured, "I hurt so much from wanting you. I am so hungry for you I cannot sleep at night. Can you not feel my desire?" How could she not, when every tempting movement was an explicit invitation? "Oh, Charlotte, you are cruel to deny me, when I have waited so long. Sweet siren, if I am not soon sheathed in you I shall run mad, I know it. Let it be soon. *Please,* please, let it be soon. I cannot wait much longer; indeed, I know not how I have resisted temptation thus far," he murmured, entreating her powerfully, with hands at her hips, easing and exciting the need equally with each urgent thrust of his body.

"Oh!" Charlotte was scandalised, breathless, and unable to believe what she was hearing. "Robert! What are you saying?" He laughed, as breathless as she, but from a different cause.

"As if you did not know! I am saying that I want to lie with you, as I have wanted to for more than a year. I want you beneath me, in my bed, mine to possess." He was rubbing his face against her throat, touching and tasting, so urgent and demanding the barriers of clothing were as nothing. "Three times I have asked you to marry me and three times I have been rejected. I shall never ask you again. In spite of this, my tormenting little witch, you will be mine when it is my birthday this year . . . and *that* I promise you."

"What can you mean?" she asked faintly.

She had long since ceased to struggle, the things Robert was saying, the distraction of his lovemaking, the vibrancy of his aroused body, all conspiring to blur the edges of reality, so that everything ran together, condensed into a sweetness that was simply the aura of Robert. How could hatred of him have deliquesced into such awesome, tempting delight?

"What do I mean?" he echoed. "I mean that from my birthday you are no longer my ward. Then, will you nill you, I shall have you beneath me, surrendered, if it is the last thing I ever do!" he promised exultantly. "I *will* know you, my lovely Charlotte. I give you my word on it. I have waited for you long enough and the next time I raise your skirts I shall take what is mine! Never doubt it."

Gazing at him mesmerised, feeling him, so powerful in the glory of arrogant manhood, Charlotte was all too afraid he meant what he said. Robert usually did.

"Incidentally," he murmured confidentially in her ear, "how could you *possibly* believe I slept with Barbara last night? I have bestowed no favours there that are rightly yours, I assure you."

Once more, he was moving against her provocatively, where it was most pleasurable to Charlotte, making her weak and boneless with want. "I have not made love in a very long time. I would have thought that much was obvious. Trust me, Charlotte, the only reason a man allows himself to be led by the . . ." Robert changed course verbally, "by the nose, as you, my darling, have been leading me this last year, is because he is so hungry he can do nothing else but follow the enticing lure."

Charlotte gasped. How often she had wished Robert would be plain with her.

Could he, now, have been plainer?

Chapter Seventeen

Life changed dramatically. Robert was a different man. At once he lost his driven look, sloughed off like an old skin, and a new spring appeared in his step. He was, for him, quite boisterous and he surprised everyone.

Mrs Treleaven was so happy to see Robert his own dear self again, and Sophie felt intensely thankful to see the tension leave him; but she did wonder, with some unease it must be said, what had caused such a remarkable turnabout.

First intimations of changed times came that evening. They were dining at home. Robert appeared last and went straight to Charlotte, sweeping her up into his arms.

"Oh, Charlotte, how beautiful you are," he said and hugged her tightly. He pressed a kiss into the curve of her neck. "Uhmmm, and how delightful you smell," he murmured, savouring her perfume with eyes closed. "I missed you today."

"Mr Hattenbury!" she protested, going very pink as she saw the mamas looking at them in astonishment.

"Did you not miss me, Charlotte?" he asked, plaintively. "It was the least you could do after this morning." He glanced across, to where sat two bemused mamas. Turning his head revealed the cuts on his face and mouth. Both exclaimed aloud.

"Robert, your face! Whatever has happened?" Sophie gasped.

"Oh, my dear life, Robert! Oh, how very painful that looks. Did you cut yourself shaving?" Mrs Treleaven was dreadfully upset to see Robert's injury, the familiarity of his greeting to her daughter driven quite out of mind. It was swiftly recalled by his answer, which effectively silenced them all.

"No, I did not cut myself shaving, Mater, since that is a task ably performed by my valet." He looked directly at Charlotte, smiling wickedly.

"Robert, no," she pleaded, making frantic signals to head him off. Unchivalrously, he ignored them.

"No, no," he replied, "Charlotte hit me . . . repeatedly. To be fair, I should point out that I was trying to make love to her at the time. I was actually proposing, on bended knee, and thought it rather unkind of her to attack me when I was so vulnerable but," he made a throwaway shrug of the shoulders, "there you are. To compound the ignominy, she tossed back my proposal as if it were rotting offal; did you not, dear heart?" He began shepherding them towards the dining room. "Shall we go in?" he asked blandly. After a moment of stunned silence, they followed his lead.

Throughout the meal, Robert was aware of two pairs of questioning eyes drawn to him. Charlotte never once glanced up from her plate.

After dinner, Robert told the ladies equably that he had cancelled the evening's engagement, thinking, he said, as he touched his injured cheek lightly, that a night in would be a beneficial change. He extended his hand to a blushing Charlotte, watched by the still bemused mamas. "Sit with me, dear heart?"

"I . . . I thought to play the piano, Sir," she said.

He came and took her in his arms. "That would be delightful . . . but later," he said softly and gave her a lingering kiss, all unmindful of their bemused audience.

Quite how it came about Charlotte did not know, since she had fully intended to resist Mr Hattenbury's blandishments, but she found herself snuggled close to Robert's side on the sofa and he was taking down her hair.

"No, Sir," she objected, trying to stop his depredations, "this is not polite behaviour for company."

"We are not company here, Charlotte. We are family. Please?" he cajoled, "I love to see your hair down for then you look *so* adorable." He continued about his business and soon the abundance of her silky hair was just as he wished it. He began kissing her again, his hold most lover like.

With his kisses, lovely warmth spread throughout Charlotte's body, despite the firmest resolution, and her embarrassment at having an audience. She knew she ought to protest at Robert's extreme familiarity, but the creaming sweetness was too seductive to resist. She had been starved of him too long. At one point she murmured in his ear: "Sir, what will the mamas say?"

"I do not care, love," he breathed; and, Charlotte suddenly realised, neither did she and so sat mute within his arms, lost to all save the magic of his touch.

While Robert and Charlotte were absorbed in each other, the mamas stitched and knitted assiduously. They were careful not to remark the extraordinary love scene being enacted before their eyes, and neither spoke; but of the conscious silence in which they sat both were aware, knowing, also, much of what was in the other's mind, to be said later.

***

"Mr Hattenbury . . . Robert . . ." unusually, it was Mrs Treleaven who first approached Robert, before breakfast next morning, "may I have a moment of your time, dear?" she asked, flustered and nervous at having to challenge male authority, but steeled to it for her daughter's sake.

"Of course, Mater. Shall we take a turn in the garden?" Robert offered an arm to conduct Alethea out into the fresh morning air. It promised to be another lovely day, the sun, still misted about, not too hot for comfort.

Once their perambulation was underway, Robert asked helpfully: "What was it you wished to say, dear Mater?" already knowing full well.

Alethea was moved by Robert's endearment, which made it all the more difficult for her to castigate him, but it had to be done.

"Well, Sir, I cannot think it right that you were so . . . so openly affectionate to Charlotte last evening. Robert, even if you were engaged, which you stated categorically that you are not, it would not be *convenable*."

"That is true, Mater," he agreed gently, "but I am choosing the lesser of two evils here. Unless I make it impossible for Charlotte to refuse me, she will end up married to Mr Neville and I feel sure you do not want *that* to happen. You must have seen how she encourages him to make me jealous; with success, I might add. But, dear Mater, she loves me and it would not be right for her to marry one man loving another, would it?"

Alethea missed a step and went pale. Had not she herself done precisely that? And had it not been a disaster? "Indeed, Robert," she agreed faintly, "but I hope you do not judge me harshly. I had no choice. Mr Treleaven was chosen for me."

Looking down to see why Alethea had stumbled, Robert saw that she had gone white. Hastily, he pressed her to a seat.

"No, no, Mater. I would not presume to censure you on any score," he assured her robustly. What old stories were coming to the surface recently? Whom had she loved, if not Jake Treleaven? "I spoke only of my situation with Charlotte. I do not mean to lose her, Mater, and shall do anything I must to prevent it. To say frankly, if it is seen by you and Mama how well Charlotte responds to my overtures, in all conscience she cannot do other than marry me. Is this not so?"

"Well, dear . . ." Alethea was torn, "it is my dearest wish to see you married to Charlotte but I will not see her constrained, Robert. I could not condone that."

"There will be no constraint, I promise you. When Charlotte marries me it will be willingly. I say this with absolute conviction because I know she loves me as much as I love her. Let me say also, that you need not worry for Charlotte's reputation. I give you my word none shall see me make love to her save you and Mama. So, dearest Mater, think of those delightful grandchildren clustered about your skirts and give me your blessing, I implore," Robert said, kissing her cheek.

Thus, with rosy dreams in her head, Alethea was won over to Robert's cause, unaware that his campaign was not totally one of necessity, as he had intimated, but was mostly designed for Charlotte's pleasure. In the last twenty four hours he had seen again what he had always really known, that she belonged to him and ever would.

'Nevertheless,' he thought wickedly, with a secret smile on his lips, *'it would not hurt her to be chased, all the while wondering if she were about to be made unchaste.'*

His mother was not so easily persuaded.

"Tell me, Mama," he said musingly, "with whom was Mater in love if not Mr Treleaven?"

Sophie was taken aback. "How do you come to know of this?"

"I stumbled upon it by chance when we talked this morning. Who was it?"

She gave a dry laugh. "Can you not guess? Your father, of course; all the girls were in love with him."

"He was a busy man, it seems," Robert observed, his tone as dry as Sophie's.

Mrs Hattenbury took the opening this gave her. "As were you last night, Sir," she said bluntly. "What were you about with Charlotte; and why? You were so libertine it was difficult for Alethea and me to keep countenance. I also think you owe us an explanation as to why, suddenly, all is well with you, when only yesterday you were in black despair over Charlotte; and, pray, do not say it is not my business. If you have been doing what you should not with Charlotte, it is very much the business of a mother, Alethea or me."

Robert laughed at his mama's plainness, so unlike her. He reciprocated equally. "If you wish to know have I been in her bed, the answer is no, much as I'd like to. No, that is to come when we marry shortly."

"Marry? You said yesterday she had refused you," Sophie objected.

"Yes, but only from pique because she thought I was having an affair with Mrs Lerpiniere. I *was* last year but there has been no-one since I met Charlotte. She knows that now. Do you seriously think she would otherwise have allowed me to make love to her, let alone in front of you? She would cut my throat sooner. Charlotte is no milk-sop miss, as you well know," Robert declared, with something of amused rue and a good deal of pride.

"If she knows you are faithful, what need of such shameless persuasion as you used upon her last night?" Sophie asked directly.

"Mama . . ." a half smile raised one corner of Robert's mouth, "it was for Charlotte's pleasure, my own also, but safely done in your company. No, wait, Mama," he said, as he saw Sophie prepare to register a further objection. Robert paused to marshal his thoughts. Then he said: "I cannot tell you how often I have regretted that I did not get her safely attached when you recommended it. What relief if I had. This last year has been a complete misery for us both. Why do you think she has been leading me such a dance? Indeed, you must know that it is from frustration, because she wants what I want and has it not. It is absolute penance to be living in the same house with her, and not . . . well, I need say no more."

Sophie did not need more to read his trend. "That does not make your conduct either right or proper."

"No, but I am past caring. What does it matter when we are so soon to be married? I have already addressed Mr Rodd[5] for the calling of banns. We shall be man and wife three weeks from my birthday. But you are not to tell Charlotte."

"Not tell Charlotte," Sophie echoed. "She does not know?" she asked in amazement.

Robert grinned. "No. It will be a lovely surprise when *I* tell her . . . eventually. You know, Mama, the last time she refused me I vowed I would never ask her again and I meant it then. Of course, that was before I realised what was wrong with her, but now . . . well, I mean to keep her on pins for a while. It will be just retribution for the hoops through which she has put me these last months." As he spoke Robert was smiling. Clearly he meant no malice.

"What of the wedding arrangements? What of her bridal gown?" Sophie asked, aghast. "Do you not know, Robert, what work is entailed in a nuptial?"

"Ah, you and Mater shall see to all that, but don't be alarmed," he

---

Mr Treloware retired at Easter.

reassured hastily, seeing his mother go pale with horror at the very thought. "I have everything in hand," he added, looking inordinately pleased with himself. "Here is my plan."

***

There followed seven days of seclusion, during which the household neither visited nor received, it being given out that Mr Hattenbury was indisposed. There were no complaints from Charlotte over this prevarication. Most of her waking hours were spent in Robert's company and his attentions to her were such as she had long wanted, keeping her in a delicious dither.

Finally, came a day when the condition of Mr Hattenbury's face allowed him out. What a day that was for Charlotte! He was up betimes, and away from the house before the ladies rose, but back in time for breakfast. Charlotte was not yet down. He ran lightly up the stairs to fetch her. He beat a loud tattoo upon her door and went in.

"Come along, sleepy head. I am starving and breakfast must be out of the way by eleven at the latest, but there is something I want to give you first."

The 'something' was a fine pair of kid driving gloves. His comment, as he handed them over, made Charlotte blush rosily, a thing she had been doing regularly of late. "These are in exchange for the gauntlet you threw down to me last week. I have not forgotten, you see," he murmured, with a seductive glance.

Clutching the gloves to her breast Charlotte began: "Robert, I did not mean . . ."

"Not now, dear heart," he breathed as he silenced her with a kiss, one which, he observed, when he drew back his head, had brought them both under love's compelling influence. "What a pity we are in haste," he whispered, his hands caressing Charlotte lightly.

At the appointed hour of eleven, Charlotte discovered the reason for Robert's hurry. A bright new chaise was driven to the door. Between its shafts was a glossy chestnut horse of the sweetest proportions. Charlotte looked at this smart equipage with admiration, never realising what was to come.

"What a beauty, Sir. I did not know you thought of acquiring a new carriage. But is it not rather small for you?"

"It is not for me. George?" The coachman came to them. Robert made an oblique signal and George Coachman offered the whip he was carrying to Charlotte.

Not being a slowtop, comprehension dawned on Charlotte immediately. She put both hands to her lips in a gasp of bemused pleasure. "It is for me!" she exclaimed incredulously. "Oh . . . how wonderful!" She began to reach for the whip but stopped and turned to Robert, her face alight with excitement. "My gloves, I forgot my gloves," she cried and ran back to the house, no thought of any unfortunate connotations occurring to her. She was drawing them on when she re-emerged.

Robert helped her into the driving seat and got up beside her. Not in the least nervous, she whipped up her new horse stylishly and away they went. Albeit rather too fast, as Robert was obliged to point out, advising her to slow down for the rapidly approaching corner. Luckily, the park was close at hand, much safer than the open road for a first drive, giving of a very pleasurable half hour's practice.

At the end of this time, Charlotte obediently turned for home on Robert's suggestion. Once the equipage had been handed over in the stables, Charlotte tried to express her thanks to Robert. And as so often before, love, and the compulsions of gratitude, betrayed her. In a sudden access of joy she threw her arms around his neck and hugged him, quite without meaning to.

Immediately securing her about the waist, he swung Charlotte up and kissed her, (in front of a startled stable lad, who lost no time in spreading the news), before returning a thoroughly confused and blushing young lady to terra firma.

"How sweet a reward," he murmured. "I wonder what would be the effect of a high perch phaeton. Now *that* could be interesting but, alas, not useful for our narrow Cornish lanes."

"I beg your pardon, Sir. I did not mean to . . . I hope you do not think that I was . . . that I . . ." she stopped, her confusion spreading.

Robert thoughtfully rescued her before she got in too deeply. "I shall think whatever you wish me to think, darling," he said kindly, leaving her to wonder what exactly he meant. "By the bye, did you notice that the mare's coat is the colour of your hair?" he asked as they walked into the house. "That is no coincidence, I assure you."

Charlotte stopped and stared at him bemused. She had, indeed, noticed the mare's colour but never would have imagined it a deliberate thing. At which point, Robert took Charlotte into his arms again.

"You have not thanked me for the gloves," he prompted, with his bewitching smile, and kissed her once more. When he eventually freed her mouth, Charlotte was quivering and reluctant to be outwith Robert's embrace. He put his cheek to hers, lips close to her ear, and murmured: "Make a list of all the things that you want, but be sure to put me at its head, dear heart." A caressing pressure, low at her back, reinforced his message and sent frissons of pure pleasure coursing through a much shaken young lady.

***

After noon, Charlotte was engaged to visit a new friend, Mrs Stockdale, for her children's playtime. Alethea meant to go with her. On the point of departure she discovered that Robert was to escort her instead. He said Mater preferred to go shopping with Mama.

Charlotte looked her doubts. "You will be bored, Robert."

"I am never bored in your company, Charlotte, no matter the circumstance. I certainly shall not be today," he assured her affably.

In the event, he appeared to be speaking the truth. To Charlotte's astonishment, (not to mention Mrs Stockdale, who knew Mr Hattenbury as a very aloof young man), he cheerfully played ball with the two Stockdale infants, seeming not to mind when grubby fingers clutched his kerseymeres for balance, or when the children inadvertently stepped on his toes.

Charlotte tried not to be affected by the morning's enchantingly domestic ambience because she knew, from past experience, how dangerously easy it would be to fall under Robert's spell again. But she could not help noticing how handsome he looked, with his usually immaculate hair standing in a golden halo of ruffled curls about his head. Her eyes were drawn to him constantly and, dangerous or not, she wanted very much to touch him, wanting him to be as accessible to her as he now was to his two small playmates.

Home again, she was granted her wish. Indeed, she got more than her wish and could not say later which was uppermost, the pain or pleasure of the encounter, since it left her with a painful and overwhelming desire for Robert.

She meant to take her bonnet upstairs straight away. Instead, Robert drew her out to the garden and sent for a tray of lemonade. Refreshed by a cooling drink, he discarded his jacket and stretched his length beside Charlotte. She sat with her back to the magnolia tree. He took her hand and began kissing her fingers. Smiling, she ruffled his hair, feeling safe with the paternal Robert who had emerged that morning. He represented no threat, unlike the man whose eyes sent her dangerously intimate messages, or whose body mocked her with its assertive claims to her allegiance; not without justification, she had to admit.

Eyes closed, Robert turned his face into her hand and began to nibble her pink-nailed fingertips. Charlotte's pulse quickened; her heart beat faster. "I should go in, Sir," she said, with reluctant prudence.

Robert opened his eyes. "Why? What have you to do?" As he spoke, his glance was drawn to her frantically beating heart. He sat up and took her in his arms.

Held sweetly thus, Charlotte could thing of nothing but his nearness, and said faintly: "Some several things . . . to choose this evening's dress, for example."

"No hurry, then. You may safely stay with me another hour." He drew her closer and brought her hand back to his mouth, sucking on her fingers, each in turn. "It is a poor substitute, is it not, my lovely temptress?" he whispered and Charlotte drew a choked breath, trying to push him away.

"Guardian . . . Robert . . . no, I must go in. We . . . we can be seen."

"Ah, if that is your only objection . . ." he slipped an arm around her and drew her head to his shoulder, turning his back to the house. "Now, we cannot," he said, as his hand drifted to her breast, stroking her with exquisite precision. Charlotte moaned softly and covered his hand with hers, whether to push away or press it closer to the ache of need rising into his palm, she did not know but, signally, Robert responded.

"Oh, Charlotte, this is not enough. I want all of you," he said, with a husky groan. He pressed her down to the lawn, kissing her passionately, their bodies, stretched and aching, melding together bonelessly. When the long kiss ended, Charlotte was utterly submissive, Robert thoroughly aroused and roughly urgent with her, his hands very definitely where they ought not to be about her person and certainly not in public. "I cannot wait any longer, I cannot," he groaned. "I hurt so much from wanting you. Oh, Charlotte, please let it be now."

"Robert, no!" Charlotte said, on a sobbing breath. It was frightening to think that if he persisted she might, indeed, allow that it could be now, because she wanted him equally. "In the garden, Robert? Oh, no, please, we shall be seen," she said. "How disgraceful that would be; how wounding to the mamas. It must not be, Sir."

Robert drew a shaken breath, but he was not totally lost to propriety and slowly he released Charlotte. She sat up and left him. In the house, she threw herself upon the bed and lay with trembling hands pressed to flushed cheeks until the heat in her body subsided and she was calm again.

Later, bathed and prepared for the evening's entertainment, she prayed that Robert would not make love to her again that night. If he did, she knew she would be quite unable to withstand him, for Robert, in certain mode, was irresistible, his confidence in her response to him not misplaced. Did he not prove it, over and over?

Her prayer was answered.

***

They were to watch a fireworks display in Vauxhall gardens: which they did, most enjoyably. Robert's behaviour was a model of propriety so that Charlotte was able to relax. When the display ended the assemblage dispersed and people began to walk about the gardens.

Strolling down one path, Mr Hattenbury's party met with another coming the other way. Charlotte stiffened, feeling as though an iron hand gripped her heart as she recognised one lady in the approaching quartet.

Robert felt the jerk of her body at his side and glanced down. Following the direction of her eyes, he saw that they were fixed upon Mrs Lerpiniere. His own were drawn to the lady's escort, a gentleman he knew well. It was Richard Carr, one of his father's 'other family', his own half-brother in fact, the resemblance between them too acute to be missed.

Charlotte made no effort to disguise her agitation, a compound of anger and fear, since she was fully aware that Robert's attention had been caught by the other party. From past experience she assumed he was looking at Mrs Lerpiniere.

"You dare!" she hissed. "I shall kill you if you do." To accent the threat, a small fist thumped into his back, none too gently.

"Not as you think, Charlotte. You have me firmly shackled," he said absently, eyes still fixed ahead, but he squeezed her elbow for comfort as he thought swiftly of ways to avoid his half brother in order to save his mother's discomfiture. He left Charlotte and dropped back with Sophie, urging Mrs Treleaven forward.

Looking ahead, Charlotte saw a handsome face so like Robert's there could be no doubt as to his parentage. She knew, instantly, the reason for Robert's puzzling behaviour and what he was about. With their party thus rearranged, Mrs Hattenbury was at the extreme left. They could pass the others and she see nothing in the gathering dusk. This was how it transpired; or so it seemed.

In the carriage going home Sophie disabused them. "Which one was he, Robert?" she asked. There was a pregnant silence. "You may as well tell me, darling," she added gently. "If they are universally accepted a meeting must have occurred at some time or another."

"Possibly, but there is no need of an acknowledgement," Robert replied frigidly. "Of course, their being accepted is all Aunt Jane's fault. She *will* do it," he added angrily. "As if it were not bad enough simply to know they are *there*, one even meets them in her salon unless asking for her guest list first."

"Which was he, Robert?" Sophie asked again.

After a pause, Robert said reluctantly: "Richard Carr. Now, no more, if you please, Mama," he added. Thereafter, he was morosely silent but Charlotte did not mind. He might be as absent minded as he pleased so long as her hand was tucked into his; which it was.

At home it was clear Robert wished to speak to Sophie. Tactfully, Charlotte said good night immediately, for which Robert thanked her warmly and gave her the sweetest kiss. She and Alethea went to bed but it was long before Robert and Sophie did likewise.

***

At church on Sunday Charlotte saw Mr Neville, restored to the bosom of his family. After service, he asked if she planned to walk in the park that afternoon. She hesitated and said she would consult her guardian, hoping he would solve her dilemma. He only said brusquely that he had no objection, seeming so disinterested Charlotte's heart sank. Diffidently, she told Mr Neville it was likely.

After noon Robert came to her. "Charlotte, are you intent on seeing Mr Neville, or will you come riding with me?"

"Is that what you wish, Sir?"

"Of course I do!" Would I otherwise ask?" he replied irritably.

Charlotte laughed, feeling more light-hearted suddenly. "I beg your pardon. That was silly of me. I am delighted to accept your invitation," she responded demurely.

Robert smiled a little. "Ten minutes," he said.

Within the stipulated time they were away from the house, cantering sedately until reaching open countryside, when both riders gave the mounts their head until the spring in their step had lessened.

"Where to, Guardian?" Charlotte asked when conversation was possible.

"Tut, tut, how inelegant your phraseology, my darling," Robert said with a grin. "Richmond."

When they came to Richmond's green fields, Robert and Charlotte dismounted to walk for a while. While they walked he was silent. Shortly, he tethered the horses. Then, without preamble, he began to talk, pacing to and fro as he did.

He told Charlotte the whole story of his father's Carr family, of whom Richard was only one. There were two more brothers, James and William, and two sisters, not to mention the suspect Neath girl.

"Ariadne Neath?" Charlotte asked in surprise.

"Yes," he said, resignedly, "she also."

"But, Robert, why have we not met with them before if they are generally accepted?" Charlotte asked curiously. "It seems strange."

"No it isn't," Robert said bluntly. "I take care to vet any company before accepting invitations. Also, naturally, most people have too much delicacy to invite both Carr and Hattenbury to the same function . . . except for Aunt Jane, of course." He sighed heavily. "*Now*, would you believe, Mama says she is inclined to recognise them. Why, in God's name? What does she hope for in wanting the Carrs to call?"

Charlotte hesitated, before saying gently: "If Aunt Sophie seems not to object, does it matter, Sir?"

"To me it does," he said in a constricted voice, his face sober and uncertain. "I do not want to know them. They have already had too much that was rightfully mine. Must I now share my mother also?" Robert's clear sense of grievance was tinged with pained bewilderment.

"Come and sit down," Charlotte suggested. Suiting word to action she sat. Robert stretched his length beside her, leaning on one elbow, his gaze centred on her face. She cuddled a hand to his cheek, thinking how unusual it was to see him look uncertain, and how endearing. He sighed and pressed his face into her hand. She slipped an arm about him to hold him close.

"What shall I do, Charlotte?"

She did not answer immediately, since it was no easy thing he asked. Indeed, her immediate thoughts were not of his question at all. She was basking in a wonderful realisation; that this was the first time Robert had sought her opinion over his own, or turned to her for comfort. She gave it most willingly, cuddling him close, with an instinct as sure as the impulse which had made him reach out to her.

When she finally answered, Robert had almost forgotten the question. His head was resting in Charlotte's lap and her gentle fondling of his hair had lulled him to a pleasant state where it seemed less urgent.

"I do not think you need do anything, Robert. It seems to me that if it pleases Aunt Sophie to recognise the Carrs she must have her reasons, but it need not affect you. You do not have to be present if they visit. That omission would show that *you* have no wish for a connection," Charlotte began.

"On the other hand, recognition would, indubitably, benefit them and must increase your stature, Sir. It could not be otherwise, for though it is true that the Hattenburys have less blue blood than the Devonshires, they have no less breeding. What does not belittle one, will not belittle the other." Charlotte referred to the duchess' peccadillo and the resultant child accepted by the duke, her husband.

Robert's expression was noncommittal. Charlotte continued. "These are two ways of looking at the situation. Which to take, if either, must be your decision, Robert, for only you know what you find acceptable." She ran a finger down his nose, smiling. "There is a third possibility, of course, which is to forbid Aunt Sophie, but could you do that? She asks very little of you as a rule. That she petitions you now, shows it is important to her," Charlotte ended gently.

"I do not dispute that Mama is undemanding, and ever was, but what she asks now is anathema to me," Robert declared with energy.

"Are your wishes paramount in this?" Charlotte asked carefully.

"I did not say so," he responded defensively.

Charlotte gave him a frank and open look. "That is how it appears," she said, "but I may be wrong and, certainly, I do not presume to criticize you, Robert. The decision must be yours."

Robert sat up. "So exact a summing up certainly clarifies the situation, but I cannot like it any the more," he sighed.

***

Talking to Charlotte brought Robert ease, since he recognised the essential truth of her observations. As she said, the Carrs were received, if not universally, and it would not demean him to recognise them. In fact, it provided an opportunity to right a wrong he had once done them.

After his father's death, Mrs Carr wrote to Robert, telling him Francis had promised to buy a commission for James, but had not done so at the date of his unexpected demise. She asked, therefore, if Robert would be willing to fulfil his father's pledge, at the same time giving assurances that no further favours would be asked if he saw fit to help in this.

He had not replied. The letter came at a time when he was feeling raw at losing a father who had only come close to him in recent years. To be reminded of those other children, who had had so much more of Francis than he, made Robert view the letter as gross intrusion.

Later, he thought he should have honoured his papa's pledge, but the difficulty of approaching Mrs Carr decided him to leave matters as they stood. It was not a decision taken positively; rather had he allowed it to come about. Now, if he wished, the omission could be righted and his conscience cleared. He could recognise the Carr family out of respect for his father's memory because they *had* brought joy to Francis. As his mother had said, it was not their fault the Carrs were labelled 'Fitz'. That was entirely down to her late husband. For her part, she felt only compassion for the children of his unholy alliance.

For his part, Robert was astonished by her tolerance. He might acknowledge their existence but he was not obliged to like them as well. Thus, after much deliberation, Robert came down in favour of Charlotte's logic.

She knew at once when the decision had been taken because he came out of his abstraction. He sought her company positively instead of simply being with her, as had been the case of late.

"I am going to take your excellent advice, darling. I mean to recognise Papa's Carr family," he said, with an unconscious arrogance that made Charlotte smile.

"I am so glad, Sir," she said, showing her delight, until she saw that he frowned. "Is something wrong, Mr Hattenbury?"

"Assuredly there is," he replied, irritated. "Why is it that on Sunday you called me Robert but today I am reduced to Sirs and Mr Hattenburys? You do it simply to annoy me; do you not?"

Charlotte laughed. "As if I dared," she objected demurely. She slid her hands up his jacket front, ostensibly to smooth an infinitesimal wrinkle from the lapel. In reality it was for the pleasure of possessive touch, as he was well aware.

"You would dare much if it suited you, mistress temptation," he observed ironically. He caught her in his arms, suddenly and vibrantly conscious that he had not held her close for several days. "No arguments. I *shall* be named as I want."

How very imperious, how very Robert, thought Charlotte. She glanced at her hands, resting on his chest. "Clearly, as with Richard, the one-time king, you were not born to sue but to command," she said, verecund as a milkmaid.

"Would you have me soft and sighing?" he demanded, amused.

"He who bends the neck often commands all," she answered ingenuously. There was unconscious provocation in the parting of her lips.

Robert took immediate advantage and kissed her, an experience pleasing to them both, although Charlotte reproved him, smiling. "Fie on you, for that was not what I meant and you know it."

Robert's arms tightened masterfully. "Dear heart, I have been starved of you too long. I need restoring with kisses and fond embraces."

"The question is, Sir, should I wish to see you restored, or have I something in common with King Richard's eventual wife, Anne?" Charlotte wondered thoughtfully, assiduously studying Robert's shirt front.

"So?" he asked, with a lifted brow.

Charlotte explained impishly. "She, before marriage to the sovereign, was obliged to run away from his . . . uhm . . . importunities?"

Robert dissolved into laughter, rocking Charlotte from side to side in his arms. "Oh, my lovely Charlotte, how *did* I exist without your nimble tongue to entertain me?"

"Perfectly well on *some* occasions I observed," she replied tartly, remembering those occasions clearly.

"One has to be polite, darling; most especially you, to me, right now. Repeat after me: 'kiss me, Robert', if you please," he commanded teasingly.

After some delightful cajolery and subtle caressing, Charlotte succumbed to his blandishments, following which she was richly rewarded.

"No, darling," he cuddled her close, "I do not think you will ever run from *me.*"

"I do not have cause," she responded, contentedly leaning her head against an accommodating broad shoulder.

"You should not count upon it," he said wickedly, "for if I had *my* way, Charlotte, you would have cause here and now. Alas, we are too public."

Chapter Eighteen

The remove to Brighton was accomplished at the start of the following week, later than originally planned, allowing time for the Carr family to call. Understandably, Mrs Carr did not accompany her children.

James, William, Richard, Molly and Isabel, in descending order of age, all had charming manners and Mrs Hattenbury liked them. At first sight, she was startled by their astonishing resemblance to Francis, especially Richard, who was so like Robert it was uncanny. But when each spoke differences became evident and the goose bumps subsided.

In fact, although there was some degree of pain attached to the thought, she seemed to see in the children a ghost of the family she and Francis had planned in the first year of their marriage, and so felt no resentment of these evidences of her husband's infidelity (time changes all things) but was warmed by their acquaintance.

Robert was not enthusiastic, only civil. Throughout the visit he stood aloof. For him, it was a case of hasten slowly and he was glad to leave town soon after the first meeting. It would need time for him to become accustomed to the idea of an enlarged family. At this point, he doubted he ever would fully. However, he was happy to please his mama, (although he still did not understand her remarkable tolerance, not knowing that Sophie saw Francis' other children in the light of what might have been for herself had fate been kinder), and was relieved by a sense of duty done in regard to James. As for the rest . . . he had much better things to do now.

***

The journey to Brighton was leisurely, with frequent stops for the ladies to stretch their legs. This was one of the few chaffing things Robert's new lifestyle entailed. At a time when, alone, he would have driven his curricle satisfyingly fast he was obliged to ride sedately in the carriage. This lengthened journeys considerably but it was a small cross to bear, he was wont to reflect, when taken in consideration with the benefits accruing from having three women to attend his every need.

Life was certainly satisfying, except in one particular, which he intended to put right shortly. Life, also being full of uncertainties, his plans received a check when they were settled in Brighton.

His steward had taken a house overlooking the Steine, where all the world and his wife might be seen at some time during the twenty four hours of a day. After the smallest interim, Robert was heard to say, rather loudly, and with a frown marring his noble brow, that so far they had seen every face familiar to them in town. Why, then, had they come to Brighton? Was peace to be had nowhere? he asked irately.

His outburst occurred after a visit to the lending library, Charlotte's first, where they met Charles and Xanthe. Behind them were Andrena Norris and Hadley Dean, looking set for the connubial state.

The girls greeted each other with delight and sat down to drink chocolate while exchanging news. It transpired that the Deans were not staying in town because their home at Amberly was no more than twenty five miles distant. The family was spending the summer there. Why did not Charlotte visit? Xanthe asked, and then they could talk undisturbed for hours on end!

When approached, Mr Hattenbury gave his permission. He did not relish the idea but it had the advantage of putting Charlotte beyond Mr Neville's reach.

Robert knew he was being foolish but he still disliked the younger man, and only careful control prevented him making repressive remarks.

At times, the effort required showed in a tightening of his lips, whose shapely curve hardened to a straight line. His jealousy even made him short with Charlotte, which she naturally resented, telling him so plainly.

"I have no intention of being the butt of your ill humour, Mr Hattenbury. If that is how your temper inclines, vent it elsewhere, do."

This refreshing attack immediately dispelled Robert's glooms and he laughed aloud, relieved to shed the weight of anxiety. He stretched, feeling physically lighter after Charlotte's verbal onslaught and asked, in bantering tone, if she had a specific someone in mind for the said venting.

"Someone fat, since your tastes run in that direction," she flashed with asperity and flounced away.

"Darling," he called after her, "I have no idea what leads you to suppose I care for the voluptuous. Au contraire, I am attracted to a lady with beautiful eyes and a perfect, if miniature, bosom . . ."

Charlotte heard no more. Pink-faced, she fled, but later reflected, with satisfaction, that Robert had come out of his miseries. Whatever had upset him, (she inclined to the view that it was jealousy, although scarcely daring to believe it), she seemed to have regained the ability to influence his spirits.

She came to this conclusion when Robert told her, with perfect equanimity, and no sign of his former temper, that they had been invited to Amberly. Would she like to go? he asked. Charlotte said yes please and preparations were put in hand.

Before they departed, however, she received a billet doux. It came with a posy of sweet-scented rosebuds. She held the flowers to her face, breathing in their fragrance, enjoying the touch of silken smooth petals on her skin.

Robert was down later than usual. He came up behind Charlotte as she stood in the hall, and dropped a kiss on her hair. "Good morning, darling. Have you breakfasted yet? Oh, what have you there?" he asked, catching sight of the ribbon-tied sheet she held in her hand.

"It came with a bouquet," she revealed.

"A love letter, perhaps? Do I know the sender?" Robert mooted impishly.

"I do not know who sends it. I have yet to open the note."

"Well, I shall ask nothing further. It is none of my business. Come and have some coffee. Read your note in peace." From the innocence of his expression, Charlotte suspected Robert already knew who had sent the note. If he did not, he was showing remarkable insouciance.

"For a beautiful lady: an ode to a perfect, miniature . . ." she stopped in confusion as a blush swept over her face.

What followed was a paean in praise of her physical charms, which were described with loving exactitude. It was extremely flattering and quite scandalous. It was also thrilling and was, of course, from Robert.

"Robert, you are a wretch," Charlotte reproved severely, while holding the thrilling letter to her fast beating heart.

"But truthful, would not you say?" he asked with a mischievous smile; and Charlotte blushed anew.

"You cannot know . . . I mean . . ."

He knew precisely what she meant. "You have forgotten, my beautiful Charlotte, that I once saw you in your bath and shall see you again one month from today, because that day is my birthday," he reminded her, with the blandest of looks.

She blushed even more rosily and fled in total disarray.

***

They spent eight days with the Deans. To Robert's relief Spencer was not at home. This did not mean he had Charlotte's exclusive company, but at least he was free of the miseries of jealousy. At the same time, he was sharply aware of excited anticipation of what was to be. From her looks, he rather thought Charlotte was too.

Certainly, Charlotte felt shaken by her recent interactions with Robert, and from all that had gone before she was still not certain of him. At intervals, her eyes slid to him for reassurance. When their glances met, she read in his messages of dangerous promise, spiced with threat, which filled her with alarmed anticipation. It was not precisely the reassurance she sought.

Even now, she was not absolutely sure of Robert's intentions. Would he carry out his threat? She knew he was quite capable of it, but would he? Circumstances must preclude the kind of intimacy he said he intended; and, truly, she did not believe he would ever force himself upon her. Of course, the truth was that no force would be needed but it was wickedly thrilling to entertain such thoughts, although she knew she ought not to. Alas, no matter how she reproached herself, many were the shivers of delicious anticipation she experienced.

She looked forward to Robert's birthday with a mixture of eagerness and some trepidation, knowing her fate would be decided then. She felt sure he would ask her to marry him again and when he did she meant to accept instanter, all her instincts pointing to his being in love with her again. She would get him shackled this time and no more nonsense.

One day, at Amberly, Charles taxed Robert over the question of love. "How goes it with you, Robbie?" He tilted his head in Charlotte's direction. She and Xanthe were playing tennis with Anne and Andrena Norris. Girlish laughter floated on the air.

"About the same as you, I expect. Wedding fixed yet?"

"No, unfortunately," Charles remarked with a wry grimace. Then he realised Robert was heading him off. "How about you? Have you fixed a date?" he asked, never thinking to receive an affirmative reply.

"August the tenth," Robert said, grinning to see Charles' surprise.

"Good Lord! You amaze me. Charlotte has not said a word to Xanthe, or I would have heard." At that, Robert laughed outright.

"That is because Charlotte does not know," he said, with a laconic rise of the brow.

"What!" Charles was astounded. "Not know of her own wedding?"

"Yes. It is to be a surprise. My . . . ah . . . wedding present, if you like," Robert said audaciously.

"Robbie," Charles was aghast at his friend's boldness and found it hard to believe his ears, "even you would not venture so far! Good God, what if she balks at the altar?"

"She will not, because she loves me, Charles, and naturally I shall mention the wedding before we get to the church. Incidentally, I told her of your advice to me and said I meant to do it if she did not stop kicking up a dust with all these beaux of hers," Robert revealed calmly.

"Oh, my Lord! Robert, my friend, you are the absolute outside of enough!" Charles could not contain his laughter. "What did she say?"

"She was scandalised, of course. But I mean to have her and she knows it," he replied with cool assurance. Robert's glance strayed to Charlotte, his expression softening. "Oh, yes, I mean to have her. You may be sure of that."

Charles observed Robert, thinking his friend had lately revealed unsuspected depths. Come to that, he had too. "Is there something about these Bath schools, do you think?" he asked and, of unspoken accord, the two men turned and shook hands.

"By the bye," Robert added, "you are naturally invited to the wedding ~ the invitations have already gone out ~ but do not make mention to Xanthe yet."

***

Mr Hattenbury took his family back to Brighton on Friday. To their surprise, they did not return to the house on the Steine but to a more secluded villa, set in its own gardens, on the outskirts of town.

Robert enjoyed the surprised looks of his family as he calmly explained that he could not endure the crowds in town. "Furthermore," he added, "I am going no more into Brighton. If you wish to do so, you must make your own arrangements."

This unprecedented turn of events startled them hugely but, as always, Mr Hattenbury had his reasons. It was a scant three weeks to his birthday and he meant to spend them wooing Charlotte.

That evening he set up the chess table and said to her: "I wager a kiss to a new bonnet that I beat you, my love. What do you say?"

"That you will lose," Charlotte responded confidently. Alas, he did not.

"Bad luck, Charlotte," he sympathised, when the board was packed away, but made no move to claim his prize until she was lightly tripping off to bed. "Darling, I think you have forgotten our wager," he reminded gently.

Charlotte blushed, and looked towards the mamas in confusion.

Robert calmly advised them to go on to bed. He would send Charlotte to say goodnight after a few minutes. On this reassurance, Sophie and Alethea went upstairs, leaving Charlotte standing within the circle of Robert's arm.

"Now, dear heart, it is time to pay. Remember, it is for you to kiss me not the reverse." He slid her arms around his neck and tightened his own about her waist, raising her until their lips were only a breath apart. "I am ready, my dove, my dear one," he murmured.

Charlotte's heart was beating fast. She could feel warm emanations from Robert's mouth, could taste them almost, and it was a strong inducement to obedience, as was the charm of being stretched to the length of his powerful body. It was highly evocative and gave her a wonderful sense of security, among other sensations. She wanted very much to please him. Warring instincts were at large, but, ultimately, it took only the tiniest movement to bring her lips to his. Slowly, she made it. Once committed, she clung to him unreservedly.

When the kiss ended Robert rubbed his cheek against hers, and though he stood quite still it seemed that his body reached out to hers, extending every kind of delicious temptation, all of which Charlotte's own body understood, although as yet untested. "Three weeks, Charlotte," he murmured languorously.

***

During those weeks, Robert kept Charlotte closely confined, amiably refusing to allow her out. He was pointedly attentive, taking every opportunity to make love to her. When Charlotte sat, it was usually within the circle of Robert's arm; after riding, she always descended from the saddle into a lover's embrace. Most of her waking hours were spent closely attached to an ardent pursuer, one who made no attempt to hide his desire. On the contrary, he made sure she *was* aware of it, as he whispered of his longings and counted out the days to their fulfilment.

She was not secure from his importunities even when in company with their mamas. He was just as likely to kiss her then. Altogether, he had the confused young lady he coveted in a continual state of delectable turmoil, and she began to wonder if she were as safe from him as she had believed. Many a time she shivered apprehensively; many an occasion she eyed him with trepidation.

The two mamas were not comfortable with Robert's strategy either, for all that he had explained it to them. It still seemed scandalous. Sophie, spokesman for both, broached the question of his conduct with her son.

"Robert, are you perfectly assured of the necessity for your present course of action? In view of the familiarity you use towards Charlotte, and were we not so secluded here, she would be quite unable to refuse an offer from you without giving rise to scandal. Would it not be simpler to ask Charlotte for her hand? It is quite clear that she loves you, darling."

Robert smiled. "You will have a new daughter in five weeks, and Mater a new son. Meanwhile, Charlotte is safely courted, if a trifle unconventionally, and she is happy. No-one sees us except you, so what does it matter?"

Sophie recognised from his expression, a certain firmness about his smiling mouth, that her son was not for moving and further protest would avail her nothing. She swallowed her doubts and Robert went his chosen way although, in consideration of the mamas' peace of mind, he kept his more open advances for when he and Charlotte were alone.

Poetry being an acceptable form of courtship, (if not, perhaps, the way Charlotte was moulded to Robert as they sat upon a sofa), he wooed her with the seductive beauty of Byronic verse one evening.

'She walks in beauty, like the night
Of cloudless climes and starry skies;
And all that's best of dark and bright
Met in her aspect and her eyes . . .'

Charlotte listened, absorbed in Robert, her own eyes fixed upon his face. So thorough was her enchantment, she hardly noticed when he changed source and began to quote from the Song of Solomon.

'My beloved spake and said unto me,
'Rise up, my love, my fair one, and come away
For, lo, the winter is past, the rain is over and gone:
The flowers appear on the earth,
the time of the singing of birds is come,
and the voice of the turtle is heard in our land . . .

Arise my love, my fair one, and come away.
O my dove, that are in the clefts of the rock,
in the secret places of the stairs
let me see thy countenance, let me hear thy voice;
for sweet is thy voice, and thy countenance comely . . .
My beloved is mine, and I am his:'

As Robert's voice flowed on, Charlotte nestled closer into his embrace. She listened, entranced, aware of nothing but him. Even the two mamas, who suspended their sewing activities with the going of light, heard the recital with pleasure, and Mrs Hattenbury was reassured. Here, as at home last year, it was clear that Robert and Charlotte were truly in love; "albeit rather too openly for perfect politeness," she later remarked to Alethea, as Robert then kissed Charlotte.

At breakfast next morning, such was the feeling of loving rapport Robert had established between them, Charlotte offered him a kiss quite naturally. She was utterly undone, therefore, when he gave her an embrace of unbridled passion in return, shaping her body to his with arrogant assumption of right. Being so open to him, she was aroused instantly, clinging and as urgent as he.

"Soon," he murmured, eyes clouded with desire.

"Robert!" Charlotte was frantic, suddenly. She clutched at him. "Please don't seduce me. You won't, will you? Promise me? Please?" she pleaded eloquently.

"You want me, you know you do," he demurred.

"Yes, we both know I do, but you ought not to take advantage of my weakness," she said piteously. "It is not kind, Robert; it is not honourable."

He hushed her with a kiss. "Neither is it kind to deny you that which you so keenly desire," he mocked tenderly, "and I, Charlotte, mean to deny you nothing."

***

This last encounter with Robert roused the devil of fear in Charlotte. She had been so sure he was going to propose again, but now . . . he would not force her into his bed without benefit of banns, would he?

Force? Did she really speak of force? Was this not the nub of her fear? She had long faced the truth that in being so sure of her Robert was right. He could reduce her to mute submission with only one melting glance if he chose. Then, there was nothing she would not do, because she loved him, and wanted for him what he wished for himself. But she could not bear to contemplate what might happen if she yielded to him outwith the bond of marriage.

Yet, if she allowed the situation to continue unchecked, Robert *would* have his way, as he had told her many times. How could she prevent it, especially since the two mamas seemed not to object to what he was about? What *was* she to do?

After much agonising, there was only one course which occurred to Charlotte and that she took. The solution came to her on the evening of that same, fateful, day.

Robert was standing in the glass doorway leading to the garden. He was watching her, smiling lazily, and Charlotte's heart melted with love for the arrogant, elegant grace of his tall figure. He was so very dear to her. More than anything, she wanted his love, not for the gratification of a moment but for always. She needed to know that the essence of Robert was hers, not just his body. She wanted to adore him and be adored in return. She wanted him for ever, with his ring upon her finger, anything less would not do.

So it was decided. If she could not trust herself with Robert, she must remove from his presence. She must get herself home to Cornwall, and safety. Maybe, then, when he saw she was holding out for marriage, maybe then he would reconsider. If he didn't? Well, that would be time to think again.

That night she did not wait for his goodnight kiss. She put her arms around his neck and kissed him unreservedly, the poignancy of knowing she might not know the joy of his mouth again soon, if ever, aching in her breast. Drawing his nether lip against her tongue as he had taught her, she sucked gently to pleasure them both. Robert's reaction was immediate. He expressed his joy in a flurry of feathery kisses to her palms and other sweet places, and the look in his eyes, when he raised them to her face, made her long to abandon the plan of flight and render herself up to him trustfully. Surely, he could not look at her so tenderly if his feeling for her was only an ache of the body?

But then he whispered: "I think I cannot wait for my birthday, darling."

***

In her room, she subdued the ache of longing and packed a small valise. In the early light, next morning, she let herself out of the house quietly and walked to the coaching office in Brighton.

Immediately, she met with a difficulty. There was no coach travelling to London until noon. This was no use to Charlotte. It was imperative to leave immediately. She would have to post up to town. Unfortunately, this was expensive at a shilling a mile rather than the five pence by coach for which she had budgeted. Counting out her money, she discovered she could afford a post-chaise if she caught the Falmouth Mail. As the Mail left London every evening at seven, Charlotte would avoid an overnight stay in the capitol, which she could not now afford.

She paid her fare and the postillion, looking smart in a bright yellow jacket which matched the chaise, mounted the offside horse and away they went to London.

Charlotte made only two stops at changing stages, because she was anxious to put as much space between her and Brighton as possible, in case of pursuit. The chaise rolled into town at mid-afternoon, setting her down at The Blossoms in Cheapside. From here, she was obliged to take another journey, to the Gloucester Coffee House, pick-up point for West Country Mails.

It was very confusing, for someone unaccustomed to public travel, and Charlotte was now tired and hungry. The thought of the overnight journey to Cornwall ahead was daunting, but at least she was well in time to book a seat. She also had time to make herself tidy and have a meal, albeit a frugal one since funds were low. Confidently, she advanced upon the booking clerk, only to receive a check which oppressed even her stalwart spirit. The coach was fully booked.

Seeing her crestfallen look, the clerk suggested she return a little before the coach left. There might be a cancellations or a non-arrival.

Charlotte thanked him and took up his suggestion but, alas, there were no cancellations. She was horrified, not knowing what to do. She had no money for a hotel room and could not possibly stay at the coffee house, a young girl, alone. Indeed, her singular state had already attracted attention.

The clerk, a different one from the afternoon, mooted an alternative when he saw Charlotte's consternation. She could take the Falmouth Herald, which left from the Swan with Two Necks at half past eight next morning. Charlotte thanked him for the advice and retreated to the travellers' room to think.

In desperation she remembered Meva. There was nothing for it but to spend the night in the coach house there. First, she used more of her dwindling pennies to go to the Swan and book a seat for the morning.

What a day! Charlotte felt ready to face Robert ten times over rather than relive the dreadful day; and her ordeals were not yet over. Arriving at her erstwhile home, she found the gates securely locked and chained. She gripped the gates and rattled them in fury. Then she sat down and cried, longing for the comforts kept from her by the shuttered house: a lovely bathroom, a cosy bed.

"Miss Charlotte! Be that you?" an astonished voice exclaimed. Charlotte nearly died of fright as she turned to confront a disbelieving George Coachman, staring at her through the gates. "Where've thee sprung from?" he asked in amazement.

By this time, Charlotte was too fraught to do anything but tell the truth. “I am running away, home to Cornwall,” she said and burst into fresh tears.

“There now, Missy, b’aint no need to cry.”

Old Lennox, as he styled himself, opened the gates and took a very tired Charlotte home to his missus. Here she was physically restored, and mentally eased, by good food, refreshing sleep and a promise to get her to the next day’s mail coach on time.

In the morning, George Coachman took Charlotte to the hostelry and had a word with the guard. During their talk a couple of shiners exchanged hands, as a result of which Charlotte was chaperoned at every wayside stop by the fatherly guard.

He procured refreshment for her at Basingstoke, dinner at Wincanton, and both meals she was given time to eat. Not being a seasoned traveller, she did not realise how rare an event this was.

She supped on a warming punch at Ilminster and slept as far as Exeter. From there to Launceston she dozed intermittently, leaning unintentionally upon an accommodating lady to one side. Finally, at the White Hart hostelry, early on Friday morning, she bade the guard a cordial goodbye and gave him the last of her money as a gratuity. She walked out of the yard reflecting on the goodness of humanity in general, and coach guards in particular.

***

The six miles from Launceston she trudged on her own two feet, being then without funds, but the day was fair and she was going home. It was no hardship. Even so, she was glad to turn in at the back gate of Crane Lodge. She had been two and a half days in travel; she was tired and grubby. The thought of home, food and a wash was more than welcome.

To her joy, Charlotte saw the back door standing open. Evidently, there were servants in the house. She went into the kitchen. No-one was apparent, but the copper boiler had been lit and the kettle sang on the range. It was almost as if she were expected.

She left the kitchen and, hearing a noise, went towards the drawing room. Upon opening the door in pleasurable anticipation, she came to a halt on the threshold in absolute shock.

There, standing before the fireplace, as though he had not set foot outside the house since they were last at home, in all his masculine splendour, stood . . . Mr Hattenbury; tall, blond, and beautiful!

Temptation was back with a vengeance!

"Charlotte, at last!" he greeted. "I was beginning to wonder where you were."

Chapter Nineteen

Robert heard a bustle abovestairs, loud opening of doors and Mater's voice.

"Sophie! Sophie, come at once! Oh, what is to be done? Sophie, Sophie dear, where are you?"

Another door hurriedly opened and closed. "What is the matter, Alethea?" he heard his mother ask.

"It is Charlotte . . . she has gone!" came the agitated reply. "She has run away! Oh, Sophie, what are we to do?" On this last anguished cry, Robert was at Alethea's side, taking Charlotte's note from nerveless fingers.

"May I see, please?" His words were a formality. He was already perusing the few lines of Charlotte's letter, which said she was tired of aimless gaieties and wanted to go home. When he finished reading Robert looked up, but his eyes were unseeing. He was recalled to the present by his mother.

"What is to be done, Sir?" Her voice was sharp with anxiety, her look accusing, clearly blaming him for this turn of events.

"What will happen to her all alone? Oh, dread fate!" Mrs Treleaven wailed, raising trembling hands aloft, already envisioning nameless horrors.

"Nothing will happen, Mater," Robert said firmly, to quash her panic. "Do not alarm yourself. You would do better to go and see what she has taken. I will see if the chaise is gone. Hurry now."

The chaise was in its usual place. Wherever she had gone, Charlotte had set out on foot. If she meant to go to Cornwall she must seek transport. The obvious place to look was a coaching office. So Robert reasoned.

He drew blank at the first. At the second, the booking clerk remembered a dark-haired young miss who took a post-chaise to London, leaving shortly after eight. London? Yes, it made sense.

Robert asked more questions, receiving a description which tallied with Charlotte's. Certain it was she, he made up his mind to go after her. He gave the clerk a guinea and returned to the house. Here, he told the mamas what was toward.

The ladies were hardly reassured by the news he brought, even less so by the intelligence that they were to remain in Brighton. Robert quickly explained that he hoped to overtake Charlotte by travelling speedily, and alone.

For once, they did not accept his dictates unquestioningly and valuable time was lost reasoning with them. Robert finally put his foot down, reminding them that the longer they held him back, the longer Charlotte was alone on the road. On this note he left without more ado.

It was now well after midday and he had little expectation of overtaking Charlotte. It depended on how good her cattle were. In the event he did not catch her but, to his relief, had no difficulty tracing her journey since a young lady travelling without escort was an unusual occurrence. At The Blossoms, where all Mr Gilbert's vehicles set down, they remembered a girl who wanted a West Country coach.

The trail next took Robert to the Gloucester Coffee House. Here, too, Charlotte had been seen but was not there now. Mr Hattenbury left the Gloucester, subsequently visiting every coaching office he could think of, but nowhere had Charlotte been seen. He also tried the Swan with Two Necks, but unfortunately that was before Charlotte reached the hostelry.

With the trail gone cold, Robert was, by now, tired and very worried. Still, he reasoned doggedly, she could not simply disappear. Ergo, he had obviously missed her. He must retrace his steps and try again. First, home to Meva stables, to change his tired horse before starting off afresh.

At the coach house, he found George Coachman in earnest conversation with Mrs Lennox and great was their feeling of astonishment on seeing the Master (followed swiftly by relief at having to make no awkward decisions) as they told him that his ward was even then abed in their house.

Robert's relief was even greater than theirs. Over the last few hours, he had been castigating himself as a knave, to have driven Charlotte from him in panic, for he had no difficulty in recognising the impetus of her flight. To know she was safe took a heavy weight from his mind.

He drank the ale Mrs Lennox brought and ate the accompanying bread and cheese with more enjoyment than he felt entitled to. While eating he pondered what he should do next.

"George," Robert said finally, "I want you to take Miss Charlotte to the coach in the morning as planned. Here . . ." he gave the coachman several guineas, "give this to the guard and tell him straightly to ensure that she is well looked to. Additionally, I shall write a letter which I want sent to Brighton first thing tomorrow."

"Shall you stop the night along of us, Master?" asked Mrs Lennox.

"No, thank you, I shall not. I don't wish Miss Charlotte to know I have caught up with her. She will answer to me later," he said firmly. When he had gone George said he hoped the master would not be too hard on her, pretty little maid as she was.

After a night's rest at his club, Robert set out for Cornwall, confident in the knowledge that Charlotte followed safely behind.

***

The two mamas' relief on reading Robert's letter produced copious tears initially, but the remainder of the letter soon put them to flight.

The steward was instructed to pack up the household and set out for home. They were to stay overnight in the London house, collecting the bulk of Charlotte's trousseau, which was now ready at the modiste, arriving in Cornwall no later than Thursday, the twenty eight of July. This gave them a sennight to arrange with Mrs Buckingham for new gowns for themselves. She had already made Charlotte's wedding dress, which was, even now, waiting at Crane House. If they put themselves in the steward's hands and followed instructions, everything should go as planned. Naturally, the ladies did as requested, all abustle with excitement.

***

Meanwhile, Robert arrived in Cornwall. He made a way to Crane Lodge, there to await Charlotte's coming.

She was later than expected; he had not allowed for the walk from Launceston; but at last he heard her step and the slight anxiety he had begun to feel evaporated, replaced with joy. No more rivals. No more jealousies. She was home. She was his.

A bemused Charlotte stood in the doorway. Robert welcomed her in.

"Come, love. You must be tired. Sit here while I make you tea. You would like that, would you not?" His hands were cool upon her sun-warmed skin as Charlotte allowed herself to be led forward, staring at Robert dumbly, unable to take in the situation in which she found herself.

"How . . . how did you get here? I . . . I thought you were in Brighton," she said faintly. "How did you know?"

"I know everything about you, my lovely Charlotte," he said with a smile. He put strong arms about her unresisting body and kissed her gently. "But explanations can wait. First it must be food and a bath. I expect you feel jaded after your long journey. The water is ready. Rest, darling, and leave everything to me."

Charlotte sat unmoving after he left her, wondering if it were she, or the world, which had turned upside down. How had it come about, after all her efforts to escape him, that Robert was here before her? She pondered fatalistically on her facile belief that he would allow her to leave unchallenged. Robert allowed only what he chose.

Then she remembered the date.

It was July the twentieth.

It was Robert's birthday!

He returned shortly bearing a laden tray, the sight of which brought Charlotte out of her comatose state. She was ravenous and set about clearing the plate Robert gave her. He ate little himself. He had other things on his mind.

When Charlotte finished eating Robert urged her to put up her feet and rest. He took the tray away. It was quiet in the drawing room after he had gone. Replete, and tired after her six mile tramp, Charlotte drowsed.

For the second time in her life, she awoke to the sound of Robert's voice. She opened sleepy eyes, to see him smiling at her tenderly. Without conscious thought she raised her arms to him. He gathered her close.

"Your bath is ready," he murmured, his face against her hair.

Charlotte came awake with a bang, remembering exactly where she was and with whom. Her eyes flew open and she said: "How did you get here before me, Sir? Where is everyone else?"

Robert's eyes sparkled as he watched Charlotte's awakening, and how sweet his smile of anticipation as he said, softly: "There are but two here, Charlotte . . . you and I," and in his smile was all, and more, that had long been pending.

"Oh, no . . . no," she said, with a groan, "after all my efforts."

"Oh, yes," he murmured gently. "We are come home, you and I, my dove, and shall not be parted again."

He lifted a stultified Charlotte into his arms and carried her upstairs to her bedchamber. The bath stood waiting, filled with water fragranced by rose petals floating on its surface.

Robert kicked the door shut and set Charlotte upon her feet. She stood with hands clasped to her breast, looking first at the bath and then at him.

"What now, Mr Hattenbury?" she asked, raising her chin.

Robert laughed. How happy he was to have Charlotte to himself finally, even though he could see she meant to defy him to the last. That was as it should be.

"Now, dear heart, to the bathing." He began to undo the buttons at her bodice. Charlotte stopped him with a hand over his.

"I am perfectly capable of doing this for myself," she said.

"But *I* mean to do it, Charlotte," he replied, and undress her he did, saying: "Trust me, darling," kissing her softly, his eyes, so warm a blue, sending no dangerous messages now. Strangely, she did trust him, even when she stood in his arms in puris naturabilis and heard Robert catch his breath.

"Oh, my darling, beautiful Charlotte, there were times when I thought this moment would never come," Robert murmured. He was a deeply happy man as he pressed her close, lips caressing her throat and face. For a moment longer he held her and then said reluctantly: "This will not do. Your bath awaits and I am importunate. I must get you some towels." And away he went to get them.

When he returned Charlotte had bathed and was relaxing in the water, rose petals clinging to her shoulders and arms.

Robert held up a towel in readiness. "Arise, my love, my fair one, and come away with me," he invited, sweetly coaxing.

Charlotte did not take up his invitation immediately. She studied him silently, her expression calm and serious. "Robert," she said, eventually, "are you really going to seduce me?"

A slow smile began to curve his lips and there was the wickedest light in his eyes. "Oh, indeed I am, my lovely Charlotte. Most certainly I am."

"In which case . . ." she paused, and said simply: "I have done my very best to avoid this fate but, if it is to be, I shall not resist further. It would be undignified and dishonest since I have long wanted the promise your body holds out. You have always known this, have you not? It is useless to deny it and, therefore, Robert, shall I come to you willingly."

So saying, Charlotte arose. She stepped out of the bath, with rose petals still clinging to her wet skin, and came to stand before him, clothed in nothing but her own beauty. "Here I am, Robert, for your happiness and mine, because I love you," she said softly.

For a moment he was lost in silent admiration of her candour, the sweetness of its expression. But in his heart he had always known that when she came to him it would be without artifice; and so it was.

He enfolded her in the towel and gazed at her, in his eyes an unmistakable look of love. "I adore you, Charlotte," he said, "and have done from the moment I first saw you." He examined her face tenderly, smoothing wisping tendrils of hair from her brow, refreshing himself with gentle fingertip touches to her eyes, nose and mouth, and there was a definite twinkle in his eye as he said: "You were not even a week old then and I but a callow boy."

She smiled, feeling as though drowning in his adoring blue gaze, the breath from his mouth as much a caress to draw her response as his lips and hands. "I think you indulge poetic licence, sir, but it is a pretty thought," she murmured.

"Indeed I do not," he protested, smiling in his turn, "you held my heart from the moment I saw these lovely grey eyes."

"With a small loan of it to different ladies, at intervals in between times," Charlotte said, a touch drily.

"Well, you had some growing to do first, Charlotte . . . but now you are quite grown up, are you not? More . . . you are mine," he breathed, blue eyes flaring triumphantly.

Gently, he dried her and ran his hands over her body to make sure she was quite dry. Then he carried her to the bed and looked down at her, savouring her loveliness; the sweet curves and hollows of her body; the enticement of her breasts, pearl-skinned and tender, with a rising rose-tipped invitation . . . and found, suddenly, he was shaking and had difficulty in breathing, because it came to him with stunning clarity that the waiting was at an end. He was on the threshold. She was his!

"My dear, my darling love, how beautiful you are. Oh, I want you so much." He came down beside her, mouth seeking, caressing hands gliding over her smooth skin; but it was not enough. There was still an impediment.

He swung away from the bed and carelessly threw off his clothes, until he was as natural as Charlotte, she who lay watching him and waiting. She raised her arms and he went in to them as though coming home.

"Darling Robert, I did not realise how beautiful you are, face and form equally," Charlotte whispered in awe. "Oh, I *do* want you so." She held him tightly and drew him down to be kissed, the most open and vivid expression of desire she had ever shown, because now there was no need for restraint. Now was a time for giving, and receiving, all she had ever wanted from him.

His response was startlingly immediate and prompted an equally immediate reciprocation, for both had long awaited this moment and were more than ready for its consummation. This was what had so nearly been theirs on Robert's birthday, a year since almost to the hour, their bodies assuming once more the same welcoming postures. Again, as then, he moaned softly, as Charlotte did, in a duet of love and hunger. He was exigent, as then, face flushed with urgent desire, his hands and mouth creating magical pleasures for Charlotte, feelings so astonishingly sweet there was no room for maidenly modesty.

And not this time a jarring end to dancing love, nothing to prevent their final conjoining, when they could no longer bear to be their individual selves, when nothing else would do but to be one, joyfully to sheath and be sheathed.

For Charlotte, then, came complete fulfilment. At last, Robert was hers. For him, filled with the power of love, happiness flooding him, it was the most tumultuous triumph. Held tightly within Charlotte, as he was, and propelled by a tremendous impulse to give her all that was the essence of himself, he felt the exact moment when the tide of his love broke over her. She cried out at that first awesome shattering of self which, ever after, made her a part of him, even as he too was lost in her. They were come home, never to be their separate selves again.

***

Afterwards, Charlotte cried a little from happiness, but it was all one with the pattern of love. When Robert held her face to his, murmuring sweet comfort, her tears ran into his mouth and that too was fulfilment of a kind.

They slept, and woke next to a night sky filled with stars. When Charlotte opened her eyes she saw that Robert was already awake and gazing through the window.

Contentedly she nestled to his warmth, breathing in the smell of him, that indefinable something that was delightfully, astonishingly, excitingly Robert. Robert, who now belonged to her! Amazing!

Feeling Charlotte stir, he turned and kissed her. She 'uhmed' sleepily and put her arms around him, rubbing her lips against his shoulder, dreamy and drifting.

"Do I take that to be an 'uhm' of approval?" he teased.

She murmured impishly. "My sole regret is that I was not able to express it sooner. Dear Sir, did you not dislike Morley last year . . . I mean *really* dislike him?"

"Saucy minx," Robert said, amused, "and, yes, I did, but it is no longer important. I have you now, for always."

"Are you to have me without wedlock for always, Robert?" Charlotte mused, the question unheated, her attention taken up more with the pleasure attendant on stroking down his warm body and feeling his gratifying reactions, the ripple of muscle under her hand.

"No, of course not," he said easily, his hand closing over hers and moving it a smidgeon, to increase their mutual gratification.

"You said you would never ask me to marry you again," she reminded him. Her mouth was gently savouring the taste of his smooth skin, an exercise which suspended Robert's thought processes for a while.

"Nor shall I; nevertheless, you will go to your wedding in three weeks time, my love," he said eventually, voice not quite steady although his mind had cleared. "It is all arranged. I have spoken with Mr Rodd and the banns are to be called. The two mamas will be here next Thursday with your trousseau. As for your wedding gown, it hangs in Mater's bedroom. It waits only to clothe your own exquisite self, so that when you and I walk up the aisle, on August the tenth, I may exhibit to everyone there assembled, in all her beauty, the treasure which is mine and mine alone."

By the time he had done, Charlotte was open-mouthed with astonishment. "But . . . but you said never a word! Robert! You said never a word! Oh . . . wretched, arrogant man! You have teased and harried me unmercifully, worried me so much I was sleepless at night, thinking you were going to ravish me without benefit of banns; and I, knowing I had not the will to resist you, could think of nothing, finally, but to run away . . . and all for *nought*! Oh, Robert, how could you?" She was laughing with joy but belabouring him with some less than gentle blows at the same time. "Beastly creature, oh . . . my dear Sir, I love you so much. Despoil me as you will, how could I *ever* have thought it possible to live without you and the happiness you bring me?"

Dodging the worse of the blows, Robert wrestled her to stillness, tucked half beneath him. He was laughing as much as she. "Charlotte, had you not run away you would still be virgin," he pointed out wickedly.

"How . . . when you threatened me with all manner of things I dearly wanted . . . and have now had, to my very great satisfaction, I must confess?"

"To our mutual satisfaction," he said, his lips moving in an enchanting line of descent which began with her mouth and ended between her breasts. "But, think, beloved . . . I may have threatened all manner of things but it would have been impossible to make good my threats in Brighton. The mamas were watching my every step and would soon have intervened had they seen me anywhere near your bed." His breath fanned warmly over her skin as he kissed some sweet prominences, for Charlotte's pleasure and his own.

"Of course, it would have been relatively easy had we stayed at Meva . . ." he paused to caress the valley between her breasts with his lips, "which was why I was obliged to remove to the seaside. You were too much of a temptation, and I all too likely to fall before it. For you, my bewitching Charlotte, are more beautiful than the Venus star I watched earlier and much more evocative of love. How could I resist you? You are my Venus and I a votive of love. From this day, all my devotions will be made upon your breast, dear heart."

Charlotte was entranced. "How poetically you speak, Robert, and how wounding to my heart," she murmured with a catch in her throat. Her hand, at the back of his head, was holding his mouth where pleasure was profound.

"I hope you mean as beauty wounds," he teased. He nibbled gently, and Charlotte drew a breath sharp with rapture.

"Yes and pierces the heart with its sweetness. Oh, Robert . . . you will always love me, won't you?"

She clung to him and he held her tightly, murmuring of his love, showing it to her with the daintiest of attentions to her body which did, indeed, pierce her heart sweetly. More, it began to arouse immediate and less exalted expectations, to which Robert, himself now stretching to the call of love, responded effortlessly, with soft murmurings and an entirely unexpected and imaginative placement of kisses which were a shockingly pleasurable revelation to Charlotte.

***

Much, much later, Robert carried her to the window and they stood in silent communion, gazing out over the moon-silvered garden, the mingled perfume of roses and night-scented stocks rising on the air. Everything was still. Robert began to speak softly behind her.

"Thus breaks the night upon mine ear,
And tells me, love, that thou art here;
No more, alone, my heart must sigh
For now, in love, with thee I lie.
Now thou haste been made known to me,
Two hearts, one beat, entwined we;
About me, all encompassed bright,
I have thee, love, and soft, dark night."

Charlotte nestled closer. "How beautiful, Robert. It is exactly what I feel for you," she confided. "What poem is that? Who wrote it, do you know?"

"It has no title since I have only now made it up. If I still remember in the morning, I shall call it 'fragment'."

"You are its author? Oh, Robert, how clever you are," Charlotte said, her voice filled with wonder. Robert laughed.

"No, darling, I am not a good versifier. It is an indifferent poem and best forgotten," he remarked in self-deprecating tone. "Still, I'm glad you liked it."

"Forgotten ? Certainly not! I shall write it down and keep it," she resolved. Hands at his back, she pressed him close, joyfully aware of his immediate response, as that most exciting part of him, of its own accord sought and found, nudging her with exquisite precision.

Last year, tantalisingly, she had only been able to guess at the strength and beauty of Robert's muscular frame. Now, all of him, everything he was, came to her hand, hers to command, warm and excitingly tractable. How awesome he was, and how rich the feast he had made for her this night.

"This is where I fell in love with you, Robert, here in the garden, when you first kissed me. Smelling the flowers now reminds me of that time. But," a small bubble of laughter escaped Charlotte's lips, "I must confess that it was not the first time I became acquainted with the nature of want in your regard."

Charlotte felt Robert catch his breath in surprise. "Charlotte?" He sounded a trifle scandalised and she giggled.

"No, indeed, my dearest love, the first time I recognised the alluring promise of your body," her hands were even then encompassing the lure, "and how well I recall it, was when you took me to the lake that day and threatened to throw me in. Do you remember that?"

Robert was astonished. "But I thought you only a schoolgirl then."

"No, my darling Sir, you were wrong. I was dressed like a child, from necessity, but I was *not*, I do assure you. If only you knew how many were the nights I have lain awake longing for you."

Robert groaned. "And there was I, labouring under the strongest sense of guilt because I loved you and thought I should not. What a waste! Well, let there be no more time wasted, Charlotte. Let us away to bed, where we can make reparation, each to the other."

"Yes please, my dear, kind, beautiful, and perfect Robert," Charlotte agreed, pressing herself to him in eager anticipation.

Robert raised her in his arms. "I have not always been kind to you, dear heart, but since you generously overlook my faults in your recital of praise, let me confess my love in turn, let me show it to you."

Charlotte laughed. "You must make no mention of *my* faults, either."

"Ah, but you have none, Charlotte," Robert claimed disarmingly and she blushed, a heat felt against his face, though not seen in the darkness.

Close held in each others arms, breast to breast, Robert told Charlotte how much he missed her when they were apart; of his thinking of her wherever he went; of his pleasure in planning her lovely bathroom, imagining her surprise when she saw it; of his eagerness to be reunited with her in London, after the long, lonely and frustrating months they had spent apart.

"Robert," something which had long pained her was now revealed, "if this is true, why were you so cold to me when I arrived at Meva? After what you said in Bath, I began to think you might really love me, but you recoiled when I kissed you in welcome at the London house. Why?"

Robert brushed Charlotte's hair behind her ears, simply for the joy of touching her. "To recoil was my second reaction, darling, and stemmed from a need to hide the first. You see, whenever we are close I experience a highly urgent desire to be a part of you and my body takes no account of time or place," he explained dryly. "When you embraced me, I very nearly disgraced myself. I felt such a fool, like an untried boy outwith control. I was frightened, too. If need were so urgent from the first moment of seeing you, how was I to last out my wardship? I didn't think I could!"

"Is that why you were so miserable and distant afterwards? Oh, Robert, I wish you had explained. I thought it was because you did not love me."

"So, as punishment, you treated *me* wretchedly, until I thought you did not love me, either. That was only until you were poorly, of course. After that my belief may have wavered at times of particular stress ~ as on days when I saw you embracing all my rivals, for example ~ but I knew in my heart that you loved me."

"Charles was never your rival and, in truth, neither was poor Mr Neville or Mr Dean. But to speak of when I was ill, Robert, I *did* think you unkind then, for you never came near me the whole time," she reproached, with remembered hurt.

"Did I not, Charlotte?" Robert asked whimsically. She felt his chest move under her hand as he laughed. "You do not remember it now, but that night, when I took you home from Vauxhall, you pleaded with me to stay with you. I gave you my word that I would never leave you and, indeed, I never did. I was at your side day and night, until we knew you would live. Only then did I retire to my own chamber."

"Robert! I thought I only dreamed you were there. Oh, you are such a darling idiot," she rebuked lovingly. "Why did you not tell me? Had I known the truth, I would not have resented you without cause. Why were you so secretive?"

"Dear heart," Robert said, "it was to save your blushes, since there were . . . well, how shall I say . . . certain happenings which it may have embarrassed you to recall." Charlotte gave a startled gasp and he began to laugh.

"Robert! Are you saying that I . . . actually did . . . what I dreamed I had done?"

"Actually, *yes*, my darling, and I loved you the more for it. To act as you did showed that you *must* love me. Why else would you seek to comfort me from the depths of your desperate illness? It was a very humbling experience, Charlotte, and in some way, I don't know how, what happened that night drew you back from death's edge because by morning, the fever had broken."

"It must have been because I sensed your need, Robert, and you had never shown that before," Charlotte said softly. "It is supreme enablement to be necessary to the person you love best in the world, and that night I think I sensed it beyond question. It was only afterwards I lost sight of the truth, blinded by my jealousy."

"I always needed you, Charlotte, from the very beginning. It was the first time I had ever felt such helpless longing. No-one else has touched my heart the way you do. But, my darling girl, I have never found it easy to reveal my feelings. Last year, it was such a shock to discover how absolutely essential you were to my wellbeing, to realise that I must have you for mine, no matter what; but it took the worse shock, of thinking I had lost you to bring home to me the utter futility of hiding behind senseless pride, of ranting and raving at you from fear. I mean never to do so again and tell you now, plainly and humbly, that I adore you, Charlotte Treleaven, soon to be Mrs Hattenbury, and ever shall."

"Oh, Robert," Charlotte's eyes were tear-misted, "the same is true for me, dearest, *exactly* the same."

***

They talked until dawn, before making love again, joyfully and with total commitment. They were not to know each other again until Mr Rodd spoke the blessing over them, but this was their real wedding night and both knew it.

Next day, convention to the fore, Robert went home to Hattenbury; the servants were called in to open both houses, and no-one ever knew that Robert and Charlotte had lain in each other's arms at Crane Lodge for a blissful night of love.

The two mamas came home. The wedding breakfast was ordered. Guests were summoned. Thus, it was, that Robert made vows of life-long devotion to Charlotte, on a wet Wednesday in early August, three weeks after his birthday, just as he had carefully planned.

He looked extraordinarily handsome in a wedding suit of black coat and white pantaloons, wearing a white quilted waistcoat. Charlotte found him dazzling and thought happily that Sophia Bond, recently married to Edward Baring-Gould, might sing hymns of praise to her new husband's blond hair and liken him to a silver poplar, but her own, darling Robert was more beautiful by far.

Charlotte also looked adorable, in a gown of Urlings lace over white satin, (Robert had impeccable taste), with a matching lace veil. In her hand, she carried a prayer book of Sophie's, and a fine cambric handkerchief, beautifully embroidered by her own mama. Not that she needed it for anything but decoration although, naturally, the two mamas had recourse to theirs, particularly when they waved the happy couple off on a protracted honeymoon.

True to his word, Robert took his wife to all the places of which he had spoken on that fateful day in London, and did with her all the things he had romantically promised, but first they made a detour to Scotland, to take Jacinta a slice of wedding cake and a budget of news.

They became acquainted with Christina, Jacinta's sister by marriage, and the two sturdy Macgregor boys, who gazed at Robert and Charlotte solemnly and would not come out from mama's skirts at first. But Charlotte soon charmed them out of their shyness, watched by Jacinta, who was astonished at the change in her sister since last they were together. Marriage obviously agreed with her. She was also amused to see the arrogant Robert of old so unashamedly in love with his wife and uncaring of who knew it. Never would she have thought to see such. What? Lordly Mr Stiff & Starchy reduced to a doting husband? What was the world coming to?

***

Mr Hattenbury's first born, named for himself, came into the world in April, Eighteen Thirty Two, a scantish nine months after his wedding day. Robert smiled at his wife, privately counted up the weeks and kept counsel.

His second son arrived close on Charlotte's birthday the following year. By October of that same year, Eighteen Thirty Three, Francis, the baby, was having trouble finding purchase on Mama's lap. He was obliged to drape himself around a large bump, which effectively shortened the length of knee available to perch upon.

On that golden October day, the Hattenbury family was in the drawing room at Crane Lodge where, contrary to the original plan, they still resided with their growing family and the two mamas. In fact, they did not move down the lane to Hattenbury House for several years more. Not, in truth, until the doting grandmamas became rather weary of hearing the patter of tiny feet.

To return to that golden October day: Mr Hattenbury held little Robert in his arms. The glowing infant, so like his father, was blowing wet bubbly kisses against Papa's cheek and dribbling into his crushed neckcloth, but Papa seemed not to mind.

Erstwhile acquaintances of the elegant man about town would have been astonished to see him in his new fatherly role. As was his half-brother, Richard Carr, (who was then visiting Crane with his new wife Jane, to bring his sisters, Mollie and Isobel, down to Cornwall to make a new life with their half-brother's family). Even Robert's friends were slightly taken aback at the change in him, but Robert had come into his own. Contentment sat upon him like a well fitting coat.

He adored his diminutive wife, whose figure never did increase significantly, though it fluctuated regularly for some years. He loved his two children and looked forward to the birth of their third with happy expectation. While it was true there were times at night when the present incumbent of his wife's abdomen prodded him sharply in the back, this was small recompense for the happiness of knowing that if he turned to her Charlotte would welcome him into the fastness of her body as lovingly as she welcomed his children.

By the time he reached his fortieth birthday, Mr Hattenbury had fathered eight children. At this juncture, Dr Henders, from Callington, son of the Dr Henders who had brought Robert into the world, felt he should speak to his patron in this regard. Enough was enough he said firmly. Mrs Hattenbury, with remarkable good fortune considering her small stature, had sustained eight live births, five boys and three girls. She was now in her twenty fifth year and it was high time to call a halt. Reluctantly, Robert agreed. He liked his wife to be pregnant (fortunately, so did she) but eight was a good family.

As already indicated, it was rather too good for the grandmamas at times. They watched the removal of all the Hattenburys with more relief than they would have believed possible at one time. After this, all was peace, with the exuberant blessings of grandmotherhood less than a mile down the lane; when they chose to avail themselves of them.

Naturally, with such a lively family, there were times when Robert, normally the most indulgent of parents, lost his temper. Then it was that his autocratic disposition showed itself to the full and a thunderous 'go to your room!' was likely to be heard.

Fortunately, dear Mama was never at a loss and always managed to bring Papa round her thumb until tranquillity was restored.

As Papa said, she had a way with her.

***

Words: 134,974

N.B. If you enjoyed Charlotte's story, there are others to come in the series. Presently in preparation:

1828. Isobel Latimer's Bath Season.
1829. Briege Faversham: An Unexpectant Bride.
1830. Emily Williams's Incredible Courtship.

Historical Notes.

The background material for this Cornish novel is authentic, as are most places mentioned, some events and many of the families. So, for example, the woman who was sold for sixpence at Bodmin fair was only one of other women who really did suffer this unhappy fate. Of course, it may not have been unhappy ultimately. She might have preferred the soldier over her erstwhile husband!

Again, if you visit Cornwall do go to lovely Stoke Climsland church, near Callington, where you will find a memorial window on the north side to Miss Georgina Mary Call who died in 1837. It was commissioned by her sister, Mrs Augusta Hornby, so Miss Augusta's suitor obviously came up to scratch!

The Reverend Charles Lethbridge, parson at Stoke Climsland, whom Robert mentions in his note to Charlotte when he was visiting the Calls, was something of a character even for those days. It seems that his parishioners *would* be in church on Sunday, come what might, being rounded up if necessary, and heaven help those who tried to slide out of their spiritual duty. This regular attendance may have been why the congregation sang so beautifully, as recorded by the Rector himself in a letter to his Bishop. He was also, apparently, a man who liked his food and wine, a gourmand perhaps, and one whose language, so it was said, was rather robust and not always edifying (!) but for all that he was popular with his parishioners.

The Calls were a family prominent in this area as bankers and parliamentary representatives for the town of Callington, and Stoke Climsland was their parish. Their house, Whiteford, no longer exists unfortunately, although I believe some of its doors were incorporated into the Duchy Home Farm when the house came down.

There is another link between the Duchy and Stoke Climsland church. In 1337, Edward III constituted the Duchy and made his son, Prince Edward, then seven years old, Duke of Cornwall. Edward was later known as the Black Prince, Restormel, (where Charlotte incurred Robert's displeasure) being one of his Cornish castles.

On 22nd February, 1351, the Black Prince presented the living of Stoke Climsland to one, Peter de Brompton, also giving him several costly gifts. On the 2nd March, 1356, he instituted Richard de Wolverstone the next Rector at the church and among his costly gifts to this cleric were two tuns of wine. The last Rector presented to Stoke Climsland by the Black Prince, on the 9th of February, 1362, was John de Gourmoncestre and he received a generous yearly grant of 'robes for the winter'.

Why these three men were singled out by the prince is not known for certain, but it is believed that they were his loyal battle companions at Crecy, and this is quite possible since there was a force of Cornish Light Infantry present in the field that day.

The Baring-Goulds were another prominent West Country family. They lived in Devon. The Charles Baring-Gould named in the book (the one Sophia thought unsuitable for Charlotte ~ I beg his pardon for that licence. I'm sure he was perfectly charming in reality,) came from a prominent clerical family. Between them, they wrote numerous books of sermons and religious tracts which were to be found in every large country house of the time. They are still to be seen to this day in some English National Trust properties. They were also great composers of hymns which can also be found in some church hymnals of today. I have a hymnal printed in 1975, given to me by a friend, and it has one of Sabine Baring-Gould's hymns in it ~ 'Now The Day Is Over'. My husband remembers singing it when he was a choirboy.

The Baring-Goulds' home at Lew Trenchard, just over the border from Cornwall, became an excellent restaurant and hotel some years ago. In the reception area of the Manor Hotel, next to the staircase, you can see a full length portrait of Edward, Charles' older brother, looking absolutely splendid in scarlet regimentals and fully deserving of his wife, Sophie's appellation 'the Silver Poplar'. He was a very handsome young man.

Charlotte's desperate illness, a putrid sore throat, doesn't sound much but it was a killer in the days before antibiotics. It was tonsillitis.

As for the parliamentary Reform Bill, after a very stormy period, it was finally made law on June 4^{th,} 1832, so the illuminations the Mayor of London ordered for April 27^{th,} 1831, in anticipation of parliamentary reform, were a little premature.

Finally, to end on a light note, the Cornish will tell you jokingly (but with a straight face) that if you want to experience a quick trip from heaven to hell take the road from Blissland to Helland on Bodmin Moor: or vice versa, if you prefer, of course!

1828

Isobel Latimer's Bath Season

Patricia. R. Olds

Preview

When one is starting out on an eagerly anticipated Bath Season, Milsom Street is the very best place for a Young Lady to be seen, for everybody who is Anybody will be here; as well as a good many Nobodies besides.

Of course, now that Bath has grown so large the Season was no longer as refined as in its heyday, by reason of too many Nobodies. It was now conducted more from private houses than public assemblies. This is not to say that the upper echelons of society never took the waters or frequented the Assembly Rooms: the Latimers certainly meant to do so.

Newly arrived at the Spa town, Lady Eugenie Latimer was walking down Milsom Street with her beautiful daughter. Isobel Latimer's glorious red-gold hair was haloed about her head by the sun of this late September morning and her loveliness was attracting attention from gentlemen and ladies alike. Lady Latimer was gratified to see how many were the admiring glances directed at Isobel. It seemed a good auger for the season ahead on this, their very first outing.

Indeed, the lovely Miss Latimer attracted attention from a forward-sitting occupant of a passing carriage. This elegant vehicle, resplendent in livery of dark and sky blue, with high-gloss lacquer paintwork and crested central panels, was most imposing, clearly belonging to a personage of substance.

"Oh, there is Miss Latimer!" exclaimed Anne Ward. "Oh, Duke,

Cousin Nicholas, may we stop for a moment to renew acquaintance?" she asked, smiling in anticipation. "I know Isobel from school in Harrogate."

"I fear not," responded Nicholas, The Most Noble the Duke of Sommerton, his tone disinterested. He did not so much as glance out of the carriage, his handsome profile and black curling hair reflecting in the carriage windows exactly as before. "Were we to set down in all this traffic it would cause chaos. However, Bath society, being what it is, you will soon enough meet up with your erstwhile friend."

Mrs Ward, Anne's mother, saw her daughter's disappointment and leaned forward to touch her hand consolingly.

"Do not be disappointed, Anne. His Grace is perfectly correct. One meets all one's acquaintances eventually, usually at the first assembly; and of course we shall leave cards," she comforted, and smiled to see Anne's pretty face begin to lighten.

From the circumstances of their life up to this time, Anne frequently wore a serious expression, ever conscious of where lay her duty and always ready to do it. Thus, it was now a pleasure for Mrs Ward to see her daughter smile more readily. She reflected thankfully that her much-loved Anne would soon have all the gaieties of a carefree season to enjoy, with nothing but conviviality and pleasure to look forward to; to be free for a while.

Mrs Iona Ward, the duke's aunt, sister of his late father, then favoured her nephew with a smile but it was not as openly affectionate as the one bestowed on her daughter. It was in the nature of a two-fold device; first, an apology for Anne's impulsiveness, but also an expression of gratitude because it was the duke who was sponsoring his cousin's launch into society; and what girl could hope for better? Under the aegis of a duke, Anne was assured of a successful season, for everyone wanted to make the acquaintance of nobility. Every house would be open to them.

For all this, gratitude did not sit easily upon one of so independent a nature as Mrs Ward and her smile was a little forced. However, a twice-widowed woman of small means could not afford to be *too* independent when she had a daughter of marriageable age to be launched.

Anne was Mrs Ward's raison d'etre. She wanted for her the very best that life could give. For this reason, since she had no money of her own, she bent the neck and asked for help from her estranged family. The estrangement was of Mrs Ward's choosing rather than theirs it should be said, dating back to an impulsive action in her youth with far reaching results.

The duke's mother, Christina, Duchess of Sommerton, still titled thus because her son was not yet married, was presently in Italy, caring for her sister Rose who had been morbidly ill for some months. When the duke wrote to his mother, mooting a season for his cousin Anne, the duchess wrote back, wholeheartedly endorsing her son's lukewarm-sounding endeavours and coming up with more interesting suggestions of her own, saying she was only sorry she could not be at home to assist in them. At present her sister, the Contessa de Sirmione, was still not fully recovered and could not be left.

In fact, the duchess thought that Nicholas sponsoring his cousin would be an excellent way to mend the rift between their two small families, a rift that she had often wanted to heal over the years of Iona's estrangement. It was no fault of hers that the family bond was not closer. She had made every effort to remain friends with her sister-by-marriage but had been politely repulsed.

She had another reason: she hoped that by squiring his cousin about Bath, and being exposed to feminine company, as he must be, Nicholas would find a wife at last. She did not think this was hoping for too much. Where were the grandchildren for whom she longed? And what a waste of a good man that at eight and thirty her handsome, kind and loving son was still a bachelor and showing no sign of marrying.

This, the duchess felt, must be put down to that most unfortunate entanglement in Italy when Nicholas was touring Europe in his youth. He was only eighteen when it happened and was so badly hurt by the disastrous affair he became distrusting of women ever after and was inclined to eschew their company.

But that was then and this was now. As an only child it was incumbent upon Nicholas to secure the line; it was his duty, no matter a distrust of the opposite sex. Naturally he had always enjoyed his 'conveniences' in the village, but what use were they? They could not provide Sommerton with an heir. Only a child born in wedlock could do that. So he had to marry. He would need to be reminded again.

The duke, sitting in his comfortable carriage and entirely unaware of his mama's hopes for him, returned his aunt's polite smile and said: "As to the assemblies, you are perfectly correct, Mrs Ward." He knew so from experience because he had attended many a Bath assembly in his youth; too many for his taste and not always to his pleasure, Seeing his cousin's crestfallen looks he relented his disinterest and to cheer her said, more kindly: "Of course, cousin Anne, you may invite your friend to call when we are established."

"Thank you, Duke," Anne responded, as they continued on to Royal Crescent where the duke had taken a house for the season; No 1, to be precise.

Nicholas would have preferred to stay at his own home, Sommerton Court, on the family estate in Somerset, but he recognised that this would not do in the present circumstances. But if one *had* to stay in Bath the Crescent was perfectly reasonable, (if decidedly cramped), with not too much walking entailed when out and about. This was a consideration for the duke because he had a crippled leg, the result of an accident on the hunting field at the age of ten.

That long ago day his pony had taken fright and bolted when the stag turned at bay. His father, Miller Rutherford, the then Duke of Sommerton, tried to head of the bolting horse but without success. The tragic result was that the duke had been killed and Nicholas thrown, with his left knee crushed almost beyond repair when his father's downed horse fell on it. The knee had subsequently been cobbled together but was never robust again.

However, the art of a good tailor meant that his disability was not obvious sartorially. He could also conceal it when moving for the most part, and by dint of firm concentration walk with a reasonable facsimile of ease, controlling his limp quite well unless he was tired and then he tended to dip sideways a little at each left step. Since he did not care to be exposed to ridicule, as he feared he must be if seen to be lurching, Nicholas preferred to ride rather than walk. His tall, well made figure suited horseback admirably, but if he *had* to take to his feet, as one often must in Bath, staying in Royal Crescent meant that one was never far from the town's pleasures, and that suited him very well. On horse, or afoot, he would do his best to forward Anne's season.

As they neared the Crescent the duke spoke to Anne again in Isobel Latimer's regard. "Why not invite her to tea when you have found her direction," he suggested, a smile curving his shapely mouth and lighting his dark eyes; at which Anne's pretty face was transformed with pleasure.

***

Isobel and her mama, not having seen the carriage, nor being aware of Miss Ward's notice, sailed on down Milsom Street before turning into the Arcade, where they fully intended to squander a few shillings on some quite unnecessary fripperies, this, after all, being the nature of idle pleasure anywhere in the world: especially for ladies, according to Isobel's papa!

Lady Latimer, at eight and thirty and still having much of the girl about her, was as enthusiastic as her daughter in the matter of shopping. It was a pleasure not recently afforded to either because family finances were not presently robust.

Then, with their small indulgence over, and in pursuit of the Season's agenda, the ladies made it their business to discover the coming program of attractions at the Assembly Rooms and the Playhouse, besides enrolling at the Milsom Street Reading Rooms, where they checked the lists to see who was now resident in Bath.

Lady Latimer's brother, George Fellowes, and his wife Margaret, who lived in Gay Street, and with whom she and Isobel were staying for the season, would willingly have done this for them, but their excited visitors were not prepared to render up the pleasure to any but themselves.

Before returning to Gay Street they left a card in Laura Place, seasonal residence of their Leigh acquaintances in Yorkshire, apprising them of their tenure in Bath. The ladies already knew that Mr Michael Harding, the son of their closest neighbour in Yorkshire and well known to them, was staying with his university friend, Augustus Leigh and so were anticipating a good deal of pleasant socialising to be had of all the residents in Laura Place.

What they could not know at this juncture, and would have been astonished if they had, was how much pleasurable and extraordinary social interaction they were to have with Nicholas, His Grace, The Most Noble the Duke of Sommerton!

Lightning Source UK Ltd.
Milton Keynes UK
03 January 2011

165116UK00001B/3/P

9 781609 763817